DARK DAYS TO COME

TONY J FORDER

A DI Bliss Novel

Copyright © 2022 Tony Forder

The right of Tony Forder to be identified as the Author of the Work has been asserted by him in accordance Copyright, Designs and Patents Act 1988.

First published in 2022 by Spare Nib Books

Apart from any use permitted under UK copyright law, this publication may only be reproduced, stored, or transmitted, in any form, or by any means, with prior permission in writing of the publisher or, in the case of reprographic production, in accordance with the terms of licences issued by the Copyright Licensing Agency.

All characters in this publication are fictitious and any resemblance to real persons, living or dead, is purely coincidental.

tonyjforder.com
tony@tonyjforder.com

Also by Tony J Forder

The DI Bliss Series
Bad to the Bone
The Scent of Guilt
If Fear Wins
The Reach of Shadows
The Death of Justice
Endless Silent Scream
Slow Slicing
Bliss Uncovered
The Autumn Tree

Standalones
Fifteen Coffins
Degrees of Darkness

The Mike Lynch Series
Scream Blue Murder
Cold Winter Sun

The DS Chase Series
The Huntsmen

ONE

Even in the early hours of a new day, the city is never still. Its pulse continues to pump a steady flow of people through its vast array of arteries. Keeping it breathing. Keeping it alive. Detective Inspector Jimmy Bliss enjoyed the night and all its many possibilities. Darkness heightened his senses. His vision became sharper, hearing more acute, and he could both smell and taste the air in addition to feeling it brush against his flesh. He was at one with its rhythms, attuned to its disparate frequencies and patterns. He was part of the city's lifeblood. But it was also part of his.

To Bliss, night drives were best described as aimless and mundane pursuits. He took them in order to declutter his mind, with only the road and its fellow users offering the occasional distraction. The ruse worked often enough for it to have become a habit over the years. But on this occasion, he had a rare purpose. For this reason, he was not his usual calm self behind the wheel; his demeanour edgy and on high alert.

Increasingly so, as it had turned out.

He bumped the pool car off the A1 northbound, before weaving between fuel pumps standing to attention like forgotten soldiers on the empty BP station forecourt. He continued over the broken surface of an adjoining roadside diner's parking area, avoiding the deeper potholes as he slowly closed in on his destination. A handful of low-wattage bulbs ranged along the length of the far wall provided scant illumination. The car park was quiet, jammed with lorries inside which their drivers slept off the rigours of the day. But of the man he'd arranged to meet, there was once again no immediate sign.

Bliss had already driven through without stopping on two previous occasions. This was his last attempt. If it was another no show, then he was going to head back home having learned a valuable lesson. If he was lucky, he might yet grab a couple of hours' sleep, so figuring out the best way to punish the time-wasting miscreant could wait.

As the wheels of his pool car juddered on the uneven surface, stones crumbling beneath fat tyres, he spotted a vehicle parked up close to the point Baqri had suggested they meet. Bliss touched the footbrake, the rest stop area taking on a deep red hue in his rear-view mirror. From this distance he couldn't make out how many people were inside, although he noticed the motor was a Jaguar coupe. Only, a Jag was not what he'd been told to expect.

Not for the first time, Bliss wondered if he'd been set up, lured into a trap designed to ensnare the curious nature of a seasoned detective. Another instinct, far more deliberate and insistent, suggested it was already too late to avoid whatever fate had in store for him. He swallowed thickly and checked the dashboard clock.

1.17am.

Early morning, darkness thick and soundless other than the hiss of traffic hurrying by at speed. He edged the car forward in a wide arc, a full lock on the wheel that might provide an advantage should the Jaguar be populated by people Bliss did not want to meet alone on this or any other night.

He'd been expecting an Audi Q2 SUV. The Jag, its windows dark and threatening, was an unknown quantity. Bliss came to a halt once again and sat looking at it for a few seconds, still unable to work out the number of occupants. Just at the point at which he had decided to floor the accelerator, the Jag's offside door opened and stayed that way. Bright pillar lights pierced the darkness like torch beams, and when his eyes adjusted, he finally recognised Ejaz Baqri. With the interior lit up, Bliss could tell the man was alone.

'Where's the sodding Audi you promised me?' he demanded to know as he pulled up alongside the other vehicle. 'When a bloke who knows his motors as well as you do tells me he has a Q2 for me, that's what I'm expecting to see. Why the change of plan?'

Baqri, short, thin and lightweight, exited his car and began shifting from foot to foot, his head on a swivel. 'To be fair, I never said I'd be in it. I wasn't sure if I could trust you, man. I wasn't going to have the wheels here waiting for you. Know what I mean?'

Unhappy with the explanation, Bliss climbed out to join him. 'Not really, no. That wasn't our arrangement. So, what… do you have it stashed close by? Is that the new plan? The Audi's parked up elsewhere and you'll have it driven here when you know it's safe?'

The anxious man shook his head. 'I had to check you out, bruv, you feel me? I told you to come alone, but you coulda brought an army with you.' He looked Bliss up and down, took one last glance around, before eventually shrugging. 'But it's sweet, bruv. All good. The motor ain't far away. I'll take you to it now.'

This was not what Bliss had expected, and the change in plan gave him pause for thought. The Baqri brothers had been useful to the police on one occasion in the past, helping them mount a sting on an aggressive fixer up from London. The pair ran a number of garages in and around the city. Each was a legit business, but several were also a front for the processing of mostly high-end stolen or jacked vehicles. Numerous prior arrests had led to a handful of charges, but so far no criminal convictions. Their previous assistance had brought them some latitude where Bliss was concerned, but he wouldn't trust either not to steal pennies from a dead man's eyes.

He kept his gaze fixed on Baqri while he took out his phone and spoke into it. 'You can relax for the moment. Yeah, I know. I was expecting to find the Q2 here, but apparently it's not far away. Ejaz tells me he was taking precautions. Have a word with command. You can all stand down. No need for the cavalry at this point. But cover me when we leave.'

Baqri screwed up his face, sneering down his nose at Bliss as he spread his arms out wide. 'What the fuck, man? You don't trust us? Have a bit of respect. You got your people out there spying on me?'

Nodding, Bliss pointed towards the Travelodge hotel across the four lanes of carriageway separated by a central reservation. 'See those motors in the car park?' he said. 'They're all ours. I wasn't about to take any chances.'

'Fuck, man! You got firearms out here?'

'Of course. I had no idea what to expect.'

'I'm hurt,' Baqri said, his nasal whine irritating Bliss. 'Where's the trust these days?'

'It cuts both ways, Ejaz You didn't have much faith in me, either.'

'Looks like I had a right not to, don't it?'

'Me too, old son. Me, too. I don't wish to offend your sensibilities even further, but of the two of us you *are* the criminal here.'

'Fuck that, bruv. I'm also the one doing you the favour. Look, you want me to take you to see this motor, or what?'

'I want you to lead me there, Ejaz. You drive, I'll follow.'

The man muttered once again about a lack of trust, but nodded and got back into his car. Bliss did the same, and when the Jaguar pulled back onto the A1, the Mondeo was not far behind.

TWO

Almost immediately, they turned off the A1 and began heading west. A few minutes later as they slipped into the village of Elton, the Jag indicated and took a right. Bliss knew the road well; it was often used as a bypass rat-run when the A1 was blocked due to an accident. Once again he felt himself grow tense, wondering if Baqri was acting on the orders of somebody who wished Bliss harm.

They turned left moments after passing the small Sibson aerodrome. Here the way ahead became more of a narrow dirt track. A couple of hundred yards further on, Baqri pulled over at an angle and stopped. As Bliss rolled to a halt behind him, he followed the path of the Jag's headlights. Captured in the beam was the Audi SUV he'd been told about.

Stepping out of his car, Bliss walked across to where Baqri waited for him. 'You're a man of your word after all, Ejaz,' he said. He gestured towards the vehicle parked further off the trail on a rough patch of land. 'You coming with me or staying put?'

'I'm going no further than this, bruv. Not this time.'

Bliss nodded. He caught sight of an expanse of water beyond a clutch of trees. 'What is this place?' he asked.

'Sibson fisheries. The river's just over the back, too.'

About to reply, Bliss's attention was drawn along the way they had come. A set of headlights bounced slowly towards them. Bliss turned to Baqri, his eyes shooting fiery daggers. 'This had better not be loaded up with people, Ejaz. My backup team will have followed us, and at the first sign of trouble they're going to swing into action. We had snipers up on the hotel roof since before nightfall, and now they've had to switch locations on the fly. They'll all be dying for a piss and itching to end this on a high note by sticking two in your chest before slotting you one in the forehead.'

'It ain't nothing like that,' Baqri complained, his voice whiny once more. 'This is us helping you out, remember?'

'Yeah, I do. And that's what makes me nervous.'

Baqri shook his head in obvious disgust. 'I thought you had more class, Mr Bliss. Is it the brown skin making you feel vulnerable?'

'As it happens, no it's not, Ejaz. And don't play the race card with me. I'm suspicious because, as I mentioned before, you're a criminal. And on the odd occasion, villains have been known to mix with other villains. I can't ever be certain who has what kind of grudge against me. And for damn sure I don't know who has clout with who, who owes who a favour, or who is running scared of who at any given time.'

'Fuck all that shit, man! I'm disappointed in you.'

'Well, I'll just have to get over that, Ejaz. I don't think you have any reason to harm me, but others do. And they can be convincing, especially those who carry a genuine threat. Any of them might have put you up to luring me out into the night.'

Baqri appeared to have lost interest in Bliss's explanation. The car that had been approaching them crunched to a halt and Ejaz's brother climbed out, a big grin on his face. 'Everything golden here?' Rachid asked.

'It is with me,' Bliss replied. 'I'm not too sure about Ejaz. It seems to have come as something of a shock to him to realise he's on the wrong side of law and order. Wonders about the lack of trust.'

The newcomer looked between the two men. 'To be fair, Inspector, we are handing over a nice set of wheels to you on a plate. How were we to know you didn't have a crew sitting close by waiting to grab us up?'

'He does,' Ejaz said excitedly, throwing up his arms and stabbing the air with pointed fingers. 'They're out there now somewhere. We're in their crosshairs, bruv.'

'Wind your bloody neck in,' Bliss snapped. 'If I had any intention of nicking you both, you'd already be wearing a nice shiny new pair of bracelets each. But there's no need for any argy-bargy. I gave my word. That should be enough.'

Without further comment, Rachid started walking towards the Audi. Bliss followed, still wary but less so now the more sensible brother had arrived to take charge of proceedings.

'Everything just the way you found it?' he asked.

'I found it,' Ejaz called out, edging closer. He seemed eager to share his story. 'The windows were all down, but I could still smell the bleach from six feet away.'

'So whoever stole it cleaned up after themselves.'

'Nah, more than that. They cleaned up all right, but they missed bits.'

The back of Bliss's neck froze, stubby hairs springing erect. He stopped walking. 'Bits of what?'

'Blood. In the leather stitching of the driver's seat. Just a few smears, but it wasn't old. The moment I saw it, I walked away.'

'Sounds like the smart move. So why not keep schtum? Why call me to arrange a meet?'

'Two reasons,' Rachid told him matter-of-factly. 'I thought we could work something out for both our sakes. I didn't want this motor falling into the wrong hands, especially our competition.

But no way was I going to keep it, either. I don't know what happened here, but it wasn't nothing good. And bad shit going down means the involvement of bad people. We don't need rubbish like that sniffing around us or our business. That kind of nonsense ain't good for our health. You're a reasonable enough bloke for a copper, Inspector. I knew if we could reach an agreement, you'd keep to your end.'

Bliss drew in a deep breath. The early May night was cool, a steady breeze stirring the bushes and wild grass around them. Nearby trees flexed, offering tantalising glimpses of moonlight glittering on the lake behind them. He thought about what Rachid had said to him. 'And I will stick to my word. On this job only. You're fair game again as of tomorrow, though. You do realise this one-off deal buys you no additional favours from me down the road?'

'Yeah. It's all good. We do our thing, you do yours.'

Bliss held Baqri's gaze. 'I'll have the pair of you one day,' he said. 'But you get a free ride on this one, just like I promised. And be thankful you're small change at the moment.'

He was about to say more, but by then he'd ducked his head inside the car and the words cut off in the back of his throat. The stench of cleansing products and bleach was intense. He took a torch from his jacket pocket and switched it on. A close inspection of the stitching between the driver's seat panels revealed what looked to be dried, caked blood, fully oxidised and more black than deep red. Bliss played the light over the rest of the interior, paying particular attention to the remaining seats and carpeted floor. He leaned further in to check out the rear of the compartment, but found nothing of interest. He had one last look around, inspecting the windscreen and dashboard for further signs of blood spatter. The sensory overload became stifling, and he tried not to breathe in whatever particulates remained trapped in there with him.

'I take it neither of you touched the blood, did you?' he asked as he pulled himself back out and stood upright, looking over the roof of the vehicle at the two men.

Ejaz shrank further away as he spoke. 'No way, man. Soon as I saw it I knew what it was.'

'How did you come to notice it? The blood's not exactly obvious.'

'It was the stench, man. I wondered what they'd had to clean up, 'cause you don't need no bleach and shit just to wipe off prints. After that, it didn't take long to spot.'

'Speaking of prints, we're not going to find yours in or on the vehicle, are we?'

'What am I, an amateur?'

'Did you check out the rear compartment?'

'No chance, man. Could be anything inside.'

In silence, Bliss found the Audi's tailgate release and sprang it open. As it rose, he glanced over at Ejaz and offered the man a tight grin. 'Believe me, if there was a body in here you'd smell it. Sickly sweet, mixed in with all manner of foulness. Bit like a bowl of fruit salad left out in the sun for a couple of days. Pungent and over ripe.'

Ejaz winced and turned his head away. 'You're sick, man.'

Bliss chuckled. 'You have no idea.'

The rear compartment was clean, empty other than a backpack lying on the carpeted flooring. He stroked his chin while he thought about what he'd seen and what it all meant. Not everything was adding up, but he was building a picture and did not like it at all.

'You two telling me the truth?' he asked, eyeing both Baqri brothers this time. 'Because if forensics says otherwise, I'm going to be really pissed off with the pair of you.'

Rachid took a step forward, bristling with indignation. 'We were told about the car, how it looked like easy pickings for us.

FOUR

BLISS AND CHANDLER STOOD to the rear of the northernmost section of a retail estate on Maskew Avenue, in the corner of the staff car park and delivery area where a break in the wild undergrowth provided a narrow pathway. This led through to a gap in the boundary fence and up onto the railway lines. They huddled together with duty officer Lennie Kaplan, Neil Abbott the crime scene manager, plus two men from the city's British Transport Police. A constant rumble of vehicles passing by on the Soke Parkway running above them made it difficult to think, let alone talk, but Bliss heard each of them out.

Fatality Inspector Gwyn Williams, and Constable Phil Stimpson, spoke jointly on behalf of the BTP. According to them, the train was travelling down from Leeds into London King's Cross, and had not been scheduled to stop at Peterborough. The driver saw the victim step out onto the line, Williams confirmed. Having brought the train to a halt as swiftly as his reactions allowed, he immediately made an emergency call to his supervisor. This set in motion a series of procedures, culminating in the pair rushing to the scene. Quite by chance, Williams had been working out of the city's BTP offices when the call came in. He found the driver still

Ejaz came to take a look. He called me right away. Whatever he tells me, I believe. Now you must believe me.'

Bliss nodded. 'We'll see. There's more to this than meets the eye, so the three of us are not yet done.'

'You going to call your team forward now, then?' Rachid asked him. He looked out into the darkness and gave a cheeky wave.

Bliss drew in a deep lungful of air. 'There was no team. There is no team. I lied.'

'What the…? We could have had shooters in the car. And the kind of daft bastards who'd use them. You could've walked into a trap and pegged it back in that car park.'

Bliss spread his hands. 'I thought I'd probably be able to handle this on my own,' he said. 'But as it goes, I now have to call forensics in and also have someone remove this bloody motor.'

Baqri gave him a long, hard stare. 'You really don't have more filth standing by mob-handed?'

'No, but if you'll excuse me, I do have the numbers for SOCO and our tow truck office on my phone.'

'You're a bloody crazy man, Inspector.'

'Perhaps,' Bliss said. 'But at least I'm not insane.'

THREE

'You must be insane,' DS Penny Chandler said to him.

'Perhaps,' he replied. 'But at least I'm not a crazy man. And talking of crazy, what the fuck have you done with your barnet?'

His partner's left hand shot reflexively to her hair, fingers raking over the top and smoothing down the sides. 'What…? Don't you like it? I felt like going shorter.'

'Shorter and shaggier, it seems.'

'You do mean the style, right?'

Bliss shrugged. 'Not necessarily.'

They'd bumped into each other on the stairs at Thorpe Wood police station, at which point Bliss had relayed the salient elements of his nocturnal enterprise. His mood was breezy enough, but his colleague was not so easily deterred.

'You had no idea what you were walking into, Jimmy. You ought to have requested backup.'

Bliss heard the heat in her tone, but he dismissed her objections with a smile and a shrug. 'First of all, I didn't walk, I drove. So I was fully prepared for a speedy getaway should I need it. Second, this is Ejaz and Rachid Baqri we're talking about. For villains, they're reasonable enough blokes, and hardly the violent type.'

Chandler shook her head at him, frustration revealed in her every mannerism. 'For one of the supposed ancient and wise ones among us, you are so naïve. Did it not occur to you that somebody with a grudge could have been using Ejaz to lure you into a trap?'

'No, I'm as thick as pig shit, Pen. The thought never entered my mind.'

'That's a given. But please tell me you at least suspected the meet might be iffy.'

'Of course I did. I was prepared.'

'Oh, really? Were you armed with your wit or charm this time?'

Bliss grinned as they reached the MCU offices. 'Both. Why? Was that not enough?'

'No, because sadly you're long out of ammunition. If you were ever fully loaded.' Chandler gave him a familiar eye roll. 'Jimmy, you are such a–'

Bliss stuck out a hand to bar access through the doorway leading into the unit. He winked at Chandler and put a finger to his lips. Inside the room, DC Hunt was speaking and his voice was loud and pitched higher than usual.

'... the rest of you don't see it, that's all. But just think about it. Of course he can throw himself into every case and work all the hours under the sun, because he's got bugger all else in his miserable life to keep him occupied. I mean, what does he go home to? A few poxy fish and his awful bloody music. If that was all I had going for me, I'd want to be here all the time as well. That, or top myself.'

'Morning all,' Bliss said perkily as he rushed across the threshold.

The team responded in kind, including Hunt, whose cheeks coloured up. Bliss caught his eye, but remained calm.

'John,' he said as he strode by. 'My office, please.'

When Hunt joined him barely ten seconds later, he asked the DC to close the door and take a seat at the cluttered desk overflowing as usual with paper produced from his paperless job. 'I realise you're still pissed off at me for recommending you for a stint in CID,' Bliss said without further greeting or preamble. 'But however you feel about me personally, laying into me behind my back is not the way to behave. If you have something to say, say it to my face. Or wait until you and your mates are down the pub. Or even whinge about me to your girlfriend. But not while you're on the clock, John, and definitely not to colleagues who still have to work with me when you're no longer around. I'd remind you it's still my clock for the next few hours, so save it until you're off duty. Or at least until your next shift, because DI Bentley is not a fan of mine, either. You two can bond together over how awful I am.'

'I'm sorry, boss,' Hunt said, looking down at the shine on his brown shoes.

'For what you said, or sorry I overheard?'

'Both. I was just mouthing off. I had no right to make it personal. But the truth is, I'm gutted that you felt the need to transfer me to another team, and I was… letting off steam.'

Bliss exhaled a huff of disappointment. 'John, I wish you'd get this straight inside that thick skull of yours. I suggested the move because I think it will make you a more well-rounded officer. That's why the internal transfer has been arranged as a temporary exchange, with us getting DC Virgil for the next six months. You've been frustrated with your role under my leadership for the past year, so to provide you with a different working environment and a fresh set of experiences, I sorted out the swap. Learn from it, John. See another side of the job.'

'What, so this is all about you doing me a favour?' Hunt sneered. A tic pulsed in his cheek.

'No. Not at all. There's nothing altruistic about it. Truth is, I'm doing the right thing for both of us. You haven't been happy here for a while. When you're not happy you don't give your all, and your negativity can be corrosive. I need the best of you, and I thought a change might bring that about. Then when your time is up, you can decide to come back or not. The door to major crimes is always open to you.'

Hunt lifted his head. 'Right. If you say so. Thanks, boss.'

Bliss heard the cynicism in his colleague's voice. He'd invariably found Hunt to be a decent man and a good copper, but he needed to mature, and for that it was better all round if he got a taste of another environment. He was embarrassed at being shifted sideways, and it showed.

'Make the most of your time in CID, and come back here ready to up your game if you decide major crimes is still where you'd rather be.'

'I'll give it my best shot.'

'That's all we can ask. Oh, and John…'

'Yes, boss?'

'My fish and my music are out of bounds when it comes to taking a pop at me. Understood?' Bliss stared hard at his colleague, before allowing the edges to soften and become a mischievous grin.

He was content to receive a faltering one in return. After dismissing Hunt, he allowed him five minutes to return to the unit, where he would no doubt unload to his colleagues once more. It was the man's way, and Bliss had always made allowances for this quirk of character. For some time, however, he had sensed the DC's restlessness, and genuinely believed time spent working with CID under a different leadership style would be of benefit to him.

As he strode back out into the main open plan work area, Bliss spotted DCI Warburton coming through the entrance, looking somewhat distracted. 'They're just about to pull a vehicle out of the river,' she said. Then she stopped, turned to look directly at him as if a thought had suddenly occurred to her. 'It's not one of yours is it, Jimmy?'

Bliss laughed along with the rest of his colleagues. His reputation for writing off cars was not unwarranted, and one *had* taken a nosedive into a lake. 'Not guilty on this occasion, m'lud,' he said. 'But I do have a car story of my own to tell before morning prayers.'

'So I gather from my early meeting with Superintendent Fletcher. She fed me the bare bones. Do you want to flesh them out for us all?'

He enjoyed the easy working arrangement they had slipped into right from the start of their relationship. Diane Warburton was not one for cluttered thinking, and she expected her team to operate in a similar fluid style.

'Only Penny is aware so far, boss,' Bliss said, perching himself on the edge of a desk. He assembled his thoughts before speaking again. 'I got a call from Ejaz Baqri late last night, who said he'd driven out to a secluded area to acquire an Audi Q2 and what he discovered when he arrived made him suspicious enough to give his brother a bell. Together, the Baqri boys decided to earn themselves a favour from me by showing me the motor. Apparently they wanted to hand it over personally because despite someone's best efforts to clean up after themselves, they'd noticed blood still on the driver's seat.'

The room immediately erupted in a tumult of quick-fire questions, with Warburton having to shush them until all was quiet once more.

'The Baqris were gifted a pricey motor and they not only refused to take it, but also called us?' Acting Detective Inspector Olly Bishop arched his eyebrows in disbelief as he asked the question. 'Irrespective of the condition they found the car in, I can't help but find that extremely out of character.'

Bliss nodded. 'Yeah. I must admit, it took me by surprise, too. Believe me, you're not the only one who had trouble reconciling that unexpected act of generosity with their reputation for being lying, cheating, conniving, thieving bastards. But they have no idea what the blood means, only that it can't be anything good, and they don't want it tracing back to them. I'm going to make it clear we seized the car, so nobody will sniff around the brothers or anyone else in their line of work.'

'Do we know who it belonged to?'

'Not yet. The plates were removed, so I couldn't run a PNC check. We have to wait for forensics to inspect it more closely to see if they can locate the VIN. Oh, and the multi-media interface had been reset to factory defaults.'

'That's clever,' DC Gratton piped up. 'Few people even consider doing that, let alone take the time to.'

Bliss had been thinking much the same. 'As you might imagine, without the plates I've been unable to trace the owner, and the blood makes me think the motor was jacked. But since we have no reports along those lines, and nobody in hospital with injuries resulting from an attack last time I checked, I'm concerned about what became of the driver. Questions so far?'

'How did the brothers come upon this Audi?' DC Ansari asked. 'Or should I say, who led them to it?'

Ansari was another who got straight to the point, something Bliss appreciated. 'They claim they were told about it by somebody local looking to ingratiate themselves with the brothers. Just a voice on the phone to them who said they'd be in touch again later. Ejaz claims he'd recognise it if he heard it again, but we have no name, no contact details.'

'And we're supposed to take all that at face value?'

'You know the Baqri boys, Gul; shady as shit, the pair of them. I could be wrong, but I think they were telling the truth about why they gave the motor up to us. I'm happy to push them harder if we decide to pursue that line of inquiry. I can request access to their phone records, see if we're able to trace this mystery caller. Probably going to be a prepaid burner, but we can go through the motions if we think it's justified. Any more questions?'

Bishop had one. 'You say you're concerned about the owner, boss. You don't suspect the Baqris of knowing more about that than they let on?'

Bliss shook his head adamantly. 'No, I don't. It's not their game. Neither has ever so much as been involved in anything resembling real violence. Also, if they knew more there's no way we'd have been given a sniff of that car. With their contacts, the Baqri boys could easily have made it disappear and we'd've been none the wiser.'

'But they do jack motors, and it's not unknown for them to make threats if drivers fail to comply.'

'True. But we've never looked at them for more than that.'

'So maybe this time things went pear shaped.'

'I'm not denying the possibility, Bish. But I keep coming back to why they'd call me and give us the motor so readily. Plus, I spoke to them both and I didn't get the impression they'd played any part in the actual jacking. I won't close my mind on them, and I'm happy for someone else to question them. But in my opinion, they're clean. In fact, I'd say both were a little fearful. Anything else?'

There wasn't, so Bliss pushed on. 'I know we're all as busy as a one-armed paper hanger with crabs, but finding this missing driver is our new priority for the rest of the day, at which point we'll review. Hopefully it will resolve itself before lunchtime and not take up too much of our time, but if we are looking at a physical attack with resulting blood loss, then this has the potential to become serious. The Audi has been transported to the forensic yard in Huntingdon. It's obvious to me that violence took place inside that car, but given it was scrubbed down, I can't be sure how significant it was. However, since nobody has come forward to report it, we must regard that as a bad sign. I'm confident forensics will work their magic and find us some DNA to run with. If you were SIO on this, what would you be considering, Bish?'

Olly Bishop, who had recently returned from a senior investigation officer training course, took a moment to collect his thoughts. 'The VIN will give us the motor's data, which then gives us the registered keeper. From what you've already said, he or she might be in trouble. That's something to follow up on at the hospital as a matter of urgency. I'd also want to know if our victim was hurt and extracted from the car at the spot where the Baqris found it, or if the action took place elsewhere and the motor was later dumped. I'd ask for records of all triple nine calls over the past few days in which a potential jacking or street robbery was witnessed. And check ANPR, naturally.'

'The site is still sealed off,' Bliss confirmed. 'CSI are on it as we speak, having inspected the scene while the Audi was in situ. Early thoughts are that whatever happened did not take place there. I also have a small group of uniforms scouring the immediate area and we're seeking permission to access the water belonging to the fisheries people.'

The creases spread across Bishop's forehead deepened further still. 'Bloody hell. Have you been at it all night, boss?'

'Pretty much. Just putting the basics in place, mainly because I don't know precisely what we have going on here. So, what next?'

Bishop stroked his chin. 'There's not a great deal we can do until we've identified the owner. Once we have that, we can pay a visit to their residence and take it from there. I suppose there's always a chance they'd loaned it out and weren't behind the wheel at the time, so we have to be prepared for that eventuality.'

Bliss nodded. 'Good. Thanks, Bish. I'm happy enough to keep our sights locked on who might have been attacked inside the car. To that end, until we have further information, Pen and I will stick with the Baqri brothers. I told them both to make themselves available to us at short notice.'

'I thought you said they were clean on this, boss,' Phil Gratton reminded him.

'I'm sure they are. But in the cold light of day, they might remember more than they did last night. You and John check out local hospitals, see if they've had any unexplained casualties over the past couple of hours. That leaves Bish and Gul working the car. We might have a body out there somewhere, but as yet no place other than where the Audi was dumped to even begin looking for them. So let's see where forensics takes us, then we'll reconvene.'

'We might as well drive over to the hospital,' Gratton suggested. 'That way, if they've had anybody in with unexplained wounds since you last called, we'll be on the spot to have a word.'

'Good idea. But I have one further item to discuss with you all before we disperse,' Bliss said. He studied their expectant faces. 'I'm extremely interested in something I found in the boot of the Audi. It was a backpack. But this is not just any ordinary backpack. This one belongs to a certain Marty Lipman.'

'Marty Lipman the solicitor? That Marty Lipman?' Chandler said in a voice barely more than a whisper.

Bliss nodded; he hadn't got that far into his story earlier. 'The very same.'

'But it's not his car, otherwise you'd have said.'

'Not according to PNC, no. Lipman is the registered keeper of two vehicles, neither of which is an Audi Q2.'

'So how does his backpack end up in the boot of a jacked motor?' Bishop wondered out loud.

'That's what I'd like to know. However, we have to tread carefully. Our legal advisors tell me we're on dodgy and potentially unsafe ground with this backpack and its contents. That said, it was found inside what is likely to be a stolen car, which makes the vehicle and everything inside it fair game. I can massage the records as to how we came to find the car in the first place, given Rachid Baqri is a registered CHIS. Because of that, searching the backpack was a perfectly legit procedure. But there's a grey area. Of course. This is the law I'm talking about, after all. The question is, at what point should I have stopped my search of the backpack? Was it lawful for me to continue with my search once I became aware of who it belonged to?'

DCI Warburton puffed out her cheeks. The Chief Inspector sat in on as many office meetings as she could, an approach Bliss liked about her. 'That sounds like dangerous territory, Jimmy.'

DC Gratton, whose legal knowledge had proven to be extensive and decidedly more current than Bliss's own understanding, injected himself into the conversation once more. 'Seems to me as if you were well within your rights to search it, boss. However, I'd say the moment you realised it belonged to a solicitor, you should have broken off your search to inform him.'

Nodding along, Bliss said, 'For argument's sake, let's say that's precisely what I did. However, again for argument's sake, let's also say that I acquired a certain piece of information as a result of that initial search before I realised whose property it was. The general feeling is that I can still use that intel, because at the point of discovery I had no idea who it belonged to.'

Gratton nodded. 'That sounds reasonable to me, boss. The timing is critical.'

'Good. Then we're agreed. I'll make sure I'm on the right side of that timing, Phil. And we'd better hope we're correct, because our Mr Lipman has some hard questions to answer.'

Before the next logical question could be asked of *him*, the door was thrown open and Detective Superintendent Fletcher exploded through at a canter. 'Sorry to interrupt. I won't take up too much of your time, but I've just received further news concerning the vehicle pulled out of the river.'

'Please don't tell me there was a body inside,' Bliss said with a desperate sigh.

Fletcher shook her head. Then she slapped her palms together and began rubbing. 'No, there wasn't. In fact, there was no sign of foul play whatsoever. But the curious thing is, the car belongs to a local man who a short while ago stepped in front of an express train.'

Bliss failed to hold his tongue. 'Bloody Hell!'

'Indeed. Quite the puzzle. And the reason for my interruption is that Inspector Kaplan, who attended the scene after being called out by the transport police, has asked for you to join him there, Inspector.'

inside his cab and refusing to leave, shock rippling through him in a series of sudden jerky shudders. With announcements to passengers having been made, Stimpson was sent to talk to other staff members aboard the train while Williams interviewed the driver.

'He was inconsolable,' the investigator told them. 'There was nothing he could do except hit the brakes, knowing it was already too late. I placed him in what we call the chain of care and support, and when the paramedics arrived I allowed them to take him to hospital, where a counsellor will visit with him. At times like this, you know you're not going to get much out of these poor men and women. All he kept repeating was that the man stepped onto the line just as the train approached the bridge.' Williams paused to look back over his shoulder at the parkway. 'As you can see, given the speed he was travelling, that gave him no time at all to prevent the inevitable.'

'So he wasn't slowing for the station?' Chandler asked.

'He will have decelerated, but like I said, following its last stop this was an express all the way through to Kings Cross.'

'We've taken the train off into the sidings close to the station,' Constable Stimpson told them. 'It'll need cleaning, but not until your forensic team has released it back to us, of course.'

Bliss didn't want to think too long or hard about the devastation wrought upon their victim's body, but he could delay the inevitable no longer. He turned to the scene manager. 'Any ID so far, Neil?'

Abbott nodded. 'Looks like it. We found a blood-stained wallet eighteen feet from the estimated point of impact. Inside it we have a driving licence, debit card, and credit card all in the name of a Mr Morgan Latchford. The leather is in good condition, not weathered or grubby, so it hasn't been out here for any length of time. As you might imagine, the man himself – if indeed it is him – is spread all over the tracks and far beyond. I don't see us finding anything immediately identifiable. Perhaps our best early chance will be a print, provided we can find a hand or even one or two fingers. If we don't have him on record, we can always print his home. Same with DNA. Additionally, if we're lucky we might get some good DNA hits off the wallet, which we can then match to the samples we've already taken.'

'Which leads me to wonder why we're here at all,' Bliss said, turning his attention away from Neil Abbott and back to Williams. 'I take it under normal circumstances you'd process a suspected suicide scene yourselves rather than have our SOCO here. Why is this one any different?'

The investigator agreed. 'You're right, of course. Usually I'd organise everything myself, after which I'd contact the coroner and compile a sudden death report for our officers and your own. Only, during the initial stages of my investigation, we were approached by a young woman. English is not her first language, but she does understand more than she can speak. She's Latvian, and although she's found the local community from her homeland to be helpful, she's currently homeless. She and another girl, who didn't want to get involved, have been sleeping in a tent in the undergrowth at the back there just by the bridge. Anyhow, she told me what she saw and heard, and that was enough for me to call in your duty officer.'

'Communication has been a bit of a struggle,' Kaplan confirmed. 'Even through the translator I managed to rustle up on the phone. But although the girl turned away when she saw the train coming and realised what he was about to do, she was adamant about what happened in the minutes leading up to the bloke stepping in front of it. According to her, the man was on his mobile pleading with someone, sobbing as he spoke. She reckons he was attempting to bargain with somebody, trying not to walk onto the tracks, that he kept asking if there was a different way. She claims our vic was begging, but also sounded concerned about somebody else. But then he seemed to accept defeat and just walked in front of the train.'

Bliss was puzzled. 'So what's your thinking, Lennie? Sounds to me as if it could easily have been a genuine suicide rather than him being coerced. Even if the girl understood everything that went on – which is debatable given what you've said about the language barrier – what she overheard could still have been the bloke having one final disagreement with whoever put him over the edge.'

Kaplan shrugged. 'I'm not calling it one way or the other. Without a witness this would be recorded as a suicide and we'd not be involved. But the fact is, we do have someone who saw and heard a lot. We can't ignore her gut feeling, can we?'

'I'm not saying we should. Just that bringing in all of these resources might have been a bit previous, pal. I realise no man likes to think of himself as premature, but are you sure you didn't shoot your wad a bit too soon this time?'

Laughing, Kaplan shook his head. 'Don't you worry about me on that score, Jimmy. I'm a considerate and sensitive man. I wait my turn. Look, you may be right. I told you, I'm not convinced either way. But the girl was… sincere. Earnest. She came forward, and she has nothing to gain from doing that. Perhaps she even has her freedom to lose if she's here illegally. If you'd been here, if you'd heard her and the way she got emotional about it, you'd be asking yourself the same questions I did.'

Bliss accepted this with a nod. Even if the witness was credible, it still didn't sound as if what had happened was of interest to his unit. He wasn't yet seeing why he'd been asked to attend. 'All right. So then what? I know you didn't go from there to calling us out.'

'If we'd been certain about the ID, I would have sent a car out to the home address to give the death notice – I had control make enquiries, and our Mr Latchford is married with a young daughter. But we had his wallet, and I didn't really know what we'd be walking into nor how to approach it. At that point I decided to speak to the wife myself, and Gwyn accompanied me to the house not far from here in Netherton. Only, I got no response to my knock on the door or front window, and although there was a car on the drive, there was no sign of the wife or kid. I guessed the kid would be at school, the wife at work. But while we were having a cursory snoop around back, Gwyn noticed the lights were still on. And when we took a closer look inside, it was obvious someone had turned the place over.'

'For fuck's sake, Lennie,' Bliss complained, fixing his colleague with a quizzical look. 'You could have led with that.'

Kaplan waved him away. 'I have my own way of telling things. I like to dish it out chronologically.'

'So assuming we have the right wallet, our victim here takes a short stroll in front of a long train, while back home his gaff has been ransacked and his family are nowhere to be found.'

'That's about the strength of it, yes.'

'Shit! You think we could be looking at a murder-suicide?'

'No. I very much doubt it. The house wasn't just wrecked, like it might have been had there been a fight of some sort. No, from what we could tell, the rooms had been thoroughly searched. Somebody stormed through their place looking for something specific. Oh, and Mrs Latchford is the registered keeper of the car still on their drive.'

Bliss composed himself. It was a lot to take in. If the owner of the wallet was the same man who'd stepped onto the railway line, then his wife and child were possibly missing after some kind of home invasion. All of which was suggestive of something other than a clear cut suicide.

'I hate to say this,' he said to Kaplan, 'but you could be right. There's more to this than the obvious. Kudos to you, pal.'

'So now you're interested? Finally. Good. Because none of it feels right to me, which is why I thought of you.'

'I'm still not convinced this is a major crimes case, but I'm intrigued by what I've learned so far. If something smells off then it usually is, and this definitely has a rank odour about it. Now, I'm sure you'd have mentioned it – eventually, in your own sweet time – if you'd found the phone he was using, but clearly locating that is now a priority.'

'If he was still carrying it when he got hit, then it's probably smashed to buggery,' Williams said, sniffing and turning to look over at the scene. 'That would be my experience. And even if it's out there, it could take days to find. Let's face it, being hit by a train generates a lot of velocity and it could have been thrown a considerable distance.'

Bliss agreed; it was a sobering thought. 'Well, I'm sure we can help with a search if necessary. Should neither our forensic people nor your cleanup crews come across it, we'll get some officers scouring both sides of the track.'

Williams was clearly uncomfortable with that, and made his feeling clear. 'We've got five lines here, Inspector Bliss, including busy sidings. There's no way we can run our rolling stock with a search team so close to the lines. You'll completely disrupt both north and southbound services, throwing a spanner into the works of the entire eastern network. My cleanup crew is experienced, and together with your forensic team led by Neil here, we'd expect to return to a full timetable by tomorrow morning.'

'So leaves on the line can disturb your services for days, but I'm not allowed a search team?'

'With respect, that's a wild exaggeration. We expect to have the line closed for a period, no question. That's standard operating procedure. But what you're saying is you can't search until CSI have cleared the scene for you, so you'll be adding between twenty-four and forty-eight hours to the current closure. I'm telling you now, my bosses will demand this line opens up again the moment we're done. Your bosses can argue the toss with them, but I'm giving you the benefit of my own experiences, Inspector – that's an argument they are not going to win.'

There was little point in debating the matter further. Bliss understood how the game was played. The little cogs in the wheel like him and Gwyn Williams might be willing to take their time to complete a thorough examination of the site, but the mandarins responsible for public transport needed only to speak into the right ears for senior police officers to genuflect and cave.

He glanced across at Abbott and said, 'How about it, Neil? I know your people will bag and tag a phone if they find it, but your search radius might not be as wide as I'd prefer. Is it okay for me to send some boots over to scour the fringes? I'll make sure they're suited up.'

The crime scene manager was a stickler for correct procedure. Bliss hoped the man would see sense in the suggestion, and was delighted to see him nod. 'Provided they know they are only to collect a phone. If they find anything else, they flag it. Okay?'

It was a rare concession, and Bliss was happy to go along with it. The question before him now was how to proceed. Bringing in a PolSa team at such an early stage, especially when even Bliss himself had yet to be convinced this was a case for major crimes, was a big call. The Police Search Advisor unit could be expensive in respect of manpower, and with eyes on budgets at all times he suspected any request made at this juncture would be denied. However, uniform might be in a good enough mood to spare a few bodies for a worthy cause. Satisfied with the result of his ruminations, he asked Chandler to put in a call to ask for some troops to attend the scene to work with the three men currently in charge.

'Thank you all,' he said to those same men now, genuinely grateful for the cooperation. 'One last question: any idea how our victim got here? I'm mystified as to how he ends up out here when his wheels have been dragged out of the Nene several miles away.'

Kaplan reacted to the query. 'I can't imagine him walking, so either he got a lift or came by cab, I reckon.'

Bliss scratched the back of his head. He found the scene confusing, raising more questions than it gave answers. He still believed they were looking at a suicide, but the circumstances were suspicious enough to warrant an investigation. It was more a question of who carried that out: uniform, CID, or his MCU team. Undoubtedly, the man's death on its own raised concerns, but his family being absent from their home and that home showing signs of having been ransacked gave Bliss pause.

Turning to Chandler, he said, 'Any initial thoughts, Pen?'

She glanced around at the scene. 'It's tragic, whatever led to it. If you're asking me if I think this is a case for major crimes, I'm reserving judgement.'

'Also known as sitting on the fence.'

'If you like.'

He thanked everybody, asked the fatality investigator for a copy of his report and suggested it might be a good idea for them all to reconvene either later in the day or the following morning. Everyone agreed, provided they were not urgently required elsewhere. As he and Chandler made their way back to the car, the two were unusually silent. It felt as if even gallows humour was not welcome at this particular moment. The brutality of Morgan Latchford's awful and instantaneous demise was too horrific for words. Bliss had no intention of intruding onto the scene itself, and his stomach churned at the thought of investigating it.

FIVE

WHEN HE ENTERED THE conference room on the third floor of the Thorpe Wood building to find DSI Fletcher, DCI Warburton, and DC Chandler waiting for him, Bliss felt as if he'd been cast adrift on a sea of oestrogen. Ahead of the hastily arranged meeting, he had spoken to the forensic team working on the Audi, and briefly afterwards with DS Bishop. His subsequent climb up one flight of stairs had been lethargic, as if already burdened by the full weight of two new investigations. On the landing he encountered the equally ponderous DCI Edwards coming in the opposite direction.

'How are things with you, Jimmy?' she asked.

He and his old boss had not always seen eye to eye, but along the way they had discovered a mutual respect somewhere amidst the debris of their relationship. At the point at which Warburton came on board to take charge of major crimes during a reshuffle, Edwards had moved across to head up CID. She appeared to be thriving there, and he was happy for her. Distance had mellowed them both.

'Same old, same old,' he replied. 'Shovelling shit from one pile to another.'

'You always did have a lovely turn of phrase. Oh, and I hear it's you I have to thank for landing us with DC Hunt.'

Bliss detected a tone to match the phrasing. 'Is that how you see it? Landed?'

Edwards regarded him shrewdly. 'He was consistently the weakest link in your team, Jimmy. Which is why you're shipping him out.'

'That's simply not the case. I actually shipped him over to your department so's he could irritate the fuck out of DI Bentley instead of me.'

This time, the DCI laughed. 'That would not surprise me.'

Bliss gave a chuckle, but then grew serious. 'The truth is, John is a good copper stuck in a rut. I don't seem to be able to get him out of it, which is possibly a failure of my management style rather than any reflection of him. I'm hoping six months elsewhere will shake him up, and if so I'll be happy to take him back off your hands.'

Edwards took that in, then nodded towards the rise of steps. 'I've just come from the conference room. They're all waiting for you.'

'Sharpening their pitchforks or sticking pins in effigies?'

'Both. So I won't keep you. Good luck.'

'Cheers, boss,' he said before hurrying up the stairs.

His Superintendent kicked off the meeting by requesting an update. It was a question Bliss deliberated over for a few moments before answering.

'It's still early days, with plenty of confusion all round,' he confessed. 'I'll do my best to walk you through it, however. If I start with the apparent suicide on the railway line by the A47, that scene is a complete mess. And I don't just mean in terms of body parts and claret. The transport police investigator tells me he would have called it a suicide had a witness not suggested otherwise. The driver says the man appeared out of nowhere, then walked in front of the train and did nothing to avoid being hit by it. But a young homeless girl, who admittedly doesn't have much English, insisted the man did so reluctantly, perhaps even pleading for his life as he spoke on the phone.'

'Have you taken a statement from her?' Warburton asked.

'I've not had time. She wasn't at the scene; the BTP drove her back to their offices at Peterborough railway station. The translator Inspector Kaplan spoke to on his phone is on her way there to meet with the witness. Myself and Pen will head down there later on.'

'What about the phone, Jimmy?' This from Fletcher. 'Is that why you requested a fingertip search of the line and the surrounding area?'

'Yes, ma'am. I take it you've already received complaints about that?'

She wrinkled her nose. 'Not so much a complaint as a request. I was asked for assurances that the delay in reopening the line would last no longer than it took to clean up and secure the site.'

Bliss adjusted his shoulders. 'And you agreed to that?'

There was a hint of humour in Fletcher's eyes when she said, 'Not yet I haven't. I told them I'd make a final decision after I'd spoken with you and DS Chandler. So, now that I have you both here, how critical is this phone?'

Bliss glanced at his DS, who shrugged. He turned back to his superintendent. 'I have no answer for you, because at this stage we can't know for certain. That's the truth of the matter. The British Transport investigator suggested it would have been damaged beyond all recovery by the impact, and I'm inclined to agree with him. However, if it survived and we can find it, we may discover who he was talking to moments before stepping into the path of the train. It could be a useful lead. Perhaps our only one at this point.'

'Unless you're able to locate his wife and daughter. I assume you still have no news on their whereabouts?'

Bliss inclined his head. 'None. Their absence from the family home wouldn't usually be a concern; the wife may be at work, their daughter at school. But when you factor in the apparent ransacking, it all makes for a bit of a mystery, ma'am. But then, if Mrs Latchford was not the person speaking to her husband and she wasn't with whoever was, then without the phone itself we might still be stymied.'

Warburton, who had been furiously jotting down notes, looked up from her pad. 'So, what do you two make of it so far?'

'Not much, if I'm being honest,' Chandler admitted. 'We have a man who took his own life. No doubt about that. How willing he was to do so is the troubling aspect, one full of all kinds of possibilities and doubts. We have the call he made immediately prior to his suicide. We have an absent family whose home has been turned over. You have to assume it's all connected. We just don't know how or why. And, to be fair, we've had no time to even thrash it out with the team.'

'Priorities, therefore, are to trace the family and find the phone.'

'Yes, and let's not forget the fact that our victim's car somehow ended up in the river,' Bliss added. 'We can't explain that yet, either. If we were presented with each incident individually, I wouldn't think twice. But you put them together and it doesn't feel right.'

'Something bad happened last night or early this morning,' Chandler said, nodding to emphasise his point. 'We don't know what that might be, but then we haven't had time to look into it as yet. I'm sure we'll find a hook just as soon as we can crack on.'

'Very well. So, what more can you tell us about this abandoned vehicle you were led to, Inspector?' Fletcher asked.

'As for the vehicle itself, not a great deal, ma'am. Forensics at Hinchingbrooke tell me they found a few more specks of blood and, with the use of Luminol can also now see where it was before it was cleaned up. Samples of the spots they discovered have gone off for analysis, though it'll be a while before we get results back. However, they could confirm the blood was all the same type. It was all O-neg, though not necessarily from the same individual. Which means there's still a chance there was more than one person in the car when it was jacked. If it was jacked.'

'That is your working hypothesis, though, yes?'

'It is. I'm convinced the driver was assaulted, hence the blood. Why and how, who and when, are all still to be confirmed. But this leads me to even greater complexity: the backpack.'

'Which I'm reliably informed belongs to Marty Lipman,' Fletcher said, shaking her head in obvious astonishment. 'But just to be clear, the vehicle it was found in does not. Is that correct?'

'It is, ma'am. Even so, we have to wonder if Lipman was in the motor at the time it was jacked. That's one concern. The other is what I found inside the backpack.'

'You searched Marty Lipman's property?' The Detective Superintendent's voice rose, together with a single eyebrow.

'What option did I have? We had no idea who it belonged to, and as it was inside the car, it became part of the overall search. The thing is, when I looked inside I discovered something relevant to the case currently being taken forward against PC Barry Griffin. Given that matter was handled internally by uniform, I don't know how familiar you are with the details. I'll give you the broad strokes before I come to the relevance.'

Bliss cleared his throat and took a sip from a glass of water set out for him on the desk. His mind was still juggling all manner of possibilities, and he didn't want to lose sight of them.

'As you are aware, PC Griffin was accused of causing actual or potentially grievous bodily harm to a man being booked into detention. CCTV footage from the custody area backs up statements from Barry himself and several colleagues. It shows the prisoner, a low-life thug by the name of Porter, kicking it all off by carrying out an assault of his own during the booking process. The moment his cuffs were removed, Mr Porter went from meek and mild to Mount Etna in a nano-second. Also, he's a bit of a unit and was clearly off his head on something. Barry weighed in to help control Porter, which he did effectively and legally. Unfortunately, as the two of them scuffled on the ground, the prisoner struck his head against a wall. This resulted in him being hospitalised with what was subsequently diagnosed as a brain injury. Barry was cleared of all wrongdoing, but Porter's family engaged Lipman to represent them. Despite the evidence we've shown him, he is continuing to put charges together and making a song and dance about it in the media.'

Fletcher pulled herself upright, her gaze narrowing as she adjusted her blouse to remove a crease. 'Wait a minute. You're saying Lipman knows our officer did nothing wrong, but is pursuing the matter anyway?'

'Precisely. What happened to Porter was a complete accident. But, as is so often the case these days, the man's family needs to blame somebody. Lipman is running with it because he hopes the current anti-police climate will compel our side to blink first and settle out of court.'

'If this is a situation you want me to take further, I'm going to need more.'

'No, ma'am, that's not the story. Not entirely. It actually gets worse for Lipman. I'll begin with the results of my search of the backpack. Most relevant to us was a writing pad and the notes I discovered written on it. Those notes, together with accompanying digital security footage of an incident featuring Porter that occurred earlier the same day as he was arrested, all point to reasonable doubt as to PC Griffin's guilt.'

'Hold on a moment. Are we allowed to know this part?' the Superintendent asked, edging forward in her seat. 'By that I mean, are we squeaky clean as far as the CPS is concerned?'

'We are, ma'am. Any questionable details I will keep to myself. Some of what I have may be cloudy, but you are entitled to know what it is. In retrospect, as soon as we realised who the backpack belonged to, I realised the notes were obviously bullet points made by Lipman. They didn't make a great deal of sense to me at first, but they referred to the security footage on a memory stick, which I then discovered and watched. It all clicked into place at that point, because the video shows the same Mr Porter earlier in the day being assaulted inside a pub doorway. In the film, you can clearly see him striking his head first against a heavy doorframe, and then again when he was bundled outside and thrown to the pavement. Two solid thumps on his head in the exact same place he hit when PC Griffin later tackled him in the custody area.'

Silence followed an audible gasp from those gathered around the table. It was DCI Warburton who broke it. 'You're telling us Marty Lipman has evidence that, while perhaps not strictly exonerating PC Griffin, at the very least casts doubt on his sole responsibility for the man's brain injury.'

'Yes, boss.'

'And Lipman has not disclosed this to us?'

'No, boss. Worse still, the notes he made to himself suggest he isn't about to, either.'

'Do we know how long he's had this evidence?' Fletcher asked.

'Not precisely, but it won't be hard to find out. The name of the pub is not mentioned and nor does it appear on the CCTV clip, but either Lipman or an investigator working on his behalf acquired the security footage and the identity of the man who assaulted our prisoner. I reckon we can work out which pub it is and make our own inquiries. It's actually familiar to me, but I can't quite recall why.'

'That all sounds well and good. But, playing devil's advocate here, we can't know for certain that Mr Lipman was not intending to disclose the evidence to us.'

Bliss shook his head. 'No, we can't. That's why I see two approaches here, ma'am. First, we begin our own inquiries as soon as possible. We locate the pub, grab our own evidence, so that at the very least we can hand it over to PC Griffin's legal team. It's obvious to me that our prisoner hit the same part of his head on two occasions prior to his arrest, and both appear to be harder or at least equally hard as when he smacked it against the wall in the custody area. I very much doubt their medical evidence is going to pinpoint which blow caused the brain damage, but we can make a case for Barry's lawful actions having only exacerbated what was already a weakness.'

'And the second approach?'

Bliss settled back into his chair, tension in his muscles not allowing him to feel comfortable. 'That relates to Lipman himself, ma'am. We could steam in all guns blazing, but as you rightly pointed out, he could make a case by saying he'd intended to hand it all over but had never found the opportunity. I'm not ignoring his apparent connection to a vehicle in which somebody looks to have come to harm, but if he wasn't involved in the jacking, and if we can locate him easily, then we need to speak to him about both issues. If he did decide to withhold this information concerning his client and the incident in the pub, then he has to pay for that. To tackle the situation, I aim to toy with him a little.'

'And how do you propose to do that, Jimmy?' Warburton asked.

'I'm suggesting we let him know we have his backpack, and that he can pop in to collect it as and when. We say nothing about what we discovered during the search. We allow him to leave with it, then we give him sufficient time to come back to us with the evidence he has. If he doesn't, then we have a better case against him.'

'But what about the car the backpack was found in?' Chandler said. 'The driver looks to have been wounded at the very least during the jacking. I know you said you're not ignoring the possibility, but even so we surely require Lipman to explain to us why his personal possessions were in that vehicle. For that matter, some of that blood could still be his?'

'I have the team working on tracking him down via his office as we speak.'

'Okay. So even if we find out he's safe and well, we still want to learn more about his possible link to the Audi.'

'Are you absolutely certain this stolen Audi does not belong to Lipman?' DCI Warburton asked.

'Anything is possible, I suppose. There's certainly not an Audi registered to him or his company, but proving a connection might not be as tough an ask as it might have been. These jacking crews usually go around stealing legit high end motors and then take them to people like the Baqri brothers, leaving it to them to make all the VIN changes or strip them for parts. This one was clean as far as we are aware. I had a quick butcher's in obvious places, but couldn't find the VIN. Even so, I'm confident it'll be there, probably on the chassis, and forensics will find it.'

Warburton nodded. Bliss noticed her hair had recently been dyed with a copper tint, and he thought it suited her. 'But Mr Lipman's backpack ends up in its boot one way or another,' she said. 'So, perhaps he has use of the vehicle, or he possibly spent some time inside it with somebody who does. Either that or it was stolen from him.'

Fletcher sat back, folding her arms. Her crisp white blouse was flawless; whatever he wore, Bliss always felt like a bit of a scarecrow by comparison to his DSI. 'What's your own take on this particular aspect, Jimmy?' she asked him. 'Where's the connection between Lipman and our vehicle?'

He was ready for the question. 'I'd say it's likely to turn out to be tenuous at best, ma'am. Lipman is a defence brief, after all. The Audi might belong to a client. Could be whoever owns it gave Lipman a lift somewhere and drove off with the backpack still in the boot. It might be as simple as that. Personally, I'm more interested in the evidence he's keeping from us.'

DCI Warburton's phone pinged. She excused herself and thumbed her way through a text message. When she was done, she let out a long sigh. 'The vehicle fished out of the river is coming up clean other than river water,' she said sourly. 'No suicide note, nothing to indicate why Latchford killed himself.'

Bliss closed his eyes. Ran a finger over the tiny scar on his forehead. He took a breath and said, 'I suppose it's not beyond the realm of possibility that whoever dropped Latchford by those railway tracks used the man's own vehicle and then later disposed of it. We need to firm up on timelines for the entire series of events, but that seems feasible to me.'

'Which all depends on whether the team continues to investigate this incident,' Warburton said, looking around the room at each of them. 'Or the other one, for that matter. Neither of them stands out as major crimes work.'

Bliss had been expecting some pushback. He'd already planned how he would respond, and he met her gaze with equal firmness. 'I understand what you're getting at, boss. Superficially, I agree with you: neither of these looks as if they belong to us. I got involved in what now looks to be a violent carjacking, but that violence and probable wounding, plus the fact that we found no driver in the vehicle, makes me think this will end up with us anyway.'

'Fair enough. And the suicide?'

'Admittedly, that one is harder to justify. But again, if the witness heard correctly then he might have been coerced. We will of course make inquiries in connection to Mrs Latchford's employer if she worked, as well as check out schools to see if the daughter is in class. If we locate them and the wife can fill in the blanks, all well and good. But until then, the state of the family home gives me reason to believe we're dealing with something other than a marriage gone wrong and a tragic waste of life.'

Detective Superintendent Fletcher rose slowly to her feet. 'These are clearly challenging incidents, both in the very early stages. Run with them for the time being, Jimmy. But get me some answers and make it quick. I can't justify you holding on to these investigations if they aren't major crimes. When it comes to Marty Lipman, I'm not ordering you to tread softly, but I do ask you to think before you leap. Let's all remember how much scrutiny we're under, people. Some sections of the community would like nothing better than to see us fail miserably. Remember, they are watching and most likely filming everything we do out there, so please let's not give them any ammunition.'

Bliss felt the advice was aimed at him more than anyone else at the table. What's more, he knew it was warranted.

SIX

Bliss wolfed down a sandwich and a stale blueberry muffin purchased from the canteen, before catching up with the team in the incident room secured by DS Bishop. His robust sergeant confirmed it would function as the base for operations Fledgling and Understudy.

'Fledgling was allocated to the abandoned Audi,' he clarified. 'Understudy relates to the sudden death on the railway line. I might have jumped the gun assigning these incidents as official ops, but one way or another they're both going to be major crimes investigations. I thought we'd get a head start.'

'You did well, Bish,' Bliss told him, offering a cheery smile and a congratulatory wink. 'I'm always telling you lot to go with your instincts, and you did. I appreciate it.'

Bishop nodded, clearly pleased by the reaction from his DI. 'Now that the boss is here, I have some important updates, so listen up, people. Two significant items of news regards Fledgling have been confirmed in the past few minutes. First, vehicle forensics located the VIN on the Audi, and second, its registered keeper is a Callum Oliver.' The acting DI paused, turned his gaze upon Bliss once more. 'He's a journalist with the *PT*. Any chance you and he have crossed swords, boss?'

The name had caught Bliss by surprise. The *Peterborough Telegraph* was the city's local newspaper, with whom he had a chequered relationship. 'I know of him, Bish. He works the crime desk with Sandra Bannister. Last time his name came up in conversation, she was having to beat him off with a stick. Young pup hoping to usurp the old dog.'

'Sandra's not that bad looking,' Chandler said, laughing at her own joke.

Bliss suppressed a grin. 'If I'd said that, there would have been uproar. You'd have called me a sexist pig and all sorts.'

'If you'd said it, you would have *been* a sexist pig. But I did, so all is well with the world. We women have a code, and same-gender bitch-slap is not just acceptable, it's encouraged. Isn't that right, Gul?'

DC Ansari snorted and did her best to look haughty. 'In your culture, perhaps. Not mine, Sergeant. Not mine.' That drew yet more laughter from the team.

'Anyhow,' Bishop said hurriedly, 'I asked for a couple of uniforms to pay a visit to his home address. If they don't find him there, we might need to ask questions at the newspaper.'

'Let's see how that pans out,' Bliss said. 'If he's safely tucked up on his sofa playing video games or bingeing a DVD boxset, all well and good. We can have a word with him there, get the SP on his motor and take a lead from whatever he tells us. If he's not at home, I might speak with Sandra before we approach his bosses at the *PT*. Could be he was working on something that got him into trouble, and she might give me enough to go on before his employer discovers he's missing.'

'Fair enough, boss. We'll be guided by whatever we learn from the home visit, which I'd expect to hear about pretty soon. This leads me to the related matter of Marty Lipman's backpack. Following the boss's instructions, I had uniform call his office.

Lipman is alive and well and hard at work. Using the script they were given, uniform had a word with the man himself and told him we had a walk-in looking to discuss his role in a serious crime, and had insisted on Lipman representing them. He bought the story, and is on his way in as we speak.'

'I'll see him on my own,' Bliss said. 'I came up with that plan at the last moment just to lure him in here, as it occurred to me that he might send a junior to pick up the backpack. I want to make sure everything is kept low key to begin with, try to suss him out. My plan is to let him walk out of here with it. If he reveals what he has inside, fine. If he doesn't, I'll give him a day. That way he can't say he'd intended to tell us, but just hadn't found time to get around to it.'

'What about the fact it was found in the boot of what appears to be a jacked motor?' DC Gratton said. 'Are you going to push him hard on that?'

Bliss had already considered this angle. 'That may depend on how the rest of the conversation goes. I'll have to play it by ear. We can't be certain how significant it is in respect of the carjacking, but this evidence he's carting around is crucial for the case against Barry Griffin. I'll see where our chat leads us. I don't want to put him on the defensive if I don't have to.'

Bishop made a couple of notes dedicated to Fledgling. He then tapped on the second board with the marker pen and turned his attention to his boss once again. 'You want to step up and tell us what's going on with this one?'

After gathering his thoughts, Bliss took a sip of water from a bottle he'd pulled from the vending machine. Using the boards was more a matter of habit than anything else. To present every piece of information discovered during a major inquiry, they'd have to fill an entire room with them. The electronic versions had never proved reliable enough, so his team still used the large plain whiteboards to itemise the most important details, including the names of those involved. He laid out the case in much the same way as he had for the chief inspector and superintendent. As he went over the minutiae, he made accompanying bullet-point notes with the black marker pen. When he was done, he stepped back to assess the list he had created.

DEATH? Suicide. But how willingly? Coerced?

WITNESS? Does what she overheard amount to coercion?

PHONE? Who was the victim speaking to moments earlier? Could be crucial?

CAR? How did this end up in the Nene?

WIFE AND DAUGHTER? Where are they now? Work? School? Unexplained?

RANSACKING? What were they looking for? Did they find it?

TIMELINE? Establish order – sequence of events.

'Any of these on their own might not be significant,' he said. 'But you put them all together and you have a real mystery. Our mystery, at least for now. Taking each of them in turn, let's brainstorm this.'

'You're not allowed to use that word any more, boss,' Bishop pointed out, his broad shoulders heaving as he chuckled to himself. 'Apparently, it could trigger any of us at any moment. I think you have to call it a "thought shower" or something like that these days.'

Bliss glowered. 'You do that, Bish. Make it golden if you like. Meanwhile, the rest of us will get back to brainstorming. To begin with, that Morgan Latchford deliberately walked in front of a train is not up for debate. He wasn't pushed, he wasn't dragged kicking and screaming. There was nobody else with him at the time. Two separate witnesses confirm this, one being the train driver. The question, then, is why did he do it? Did he do so willingly, determined to top himself? Or was he pressurised somehow, forced into the act following some kind of intimidation? Thoughts?'

'The phone call overheard by the witness, and the missing wife and daughter come into play here, boss,' Ansari said confidently. 'Without them, I'm sure we wouldn't even be investigating this.'

'I agree. We'd be getting a report from the BTP and it would be filed away somewhere. So three other items noted on the board are not only relevant, they are critically so.'

'How reliable is the witness?' Gratton asked.

'We've yet to meet her, but from what we were told, she is at least credible. Given her deficiencies in speaking English, there's every chance of a misunderstanding, but she came forward when she didn't have to and she was adamant about what she overheard. Pen and I will talk to her as soon as we can. As for the phone, last we heard, it had still not been found. From what the investigator told us, we probably shouldn't expect that angle to provide us with any leads. He was confident it would have been obliterated. Still, if we can track down his provider, we might get a look at his texts and hear his voicemails, so let's not abandon all hope.'

'The business with his car is also dodgy,' Bishop said. 'Unless he's like the boss and just enjoys trashing his wheels for fun, his motor ending up in the Nene is another sign that there's more to Morgan Latchford's death than first appears.'

Bliss ignored the friendly dig and jabbed a finger at the board. 'These ops are complex and confusing as they stand. The timeline, therefore, becomes important at this stage. We need to establish the order of events. The only thing we know for certain right now is that train came through at approximately ten past eight this morning. So we work backwards from then. Whatever happened inside the family home has to be assessed with an open mind. For instance, did it begin with a disagreement and escalate into what took place on the railway line? The poor sod's wife may be the only one who can help us there, but a door-to-door canvas of close neighbours might provide key evidence. Either way, we have a lot of pieces here, but as yet they don't present a clear picture.'

Ansari cleared her throat. 'Of course, we don't actually know if Mrs Latchford and her daughter are missing at all. As you mentioned earlier, she could be at work for all we know, or staying with family, maybe even away on a break… there are probably dozens of reasons to explain her absence.'

'Gul is absolutely spot on,' Bliss agreed. 'We can take nothing for granted until we have further information. Uniform are out there now asking neighbours if Mrs Latchford had a job and if so where. They're also making enquiries at local schools to see if the daughter is marked as attending today. Once we have answers from them, we may see our next move more clearly. After I'm done with Lipman, Pen and I will visit our witness while you all organise yourselves effectively. I'm not sure how much more help she can be, but I want to hear what she has to say for myself. Different questions will hopefully elicit different responses.'

'We'll need an interpreter,' Chandler reminded him. 'I'll sort that out.'

Bliss jabbed the board marker in Bishop's direction. 'Bish and I had a chat about this before I went into my meeting. As things stand, there are no major crimes here, so for now we'll work without an SIO. Nor will you all take up your usual roles as if these were standard A+ crimes warranting the MCU. HOLMES, exhibits, office manager, CCTV gurus can all wait until we know precisely what crimes we're dealing with – if any. Bish, you and Gul can follow up on our missing reporter. If uniform track him down, interview him and take a statement. If they don't, go through the usual TIE procedures.'

Bishop's face contorted. 'Um, the interview and eliminate part of that is fine, but what do we do about tracing? Usual methods would entail having a word with the *Telegraph*. But you said you'd prefer to speak with Sandra Bannister first.'

'So I did. Okay, if Mr Oliver is not found at home and we still don't have a clue where he might be, give me a bell and I'll make a final decision then.'

'What do you want us to do, boss?' Gratton asked, waggling his hooked thumb between himself and DC Hunt. 'We had no joy at the hospital, and I didn't think you'd want us hanging around there too long.'

'First of all, have a run down to Huntingdon. I realise forensics is still working on the Audi, but take a look at it yourselves, ask questions of the team if you need to. Any additional information you can squeeze out of them will only help. On your way back, drop in at Sibson Fisheries to ask them about the Audi. It'd be good to know if anybody saw it there, and when. Operation Understudy is not the only op in need of a timeline.'

'Those maintained lakes often have a mobile bailiff, boss. Before we drive down to Huntingdon, I'll see if Sibson Fisheries has a website with contact details.'

Bliss nodded with no small amount of enthusiasm. Gratton's response showed his mind was on the job and his approach sharp, already looking at the angles involved. If his usual partner had half that attitude, this wouldn't be his last day in major crimes for the foreseeable future.

At the conclusion of the review, Bliss pulled his acting DI to one side. 'I haven't yet decided how I want to split the workload,' he said. 'If these two investigations turn out to be full-on major crimes, then I may need you to run with one of them.'

Bishop's brow corrugated. 'In some ways I can't wait for this next six months to be over. In others… I'm terrified of getting my promotion and either not really wanting it or not being ready.'

Bliss understood his colleague's reservations. 'Friendly advice?' he offered.

'Always.'

'The bean counters frown on those who receive the training and go through all the other framework procedures, only to back away from the jump in rank when push comes to shove. It'd be a bad career move, Bish. If you truly don't know what you want, better to remove yourself now than complete the framework and reject it after you have.'

Bishop exhaled deeply. 'The problem is, if I don't know then I don't know. Some days I wake up and get ready for work thankful I'm still only a DS acting up as DI. Other days I want it all behind me and be running my own team.'

'What's the split like in your head?'

'Fifty-fifty.'

Bliss recalled his own decision-making process, which had been far easier. The role of DI had changed beyond all recognition over the past couple of decades. He was thirty-six when he took his promotion late in the final year of the previous millennium. His wife, Hazel, had prepared herself as much as he had for what the jump in rank meant when it came to greater responsibility and accountability. Longer hours was the real downside, but as a couple they had gone into it with eyes wide open. The main difference between then and now, as far as Bliss could tell, was the tilt over those almost twenty-two years from working the streets towards working a desk. In his friend's shoes during the current climate regarding job requirements, he knew he would never have taken the promotion.

But that was him. That was then.

'You know my thoughts on the matter,' he eventually said. 'You'd be a great DI. And you've earned your spurs the hard way. You've nothing left to prove, not to any bugger. I'm sorry, but it falls on your shoulders, mate. You need to be honest with yourself. Either you can be all the modern police service demands from its DIs, or you can't. You won't get away with my kind of shenanigans, that's for sure. I don't envy you, Bish. But I do know you'll make the right decision for you and your family.'

Secretly, he was confident in his friend's abilities should he choose to move onwards and upwards. Bishop had enough about him to climb that next rung on the ladder and beyond. You had to do that if you wanted to end up in Fletcher's office, something he believed was the man's goal.

Bishop stretched out his big frame, groaning as he over extended slightly. 'Cheers, boss. I'll put my thinking cap on, chat about it some more with the Mrs. And talking about moving on, how do you really feel about John shifting across to CID?' he asked.

Bliss shrugged. 'He needs time to get his head on straight. Half a year in broader CID work will help him decide for himself how invaluable or otherwise he is. I told him he's welcome back in November, if that's what he wants. But if he comes back, he has to be with us at all times. No more half-hearted nonsense when he's put on a shit job.'

'I'm not disagreeing with you, Jimmy. He's good at what he does, but he won't push himself out of his comfort zone.'

'And yet he sees himself as deserving of greater things when it comes to workload. For me, John has no desire to step up. That's fine, because it takes all sorts to make an effective team. But I still demand his best efforts, and I expect them without complaint.'

Bishop gave him a mock hard stare, a tight V appearing above his nose. 'Ooh, you're such a hard taskmaster. Cracking the whip all the livelong day.'

Bliss laughed. 'Yeah, that's me. Bang to rights.' He paused, rubbed the pad of his left thumb across the tiny scar on his forehead. 'But seriously, I don't like to disrupt the team. You know that. I gave John the benefit of the doubt when he blew his top over the assignments he was receiving. But nothing changed. I'm hoping this will shake him out of whatever funk he's got himself into.'

'I hope so, too. I get the impression he's had some trouble with his girlfriend as well, so he's probably just going through a bad patch personally and bringing that into the office.'

'Let's see what DI Bentley makes of him. For better or worse.'

'That'll open his eyes. How are you doing with the things you overheard John say about you? Did you give him much of a bollocking?'

'Not much at all, really. And I'm fine, Bish.'

'Really? I thought he was harsh, and I told him so later on.'

'No, it's all good. I told him he ought to consider his audience more if he wanted to rant, but I didn't get arsey with him.'

'I'm surprised. You must be mellowing.'

Bliss laughed it off. 'Let's just say I'm adapting to change and leave it at that. As for John, it's down to him to make improvements now.'

Rubbing his hands together, Bishop said, 'Yeah, time will tell. But right now, I wish I could be a fly on the wall when you meet with Lipman. I'd love to see that slick bastard's face when you tell him.'

Bliss agreed. 'I can't wait to find out if he's as good at lying as those he represents. Either way, the man has some explaining to do.'

SEVEN

As Bliss had come to understand over the course of his career, the vast majority of defence solicitors were ordinary men and women looking to do the right thing for their clients. Occasionally they steered them toward a guilty plea if they were, especially if the evidence against them was considerable. This was only ever recommended when deemed to be suitable for the client, and Bliss accepted the opposition role these briefs had to play within the judiciary system.

Marty Lipman, however, had crossed swords with Major Crimes on a couple of previous occasions, and Bliss detested the man. He regarded Lipman as an odious chancer, a solicitor who considered his own role more one of working against the police as opposed to advocating on behalf of his client. If there was a 'defund the police' hashtag doing the rounds on social media, Lipman was always at the front of the queue to use it.

The first thing he asked when Bliss led him into an empty consultation room was what had become of his new client. 'Apologies, but unfortunately he accepted a duty solicitor instead,' Bliss told him. He indicated one of three chairs in the room. 'But please, take a seat for a moment.'

'For what purpose? If I have no business here...'

'Actually, I have some good news for you. But it does first require a discussion. Hopefully a brief one.'

Lipman huffed out a sigh. He wore the disgruntled expression of the terminally exploited. A man of average height, build, and weight, he nonetheless managed to appear short and stout, with a throat like a toad's inflated vocal sac. 'This is unacceptable, Inspector. You drag me over here only to tell me you allowed my new client to seek alternative representation, and then you insist you have good news for me that apparently comes with strings attached.'

Bliss said nothing as he pulled out a chair and took a seat. He smiled casually, making it clear he was happy to wait while Lipman got whatever anger he harboured out of his system. The huff came again, deeper and louder. Only this time, the man sat down without another word. He did, however, make a show of shooting his cuffs á la James Bond before folding his arms and sitting upright.

'Are you done posturing?' Bliss asked, raising an eyebrow at the antics.

'I'm ready, if that's what you're asking.'

'Perfect. First, then, Mr Lipman, the good news: an item of property belonging to you has come into our possession.'

Lipman's bushy black eyebrows angled downwards like two furry caterpillars rushing to meet. 'Belonging to me? You mean something I left behind last time I attended?'

'No. In fact, this leads me neatly into the discussion I said we needed to have. You see, the item in question is your backpack, Mr Lipman. Tell me, did you know it was missing?'

Bliss watched in delight as the superciliousness evaporated, replaced by tics of panic and quick, anxious body movements as the man took it in. It was as if his skull was transparent and the cerebral machinations on full display. Lipman's eyes flickered up and down, side to side.

'How do you know this backpack you found is mine?' the man asked, visibly rattled. He stiffened as he tried to regain his composure. 'Did you look inside? Did you search my property? If so, I must strenuously complain about such an intrusion.'

'Relax. Wind your neck in. The item found its way to us via a questionable source. We had no way of knowing who it belonged to, therefore one of our uniforms opened it up hoping to find some ID.'

'Questionable source? What exactly do you mean by that? You're on muddy ground here, Inspector Bliss, so please do explain yourself carefully.'

Bliss kept his cool. 'You haven't answered my question yet, Mr Lipman.'

'Which was?'

'Did you know your backpack was missing?'

Lipman cleared his throat and fingered the knot of his tie. Bliss wanted to grin; he enjoyed seeing this man put off his game, uncertain and ill-prepared. 'Well?' he prompted.

'What does it matter? Just hand over my property and I can be on my way.'

'So you did or did not know it was missing?'

'I wasn't consciously aware of it being missing, no,' Lipman admitted.

Bliss leaned forward, hands now clasped together on the table. 'How can that be? Surely it's something you take around with you for business.'

'That... that depends. It's for attendance purposes, yes. But I've not visited with a client in a day or so.'

Nodding, Bliss said, 'I see. Yes, that seems reasonable enough.'

'So I can have it back and get out of here?'

'You can. Of course. I'll have it brought to you. But I have to wonder why you've not yet asked how it came into our possession.'

Lipman heaved another heavy sigh, ending with an exaggerated shrug. 'I assumed you would tell me at some point during these interminable proceedings.'

Bliss had been weighing up the pros and cons of telling Lipman the truth; it would be just as easy to lie and tell the man the backpack had been handed in anonymously at the front desk. But having seen the solicitor's reaction, he wanted to apply a little more pressure.

'I see. Good guess, as I'm about to do that right now. Mr Lipman, your backpack was discovered in the boot of what we believe to be an abandoned or, more likely, stolen vehicle. A vehicle we don't have any record of being registered to you. I don't suppose you own an Audi Q2, do you?'

'Me? An… no, I don't.'

'You don't lease one?'

'No.'

'Don't own a company that leases one?'

Lipman settled himself in his chair, fussing over his cuffs for a second time. 'Inspector Bliss, this sounds very much like an interrogation. If it continues in this manner, I will be forced to report you for harassment. I'm sure a man with your tarnished record would not welcome that.'

Bliss gave an extravagant shrug. 'To be honest with you, Mr Lipman, I'm pretty ambivalent when it comes to threats like that these days. I'm the one sitting here doing you a favour, and not getting a great deal of cooperation in return. So please, tell me, do you know anyone who has access to an Audi Q2, or anything at all about it? Like I say, the circumstances surrounding the vehicle are suspicious. We'd like to trace the owner, naturally. I'm sure even you will agree that's a good thing. We're just puzzled as to how your backpack came to be in its boot, that's all.'

'Then let me be as clear as I can be, Inspector. I don't know the car, I know nothing about its owner. Nor do I know how or why my backpack ended up inside it. I can only assume that at some point my property was stolen and placed inside the vehicle in question.'

'But you have no recollection of misplacing it, or when you might have had it last.'

'Not off the top of my head, no. I will give it some thought, though. If I remember anything, I will call you.'

'Of course you will.' Bliss smiled and rapped his knuckles on the table. 'Fair enough, then. I'll step outside and whistle up your property. I'll have it brought to reception. You'll need to sign for it, obviously.'

The solicitor licked his lips. 'Out of interest, what ID did you find inside?' he asked casually, glancing away as if the answer were immaterial.

'I really couldn't tell you. Uniform handled that side of things. They went through it until something clearly told them whose it was.'

'At which point they immediately stopped their search of my property.'

Bliss met the man's gaze, which had found its steel edge once more. 'They would have had no need to continue once they'd secured an ID. Though of course there's still the nagging issue of it being inside a motor vehicle currently suspected of being stolen. I'm sure you'll know or be able to find out, but I suspect we'd actually be well within our rights to hold on to it until our investigations are complete.'

'Are you now suggesting my backpack might be held in evidence?'

'Not at all. I'm saying we'd be within our rights to.'

'But not to search it further than you already have.'

Bliss pretended to give that some thought. 'I'm not sure about the legal efficacy of that, but I dare say we could if we did indeed place it into evidence in connection with the stolen vehicle.'

'Which you've already decided not to do. That is what you said, isn't it?'

Lipman was unravelling again. Clearly he had bought the ploy, leading him to believe he was getting away with something here. Provided no further searches were carried out. Bliss was satisfied. He'd toyed with the man long enough, and didn't want to overplay his hand. He stood and gestured towards the door. 'I think our business is concluded. I'll have your property sent through to the front desk.'

But not without instructing uniform to take their time about it. Why not make the man sweat a little more, have him worry in case his backpack was held after all? Or potentially even searched one last time before it was released. Anything to put the creep off his stride. Now it was all about waiting. One day was all Lipman had to bring the CCTV footage he'd obtained to their attention. Bliss thought about that some more and decided to give one final nudge.

'Mr Lipman,' he said. 'You seemed surprised when I told you we were giving you back your property. Did you think we'd be petty enough to hold onto it just because of what you're doing to our colleague, Barry Griffin?'

'You know I cannot discuss the case with you, Inspector.'

'I do, and I'm not asking you to. Just trying to push the point that we don't hold those kinds of grudges here. You're doing your job because you were hired to. We understand that. Which is why we are being cooperative.'

'I'm pleased to hear it,' Lipman said, unable to resist a final sneer. 'But don't for one moment think that's going to make me go any easier on your colleague. The police have one view about what happened to Mr Porter, while his family and I have another. The courts will decide whose view is the correct one.'

Which was all the answer Bliss needed. The solicitor knew precisely the contents of his own backpack; the notes and the footage. This was his perfect opportunity to bring them both to Bliss's attention. Lipman's inaction told Bliss they would hear nothing from him if they waited twenty-four days, let alone hours. It was unconscionable, yet Bliss was not at all surprised. He thought of the photos they had of the backpack and the items it contained, the copy of the bullet-pointed notes, the backup film. He nodded at Lipman as they parted, looking forward to seeing the man again soon.

EIGHT

They found Zinta Balodis being cared for at a community centre inside the New England complex. After being released by the BTP, the young Latvian woman was taken by car accompanied by a uniformed officer. The interpreter Chandler had arranged was waiting for them when she and Bliss arrived. Balodis herself looked frail and appeared anxious, both feet flexing in tandem on the floor, eyes darting rapidly. She chewed on her fingernails, alternating between hands. Bliss smiled warmly as they exchanged greetings, hoping to put her at her ease.

Originally from the small coastal village of Kolka, on the Gulf of Riga, Balodis had entered the UK only months before the implemented UK migration reforms following the European Union withdrawal. Uncertain whether she could apply for citizenship, she'd attempted to drop off the grid, hoping to pick up enough cash-in-hand work to keep a roof over her head. A variety of circumstances operated against her, and she had reluctantly agreed to become one of Peterborough's 'tent people', sharing her meagre accommodation with an Estonian friend.

The woman's background explained, Bliss focussed on the events Balodis had witnessed. As they spoke, he appraised her without making it obvious, searching for signs of avoidance or even outright lies. She claimed to be 30 years of age, but he estimated her to be considerably younger. It wasn't only her slight build, though she was thin and undernourished. When he studied the smooth skin of her face, and took in her sparkling brown eyes, he didn't believe she had been out of her teens for long.

Working through Stephanie Ellis, the translator, a much older woman who already looked to have struck up a maternal relationship with Balodis, the two detectives learned more about Morgan Latchford's demeanour and actions immediately prior to taking his own life. The homeless woman had no idea what time she first noticed the man, only that her attention was first drawn to his voice.

'When you live the way this lady does, you evidently come to know your surroundings,' Ellis told them. 'Staff came and went throughout the day, so the car park was busy at certain times. If they spoke to each other in passing their voices were distant, muffled and indistinct. It was not natural to hear anybody talking so close to the tent she sleeps in, and Zinta was a little afraid of being discovered. Even so, she peeked out to see if people were headed her way.'

'But the man you saw was on his own, yes?' Bliss said, scrutinising their witness. 'He was speaking on his mobile phone?'

Balodis nodded emphatically. 'On his own. Talking on phone.'

'How much of what he said were you able to hear, Zinta?'

The young woman and the interpreter conversed, before Ellis turned to Bliss once more. 'She heard a great deal but understood little. She believes he said he didn't want to do it, that there had to be another way. This is something he repeated several times.'

'Okay. This is good. Did he mention anybody else at all? Or did it ever seem as if he might be talking *about* somebody else?'

Almost before he was finished speaking, Balodis sat fully upright and began chattering urgently at Ellis in her native eastern Baltic tongue. She gestured with her hands in an animated fashion, eyes wide and darting between Bliss and Chandler.

Ellis held up a finger, breaking the flow. She turned to the two officers. 'Zinta had forgotten until you mentioned it. She believes the man said something like "Don't hurt her. Please don't hurt her." She is adamant about this and wants you to know she is telling the truth.'

Bliss flashed the smile again, hoping it conveyed his gratitude. 'I believe you, Zinta. I have no reason not to. But, could you be mistaken? Could the man have said "them" instead of "her"?'

After a further brief exchange of words Bliss couldn't understand, it was Balodis herself who started to nod. 'Yes. It might be. I think I maybe hear both.'

His thoughts in a whirl, Bliss felt his pulse quicken. The phone call was taking on a different slant altogether. This wasn't Latchford venting prior to ending his life. It sounded very much as if he were pleading, perhaps begging somebody not to hurt his family. He doubted the Latvian could interpret nuance, but he had to complete the mental image forming in his head.

'And the man was upset when he walked onto the track, Zinta? He didn't seem to do so willingly?'

It was Balodis who answered again, shaking her head emphatically. 'He not want to. He afraid. He cry... a lot he cry. He say "No, no, no..." He cry again. Say he not want to again. But then... then you know what happen next.'

Bliss was reluctant to push deeper into that precise moment. Clearly Balodis had experienced a traumatic shock. Despite having turned her head away at the last second, she'd heard the terrible impact and knew what had happened. Eyes on Ellis he said, 'Ask if her friend might have seen or heard more, please.'

The answer was equally firm. Her friend had been asleep having suffered a bad night, and reacted only after Balodis herself had panicked. Bliss saw no outward sign of avoidance or reluctance to continue. There didn't seem to be any more information to siphon out of her at this point. She may well have been right about Morgan Latchford's behaviour in those minutes leading up to his final action, but given the language differences, it was possible that she had mistaken his emotions. He could have been sobbing in reaction to an incident that drove him to take his own life.

Yet the mystery surrounding his car, the ransacking of his home, and the continued absence of his wife and daughter, could not be overlooked. And then there were the words Balodis claimed to have heard. They didn't fit the profile of a man willingly embracing suicide. Other than the young woman's recollections, there was nothing definitive to be learned here; of that, Bliss was certain. Now came the most difficult part.

'Zinta, I want to thank you for your help. It is genuinely appreciated. But I have a duty to ask this: what is your immigration status, please?' He did not avoid her anxious gaze. 'I'll find out either way, so please just tell me: to the best of your knowledge are you in this country legally or illegally?'

The shrug she gave was tired and desperate, yet one of pitiful acceptance.

'You don't have a biometric residence permit or visa?'

'No.'

'In that case I'm truly sorry,' he told her. 'I really am. But I have no option other than to detain you until immigration officials have the opportunity to speak with you. You are our only witness to what is now being investigated as a suspicious death. That means it's official, and we will need a formal statement from you. So unless you can offer some evidence that you are living here legally, your situation has to be examined. You will have the chance to speak up for yourself, to explain how you came here, why you came, and why you remain.'

'And then they send me back,' she said following the rapid translation.

Bliss shook his head, though he knew she was probably correct in her assumption. 'Not necessarily. You have well over a month remaining to apply under the EU settlement scheme, so that works in your favour. I won't lie, your current circumstances and you not coming here with valid documentation won't benefit you. But, I will vouch for your good character, because you came forward when others perhaps would not have done. I hate to see you punished for doing the right thing, but it's out of my hands.'

Balodis nodded every so often as Ellis related this fresh information to her. Bliss was genuinely distraught at having to hand her off to the uniforms, knowing she'd be taken back to Thorpe Wood to await her fate. She could have remained in her tent, said nothing, but instead she had acted humanely to a situation taking place right in front of her. When the interpreter finished speaking, Balodis blinked and through hooded eyes stared at him beseechingly.

'I will do whatever I can to help you,' he said gently. 'Please believe me. I have no wish to cause you any trouble. But for now, our officers will take responsibility for you and will see that you are taken care of while you wait elsewhere. Thank you for coming forward, Zinta. You are a brave young woman, and that's to be admired.'

Upset at having to leave her in such an awful situation, Bliss left the centre feeling sick to his stomach. Border and immigration issues were way above his pay grade, but he was dismayed at what he assumed would happen once the system swallowed her up. Balodis had seemingly entered the country intending to take advantage of the black economy, and he accepted it was wrong for her to have done so. She had come to the UK with every intention of working, but timing was everything and she had found it impossible in the existing economic and social climate. He was torn, but she seemed like a decent person and given half a chance might end up contributing valuably. He made a mental note to check in on her later in the day and to make sure she was not removed from Thorpe Wood before he'd had another opportunity to speak with her.

'That was rough,' Chandler remarked as they exited the building.

'Yeah, poor thing. Thanks for your help, love, now fuck off back to where you came from.'

'Oh, come on, Jimmy. You know that's not how it is. You're not one of those rabid idiots on Twitter. And how do you imagine you'd be treated if you did the exact same thing in her country. Look, I don't blame her for taking a chance, and there are ways and means of legally moving around to look for work. But if you don't have rules and abide by them, then why have borders at all? And please don't tell me you think we shouldn't have them.'

'No, I do. You can't have people drifting in and out of a country at their leisure and then demanding to be part of the system. That's anarchy, and I'm no fan. But genuine people surely deserve an individual response.'

'Of course. But we both know some people are creative and wonderful liars. We have enough home-grown liars and spongers without importing more. There are deserving cases, that we can agree on. But an individual approach isn't practical. Nor is it cost-effective. I realise it's people's lives we're talking about, but don't you think the east of England has been more than generous in settling immigrants and asylum seekers?'

Bliss gave a resigned shrug. He understood the politics and the attitudes of those born and raised in the area; many of them had been against the influx of Londoners to their city in the 1970s, let alone those from abroad. He accepted the humane alternative. But knowing he could do nothing to make the two work seamlessly was a source of frustration, and he got annoyed even talking about it.

Before heading back to HQ, Bliss wanted to have a look at Morgan Latchford's home in Netherton. It was a short drive from New England, even in dense traffic. Chandler asked him how he was feeling about Hunt, which made him chuckle.

'Bish asked me the same thing. As I told him, I'm all right about it. John and I spoke and then we both moved on. Honestly, the way you and Bish are acting you'd think I'm some kind of tyrant who can't tolerate criticism.'

'No, it's not that. Not at all. But I was a bit concerned that John might have rubbed you up the wrong way this morning. We can all agree you've taken huge strides in controlling your temper, but I thought perhaps something like that might've been a step too far. I'm not speaking out of turn here, Jimmy. You know how you can be sometimes.'

Chandler was right. He wasn't known for being sanguine in the face of what amounted to disloyalty from a colleague. It was something he'd been working on, and a recent change of attitude was serving him well. 'I do know,' he agreed. 'And I'm too long in the tooth to change my ways completely. But I am a work in progress, Pen. Things are looking up.'

'Really?' She gave him a lascivious wink, a smile plastered across her face. 'You found yourself a lady friend?'

Bliss rolled his eyes and groaned. 'We poor, feeble men don't always need a woman to improve our mood. Every so often it comes from within.'

'Fair enough. That's me told. So why now? What's different?'

They'd arrived at their destination, so Bliss shook his head and said, 'Another time and place, Pen. I promise.'

A uniform stood outside the front door, whose entrance was sealed off with tape. The crime scene investigators were finished, so there was no need for him and Chandler to don protective clothing. The pair signed in and entered the two-storey semi, in which evidence of ransacking blighted every room they visited.

'Whoever did this was clearly looking for something specific,' Chandler said.

'I wonder if they found it,' Bliss responded, distracted by something he couldn't put his finger on. Something he'd seen. Or perhaps not seen. 'There's no obvious sign of either Mrs Latchford or their daughter coming to any harm here. If forensics found no blood, then at least they were spared being attacked – if they were even here at the time. I have to say, though, having seen the damage for myself and still not knowing where they are, makes me all the more concerned for their safety.'

Bliss got no argument from his DS. He retraced his steps, hoping to prod whatever had made him preoccupied during their initial sweep of the house. In the bedrooms, drawers had been pulled out, their contents scattered over the floor. Same deal in the kitchen, and in the living room they encountered empty cabinet shelves and mounds of books, CDs, DVDs and video games spread out across the floor. Cushions had been removed, leaving the dusty and crumb-ridden lining of the sofa and matching armchairs exposed. In the doorway of every room, Bliss stood on the threshold taking in the entire scene.

'What's wrong with this picture?' he eventually said to Chandler as they both peered into the main bedroom.

Chandler regarded him with wide eyes. 'You mean beyond the obvious?'

'Yeah. Think of other homes we've been inside in the past, Pen. Other places rifled through, clearly having been searched.'

'Okay.'

'Now match those mental images against what we're seeing here.'

'All right.'

'What's different?'

She gave it half a minute before shaking her head. 'I'm seeing what you'd expect to see after someone's gone through it like a cyclone.'

'Every room? Exactly the same? How likely is that?'

'If they didn't find what they were looking for, then extremely. It's absolutely consistent.'

'And how often in your long and illustrious career have you ever seen a place turned over so entirely, so… consistently?'

'Rarely, but I have. Sorry, I'm just not seeing what you're seeing, boss.'

Bliss exhaled deeply through his nose. His gaze became more intense and focussed. Something wasn't right here, but whatever it was continued to elude him.

'Perhaps you're right,' he said. 'It's one of the more thorough I've come across myself. Now we've seen it we have no option but to turn our attention away from Mr Latchford and instead focus on his wife and daughter. If they were here while this was being done to their home, then perhaps they've been taken by whoever created this mess. If they weren't, then where were they and where are they now? Because if we find her, we still have to tell her about her husband.'

'If it's him. We only have the wallet to go by at the moment, remember.'

'Fine, but why would his wallet be right there on the tracks if it wasn't him? Besides, we also have to tell her what we suspect. Right now my main concern is her and their kid. With this kind of damage, you'd expect a close neighbour to have heard something. Hopefully the door-to-door will turn up some usable intel. A timeline, at least.'

As they came back downstairs and walked into the kitchen,

the discrepancy his mind had earlier snagged upon became immediately apparent. He froze in place and pointed. 'Look at the counter tops,' he said.

Chandler peered ahead. 'Yeah. They're bare. Everything's now on the floor.'

'Precisely. There's not a flat surface in the entire house that's not completely bare. That's what's different here, Pen. Think back. Have you ever seen this before, where every single item has been swept onto the floor? That's not ransacking, it's not searching, it's just vandalism for the sake of it. Yet there's nothing smashed, no spray painting on the walls, nothing slashed up, like the mattresses or sofa cushions.'

'So… it's ransacking, but not quite. Vandalism, but not quite.'

Bliss nodded. 'Yep. It's exactly what a person might do if they wanted the place to appear to have been turned over. Just go along with your arms and scoop everything onto the deck without a care in the world. In other words, it's been staged.'

Chandler glanced around. She went back to the living room, marched across to its centre and turned a full circle. 'You're right,' she said, looking up as he stood in the open doorway. 'It's every single item. It's not been checked and searched, it's literally been swept off the shelves and flat surfaces. It's somebody's idea of what a ransacking might look like.'

'Good. Then we're agreed.' He shook his head. 'Only I'm not at all sure that brings us any closer to understanding what really went on here.'

As he stood still and silent for the next few moments, his mobile ringtone warbled. 'Bish,' he said glumly. 'I could do with some good news.'

'I have news, boss,' Bishop told him. 'But not the good sort, I'm afraid.'

Bliss mentally cursed their bad luck. 'Okay. Go on.'

'Uniform located the daughter's school. The wife's workplace, too. They're one and the same; Mrs Latchford works as a teaching assistant in the same school as her daughter goes to.'

'So they're both there?'

'No, that's the bad news.' Bishop's voice was laden with disappointment. 'Mrs Latchford sent a text first thing this morning. She was taking a sick day. A virus, apparently. One that also kept her daughter out of school today, too.'

Bliss closed his eyes. That didn't mean they were both here inside the house when somebody went through it, but if they were supposedly ill yet not at home it did suggest they were missing. And in circumstances he found immensely troubling.

NINE

Phoebe Latchford hadn't questioned the blindfolds; the man's reasoning was sound. It all made perfect sense to her. But she did question why they were stopping so soon on their journey.

'Out of necessity, these types of arrangements are always last-minute processes,' he told her. 'Secrecy is paramount, so the less preparation the less chance there is of anybody saying or doing the wrong thing. These people take their security measures seriously. You seem anxious. Do you not trust me even now?'

She nodded emphatically. 'I do. Of course I do. I just… this is so difficult. You can't imagine.'

'I think I can.'

'Sorry. I hardly know what I'm thinking, let alone blurting out. I must seem terribly ungrateful.'

'No, not at all. It's perfectly understandable. This is a traumatic time for you. Don't worry, everything is going to be fine. Now, look, I'm getting out of the car and I'll be back before you know it. Okay?'

'Yes. And thank you. Thank you so much for all you're doing for us.'

A door opened, warm air rushing in. The vehicle rocked, and then the door closed again.

'Mummy, when's the game over?' Beccy asked. Her voice sounded uncertain and a little afraid. 'I don't want to wear this thing over my eyes anymore.'

Phoebe clutched her daughter's hand as tight as she could without harming the girl. The guilt she felt at putting her child through this nightmare stung like a vicious slap. 'It's okay, baby. Not long now. Did you feel the car stop just a few moments ago? That means we're here. Once we're inside, we can take off our blindfolds and the game will be over.'

'But where are we, Mummy?'

'I don't know, sweetheart. That's all part of the game, because Mummy can't see, either.'

'Did we go to France?'

Despite herself, Phoebe smiled and hugged her child close. Recent conversations at home around the dinner table had mentioned France as a potential holiday destination this coming summer. That would not happen now for so many reasons, but her daughter's innocence and lack of awareness about such matters gave her hope she would recover quickly.

'No, because France is much further away,' she said, nuzzling Beccy, who giggled. 'And we won't be here long, because we have another adventure to look forward to after this one.'

'Will Daddy be coming?'

Feeling her embrace tighten reflexively, Phoebe shook her head, though her daughter could not see the movement. 'No, sweetie. Not this time.'

'But Mummy...'

The car door flew open. 'Come on,' Phoebe said, releasing her grip slightly but still holding on tight. 'We can go inside now and then we can see where we are.'

'Let me guide you,' the man said, gently taking Phoebe's arm. 'We'll take it slowly. Don't remove the blindfold until I tell you to. I'm not allowed to tell you if there's anybody else staying here at the moment, but if there is, we can't have you seeing them nor them you two. Once we're inside I'm going to take you up a flight of stairs and then into the room you'll be using. You're restricted to it for now, plus the bathroom, naturally. So, just another couple of minutes and all will be revealed.' He laughed. 'Don't be expecting the Ritz, will you?'

'It doesn't matter what it is. It won't be for long… will it?'

'No, no, no. It's a way station. A means to an end. You'll both be grand.'

Phoebe opened her mouth to thank him once again, but had to slam it tight on a sob that had been threatening to escape since they had first climbed into the back of his car.

TEN

Detective Superintendent Fletcher was surprised to receive a call from the ground floor desk to tell her Chief Superintendent Feeley was on his way up to her office. His dropping into Thorpe Wood without prior notice was not exactly unprecedented, but her boss usually had the courtesy to call ahead of any unscheduled visits. Her mind quickly attempted to calculate why he had chosen to today, but she came up empty.

They greeted each other warmly before taking their places in her less formal seating area rather than at her desk. Feeley declined the offer of coffee, insisting he would not be staying long.

'I really popped by to have a word about your favourite Inspector, Marion. Wondered how things were going.'

'My favourite… sorry, sir, who are we talking about?'

'Bliss. Who else?'

'Ah, I see. I couldn't tell from the description you gave.'

Feeley flashed one of his more supercilious smiles. He'd had his teeth whitened again, she noticed. 'You certainly come across as excessively supportive of the man, Marion. Let's be honest, he would no longer be here if it weren't for you.'

Fletcher could not imagine where this was leading. With Bliss having served out a six-month demotion with good grace and no subsequent lack of enthusiasm for the job, she had considered his issues with Feeley to be in the past. Not so, apparently. The pair had clashed during a case debriefing and examination of the Inspector's actions, contributing to an unpleasant disagreement which resulted in the DCS making a disciplinary complaint. She told herself to be wary, but could not help but stand her ground.

'I wouldn't say that, sir. In fact, if I remember rightly, it was you who had the final say-so following the Inspector's moment of insubordination. You suggested his demotion and probationary period rather than seeking dismissal.'

'True, but only after listening to your counsel, Marion. Both yourself and DCI Warburton were extremely persuasive in that regard. You like the man – or, should I perhaps say, you like the results he achieves on your behalf.'

Meeting Feeley's mildly mocking gaze, Fletcher said, 'I like to think he and his team achieve results on behalf of the people of this city, sir. But as for your visit today, I'm delighted to report that all is well. The ceremony held out on the Cambridge chalk pits last autumn was a success in every way, earning us all a huge amount of credit, and Inspector Bliss appears to have thrived since then.'

The Chief Super arched his eyebrows as he hooked one leg over the other. 'The ceremony certainly went down well with the media, which is to be applauded. Still, the operation Bliss led was hardly a complete success. A young woman did lose her life on his watch.'

'Virtually in his arms, sir. A matter of minutes earlier and the Inspector would have saved that young woman. It was remarkable that he got so close. As it was, his actions prevented further deaths and led to us taking down a hideous criminal enterprise.'

'Are we talking about the same action for which he was accused of assaulting one of the men he arrested?'

'Accused of but not charged with, sir.' Fletcher was growing weary of the vague threads being unnecessarily picked at. 'Please, where is all this leading? It sounds to me as if you believe Inspector Bliss has stepped out of line again. If that is the case, I'm unaware of it. Would you care to speak freely, sir?'

Feeley cleared his throat. 'Very well. Marion, perhaps you can tell me why I'm hearing unsettling news through unofficial channels concerning Bliss. I'm being told he's rather lost the plot recently, and even more so today.'

Bemusement etched itself into Fletcher's brow. 'I'm sorry, sir, but I have no idea what you are talking about.'

'Well, let me enlighten you.' He unhooked his leg and shuffled forward in his seat. 'First of all, I hear he's removed DC Hunt from major crimes and sent him packing to CID with a flea in his ear. Now, you will have had to sanction that internal transfer, Marion, and in assuming you did so at Bliss's behest, I have to ask why. From what I can tell, DC Hunt is an able, reliable officer with an impeccable record. Just the kind of officer any unit would be glad to have.'

Fletcher was taken aback. This was not something a DCS would usually involve himself in. She took a breath before responding. 'DC Hunt is all of those things, sir. But he is also a nine-to-fiver who fails to excel despite having the capability to do so. Even Inspector Bliss himself will happily admit to feeling a sense of failure over Hunt, and he believes a spell in CID working under DI Bentley and DCI Edwards will do the man some good. Or, at the very least, provide him with some perspective and a wider appreciation of the job. And you're right, I did sanction the move. A *temporary* one if DC Hunt is inclined to return to major crimes. Bliss thought it was for the best, and I have to say I agreed.'

'And you're happy to stand by that, Marion?'

'Evidently, sir. I thought I just had.'

He raised his eyebrows at her impertinence, but moved on. 'Very well. But please don't tell me you are backing Inspector Bliss's wild gamble today on two operations nobody else regards as major crimes.'

Now Fletcher knew what this visit was all about. News had reached Hinchingbrooke of the decision to allow major crimes to investigate operations Understudy and Fledgling. In her judgement, Feeley was by no means a mean-spirited person, and neither was he a poor copper. He was, however, a man who believed in running his ship by budget as opposed to the demands of the job. It went with the rank, and she couldn't rule out the possibility that she would not have been lured over to the dark side had she been promoted to Chief Superintendent instead of Feeley coming in from another area.

Realising they had strayed into dangerous territory, she took great care with her next choice of words. 'How much do you know about these investigations, sir?'

'Enough to question the wisdom of handing them over to major crimes.'

'Very well. As you raised the matter, let me explain to you what we're dealing with. Let's see if I can make things clearer for you. In the early hours of the morning, Inspector Bliss was shown an abandoned vehicle by a CHIS he and his team had used successfully in the past. Not only had the vehicle been abandoned, but its interior had also been cleaned down. Despite this, blood was discovered on the driver's seat, suggesting an act of violence had occurred inside. Now, granted, an abandoned vehicle with no report of a carjacking and no obvious missing person, either, wouldn't normally warrant the attendance of major crimes. But Inspector Bliss was curious enough and suspicious enough of what he discovered to ask for a bit of time, which the detection of blood alone warranted. We now know the vehicle belonged to a *Peterborough Telegraph* reporter who, although not technically missing, cannot be located. The inspector asked for a day and I gave it to him.'

Fletcher had driven home with some emphasis the status of the car owner, and judging by Feeley's reaction, it had found its target as intended. 'As for the suspicious death on the railway line,' she continued without further pause, 'the major crimes unit was asked to attend by the duty officer, Inspector Kaplan. Had it been a standard suicide, Inspector Bliss would, I'm certain, have had no interest in it. But a witness statement bothered Kaplan enough to make the call. After attending, Bliss himself was unconvinced, but agreed there was more to it than met the eye. Subsequently, after discovering the suicide victim's home had been turned over and also being unable to locate the man's wife or daughter, it was felt there was enough there to look into further.'

Reason alone did not seem to be enough for Feeley, however. 'In case you need reminding, Marion, major crimes operations require major crimes funding. Inevitably, more detectives, more uniforms, and more civilian workers will end up working on this than would otherwise be the case if uniform or even CID had handled these investigations. Not to mention the overtime claims we're bound to receive.'

'And I took the same view DI Bliss did, sir. He believes both are likely to become major crimes cases, and simply wanted to cut out the middle man. Once again, I agreed with him.'

'Which is all very well, but it's not as if they don't have enough on their hands already. The Inspector himself should be preparing for court next week, and I know the CPS have their doubts about how that is likely to go.'

'He and I have discussed next week, sir. Inspector Bliss is prepared. You know how complex that operation was last summer.

Managing a joint task force is never easy, and let's not forget that one included the City of London Police.'

'I'm unlikely to ever forget that, Marion. Not after what Bliss did, and the shame he brought upon us all in this area.'

Fletcher had to concede the point. Bliss had suspected an officer he was working closely with of leaking critical evidence to a daily newspaper. His actions, in bugging their phones without authorisation, were inexcusable. It had led to his subsequent demotion, and caused a rift between Feeley and Bliss. One Fletcher saw no signs of abating.

'The Inspector admitted wrongdoing. He apologised. He was punished, and he served his sentence. He's moved on, sir. I don't know what else I can tell you.'

Feeley looked aggrieved. 'Your relentless support for the man is clear, Marion. But I have to say I don't know whether to find that loyalty inspirational or concerning. I wonder if you are too close to be fully objective. I sometimes think you have a blind spot where he is concerned. Or are you defensive of him because you feel you have to be, having stuck your neck out for him in the past? After all, his failures could be regarded as your failures, as well.'

Unmoved, Fletcher replied immediately. 'I'm positive they will be, sir. Sadly, that's the way things seem to work. Though I'm not sure what failures you're referring to. I don't have the figures to hand, but I suspect Inspector Bliss has some of the best clear-up rates in this authority. Perhaps in any of them.'

'That's as maybe, but the past is the past. You say he's moved on, but has he simply unravelled? This business between him and DC Hunt ought surely to have been nipped in the bud. Instead, we have a hard-working member of his team being booted out, and I can see no good reason for it.'

'And I'm sorry, sir, but I have to respectfully disagree with you. Hunt has not been booted anywhere. It's a sideways move, and as previously stated, it's a temporary one provided Hunt steps up and decides he wants back in. Inspector Bliss has been quite clear about that.'

'Then I suppose we will have to wait and see. By then Bliss will be halfway out the door, thankfully. Precisely when is he due to retire?'

'This time next year, sir.'

'Then I, for one, will be glad to see the back of him. He may not always court disaster, Marion, but it has a nasty habit of finding him. And as for these two ops, if you've given him a day, then be it on your own head if they turn out to be nothing. But a day it is, you understand. Not an hour more.'

'Understood, sir.' Fletcher swallowed back her irritation as Feeley stood to leave, but then something occurred to her and she could not stop herself from asking about it. 'Although presumably if they do discover evidence of serious crimes being committed, you won't want the team to ignore it and sit on their hands.'

'Well of course not!' His impatience came to the fore, and she had now become the source of his ire. 'Don't be absurd.'

'I apologise. But there is one final thing before you go. You began by asking why you were hearing tales about Inspector Bliss. I'd very much like to know how you heard them, and from whom.'

ELEVEN

Bliss and Chandler met up with Bishop and Ansari in the food court at the Serpentine Green shopping centre in Hampton. Bliss treated everybody to a hot sandwich from Sub-Express. The four detectives sat at a table far away from other diners, allowing them to discuss both operations without having to lower their voices. Bliss filled them in on his chat with Balodis and the scene he and his partner had discovered at the Latchford property.

'You're right,' Bishop said after Bliss had outlined his theory relating to the apparent vandalising. 'The way you describe it does sound suspiciously like it was faked.'

'The more I think about it, the more certain I am. Afterwards, Pen checked with the canvassing team. One immediate neighbour has not been out of the house since yesterday morning, but they neither saw nor heard anything untoward. I can't believe anybody could crash around in there, creating that level of disarray without it being overheard.'

'Seems unlikely,' Ansari agreed with a firm nod.

'Also, somebody living a few doors further down the street mentioned a red minivan type of vehicle. Said it was parked outside the Latchford house for a while first thing this morning. They didn't recognise it, but neither did they take too much notice.

So no real description and no plate.'

'A number of residents were not at home during the door-to-door,' Chandler added. 'Presumably, many were at work. So we might still get something from them later on when the canvassing team pay a second visit.'

'Not a great deal to go on from the witness, either, by the sound of it,' Ansari observed. 'It'd be good to nail at least one thing down on that op.'

Bliss agreed and voiced his apprehension. 'I'm worried about this one. There's not a lot about Latchford's death, his car being dumped in the river, nor what took place inside his home that makes a great deal of sense. You're spot on Gul – we have not a scrap of solid evidence. All we're working with is whatever's left of a body, the contents of a wallet, a dripping wet motor, and a home that's clearly been staged to look as if it's been turned over. To be honest, I don't know what to make of any of that.'

'Other than the elephant in the room,' Chandler said between bites of her BLT. 'The most obvious scenario sees Latchford murdering his wife and daughter, faking the mess inside his house, dumping the bodies, and then topping himself.'

'I don't even want to go there,' Bliss admitted. 'Plus, now that I've had more time to consider that prospect, the entire sequence of events doesn't add up. If he killed them, faked the ransacking to make it look as if somebody else was there, then got rid of the bodies, why step in front of a train afterwards? If you were going to commit suicide, why would you take steps to obscure what you did beforehand?'

'Perhaps killing himself was a late decision,' Bishop suggested. 'Maybe he couldn't live with what he'd done.'

Reluctantly, Bliss realised the scenario made more sense that way. Latchford had hoped to cover up his crime and get away with it, but the reality of the situation got the better of him. Then he remembered both the phone conversation and the man's vehicle. 'If he'd already murdered his wife, then it can't have been her he was talking to on the mobile. So who else could it have been?'

'Perhaps he was having an affair,' Chandler suggested. 'That could explain why he got rid of his family. He could have been on the phone with his bit on the side.'

'Then why was he seemingly so reluctant to go through with it? Also, how does any of that tell us how his motor ended up in the Nene?'

Chandler clicked her tongue. 'I keep forgetting about that. Plus, now there's also this red minivan to consider. No, you were probably right first time: it doesn't make an awful lot of sense.'

'How about you, Bish?' Bliss asked. 'How did you get on?'

The acting DI heaved a heavy sigh, his wide shoulders slumping. He'd dripped tomato sauce down the front of his white shirt without noticing. When Bliss pointed it out, Bishop scooped it off with a pudgy finger and sucked the evidence away. He smacked his lips before answering.

'No sign of Callum Oliver anywhere, boss. He wasn't at home – well, we got no answer – and those neighbours we were able to raise had bugger all information for us. Gul called the newspaper, and according to them he's on annual leave.'

Bliss scowled. 'I asked you to contact me before you went that far.'

His colleague held up a hand. 'It's fine. We went about it in a different way. Gul didn't give her name and made it seem like a personal call.'

Pacified, Bliss gave that some thought. 'Did you press them on that, Gul?'

'In what way?' The DC looked at him in bemusement.

'Did you ask if it was a planned absence or a sudden request?'

Ansari winced. 'No, sorry, Jimmy. I didn't think to ask.'

'That's okay, it's not a big deal. It might have sounded like a strange question to ask anyway. I'd love to know if this holiday was planned, or if it was a recent request, but it's probably best to leave it alone for the time being. Let's see if we can get in touch with family members, find out if they know where he might be. I'm sure you can come up with a reason for asking that won't alarm people. Also, try scaring up a warrant to have his front door off its hinges; I want to search his gaff. We have his car abandoned and most likely his blood on the seats, plus we're unable to locate him. That ought to be enough reason to get in there to see if we can find anything to explain it.'

'That won't be enough for a section 16.'

Bliss knew she was probably right. To secure a warrant to enter and search any premises, you had to satisfy section 16 of the Police and Criminal Evidence act, which was necessarily strict about having adequate reason to do so. 'Add welfare check into the mix,' he said. 'That might appease a judge.'

'I can but try.'

They fell into silence for a short while as they finished consuming their food and beverages. It was still early days in both cases, yet neither was offering any clear explanation. Bliss was the first to speak his mind. 'Disturbingly, we don't even know if a single crime has been committed. On the one hand, we have what looks like a suicide and a mystery as to the whereabouts of the victim's family, plus a ransacked home and a set of wheels floating in the river. On the other we have a car found off the beaten track, with traces of blood on the seats and no firm idea of how the claret got there. Neither op is straightforward. We need some answers. And double quick.'

'Speaking of which,' Bishop said, 'what happened with that shyster Lipman?'

Bliss raised his eyebrows. 'Ah, now there is one slippery

bastard. I didn't go hard at him about his backpack and where we found it. I was more intent on the contents in connection to Barry Griffin, but I gave him the opportunity to cough it up. He didn't, so I got him to admit his intention to proceed with the court case. I decided to give him twenty-four hours, taking the gamble that we might learn more from the owner of the Audi.'

'That doesn't look as if it will pan out now.'

'No. So we might need to get Lipman back in sooner than I'd expected. This time we'll switch it around by focussing on the motor and its owner. When we've taken that as far as we can, I'll have him on withholding.'

'And what if he doesn't open up about the Audi, boss?' Ansari said. 'What if he sticks to his original response?'

'I'll move on. Who knows, once he realises we have him on the withholding, he might be persuaded to talk to us about the motor.'

Bliss raised a finger as his mobile rang. He answered hoping for a break, because he felt they were getting nowhere. It was DC Gratton.

'We're just back from Huntingdon, boss. Forensics found some more blood traces, but no significant spillage. Same type, though. But that was it. John then spoke with the bailiff for the fisheries lake, and that drew a blank as well. He never saw the Audi and had no reports of it being dumped there, either.'

'Balls! We're bang out of luck on this so far, and that cheeses me right off.' Bliss eyed his colleagues and shook his head.

'Precisely what I was thinking. However, things opened up more when we came back through the doors here at HQ. First, we noticed there's mention of a red minivan on the crime logs. Well, that might actually be in the frame. A passer-by can't swear to it, but she thinks she saw Mrs Latchford and their daughter getting into that car. Someone was behind the wheel, but we don't have a description. A vague impression only. They can't even be certain if it was male or female.'

'No plate, I'm guessing.'

'No, sorry. But we've asked the team to step it up. Also, John is working with a uniform to gather CCTV footage close to the area to see if we can find the minivan coming or going.'

'Sounds good. Finding that vehicle is now a new priority.'

'Oh, and while we were at the yard in Huntingdon, we asked about the car fished out of the river. So far that's looking like a dead end, too. There's no sign of anything dodgy. No blood, no evidence of a struggle.'

'Okay, Phil. Good job. That was always a faint hope. Have you acquainted yourself with our witness, yet?'

'Just finished doing precisely that, boss. Miss Balodis is quite a character. We're taking care of her until immigration and border officials arrive.'

'Good. Notify me the moment they show up. I want a word with them before they speak to her.'

When he hung up, Bliss told the others what he had learned. As he finished, he took another call. This one was from Lennie Kaplan. 'Please tell me you're calling to say you found Morgan Latchford's phone.'

Kaplan gave a grunt of exasperation. 'Sorry, Jimmy. We might have found the battery and a few scraps of its casing, but that's about it. If anything was going to survive that sort of collision, though, it's a battery.'

Bliss asked Kaplan to keep him informed, then turned to Ansari. 'Gul, you're my phone guru. Can a battery serial number be traced to a specific phone?'

She shrugged. 'Depends. A number of new phones don't have removable batteries, so there's every chance of serial number linkage to the main device. However, that's by no means certain and probably depends on the manufacturer. But if it's an older phone, forget it. You'd have more chance winning the Lotto.'

'I doubt it. I never do it. But I get your point. We can still find out if Mr Latchford owned a phone, though. It's just going to take a while.'

'Of course. The data is there… somewhere.'

'Get on that as soon as, please.'

Ansari took out her own phone and placed a call. Bliss turned to Chandler and Bishop. 'Have I missed anything?' he asked. 'On Understudy we have Gul tracking the phone, door-to-door on the Latchford home, CCTV being collated. We still have access to our witness, but that door will close on us soon enough. Regards Fledgling, all we can really do for the time being is try to find Callum Oliver. Bringing in Marty Lipman might help us with that, but I'm not all that hopeful. When I spoke to the man he was guarded, but I didn't get the impression he knew anything about what happened inside that Audi.'

'You want me to have him picked up?' Chandler asked.

Bliss bit into his bottom lip as he gave the question some thought. For Griffin's sake, he wanted Lipman to be cooperative. Dragging the man in only to have his attention split between the vehicle his backpack had been found in and the contents of the backpack might work against them. He decided to let it play out.

'Hold off on that for now, Pen,' he said. 'Let's see if we can find our missing journalist without having to mention him to Lipman. I don't think he knows anything about it. That's my gut instinct. So let's focus on Callum Oliver himself. We need to find him, or we need to get inside his drum. Agreed?'

Neither Chandler nor Bishop argued, and Bliss knew either or both would if they believed he'd made bad choices. He didn't like the situation they were in, but was experienced enough to realise that once they unplugged the dam, the subsequent deluge of information could drown them.

TWELVE

THE REST OF THE afternoon dribbled away disappointingly. Progress was as sluggish as an asthmatic sloth, which was frustrating for all concerned. The stall in momentum eventually led to Bliss becoming embroiled in a testy debate over entering Callum Oliver's property. He sat with DCI Warburton in her office for the better part of an hour, a CPS advisor on the other end of the phone. The solicitor was of the opinion that the magistrates' court would not issue a search warrant. He cited the lack of verifiable information, added to the fact that the journalist himself was not a suspect, not wanted for anything, and neither was he officially missing. There was simply no justification for a search.

Bliss was fine with that outcome. Having not expected a warrant to be granted, he was content to push for a section 17 entry instead. Experience had taught him that when you asked for more than you needed and were subsequently refused, it made it harder for them not to allow your next request.

'On what grounds?' the advisor asked.

'Life and limb are still the most obvious reasons,' Bliss said emphatically. 'This is a clear case for it. The man's vehicle was found abandoned, traces of blood on the driver's seat which had been scrubbed down. There's every chance the man was injured during a carjacking. If he was in shock, and likely wounded, he might have returned home in that same state.'

'I'm hearing plenty of "ifs" here, Inspector. You know full well the reasonable grounds criteria; believing the person you're after is on the premises is an absolute must, and I cannot see those reasonable grounds in this case.'

Bliss exhaled impatiently. 'Then use your bloody imagination. Let's say we're right. Let's say this poor sod got jacked, got injured in the process. If you're in shock, with your brain scrambled, where's the first place you head for?'

'You're going to suggest he'd go straight home. I'd think a hospital or the police station is far more likely.'

'Agreed. But now you're making my point for me. The fact is, he didn't come to us, and we've checked out the hospital, too. He's on annual leave, so his work colleagues have no idea where he might be. We're doing all we can, but now we've reached the point where searching for him inside his home has to be the next step.'

'I assume you've carried out your own welfare check?'

'Of course. But you know how limited that is. That's why we need to section 17 this, on the grounds of life and limb possibly being at risk.'

'I don't think you have enough, Inspector.'

Bliss felt himself becoming agitated. He understood the issues relating to police entering a person's home without permission. He also realised his request was stretching the boundaries of the PACE section on entering premises without a warrant. Yet he was convinced the reasons for doing so in this case were legitimate.

As if sensing his mounting anger, or perhaps having seen his features cloud over, Warburton stepped in. 'If Inspector Bliss is concerned, then so am I. This is not a fishing expedition. There is no ulterior motive here. I'd ask you to reconsider.'

'Without fresh information, I'm not sure I see the point. That's the decision I've reached, and I can find no reason to change it.'

'Then I'll ask you to submit our request to your supervisor.'

Bliss's head jerked up. He regarded his DCI with renewed admiration. Having a CPS advisor's recommendation referred upwards was an unusual step, and not one taken lightly by the police. Relations with the CPS were often fraught, though the more senior officers did their best to maintain good relationships with their staff. After a moment or two of silence, the advisor said he would do as requested. His voice was clipped, and both detectives knew they'd probably blown this particular association.

'This had better be worth it, Jimmy,' Warburton warned as she ended the call. 'God knows how many bridges I just burned.'

'There are no guarantees, boss. You know the score. You must think there's something to it, or you wouldn't have stepped up like that.'

'I got involved because I trust you. Or rather, your instincts. All I'm saying is, if we get the nod to go in, you'd better find something in Callum Oliver's home. If you don't, I hear the outer Hebrides are looking for a local bobby.'

'You'll fit right in there, boss.'

They exchanged anxious grins. Bliss thanked her before rejoining his colleagues. Together they worked it through until shortly before five, at which point they had a brief office meeting. There was not a lot to say, and Bliss felt deflated when he called time for the day. Chandler asked him if he fancied a drink, but he had somewhere else to be. He had a swift word with DC Hunt before leaving the building, wishing him well.

'I'm having a beer with a few people to mark the occasion,' Hunt said. 'Always room for one more, boss.'

'No can do, John. I've got to go.' He took out his wallet and extracted a couple of twenty-pound notes. 'Here, have a round or two on me. And good luck. I mean it.'

Hunt ran a hand through his hair, awkward and abashed. 'I really am sorry, boss. You know, for what you overheard me saying earlier. I admit I'm not happy, but I respect your decision. I respect you. I didn't mean it to get so personal.'

Bliss nodded. Held out his hand. 'It's forgotten, John. If you think I'm out of order, then prove me wrong. Let that be your motivation.'

'Um, I'm ashamed to tell you this, but I whinged a bit to DI Bentley. I shouldn't have, but I wanted to own up to my mistake.'

'It's of no consequence, John. He has the ear of the DCS, together with brown smears on his tongue, but he can't hurt me. He has far less clout than his ego imagines.'

The two shook on it, and Bliss headed down to the car park. He could have accepted Chandler's offer of a livener before setting off for home, but with time to kill he knew the best way to do so. Police Constable Barry Griffin had not been suspended for his part in Mr Porter receiving a brain injury, and neither was he serving out any form of unofficial gardening leave. He had, however, been advised by his union rep to take time off for his own mental wellbeing. The young constable had reluctantly agreed, but had also expressed his relief at removing himself from the firing line. Even if only temporarily. His colleagues had been encouraged not to talk to Griffin, and certainly not to visit him during his time off work. Bliss ignored encouragement of that ilk, favouring his own personal approach.

Griffin was clearly surprised to see him standing at the front door when he answered the summons of the doorbell. 'Jimmy?' he said falteringly. 'Uh, you shouldn't be here. It won't look good for you if you're seen hanging around with me.'

'Yeah, because I care so much about appearances.'

'Are you here with bad news?'

Bliss shook his head. 'Not at all. Quite the opposite, I'm hoping. Can I come in?'

'Of course. Sorry. You just threw me there for a bit.'

Griffin lived in a relatively new apartment block in Hampton Gardens, to the south of Teardrop Lake. Like so many modern homes, the rooms came in only small-to-smaller sizes, with an open-plan kitchen and living area to save on wall space. The ground-floor flat looked neat and tidy, unexpectedly so given its young, free and single male owner. Bliss accepted the offer of a beer, though he was disappointed at being handed a bottle of Corona. Its alcohol content was acceptable, but to him it tasted as if lemons soaked in dirty socks were part of the flavouring process.

'For a moment there I thought you were going to tell me Mr Porter had died,' Griffin said, taking a pull from his own fresh bottle. He gestured for Bliss to take a seat on the living room sofa, which was invitingly comfortable.

'As sad as that eventuality might be, it still wouldn't be your fault, Barry. That was just as true yesterday, but today I have something I think is going to improve your mental health by a factor of a hundred.'

Bliss outlined the day's work where it applied to Griffin and the blows on the head Porter had received on the same day as the incident in the custody area. As he spoke, he realised it had also been a full night's work on top, and he immediately felt more listless. He pushed through it, smiling broadly as he revealed Lipman's involvement.

'Bloody hell!' Griffin appeared stunned by the revelations. 'That's amazing news. Not just for my sake, but hopefully we can put a dent in that shyster's armour.'

'That's for me and my team to deal with, Barry. The main thing for you to take out of this is that the moment he realises we have the same information as him, he'll have no choice but to drop the case against you. First thing in the morning, I'm having the CPS run it by their own medical experts. They'll re-examine the MRI results, scans, and hospital documentation, and come to the same conclusion we already have: there's no way they can identify which of the three blows caused the haemorrhage and the resulting damage, because the brain bleed came much later in the day when he was already in his hospital bed. Believe me, this is the best news you could have hoped for.'

Griffin, who continued to stand, hung his head, touching the neck of the bottle to his temple. 'I can't tell you what a relief this is, Jimmy. Are you sure about the findings?'

'Yes. In fact, a similar incident went against us a while back. I think it was in Bedford. They had somebody in custody for lamping a bloke and causing brain damage, then the suspect's brief comes along with footage showing the same geezer being clobbered in a boozer earlier in the day. Unpopular, it seems. But the CPS had to drop the case because nobody could prove which blow did the damage, or if it was a combination of the two.'

'That's the CPS, though,' Griffin said, looking up uncertainly. 'Are Porter's family as likely to back off so quickly?'

'Lipman will walk away, and nobody else will touch it with a syphilitic dick once all the evidence is available. No, you're okay on this, Barry. Get used to it and make sure your uniform still fits.'

Bliss was delighted for the young copper. The previous autumn, Griffin had somehow convinced him to help with a voluntary boxing scheme for young people on the verge of becoming lost or unwanted by a largely unsympathetic system. Bliss coached the group once or twice a week depending on shifts and caseload, but found it immensely satisfying being involved once more in a sport that had brought him both dignity and self-respect, not to mention a fair few wins and several trophies. Though his initial involvement had been grudging, he now enjoyed it enormously. Griffin was as decent a man as he was a copper, and it was nice to see a win for the good guy.

'What are you going to do with Lipman?' Griffin asked.

'Whatever I can and whatever it takes. Continuing with his case against you while at the same time holding back information he knows will throw it into disarray, is unconscionable. In my view, it shows he has been dishonest and lacking in integrity. Don't you worry about that wanksplat – I'll make sure he pays.'

Bliss noticed how the pressure and strain lifted off the young officer's shoulders. His eyes were also more alert, hopeful now. 'I know how you feel,' Bliss told him. 'It doesn't matter how much you convince yourself of your innocence, there's always a part of your brain that insists mistakes get made all the time in the legal system. I've been there, Barry. I know how you were feeling, which is why I thought I should tell you as soon as possible about this. It stays between you and me for the time being, though.'

'Of course.'

Draining his bottle, Bliss rose and clapped his colleague on the arm. 'See you at training if not before.'

Griffin's smile became a frown. 'I can't believe you're leaving without hitting me with something deep.'

The pair shared a love of music. Both enjoyed eclectic tastes, and often tried to outshine the other with their knowledge. Bliss was up to the challenge. 'All right. Artist, song or album?'

'Let's go with artist for a change.'

Bliss spent the next ten seconds thinking it over, before eventually nodding. 'Okay. I've got one for you. Which band did Michael Buble sing with about an elf's lament?'

It was interesting watching the changes wrought upon Griffin's face as he worked his way through the clues. The greater the gurning, the more Bliss knew he had his friend stumped. Eventually,

Griffin said, 'I'm not convinced, but I might have pulled this off. I'm saying the answer is Smash Mouth.'

Bliss made him wait. He mentally counted off the seconds. Finally, he moved his head from side to side.

'Really?!' Griffin cried, hands slapping his sides in anguish. 'I really thought I'd nailed it.'

'I can see where you're coming from. They're a fun band who record some daft tracks, but you got it wrong, my friend. It was Barenaked Ladies. I actually gave you part of it, because the track is called *Elf's Lament*.'

Crestfallen, Griffin spread his hands. 'Another one to you, Jimmy. But it's my turn next, and I am going to slam you with something from a band so unknown even they haven't heard of themselves yet.'

'Good. I prefer to have you focussing on that than where your head has been lately.' Bliss had elected to stiffen the challenge for this precise reason. It had worked better than he had imagined.

Griffin nodded his appreciation. 'Thank you,' he said. He held out his hand, which Bliss accepted and shook.

'My pleasure. And no matter what you come up with, I'll be ready.' He smiled. 'Keep your chin up, Barry. It'll all be over soon.'

THIRTEEN

Bliss collapsed into his recliner when he got home. No food, no beer. He'd just about found the strength to remove his jacket. That's what being awake for over forty hours straight did. Especially at his age. If his memory wasn't playing tricks on him, it was Edgar Allen Poe who had once described sleep as little slices of death. Right now, Bliss was willing to take his chances. He couldn't recall being as mentally and physically exhausted in his entire life, and yet his mind refused to release him. He tried to embrace the silence, only with tinnitus in both ears, his world was never entirely without sound.

There was no point in turning over the investigations in his head. Both had rapidly become a waiting game, with momentum expected the following day; picking at loose strands served no useful purpose, because there was nothing to discover until additional information had been disclosed. Except perhaps for one potential lead he had yet to explore. It might require a little more finesse than he felt capable of, but Bliss thought it was worth a shot. He took out his mobile and placed a call to Sandra Bannister, who picked up immediately.

'Jimmy Bliss,' she said pleasantly. 'What a surprise. You must be after something.'

'You don't know that. I could be calling with information for you.'

'Well, are you?'

'No. But I could have been.'

'Yeah, yeah. Tell me what it is and I'll see what I can do.'

'Okay. Have you heard from Callum Oliver today?'

'Callum? No, he's on holiday. Why d'you ask?'

'You didn't know we'd been in contact with the paper earlier?'

'I hadn't heard, no. What's going on, Jimmy?'

'Me first,' he said. 'You still supervising his workload, Sandra?'

'Not that he cares to admit it, but yes. I told you the little creep was after my job, but I'm keeping him at arm's length for the time being.'

'Good, then you might be able to help me. I know you can't or won't tell me precisely what he's working on, but I would like to know if he's involved in anything dangerous. Is there anything that might put him in harm's way?'

'Oh, now you're really scaring me. What is it? What's happened to Callum?'

'Sandra… please, bear with me. Are you able to answer my question?'

'Sorry. Ah, no. I mean, yes I'm able to answer, but no he's not working on anything remotely dangerous. We're both following up on cases as and when they come in. Nothing out of the ordinary.'

'No investigative work, then?'

'Not at the moment, no. We're in a round of budget discussions, so all that is on hold.'

Bliss took a beat. Exchanging information with a journalist was always a balancing act. He'd developed a good rapport with Bannister, and thought he knew how far he could take matters.

'One more question,' he insisted. 'Did Callum fish?'

'No. Not that I'm aware.'

'Fair enough. Thank you. Listen, what I'm about to say must stay between you and me. You understand?'

'If you say so. Please, just tell me what's going on, Jimmy.'

Having fed her only part of the story, Bliss chose his words carefully. 'Callum's car was found abandoned out by Sibson Fisheries close to Elton. All the windows had been powered down, but there was still a substantial reek of cleaning fluids and bleach inside. Somebody had done a decent job of cleaning up, but not a perfect one. We found traces of blood inside.'

'Oh my god!'

'Our best guess is he was jacked, and in the process got hurt. If that's the case, we have no way of knowing how badly. There's been no report to us, and he's not being treated in hospital. We found no sign of Callum anywhere, not even at his home address. At least, if he's in there he's not opening the front door. Tell me, do you know if he was due to go away this week? You said he was on holiday, and your paper told us he was taking annual leave.'

'I really couldn't say. He and I rarely talk unless it's about work. We're certainly not close enough for him to mention if he was going away somewhere. And it wouldn't occur to me to ask.'

'Anyone else at the paper he's more friendly with than you?'

'Probably everyone other than me. I can ask around if you like?'

He thought about that, but decided against it. 'No, that's fine. I don't want to draw attention to his absence. Besides, I'm hoping to get inside his flat tomorrow, so that might turn up something. Perhaps even him. If not, we'll have no choice but to talk to his colleagues, so maybe it's best you stay out of it for the time being.'

'Okay. But you know if he is missing, if something has happened to him, the *Telegraph* is going to cover it.'

'I understand that. But at the moment, we don't have all the details necessary to conclude one thing or another. Of course, your paper will want to run with it if we confirm there's an issue, but there will be no formal statements until at least tomorrow afternoon.'

'Look, I don't like the man, but I'd never wish him any harm. I hope you find him at home, licking his wounds.'

'Me, too. While I have you, Sandra, do you have his phone number?'

'He has two. A second SIM card in his work phone is for personal calls, etcetera. I don't have that. But neither can I give out his work number without checking with my bosses first, so that puts us in an awkward position.'

Bliss walked back his irritation. He was trying to help find the man, and yet here was another barrier being put up in front of him.

'You could,' he said as gently as he was able. 'Nobody need know you gave it to me.'

'How about if I call him? If he answers, then we're good to go. If he doesn't…'

'You could do that. But like I said, you could also just give it to me now. I can make that call. And if I get no response, I can use the number to trace the phone if it's switched on, or at the very least pinpoint where it was when it went offline. You can only do one of those things, Sandra. So how about it?'

It took a further couple of minutes of gentle persuasion, but eventually Bannister surrendered the information. He thanked her, killed the call before she could ask any further questions, and then promptly dialled the number. He got no answer, but left a voicemail message when prompted. He then called out again, this time to DC Ansari.

'Sorry to disrupt your personal time, Gul,' he began, 'but I need some help and my mind immediately went to you.'

'No problem. If I can help, I will.'

Bliss smiled. He was taking advantage of his colleague's good nature and attitude towards the job, but assuaged his guilt by telling himself it was for a worthy cause. He explained he had the work number for Callum Oliver, but didn't want to wait until the following morning to start tracing. 'Do you have any way of doing that for me from home?'

'I can access the remote system. There's an app on there I can use.'

Bliss gave her the number, mumbled his thanks, and closed the call. Less than ten minutes later, Ansari was back on the line.

'The phone is not switched on,' she told him, her voice heavy with regret. 'Last known position was South Luffenham.'

He blew out his lips. 'Which is where?'

'Just off the A47 west of here, boss.'

'When was this?'

'Saturday afternoon. At 3.27pm, to be precise.'

'Okay. I'll have to think about what that means. Thank you, Gul.'

Bliss said goodnight and set the phone down on the arm of his chair. He yawned and stretched out his legs and arms. Rolled his head to loosen up tight neck muscles. In recent weeks, he'd not been doing his specific stretching exercises, and he felt the stiffness in every sinew beginning to pull and cause a chain-reaction elsewhere. His routines had suffered of late, though he had no reasonable excuse for neglecting his health. Over the past year, the days, weeks, and months felt as if they'd bled into each other with no discernible break. His focus had been somewhere else; anywhere other than on his own condition.

He'd been fighting on too many fronts. The demotion in rank and the six-month probationary period had taken its toll. He'd deserved his punishment, which was less than he had expected. Even so, his battle to keep his job in any form, at any rank, had taken a lot out of him. At the same time, he'd been confronted with inching closer to reaching compulsory retirement age from the job. A year away now, and Bliss was all too aware of how rapidly those twelve months would fly by. He wanted to slow down the passing of time, but the hands on the clock were spinning around the dial so quickly he couldn't keep up.

'There's a lot more sand beneath my feet than there is left to rain down on my head inside this hourglass,' he'd said to Chandler recently. 'And I'm not just talking about the job.'

Bliss recalled being shocked by his friend's response. For once she hadn't mocked him, hadn't made a joke at his expense. In fact, she made no reply at all. Instead, Chandler's reaction was one of silent contemplation. In acknowledging the truth of his words and the depth of his feelings, she had brushed against his mortality and had been frightened by it.

For a long time – longer than he cared to admit – his mind had taken him to all the same places hers had at that precise moment. He had allowed himself to become suffocated by the genuine potential of his inevitable decline.

But not any longer.

He was beyond mere fatigue, yet his head was elsewhere these days. He dwelled in a better place. Mentally, at least. Physically, Bliss realised he could help himself more and silently promised he would. For now, he needed to rest, to sleep, and to awake refreshed. Each new day brought with it a different challenge. And to overcome them, he had to be at his best.

He had his own ways of relieving stress and tiredness: sitting out in his garden admiring the Zen-like design and the koi fish generating lazy patterns in the pond; watching a film or listening to music often did the trick for him, either option able to take him out of the moment and whisk him off inside an adventure or to a different moment in time; if none of his home-bound pleasures worked, then taking a fast drive at night relaxed him by focussing his attention on the road – preferably one with many curves to concentrate the mind. On rare occasions, he simply shut his mind and body down where he sat or lay, knowing nothing other than complete rest would do the job.

This was one of those nights.

FOURTEEN

Morning briefings were often more about clearing away the fog of sleep and reacquainting yourself with the case than delving into new leads or evidence. The days of entire second teams working through the night were long gone, which meant little changed during those out-of-office hours. Bliss was therefore pleased to update the team regarding Callum Oliver.

'He wasn't working on anything controversial,' he explained. 'Sandra Bannister was adamant about that. I called her again first thing to ask if South Luffenham meant anything to her, but it didn't. Gul is going to obtain the precise coordinates for us, so at some point somebody may need to take a run out there.' He turned to Bishop, a smile twisting his lips. 'That's me done. If you want to get up onto your plates for a change, old son, let's have your plan of action for the day.'

Bishop wrestled himself out of his seat with all the grace and agility of a disgruntled bear. 'Just a quick follow up on Mr Oliver. I was able to contact his parents. I told them it was concerning an on-going investigation he'd reported on, so they're none the wiser. Anyhow, they don't know where he is and weren't even aware he was on annual leave. So no joy there. As for today, Gul and I will trawl through CCTV from around the Latchford property. The red minivan may be our best lead so far on that, because we've had largely bugger all from the neighbours otherwise.'

'Okay, thanks for the update on Callum's family. Find out everything you can about the Latchfords,' Bliss told him. 'All three of them. Let's see if we can build up a picture of their movements over the weekend. As I mentioned previously, it'd also be nice to confirm a timeline surrounding yesterday morning's events, to find out precisely when it goes cold. Speak to family and friends. Work colleagues, too. I want to know if the Latchfords were having marital problems. And remember, for the time being we're still only working under the assumption that our suspicious death victim is Morgan Latchford. Hopefully, DNA will confirm ID today, but I want everything on them anyway.'

'Yes, boss. Unless we get lucky, CCTV will probably be slow going, given we don't have a time window to work with. All we can reasonably do is work backwards from the precise moment Inspector Kaplan and the British Transport investigator arrived at the property. But I'll make sure there's a concerted effort to get information on the family at the same time.'

Bliss nodded amiably. 'Thanks. I had intended to meet with Lennie and the transport police again yesterday, but things got away from me. Still, if they had something new, we'd know by now. Oh, and as John Hunt's replacement is with us today, it might be best if you work with him. Gul can pair up with Phil for a day. And on that note, I'd like you all to welcome DC Virgil to the team.'

Following an outpouring of applause and good wishes, together with the odd back slap, the young constable eased himself away from the wall on which he'd been leaning. He seemed a little embarrassed by the fuss, but thanked everybody.

'I remember you, DC Virgil,' Bliss said. 'First inside the home of Jade Coleman, who was stabbed to death in her own bedroom.'

'That was me, boss,' Virgil said, eyebrows arched. 'I'm surprised you remembered.'

'I never forget a case. And you made an impression, the way you reacted when you discovered her. You thought about forensics, even though your heart must have been bursting out of your chest. Good work like that sticks in my mind. Oh, and when there's nobody above my rank in the room, you call me Jimmy. Save "boss" for when you actually need it.'

'Yes, boss.'

That prompted laughter, and Bliss smiled along. 'Okay, you'll find this an easy team to slot into, but I'll give you a brief rundown of roles and responsibilities. This unit is based along similar lines to the Met's Murder Investigation teams. Current SIOs are myself or DCI Diane Warburton, plus the Super is available for that role if we get really busy. Acting DI Olly Bishop is working his way up there. I am, of course, the lead investigating officer, with Bish or DS Penny Chandler operating as case officers. CCTV is usually down to Bish, with DC Gul Ansari generally acting as our intelligence and communications officer. DC Phil Gratton also operates in the same areas as Gul, and often ends up working our disclosures and exhibits if our specially trained civilian workers are not available. Both Gul and Phil are also heavily involved in interview situations, occasionally joined by Pen or Bish and if I think it's appropriate, myself as well. These responsibilities are interchangeable, but as often as we can we hand the right person the right role at the right time. Any questions?'

'No. I was told I'd mostly be shadowing the other DCs.'

'That's correct. Although Bish will steer you through your first day and bring you up to speed on our cases. Obviously we have more on the books than these two investigations, but operations Understudy and Fledgling take priority at the moment because of probable mispers.'

'Can I ask what makes them serious crimes?'

'That's a good question. One we've been asking ourselves for the past twenty-four hours or so. Usually it's fairly obvious to everybody, because either uniform or CID have to call us in. But with these two examples, I admit it's iffy. In fact, we have less than a day to prove they're ours. If not, could be we get to noon today and Superintendent Fletcher decides we've tinkered enough around the edges, trying to make the pieces fit. As to why I think they belong to us, it's more a question of what's not right, and what that means in terms of possibilities. When you have time, study the boards and look at the crime logs and HOLMES. Neither op is straightforward, we just don't understand why as yet. It's down to instinct on both, but backed up by experience.'

Bliss found himself drawn back to the Jade Coleman investigation. Virgil, then a PC, had impressed him. His first murder victim had not fazed the young officer. He'd gone about the process of investigating the call out and confirming death with a calm authority, which he retained when relating his movements to Bliss and Chandler when they arrived at the scene. He'd be a good addition to the team, one who might be persuaded to stay even if DC Hunt returned.

'Right,' he said, clapping his hands together. 'Let's bring our best game to this. We're up against the clock. We all have jobs to do, so let's get on with them.'

The team dispersed. Though the incident room provided online access, the computers and laptops available to them were less than reliable. Some officers remained to tap away at the keyboards, others used the bank of phones. The rest either went back into the major crimes area or, as with Bishop and Ansari, sought the fastest computer equipment required for viewing CCTV film.

Bliss sat with his partner, going over both operations from top to bottom, trying to find a new way in. The first break of the day came early on when DCI Warburton returned from her meeting with the Super. She motioned for Bliss to join her in the small office she'd taken over on the day she joined the team. Sitting behind her desk, she wore a wide grin of satisfaction.

'You have permission to conduct a section 17 entry and search of Callum Oliver's residence,' Warburton told him.

Bliss pumped a fist. 'Really? That's great news. Well done. You standing up to that numpty CPS advisor did the trick after all.'

'For now. However, the scope is limited. If you don't find him at home, you can use only that which is in plain sight to help with your search. This means there will be no rummaging through drawers, no checking out his clothes, no rifling through any cabinets or files. Only whatever is out in the open. Is that understood, Jimmy?'

'Yes, boss.'

'Is it? Is it, really? So if you see, say, a box file sitting on a shelf, you are not going to open it up and go through Mr Oliver's personal and private information?'

Bliss inclined his head. 'To be honest, I think the restrictions are a nonsense in this case. We're not looking to put the man away, we're concerned about his safety. That said, I hear what you're saying, so I'll work within the parameters set out for us.'

Warburton studied his face for far longer than he was comfortable with. 'What?' he said with a shrug. 'I've told you what you wanted to hear, haven't I?'

Still her suspicious scrutiny continued. 'Jimmy, let me put this more simply for you. Unless I accompany you, I'm not going to know what you did or did not do. So, what I'm saying is, you know your limits. Work within them. Or at least don't make it obvious if you don't.'

Bliss smiled. Warburton understood him too well.

Leaving his team to focus on their own areas of expertise

relevant to both operations, Bliss took Chandler with him to Callum Oliver's ground-floor flat in Orton Southgate, close to the East of England showground. A couple of uniforms waited for them, the pair forcing entry before continuing to stand outside to prevent anybody else from sauntering in. It wasn't a large dwelling to work their way through, and less than a minute after they'd stepped inside they confirmed Callum Oliver was not at home.

'What do we do now?' Chandler asked Bliss.

He had informed her of the PACE limitations attached to the search. 'If he came home wounded there might be signs of him treating himself; you know, bloody cotton wool, flannel, that kind of thing. I suggest we both take a closer look around inside different rooms. That way, if asked, you can genuinely say you didn't see what I did.'

She huffed a sigh and put both hands on her hips. 'Which tells me you're not going to do as you've been told.'

'Not necessarily. But provided you don't see me not doing as I'm told, you can't know for sure.'

Chandler fixed him with her sternest gaze, which eventually wilted beneath his own. 'Whatever,' she said, stomping out of the room. 'On your head be it.'

Bliss grinned and got to work. He went from room to room, pulling out drawers, picking his way through cupboards and shelves. Chandler remained in the passageway, rustling up a glare for him whenever he passed by. Finally, he came back to where they had both started: the open-plan kitchen and dining area.

'Did you check the bin in here and the bathroom?' he asked.

'Would I be incriminating myself if I told you I had?'

'Not at all.'

'Then yes, I did. No sign of any wound clean-up.'

Bliss nodded thoughtfully as he ran his gaze over the room they stood in. On the breakfast bar lay a notepad next to a laptop which until now he had ignored. Not so this time around. 'You might want to double-check the bathroom bin,' he said. 'I need a minute.'

With Chandler out of the way, he powered up the laptop, but was prompted to enter a username and password. He sat for a moment with his fingers drumming on the counter top, then something occurred to him.

He closed the lid and turned the device over. His guess had been correct; there was a postcode engraved into the chassis. He knew without checking that it would match the address for the *Peterborough Telegraph*. He set the laptop down again as he'd found it, considering several possibilities. Finally he shrugged and gave in to the inevitable. At which point, he took out his phone and made a call.

'Sandra, it's me,' he said. 'Listen closely. Don't ask questions, just hear me out. We're inside Callum's flat. There's no sign of him and we still don't know where he is or how he is. Thing is, there's a laptop here and I can see it belongs to the paper.'

'Then you can't touch it,' Bannister insisted. 'It's not his property, so it's excluded from your warrant.'

'If I had a warrant and time to waste, we could debate that, but I have neither. It's a life and limb safety check only.'

'So why the phone call, Jimmy?'

'I need your help. Don't get mad, but I switched the laptop on and it booted. But it's password protected.'

'Do you ever just follow your own rules?'

'I do when they make sense. This doesn't. All I'm trying to do here is find your colleague. Is that so wrong?'

The way he'd couched the statement, it was hard for the journalist to argue. 'I still can't help you,' she told him. 'I don't have his credentials, and mine won't work.'

'Actually, I think they will.'

'No, they won't. I've never used Callum's machine, and I have no user account on it.'

'I understand that. But bear with me, because you know what a technotard I am. Sandra, am I right in thinking that when these *PT* devices are brought into work, they automatically synchronise with the newspaper's own network?'

'Ye…es, they do. I'm amazed you know even that much.'

'That's what comes from working with Gul Ansari. Can't help but pick up a few tips. So, let me take it a stage further. If this device was inside the *PT* building, you could then use your network credentials to log on to it. You'd have access to the network, but also the hard drive and probably the cloud if you people use it.'

'Please don't ask me to do what I think you're about to ask me to do, Jimmy.'

'It could help us find Callum.'

'Sod Callum! He's a weasel.'

'That may be so. But he's a missing weasel right now. And I have a feeling he might be in trouble, Sandra. I understand why you don't like the bloke, but I'm sure you wish him no harm.'

'You want to bet on that?'

He laughed. 'Not really. But I think you're better than that.'

A couple of seconds drifted by before Bannister spoke again. 'Okay, so what? You want to bring Callum's laptop here to my office and have me log on and then search it for you while you wait?'

'No, nothing like that.'

'What then?'

'Okay, well, something like that. But not entirely. Yes, I want to bring the device to you and have you log on.'

'That's what I said.'

'Yes, but you then went on to say you assumed I wanted you to search through the laptop while I waited.'

'And you don't want me to do that?'

'No,' Bliss said firmly. 'I want you to log on and then give me the laptop so that I can search it instead.'

FIFTEEN

THE THREE MOST SENIOR female detectives working out of Thorpe Wood police station gathered in the conference room. Fletcher had booked it out for an hour, summoning both chief inspectors to an ad hoc meeting. She spent the first few minutes describing her unexpected visit from the Chief Superintendent the previous day. When she was done, she looked between them, ensuring she had their complete attention.

'Before we move on,' she said in a low voice. 'I expect nothing less than honest opinions and the absolute truth in all matters discussed here today. I also demand absolute confidentiality. Nothing – and I mean absolutely nothing – leaves this room. Is that understood?'

Both her colleagues nodded their agreement.

'Good. I wish, therefore, to tackle each of the DCS's concerns. I'm not above questioning myself or my actions, which is why I insist you both speak openly. First, then, I want to look at the issue of DC John Hunt. Diane,' she said, turning her gaze to DCI Warburton. 'You've worked most recently with the man, managed him for over two years. Tell me, what is your honest opinion of John and of Jimmy's decision to shift him sideways into CID?'

Warburton swallowed and leaned back in her chair. She took her time before responding. 'The arrangement did not occur in a vacuum, ma'am. The inspector and I discussed the issue in some detail. He asked for my advice, readily admitting he had run out of ideas where DC Hunt was concerned. But please don't be misled into thinking Jimmy considered Hunt to be a problem character in need of forcing out of the unit.'

Fletcher nodded for her to continue. 'Very well. Do go on. And in here, with just the three of us, please let's dispense with rank. I don't want it getting in the way.'

'Of course. You asked about John Hunt, so I'll give you my impression of the officer he is. Initially, it's hard to find fault. He is adroit, experienced, well-regarded by his colleagues, and a genuine asset to the team. That is, he was. But something has altered. I hear whispers about his personal life, and some upset there might explain changes in his behaviour. Having said that, while John was all of those positive things as an officer, he never struck me as being fully committed. He was never the first to step up, seldom volunteered for overtime, rarely worked beyond his required hours. Jimmy was surprisingly okay with that. As he said frequently, it takes all sorts to make a team, and whatever John's shortcomings he made up for in the job he did when it counted. But a while back he became… less interested in the basic functions of a DC. This led to periods of surliness, often revealing itself as a lack of respect for others. He didn't want to do the work needed to make a step up in rank, yet behaved as if he had already taken it.'

Fletcher was nodding along. 'That tallies with my understanding of the situation. So am I right in thinking you support the transfer to CID?'

'You are. I do. I think John had drifted, and while Jimmy is annoyed with himself that he failed to bring him back in line, he believes he has a lot to give and perhaps just needed to find out more about the job from a different perspective. I can absolutely guarantee there was no malice involved. Not on Jimmy's side, that's for certain.'

Turning to DCI Edwards, Fletcher said, 'What's your take, Alicia? You also managed both men.'

'I did. John is every bit the good copper Diane described. But I would also agree that he lacks a certain something. I don't know anybody else in that team who regards their work as just a job, but I'm sorry to say I saw that in him. He came in every day, did everything expected of him, and you were left with the overwhelming impression that he forgot about the cases he worked the moment he left the building. Now, I know there are some who will say that's a good thing, the sensible way to tackle what is a stressful role. And I suspect his colleagues accepted it well. However, if he started disrespecting others, became disenchanted with the job he was being asked to do, then I can imagine him being a bit of a handful.'

Fletcher made some notes in a ring-bound A4 notepad. 'Don't worry about this,' she said, looking up and smiling at her two chief inspectors. 'I am noting details but attributing them to neither of you. Should anybody ever read the contents, what I've written will come across as my own thoughts. So… the gist I'm getting from both of you is that neither of you has issues with Jimmy's decision regarding John Hunt.'

Edwards nodded. 'He's now under my command, Marion, and therefore now my problem to deal with, but even I can see how this might help John in the long run.'

'Good. Then let's turn our attention to the major crimes workload.' Fletcher switched her gaze back to DCI Warburton. 'You already had a number of open cases on your hands, Diane. We spoke about this yesterday, but please tell me how you intend approaching both Understudy and Fledgling today.'

'I'd like to give it time to breathe. And I'm well aware of our existing caseload. However, in the main, those ops have reached the point of either winding down or preparing the necessary documentation for the CPS. A few remain active but are considered to be the type of investigations we can no longer pursue until we have additional information – an unexpected break, in other words. We have room to at least see where these two new jobs take us. Jimmy is not entirely convinced about them, and held his hands up to that. However, his instinct insists there's something there in both these cases, and no matter what else you may think about him, his gut rarely lets him down.'

'I can vouch for that,' Edwards confirmed. 'Jimmy and I haven't always seen eye to eye, and he's not the easiest of people to deal with. But his experience and feel for an investigation are second to none, so if he says there's something above and beyond the obvious, then there most likely is.'

Warburton nodded and added, 'I also think it's more than just his intuition this time, because both acting DI Bishop and DS Chandler appear to agree with him. Not only that, but when Inspector Kaplan called in major crimes, he must have had his reasons.'

Fletcher let that sink in. Her thoughts drifted back to the Chief Superintendent's fleeting visit. Quite why he had a bee in his bonnet about Jimmy Bliss again was beyond her. They had all moved past that, and the team was functioning as well as they ever had. But something had stirred Feeley. She had asked him how he had learned of the DC Hunt matter, and from who. He had dismissed the questions as if it they never been asked, a lofty shake of the head his only retort. Angered by his arrogance, she had insisted that if tales were being told behind her back, she had every right to confront her detractor. Feeley's reaction echoed in her mind now.

'It's no secret that you wanted my job, Marion. I'm sure you believe you deserved it instead of me. But please don't do that job for me. I hear what you're saying, but all I will tell you is this: like any good police officer, I have my own confidential sources, and confidential they will remain.'

She had given that a great deal of thought afterwards, and her irritation came flooding back. She looked up. 'Tell me, Alicia, does DI Bentley still caddy for the Chief Superintendent?'

The question appeared to take Edwards by surprise, but she recovered well. 'I believe he does, yes.'

'Regularly?'

'Bentley is a keen golfer, but often carries the bag for the Chief Super when they are not enjoying a round together themselves.'

'And so has his ear.'

'Of that I have no doubt.'

Fletcher gave a wry grin. 'In which case, if we cannot cut off the supply of information, we must do our best to ensure that information is all positive in future. Need I say more, ladies?'

Both Warburton and Edwards nodded at the same time. Fletcher had expected them to respond well. Alicia Edwards anticipated a long and illustrious career ahead of her. She might be more inclined towards Chief Superintendent Feeley given he was a further rung above, but was astute enough to realise that no battles would be won in the future if she pissed off her immediate boss here and now. As for DCI Warburton, she played her cards close to the chest, but had been nothing less than loyal and supportive.

Fletcher despised the politics of their various positions and statures. It made her uncomfortable, with trust being the main victim in any dispute. Clearly Feeley had it in for Bliss yet again, and although DC Hunt was at the forefront of his concerns, she couldn't help but imagine there was far more to it than that.

When it came to Jimmy Bliss, there always was.

SIXTEEN

'You do know I can't just log you on to our network and leave you alone?' Sandra Bannister said to Bliss. She was impressive when she was riled, and her face was all tight knots of ill-concealed anger. 'I'm trusting you and taking a huge risk as it is. I'm willing to let you search through whatever's on the hard drive, but that's all you get. There's no way I'm allowing you to dip into shared drives or the backup cloud.'

Ostensibly, if anybody saw them together, Bannister would tell them Bliss was there to discuss the forthcoming trial at the Old Bailey. The reporter had no office of her own, so they sat in a small room set aside for interviews and meetings. Though he'd dropped Chandler back at HQ before heading into the city centre, Bliss had fully expected a measure of push back from the journalist, accepting what he could get without putting up too much of a fuss.

He raised his hands defensively. 'Okay. I understand. It's your turf, your rules apply.'

'If that were the case, you'd be leaving and I'd be locking that laptop away in the property room.'

Bannister's tired smile told him her patience with him was

stretched thin as it was. Bliss gave in to it, and not for the first time where her strong will was concerned. He waited until she had opened the device and connected to the internal network, at which point she pushed it across the desk he'd taken a seat at. 'Hard drive is all yours,' she said.

'How about the My Documents folder?'

'That synced with our servers the moment I logged in. Any new or updated files will also have been copied up to the backup cloud. But I can guarantee you, if Callum was working on something of his own, for the reasons I just explained, he'd never have saved it into that folder. But either way, none of that is yours to see. And let me stop you before you go on… you're to steer clear of his Downloads folder, as well.'

Jimmy reacted with a wide smile. 'That's fine. See, it's all amicable,' he said. Then he pulled a writing pad from his pocket and shoved it under Bannister's nose. It was the ring bound notebook that had been sitting alongside the laptop in Oliver's kitchen. 'You recognise Callum's particular style of shorthand?'

Bliss knew she would. Shorthand was a taught skill and contained standard geometrical shapes to denote letters, words and phrases, but journos often added their own individual flourishes. Callum Oliver was likely to be no different. Bliss had assumed Bannister would need to know his style in case he was ever incapable of transcribing them himself. 'While I'm busy scouring the hard drive, please run your eye over his notes. Something in them might be helpful to my investigation, and I also need to be aware of its more general content.'

Bannister snorted. 'You don't want much from me, do you, Jimmy? I offer you a hand, you take a leg, both arms, and my good intentions.'

'I appreciate your help. You know I do. But remember, this time it's not for me; your colleague is missing and the contents of this device could help to find him. If it turns out to be one of your cases after all, then pull the shutters down. I'm willing to bet that's not the case, though, Sandra.'

It was a risk, but one Bliss was willing to take. He had no idea what might be stored on the laptop, but was keen to find out. Bannister eyed him warily before shrugging and getting on with it.

'I have something,' she said smoothly after a few minutes. 'It's a series of disjoined items, so basically nothing more than an idea sketched out. But there's nothing here I recognise as being associated with the newspaper. Certainly not one of our authorised stories, nor even one we've ever discussed. I don't know what Callum is into here, but it's definitely something he intended to keep to himself.'

'Sounds promising. And timely. I just found a document containing lines of short notes. They also appear to be disconnected. You go first and I'll see if I can follow.'

'All right. I have here a series of initials to begin with, which usually indicates the names of people relevant to the story. Do you have a DN and an ML?'

'Yep.'

'SP and SH?'

'Yes.' Bliss grinned and gave a nod of encouragement. 'So what I have here on the document was clearly taken from the notepad. That's a good start. I have one more set of initials, but oddly enough it's preceded by two full names. So I have Bernadette Finch, and Edith Weston, followed by the initials OK.'

'I have something similar, but on the pad all three are just initials,' Bannister said, seemingly puzzled by this. 'I wonder why he expanded those two names in particular and not the others when he typed it up.'

'No idea. I'm guessing they mean nothing to you?'

'No. This is definitely something Callum had going on the

side. Which, to be honest with you, comes as no real surprise. He could be ridiculously competitive.'

'Unlike you, of course.'

Bannister clamped a hand to each hip. 'Hey, play fair. I'm here helping you, which so goes against the grain for me.'

'There is another name,' Bliss said, squinting at the monitor. 'But it's not *in* the document. It's the document's name. He called it Paul Foot. Does that mean anything to you?'

Bannister stifled a laugh. 'Typical Callum. He doesn't lack ambition. Paul Foot was a renowned investigative journalist. He died in 2004, since when there's been an annual award named after him for the best piece of investigative journalism in the country. Clearly Callum rated his chances with whatever this is.' She slid over in her chair to look at the file Bliss had on screen. 'Let me see what he might have added here that doesn't appear in his notes.'

She read the short file, nodding or shaking her head with each line. 'There's nothing substantial here,' she said eventually. 'Early days, I'm assuming. And at this stage, he is being extremely careful. Almost to paranoid levels, I'd say. But I am seeing the exact same pattern replicated from his notes. The initials DN and ML are on the same line, as are SP and SH. Then the OK is on the same line as the two names spelt out in full.'

'Suggesting what?' Bliss asked.

'That they're connected somehow. That they come as a batch.'

Bliss nodded. It made sense. Yet he felt an increasing frustration take hold. 'Not that it does me any good. There's nothing in either his notes or this file to tell us what he was working on, who these people are, or where we can find them. That leaves us with the names of Bernadette Finch and Edith Weston as our only real leads.'

'But presumably you'll be able to find them, won't you?'

'We can find women with those names, but it could be a substantial list.'

Bannister squeezed closer so that she could reach the keyboard. She minimised the Word window, then double-clicked the Facebook icon. Less than a minute later, they were looking at a lengthy list of Facebook members using the name Bernadette Finch.

Bliss's shoulders slumped. 'And that's just on one social media platform,' he said bitterly.

'Hmm. I don't envy you.'

He glanced sidelong at her. 'Is there anybody else Callum might have confided in? Perhaps a colleague renowned for digging up connections between people, that sort of thing?'

'No.' She gave a firm shake of the head. 'Even if there were, Callum wouldn't have risked approaching them. Writing your own pieces is frowned upon. It can get you fired. The suspicion is always that the piece is being developed in order to persuade a national that you have the chops, and so is construed as wasting paid time in order to further your own cause. I can pretty much guarantee that Callum told nobody about this.'

'Whatever it is.'

'I can't make any sense of it, Jimmy. Honestly. At the moment, it's just a series of random lines. Except to Callum, of course.'

'So what about those odd squiggles? Can you make them out?'

'I can. He was determined to conceal significant aspects of these notes, but I recognise these as numbers written out in his own take on shorthand. Some of them appear to be years. There's 1987, followed by 12. 1997, and then 22. A ten-year gap, and the lower number also increases by ten. Then we have a slight jump to 2001, followed by a 26 – so again those figures increase in line with the years. Then there's 2007 and 32, before finally, 2021 and 46.'

Bliss had been nodding along. They made no more sense than they had the first time he'd attempted to decipher them. The numbers had not been included on the laptop document, which told him they were crucial enough to initially keep hidden. He ran a hand over his face.

'Callum obviously decided not to write this up fully, but based on the notepad he was looking hard at a story in which those years feature prominently. The non-date numbers are most likely the corresponding ages of his person of interest. There's nothing else for it, Sandra: my team and I will have to track down these two women. Maybe they can make sense of the rest of it.'

'I'm sorry. I admit I was reluctant to get this involved, but now that I am, I'm concerned about him. Do you think whatever he was working on has landed him in trouble?'

Bliss gave himself time to answer fully. 'I can't rule it out. On the other hand, all we have to go on are a few notes. Plus, if they were connected to his disappearance, I have to wonder why his flat wasn't turned over. Feels like a job half done to me.'

'That's if he's disappeared at all. I mean, you still don't actually know if he's missing.'

'True. But circumstances do point in that direction.'

'His car could have been stolen while he was away somewhere. He could be sunning himself on a beach, with no idea all this is going on.'

'Anything is possible. I hope that's the case, but somebody still got hurt inside that car. Anyhow, thanks for taking things this far. Any chance you could mail me a copy of the file?'

'Of course. And good luck finding those two women.'

He nodded. 'Thanks. And Sandra… don't you go on your own fishing expedition. This is not your story to tell.'

She raised her eyebrows. 'As if I would.'

Before he left, Bliss reminded Bannister once again not to tackle any part of what they had before he and his team discovered more. 'Think about Callum's Audi,' he said as a parting shot. 'Abandoned with blood on the seat despite having been sanitised. Believe it or not, Sandra, I don't want that to be you. I truly don't.'

SEVENTEEN

B LISS REPORTED HIS PROGRESS directly to DCI Warburton. He couched his update in a specific way, downplaying his relationship with Bannister. But she was sharp, and picked up on one particular component of his story.

'Taking *Peterborough Telegraph* property back to them without being asked is an unusually charitable decision on your part, Jimmy. Normally I'd expect you to fight tooth and nail to keep hold of something like a computer device.'

He nodded. His DCI had not asked a question.

'Care to explain?' she prompted him, eventually.

'Truth is,' he said, lowering his voice conspiratorially, 'I couldn't access it. I knew I wouldn't get permission to have our tech people crack the password, so I went directly to the source. As Callum Oliver wasn't available, I tried the next best thing.'

'And what exactly will Ms Bannister expect from you in return?'

'She already has it, boss. The laptop. She knew I could've kept it from her while we fought over it like scrapyard dogs. Instead, I persuaded her to allow me to see what was on it, in exchange for handing it over when I was done.'

Warburton's scrutiny oozed scepticism to Bliss, so he moved quickly on. 'I'm not sure what good it did us, though. A couple of names, a series of initials, plus some figures which may or may not include specific dates and years. But as Sandra pointed out, while they appear random, they're not entirely. Sets of initials seem to be grouped together, as were the full names. That suggests they belong together within the story; whatever that is. As for the years and accompanying digits, I need to spend more time with them. Open it all up to the team, as well.'

'Very well. Let's move on to Marty Lipman. When are you going to give him a pull?'

'I was thinking of doing so the moment I left here. Thought I'd have uniform fetch him, which would give me a chance to fill the team in first with the info I got from Callum Oliver's laptop.'

She leaned forward. 'What makes you think Lipman will allow himself to be fetched? He doesn't have to accompany our officers anywhere unless he's placed under arrest. Something he knows better than anyone. I take it you don't intend taking it that far?'

'I'll get them to dangle it out there as a threat if he protests. Initially, he'll be asked in to help with our inquiries concerning Callum Oliver, specifically regarding the abandoned car and the presence of his backpack in its boot. If he refuses or fobs them off by saying he'll pop by as and when he feels like it, I'll have them refer to the backpack and evidence connected to PC Griffin. If he still refuses, then they can make sure he realises we'd rather speak to him with no fuss, but are quite happy to make an arrest and let as many muck-raking journos know as possible.'

The DCI gave a wry grin. 'You can be a slippery bugger when you set your mind to it, Jimmy.'

'Sometimes it's a matter of needing to be, boss. It's the murky waters we have to wade in occasionally.'

'I'd hate to get on the wrong side of you.'

Bliss shrugged. 'I'll take that as a compliment. Even though I'm not sure it was intended as one.'

Before heading over to the major incident room allocated to the Understudy and Fledgling operations, he tracked down Inspector Kaplan. They discussed events over at the railway line, where the scene had long been closed down and services opened up again. He had nothing further to add, so Bliss explained what he needed from a couple of traffic uniforms.

'If it's going to piss off Marty Lipman, you've got it,' Kaplan said. He chuckled. 'In fact, I hope he refuses and they have to drag him in here with cuffs on. Let him see the custody suite from the wrong side for a change. I'll pay him a visit myself if we can stuff him inside a holding cell.'

Satisfied, Bliss continued on his way to MIR 1, where the team were doing all they could to maintain a decent momentum. He'd already used his phone to forward Chandler a copy of the mail Sandra Bannister had sent him. He asked her to check her inbox and to print out the attached document before turning his attention to DS Bishop.

'Anything good come of the CCTV searches?' he asked.

Bishop nodded eagerly. He'd smartened his appearance in recent weeks, and Bliss was happy to see a suggestion he'd made some time ago being heeded, having advised the man to look less slovenly if he wanted to work his way up to DI.

'Good progress on that, boss,' Bishop said. 'We think we've identified the minivan. We believe it's a Citroen Picasso. According to DVLA, the car was a write-off following an accident, and supposedly no longer on the road. It belonged to a pensioner who passed away shortly afterwards. But a red Picasso bearing his plates was seen in and around the area at the time. I've alerted traffic and it may ping ANPR if it's still out there.'

Excited, Bliss nodded his approval. 'Good man. How about

the second round of door-to-door?'

'Another result, I'm pleased to say. A neighbour living two doors down from the Latchfords says she saw the wife and daughter getting into the back of our minivan. She only saw them from the side, both partially turned so actually mainly from the rear. She didn't notice the driver, but is absolutely certain she's never seen the motor before. It looks like a cracking lead.'

'Yeah, but one that petered out, I'm assuming?'

'Boss?'

'By that I mean CCTV must have lost them at some point.'

'Oh, right. Yes, but we're looking to reacquire. It's a long and difficult job, and the CCTV main desk for the city is getting priority requests coming in.'

Bliss nodded. Traffic and CID, especially those working drugs cases, often required camera-based tracking of vehicles during operations in which neither vehicle nor mobile phone GPS had been possible. 'Fair enough,' he said. 'Hopefully it'll pop up somewhere today. How about our victim's phone? Any luck with that?'

'We ran a subscriber check, which came back as Telefonica. They confirmed it was a Tesco Mobile number. Gul sent off the relevant details to have the RIPA form completed online as authorised by you, and I'm hoping to have data back on that either later today or tomorrow at the latest. Bearing in mind it's Telefonica, they may still require a manual authorisation check.'

'Okay. Good work, the pair of you. And the neighbour who saw Latchford's wife and daughter getting into the Citroen, did she happen to hear any crashing about shortly beforehand?'

'Not a thing. Mind you, she's a couple of doors down. Even the immediate neighbours heard nothing out of the ordinary.'

Bliss scratched the back of his neck. 'All that disturbance and nobody heard a thing. I have to say, that convinces me all the more about the scene being staged… carefully.'

Chandler came back with the printed document. She put it on the board, securing it with magnets, then used a marker to transfer the details across so that they could be viewed by everybody. Bliss was about to talk the team through it when his phone rang. He answered without glancing at the screen.

'This is Marty Lipman. I have two of your officers here, Inspector Bliss. I realise you have a job to do, but so do I. I'm in the middle of an important brief and I have a meeting later today, by which time I need to be entirely familiar with it and my client. Can whatever you want with me wait until this evening?'

Bliss was not about to be side-tracked. Nor was he willing to agree to a delay. 'No, it can't.'

'Then would you at least do me the courtesy of explaining why you're demanding my immediate presence? I told you yesterday, I don't know how my backpack came to be in the boot of that vehicle you found abandoned. None whatsoever. I really don't see how I can be of further assistance.'

'That's because you're not privy to all the facts, Mr Lipman.'

'So then, tell me what they are.'

'I will. Of course. Just as soon as I sit down to talk with you in person.'

'And if I refuse? If I agree to submitting to your questioning tomorrow instead? Your officers seem to think they have orders to arrest me if I don't make myself available to you right away. I told them that can't be the case, which is why I called.'

'Don't refuse,' Bliss said bluntly. 'That's my advice. Those were the instructions I gave uniform, and they'll carry them out if they have to. I warn you, though, if you don't come here of your own volition, you'll be driven through a media scrum outside, and my officers will pause long enough for you to be identified.'

He smiled to himself when the call was closed without further discussion or argument. The solicitor had caved, which he would not have done if he had nothing to hide. Bliss turned to the boards, Chandler having finished writing up Callum Oliver's notes.

'I have about ten minutes before Pen and I have to shoot off to have words with Marty Lipman,' he said. 'So, let me quickly take you through this. What you see here is precisely how it was written in his notes.'

He paused, allowing his team to read and digest.

DN > ML
SP > SH
1987 > 12
1997 > 22
2001 > 26
2007 > 32
2021 > 46
R on L
Ct Inj
Li An
Bernadette Finch, Edith Weston... OK

'I'm told by Sandra Bannister at the *PT* that the capital letters indicate the initials of people relevant to the story. In his original notes he had written BF and EW, but Sandra could not explain why he might have written their names more fully in the document he created.'

'Is it possible that Callum Oliver only had the initials of the other people to work with, but had lucked out with the full names of the other two?' DC Ansari asked.

It was a terrific question; one neither he nor Bannister had considered. It spurred an idea in his own mind. 'That's certainly a possibility, Gul. Nice thinking. It's especially possible if the information came from another journalist. Or, more specifically, their own set of notes.'

'And none of this made sense to Lois Lane?' Chandler asked.

Bliss shook his head. 'Sadly, no. The most we agreed on was that the sets of initials had been written that way because they belonged together. In what context or capacity is anyone's guess.'

'And Bannister didn't recognise the rest of the shorthand?' Gratton asked. 'Those three lines beneath the figures have to be crucial to the story, connected to everything else.'

'They're not standard shorthand, no. They must mean something to Callum Oliver, but perhaps only to him.'

'Which leaves us with the two named women,' Bishop said. 'And whoever this OK person is.'

'Could the O and the K mean precisely that?' Gratton asked. 'Might it not be a person at all? Could he have simply meant okay?'

Bliss shrugged. 'It's possible, Phil. But given his use of upper-case initials elsewhere to signify the names of people, it's doubtful.'

'So until we flesh the rest of it out, Bernadette Finch and Edith Weston become our main focus.'

'Exactly. So, while Pen and I are in the room with Lipman, you lot can put your heads together. Run those two names through PNC and see if your tiny brains can decipher the rest of these notes.'

He glanced at Chandler and nodded towards the door. 'Come along, Sergeant. Let's not keep our esteemed legal mind waiting.'

EIGHTEEN

I F EYES COULD SLICE and dice, Bliss imagined he would never have made it to the interview room table. Marty Lipman seethed in his chair; jaw rigid, chest heaving, cheeks florid and shiny. His toad throat pulsed. If ever a man needed a release valve, it was him.

'Thank you for coming in, Mr Lipman,' Bliss said drily. 'We have a couple of things to go over. Do you have legal representation on the way?'

As Bliss and Chandler lowered themselves into their seats opposite the solicitor, he exhaled through his nose in such a way that Bliss imagined steam emerging. 'Firstly,' Lipman boomed, counting off on his fingers, 'I am here because you made it abundantly clear that I had very little choice in the matter. And secondly, I have no need of representation when the best opponents this station has to offer are you two.'

Bliss pursed his lips. Nodded. 'Fair enough. Before I go ahead and make things official, however, are you willing to talk to us without caution and without any recording devices switched on? We can, of course, do so whenever you like, but I suspect you're going to be happy for us to begin off the record.'

Lipman's shoulders continued to rise and fall steadily, his breathing laboured. Bliss could tell wheels were spinning inside his head. He would feel caught, but as yet not netted. That gave him some wriggle room, and as expected, he was too shrewd not to accept the offer.

'You ask away,' he said. 'I'll answer when and if appropriate. If that becomes unacceptable, we'll make this interview more formal.'

'Quite. And that goes both ways. When we feel the time is right, we'll say so. Let me begin by asking you about the vehicle in which we discovered your backpack.'

'What about it? We've already been over this as far as I can recall.'

'We touched on it, and now we need to revisit the matter. Let me tell you what we know, Mr Lipman. Then you can judge for yourself whether your previous response was adequate. The vehicle in question was found abandoned. It had been cleaned down on the inside, yet we found small traces of blood. We believe that blood may stem from a wound to the registered keeper of the vehicle, a Mr Callum Oliver. Does that name ring a bell, sir?'

'Not that I recall, no.' The puzzled frown came a fraction too late, beaten to the punch by a blink of concern.

Bliss narrowed his gaze. 'So you were not aware that Mr Oliver is a journalist with the *Peterborough Telegraph*.'

'Once again, not that I recall.'

A stated lack of recall came straight from the *Interviews for Dummies* handbook. It represented a tactic used for many years by those experienced in such matters, deployed as a way to avoid being caught out in an outright lie. Bliss didn't blink, having expected Lipman to take this path.

'Strange,' he said. 'Because, oddly enough, Mr Oliver works the crime desk. Are you sure you haven't at least heard the name before?'

Again the one-two; genuine concern followed by a studied bemusement. And before long, capitulation. 'Ah, yes. I see. Now that you've added context, I am familiar with the name.'

'Does that mean you've met him, Mr Lipman?'

'I didn't say that. I said the name was familiar to me.'

Bliss accepted the response with a nod. 'Quite right. So you did. In which case, let me rephrase: have you ever met Callum Oliver before, sir?'

Prepared this time, the solicitor was quick to respond. 'I may have. Perhaps at a function or event. It's quite possible, though I have no immediate recollection.'

'Which is understandable if the meeting had been fleeting or took place quite some time ago. But equally, had you met with him, say, only three days ago, you would recall that quite well, I'm assuming?'

'Why would you think that was the case, Inspector?'

Bliss shifted his weight in the chair. 'I prefer it when I'm asking the questions. However, on this occasion, I would have thought the answer was obvious. If you had previously met with Mr Oliver, that might explain how your backpack came to be in his possession. Did you meet with him? If so, I can't think why you'd be reluctant to mention it. Not unless you are involved in his disappearance. I should add that if you were inside his motor, your prints are going to be found.'

Lipman took a deep breath. He blinked rapidly, eyes dropping to the table. A moment later, he cleared his throat and said, 'All right. Yes, I met with Mr Oliver, and yes, that's why my backpack was in the boot of his car. The fact is, I neglected to mention this to you before because he is a client and the subject of our meetings and subsequent conversations is protected by privilege. I didn't think it was worth mentioning, because I cannot tell you what was discussed.'

Bliss turned to Chandler. She, too, cleared her throat before speaking. 'While of course the substance of your arrangement with Callum Oliver is between you and him, the fact is you could and should have told this to my colleague yesterday. To be blunt, you lied when questioned, Mr Lipman.'

'I was not questioned as a suspect. I was not questioned under caution. If I lied at all, and I'm admitting nothing of the sort, it was simply in order not to waste your time with inconsequential matters. Which is not illegal.'

'It is if we believe you lied for the very opposite reason, sir. If your lie wasted police time, or in order to pervert the course of justice, then we have every right to take matters further in that regard.'

'And do what?' Lipman said, laughing this time. 'We all know you'll never prosecute. So let's stop wasting time, shall we? I've now admitted to knowing Callum Oliver, attested to the fact that he is a client and therefore everything we discussed is out of bounds where you are concerned. However, that leads me to ask about the welfare of Mr Oliver. Am I right in thinking you believe he may have come to some harm?'

'That will not be part of this discussion,' Chandler said forcefully. 'Mr Oliver features in an ongoing investigation. All I will tell you is that his current whereabouts are unknown. To that end, your dealings with him may directly connect to his absence.'

'In which case, I still cannot discuss them with you. Not until you have more information.'

Bliss folded his arms, drawing his attention. 'All right, sir. Let's set that aside for the time being in order to focus on the other reason we wanted to speak with you today.'

'By all means.' Lipman sat back and crossed one leg over the other.

'Mr Lipman, do you still intend to go ahead with your civil prosecution of Police Constable Barry Griffin?'

'I do indeed.'

'And there's no reason you can think of why you ought to reconsider?'

'None whatsoever.'

'In that case, I have to inform you of something. In fact, as we're off the record here, I'll put it to you in terms you can more readily understand. We want you to drop the case against PC Griffin. In fact, we insist upon it.'

'And why on earth would I do that, Inspector?'

'Because if you don't, we'll be forced to seek a judgement on your behaviour and practices. The rules on evidentiary disclosure are clear, Mr Lipman. And I don't need to tell you how things might go for you if you are found to have deliberately withheld evidence from us and defence counsel. Wilfully failing to make a relevant disclosure is not something you want on your CV.'

'What on earth are you talking about, man?'

Bliss squinted for a moment, then grinned. 'I just this second realised where I knew that pub from. It's the Anvil on Oundle Road. You recognise the name? You ought to. After all, you or one of your employees visited it recently to collect security footage. Isn't that right, sir?'

The outrage returned swiftly, along with ugly creases of flesh. 'You went through my backpack. My personal possessions. You had no right.'

'On the contrary, we had every right. We had to search that backpack in order to find out who it belonged to. We couldn't just assume it belonged to Mr Oliver. We didn't realise the property belonged to you until we'd watched the CCTV footage on the USB stick and read your notes. You will argue the point, I'm sure. Or at least, you'll want to. But I'm told we're on firm ground here. The fact that you have not disclosed this evidence to us is going to count against you because you've had sufficient time to do so. In fact, on two subsequent occasions you've made it quite clear to me that you fully intended to continue with your prosecution, despite having had access to the video and drawn several conclusions about it in your notes.'

Lipman's glare was spiteful. 'You're damn right I will argue against this.'

Bliss continued, unruffled. 'Which is your prerogative. But perhaps not in your best interests. After all, just imagine what will happen when you lose – and you will. You not only lose the case, but you might even lose the right to practice law. Even a public reprimand will severely damage your reputation. Who will ever trust you again?'

Silence.

Bliss let it sit, knowing its power to influence. After a period of reflection, Lipman said, 'What are you suggesting?'

'Three things. We go on record in a moment. At which point you freely disclose the evidence to us, offer it up for our inspection, and in the same breath withdraw the case against PC Griffin. You also tell us what we need to know about your relationship with Callum Oliver.'

'And in return…?'

'We won't make any mention of you failing to do the right thing earlier. In essence, we won't accuse you of deliberately doing so with the intention of pursuing your case.'

'That may be acceptable to me. Regarding Mr Oliver, however, I can only tell you what the law allows me to tell you. I cannot infringe upon my client's confidentiality.'

'How about you tell us more right now while we're off the record, Mr Lipman? After all, it is your client who appears to be missing.'

Blinking furiously, Lipman licked his lips and nodded. 'This is all I know: Mr Oliver sought my advice on the legality of the investigation he was running. He gave me no facts, no names. He kept to vague details only. He wanted to know how far he could go when investigating something whose results he intended to make public, and what – if any – prohibitive laws might come into effect because of a court injunction.'

'That's it?' Chandler asked.

'I'm afraid so, yes. The truth is, I met Mr Oliver just the once. He was extremely nervous about even talking to me. We met at a pre-arranged location. I got into his car and we drove around for a while as he outlined his situation. He suggested we stop for a coffee, so when we did, I popped my backpack into his boot for safe keeping. After he took a call that meant he had to rush off, I stupidly forgot to retrieve my things. By the time I realised, he'd already driven off. It was a simple misunderstanding.'

Bliss stared hard at him. 'If that isn't the truth, if I later discover any part of that to be a lie, I'll come for you again,' he said in a low voice. 'We can agree going in that once we activate the recording devices and apply the caution, we make no mention of disclosure. But that doesn't mean we won't return to it at a later date if we find out you've been telling porkies or holding out on us. Is that understood?'

'That's not much of a deal, is it? You get the information you want and walk away free to hang me out to dry somewhere down the road.'

'It's all the deal you're going to get, and better than you deserve,' Chandler snapped, contempt lacing each word. 'Make no mistake, *Marty*, we'd love nothing more than to have you for tucking up our friend and colleague. It's one thing to go after him because you've been asked to by the victim's family, but another matter entirely when you acquire evidence showing he's innocent.'

'Neither the footage nor the incidents themselves prove anything of the sort,' Lipman shot back, squaring his shoulders.

'Okay. But it ruins your case because you cannot possibly prove Griffin's was the blow that caused your client's injuries. In fact, that footage shows the more likely suspect to be whoever lamped him in the Anvil. So, like I say, we'd love to see you done for that. But we'd all rather have PC Griffin off the hook more immediately. That and the information about Callum Oliver. Bird in the hand and all that.'

Lipman turned straight on and crossed his arms. 'Let's not waste any more time,' he said bitterly. 'I imagine we all have better things to do.'

At that precise moment, Bliss could think of nothing he'd rather be doing.

NINETEEN

The closer they got to St George's Barracks, the less they could see the base itself. Sneak glimpses from afar were quickly obscured by high hedgerow and lines of densely populated trees, clearing only as the entrance opened up into plain view. The barracks and airfield sat in idle contemplation of its impending closure and planned redevelopment into a new community of homes – much against the will of local villagers.

Bliss and Chandler found themselves in Rutland because of a moment of inspiration from the newest member of the MCU, DC Virgil. Following the Lipman interview, the team had reconvened in the incident room. Together they celebrated the good news regarding PC Griffin, though the mood turned a little flat when they learned of Lipman's statement concerning Callum Oliver. As they bounced ideas around, it was Virgil who asked whether the Edith Weston mentioned in the journalist's notes was definitely a woman.

'What do you think she is?' Gratton replied with a chuckle. 'A bloody greyhound.'

Virgil joined in with the resulting laughter. 'No,' he said when it died down. 'Nor a racehorse. I was thinking more like a place.'

'You what?' Bishop asked.

'It's just that there's a village called Edith Weston. It's less than thirty minutes away, just outside Oakham.'

Blank faces turned to other blank faces. After a moment, Bliss said, 'Are you sure about that, Alan? Edith Weston?'

Virgil's nod was firm and confident. He sat close to the eboard controller desk, besides which a laptop had been permanently connected to the display screen. He shuffled over in his chair, pulled up a browser, typed in the name, then clicked the maps link. The village appeared on the southern banks of Rutland Water.

'I wasn't sure about it before,' he explained. 'But when I saw it written up on the board, it rang a bell, though I couldn't initially think why. Then I remembered hearing the name on a local TV news report about the base and its redevelopment.'

'Bloody hell!' Bliss said, louder than he'd intended. His gaze switched to the whiteboard and back again. It was a great shout from DC Virgil, but how dark a pall did it cast over the rest of their information?

Ansari must have asked herself the same question. 'So if the EW in Callum Oliver's original notes is a place and not a person,' she said, 'were we wrong to assume all the initials represented people?'

Chandler shook her head. 'Not necessarily. It is still a name, after all.'

'But then, so might some others be. Written as we have them, and as the two names now appear to be, we could have a person's name followed by a place name.'

'Could it be as simple as naming where they live?' Bishop said, following the suggested pattern. 'Does the Bernadette Finch we're looking for live in Edith Weston?'

'I'll get on that now,' Ansari said, turning away as she took out her phone.

Meanwhile, Bliss had edged closer to the boards. He ran his gaze over the notes. Then he turned to his team. 'Perhaps this explains why Callum Oliver wrote BF and EW in full when he typed up those bullet points. Maybe he did so because they're different from his other notes. Sandra Bannister was firm about initials representing names, but it just so happens this Edith Weston is also the name of a village. He might well have expanded upon the initials in order to remind himself that they followed a different structure.'

'What does that tell us about the O and the K?' Chandler asked.

'I don't know. I really...' Something lodged in his mind. He glanced over at the screen, allowed his gaze to wander across to the right of Rutland Water, following the yellow line representing the A606 road, found where it met the A1 and then followed that north.

'How about this for a suggestion?' he said. 'Callum Oliver searches for Bernadette Finch and discovers she lives in Edith Weston. He contacts her. They arrange a meeting.' He jabbed the screen. 'Here. At the OK diner.'

Breaths released in gasps as if each member of the team had been holding them in. Amidst the jumble of initials and dates, it was the only part currently making some kind of sense.

'You could be bang on about that, boss,' Ansari said as she looked up from her phone, her face gleaming with excitement. 'DVLA records are showing me a Bernadette Finch residing in the Rutland village of Edith Weston.'

All of which had had led to Bliss and Chandler driving out to speak with the woman they hoped might provide them with the breakthrough they'd been searching for. They found her at her home, a converted Collyweston stone barn opposite the village church. Clearly distressed to learn of Callum Oliver's possible disappearance, Finch invited the two detectives inside and immediately set about making them a hot drink.

'I'm not at all sure how much I can help,' she said, taking mugs down from a cupboard mounted on the wall. Of less than average height, she had to strain on tiptoe. Trim and tidy, Bliss imagined the woman doing everything with great precision. Her smile upon seeing the pair at her door had been broad and welcoming. 'I only met him the once. We left the door open to further meetings if he felt he needed more background, but to be honest with you, there wasn't a great deal I could tell him.'

'About what exactly, Mrs Finch?' Chandler asked with her own winning smile.

'About the man I had seen.'

'The man you'd… tell you what, when you're ready, let's start again, beginning with how, when, and why Mr Oliver contacted you.'

Their drinks made, the woman who looked to be in her late sixties settled at the dining table with them, having rested their steaming mugs on slate coasters.

'He telephoned me out of the blue,' she said. 'This would have been… ooh, a few weeks ago now. As for why, well, he told me one thing, but I suspected it was something else entirely.'

Bliss took a sip of his coffee, nodding for her to continue.

'He told me he'd seen an article in the *Stamford Mercury*. It's silly really, but for the past seven years on the exact same day at the exact same time, I've had my lunch at the same little diner on the A1.'

'This would be the OK diner, yes?'

She gave him a look of surprise, but nodded affably. 'Yes. You know it?'

'I do.'

'It's not fine dining by any stretch of the imagination, but my husband and I occasionally drove out there for a bite to eat. He was from America, you see, and although he often pointed out how different the food was, he enjoyed the feel of the place. Said the look and atmosphere kind of reminded him of home. The thing is, the last meal we ever ate together was at the diner, which is why I go there once a year to commemorate it. Somehow, I feel close to him there because it was where he felt closest to his own roots. It must sound silly…'

'Not at all,' Chandler assured her. 'I think it's a lovely gesture.'

Finch blushed. 'Thank you. Anyhow, last year I got into a conversation with the manager of the diner, and I told him about my annual visits. I can only imagine the manager mentioned it to others, because this year I got a call from the *Stamford Mercury* asking if they could write an article about it. I agreed – I thought my Earl would get a real kick out of it as he looked down on us – and one of their junior reporters joined me there for my anniversary lunch.'

As fascinating as the story was, Bliss couldn't see where Callum Oliver's disappearance fitted in. Or his interest in this elderly couple's anniversary. He prompted Finch to explain.

'Oh, he wasn't interested in my little story,' she said with a shake of her head. 'What drew him to me was the photograph they took that same day.'

'The photo? What about it, Mrs Finch?'

'Mr Oliver wanted to know if I had spoken to the man sitting in the booth behind me. See, it wasn't as if they sent out a photographer with the reporter. I don't know if they often still do that sort of thing these days, especially with these local newspapers, but my little story obviously didn't deserve one. Instead, the young lady who came to do the interview also took some snaps with her phone. One of which appeared in the paper.'

The woman raised a finger as she broke off from her tale. She left them sitting alone and then wandered back in a few seconds later clutching a framed photograph. 'The newspaper was kind enough to send this to me,' she said, laying it flat on the table.

In the photograph, Bernadette Finch sat in the diner staring plaintively at the camera. Caught mid-memory, Bliss thought; perhaps recalling the last time she had visited the place with her husband. Behind her, a man's slightly blurred image as he was caught on the move, sliding out of the booth across the bench seat.

'What exactly was Callum Oliver's interest in this man?' Chandler asked, her voice softened.

'I never did find out. He wanted to know if I'd spotted the man already seated there when I entered the diner, if we'd spoken, if he'd placed an order, and if I'd noticed him leaving abruptly. He had so many questions, and I could tell it was important to him. In the end, though, he seemed to focus on just one moment. I said I'd probably had the best view of the man when I went to sit down at my booth. I remember him looking up at me. Our eyes locked, I suppose. Just for a second or two. We exchanged smiles, you know, the way strangers often do.'

Chandler nodded encouragingly. 'So Mr Oliver asked you to describe the man in more detail? Or maybe was he looking for your impression of him?'

'Neither of those,' came the reply. Her eyes twinkled as she recalled their exchange. 'He produced another photograph. Took it out of his jacket pocket. He asked me if I thought it could be the same man. I looked at it for perhaps twenty or thirty seconds. The man in the photo he showed me was younger. He had longer hair and was a little leaner in the face. But the man happened to be looking up and slightly on the move in much the same way as the man in the diner appeared in the *Mercury* photograph. I told Mr Oliver that I couldn't be certain, but yes, I thought it might very well be the same chap.'

'And what was his response?' Chandler asked.

Bernadette Finch frowned, adding age to her appearance. 'It

was quite odd. He said only one thing at that point. Said it so softly as he breathed out. I almost didn't catch it, and by the way he reacted afterwards, I'm quite certain he didn't mean to say it. But he whispered a name. A man's name. I took it to be the man in the photograph, I suppose.'

'Do you remember it? The name he mentioned?'

'Oh, yes, dear. It stuck with me, though I'm not sure why. It was Dean Norman.'

A sharp tingle like a mild static shock ripped urgently through Bliss's flesh in a strong wave. Its ripples caused hair to raise on the back of his neck. He glanced at Chandler, who merely shrugged back. After a pause, Bliss said, 'Mrs Finch, did Callum Oliver ever explain why he was interested in this man?'

The woman ran a hand through her hair, careful not to get her thin fingers tangled up. 'I'm sorry, but no, he didn't. He was satisfied, though. He'd got what he came for. Oh, and he took a snap of my framed photograph. Said it was far better quality than the one from the newspaper. I told him he could take it if he wanted to make a copy, but he said he didn't need to. Would you like to, dear?'

Bliss smiled. Shook his head as he stood to leave. 'Thanks for the offer. But I'll have the *Mercury* send me a copy of their original image for our records. And thank you for the drink and the conversation. You've been extremely helpful.'

They said their goodbyes. When they were in the car and heading south again, Bliss asked his colleague to call the paper to make the request. 'Oh, you actually want it?' she said in surprise. 'I thought you were being polite and gently rebuffing her kind offer.'

'Not at all. Something happened back there, Pen. Something significant. And that image is going to play an important role in our investigation.'

Chandler studied him as if he might be pulling her leg. 'We are? It is? What did I miss? Do you know this Dean Norman?'

'Dean Norman has to be the DN from Callum Oliver's notes.'

'I'm not a complete numbskull, Jimmy, so I'd gathered that much. It looks likely, I admit, but we can't know for certain.'

'We can,' he said, feeling a familiar energetic spark flushing through his blood. 'Because the moment she said the name, I recognised the man in that diner booth, Pen.'

'So you do know this Norman bloke.'

'No. I know of him. Do you remember which initials D and N are paired with in Oliver's notes?'

'Of course. DN together with ML.'

'Precisely. Dean Norman and…?'

Chandler shrugged and huffed at him. 'Spit it out. You know you're dying to, you smug git.'

His grin was tight. 'It was right there in front of us this whole time. DN is Dean Norman, and ML is Morgan Latchford.'

Her face went through a variety of expressions as she tried to bring meaning to his words. She finally settled on a heavy frown. 'You mean the bloke caught in the diner photo is connected to our suicide victim?'

Bliss turned to her, his peripheral view still on the road. 'Yes. If by connected you mean he *is* our suicide victim. Pen, Dean Norman is Morgan Latchford.'

TWENTY

The team took their usual places in the major incident room. Just like a school classroom in that way, Bliss often thought. In many ways, actually. Chandler had printed off the image sent through by the *Stamford Mercury*. She had also obtained from an internet search the lone snapshot of Dean Norman captured by a startled passer-by in Kent when he was in his mid-twenties. Between them hung the photograph Bliss had earlier put up, taken from Morgan Latchford's DVLA record. In context and with the photos side by side, everybody agreed it was the same man.

Bishop, arms folded across his chest, blew out a long breath. 'So now we also know who the SP must be,' he said. His voice was deep and carried some heat.

'Would you care to fill me in on what this is all about?' Ansari said, looking between the two of them. 'Is anybody else here as clueless as I am?'

Chandler's arm shot up, prompting Bishop to mumble, 'No change there, then.'

Bliss raised his hands to quieten them down as additional voices admitted to being in the dark. 'I don't exactly know what this means for our two operations, except to say that they are connected by this new information. Sadly, that won't necessarily make it less complex because I'm still completely puzzled. We'll put our heads together on that as soon as I've told you what I know.'

He took a sip of vending machine hot chocolate before continuing. 'The man who stepped in front of the train yesterday morning was not born Morgan Latchford. For the first twenty-plus years of his life, his name was Dean Norman. When he was barely twelve years old, he and his closest friend, Stevie Phillips, also twelve, murdered eight-year-old Haley Deerbourne. Before sealing her up in a fly-tipped chest freezer and piling rubble on top to keep the lid weighed down, the two boys beat and tortured the poor kid. Norman admitted to it all from the word go. He was unrepentant, claiming he had no real idea of what he and his friend were doing. Phillips initially denied any involvement, but Norman insisted his friend was there the whole time, that he had joined in with everything that took place, and forensics found both sets of prints on the freezer door. Phillips eventually coughed to it as well.'

'I remember it now,' Chandler said in a hushed voice. 'I'd forgotten their names until you mentioned them. But weren't they both jailed for life?'

'Yeah, what the fuck does that mean?' Bishop said in disgust. 'Bugger all once the beardy reformers and hand-wringers get themselves involved. As I recall, the pair were both released on licence after serving only ten years each. A High Court application for new identities and lifelong anonymity was made and accepted.'

'This all ties in with the initials and the years found in Callum Oliver's notepad,' Bliss continued, nodding at the boards. 'Norman and Phillips were sentenced in 1987 when they were both still twelve. Released in 1997 when they were twenty-two.

I confess I'm not sure why 2001 is mentioned, but of course they would have been twenty-six by then.'

'I know what happened,' Bishop said. 'That was the year Dean Norman was outed as living in Kent. That photo on the board spent some time on a Wikipedia page, and was also emailed and shared across the world.'

Bliss gave him a thumbs up. 'Yes, of course. I can see he's much younger, but I hadn't realised it was so long ago. Whoever took the snap didn't have his new identity as far as I recall, nor any indication of where he was living. But the bloke who took it and exposed Norman was arrested and charged.'

'For what?' Gratton asked. 'Outing an ex-con?'

Bishop wagged a finger at him. 'Precisely so, Phil. With life-long anonymity came a court injunction preventing anybody from disclosing the new identities or locations of these two lads. That injunction stretched even to searching for them.'

'Which explains why Callum Oliver was working beneath the radar,' Virgil piped up. 'He was afraid of getting nicked.'

'Afraid, perhaps, but that didn't prevent him from pursuing it. He must have had good reason, and I doubt he was thinking about a splash on the front page of the *Peterborough Telegraph*, either.'

Bliss agreed, suggesting Oliver had been looking for a much larger audience and a far greater payday. 'Hopefully we'll find him alive and well, so he can tell us what was in it for him. I think we can now safely assume that when Dean Norman's boat was revealed back in 2001, he was relocated shortly afterwards to this city. He kept the same ID because that hadn't been compromised. I can't explain why the year 2007 is also indicated, but I think we have to assume this current year is mentioned because it's when the photo appeared in the *Mercury*.'

'How are we supposed to confirm any of this?' Ansari wanted to know.

'Good question, Gul,' Bliss told her. 'In cases like these, the only people who have that kind of information are senior probation officers and the highest ranking police officer in the area. The licensees are monitored by this tiny group of people. Those assessing him in Kent wouldn't even know he'd been moved here. It really is a need to know situation.'

'And all to protect scumbags like these two child-killers!' Bishop snapped. He shook his head in outrage.

'And to protect the financial investment in them. It costs the tax payer a lot of money to keep these people out on licence. Plus, they were only kids themselves when they did what they did.'

'My heart bleeds for them,' Bishop muttered. 'Twelve or not, they understood what they were doing when they tortured Haley Deerbourne. They knew they were hurting her, that the poor little mite was in pain and terrified of them. And they knew she would suffocate to death when they slammed that freezer door shut on her. No remorse, nothing. They should both be rotting in prison. I mean, we're looking at Dean Norman having a wife and child of his own, a life to live as he pleased, fresh air to breathe. That's more than they allowed that poor kid they murdered.'

'You'll get no arguments from me, Bish,' Bliss said calmly. 'But we have to deal with the facts as we know them. My point being, with Fledgling we have Callum Oliver nowhere to be found shortly after he confirms the sighting of Dean Norman. And we also know he linked Norman to his new name.'

'And how are we saying Oliver came by that information?' Ansari asked. 'How does he go from spotting a familiar face in a newspaper photo to contacting Mrs Finch and also identifying Morgan Latchford?'

'Mrs Finch is an easy one. Her name was in the article, as was the village she lives in: Edith-bloody-Weston.' He nodded in DC Virgil's direction. 'With that level of detail, finding her home address would be a doddle; electoral roll, most likely. As for putting a name to the face of the man swiftly exiting that booth, my guess is Callum paid a visit to the OK diner where he found somebody to ask. If he used his *PT* credentials, he could have persuaded them to search through their payment records for that specific time on that date. Either that or cash changed hands to achieve the same result.'

'We're going to have to gather evidence to that effect,' Bishop said wearily. 'Who knows why, how, or when we'll need it – or even if – but better to have it in our back pockets and not require it than be asked for it and have only speculation.'

Bliss nodded. 'Quite. Well said. And thanks for volunteering, Bish. Buy Gul a fat, greasy cheeseburger while you're there.'

'On you is it, boss?'

'Not a bloody chance. Anyway, this all overlaps into operation Understudy, because it cannot be a coincidence that Morgan Latchford, aka Dean Norman, walked in front of a train at around the same time as Callum Oliver was investigating him.'

'So how does any of that tie in with the absence of Latchford's wife and daughter, the fake ransacking of their home, or Latchford's motor ending up in the Nene?' Chandler asked.

Bliss exhaled, already feeling the rigours of the day deep in his bones. 'I don't have answers to any of those questions. We need to find that red minivan. We also need to find Callum Oliver. But… I also have to remind you all that as things stand, we haven't yet positively identified a crime being committed. Other than, perhaps, Oliver himself investigating Norman. Oliver might have been carjacked, he might have come to harm. Mrs Latchford and her daughter might have been taken from their home against their will, or they might have gone willingly. Her husband might have been talked into stepping in front of that train. But the fact remains, nobody has reported anybody missing so far.'

The team took a moment to digest this. Bliss tossed it around inside his head. Was any of it worthy of the Major Crime Unit's time? How serious was it in terms of resource and budget allocation? The blood clean up remained of interest. So too the conversation the man known as Morgan Latchford had moments before stepping onto the railway line. Yet how significant was any of it?

'I'm considering taking this upstairs,' he said. 'DCI Warburton and I can have a word with Superintendent Fletcher. It's obvious to me we have something here. There's nothing right about any single aspect of these two operations. But what's not clear to me is our role in working them. I wonder if they are more a CID matter, and yet I still believe these two ops belong to us. But I'm happy to listen to what any of you have to say before I make a final decision.'

'I vote we keep them,' Chandler said immediately. 'No doubt in my mind.'

'You don't want to give it a bit more thought?' he asked, arching his eyebrows.

'Don't need to. I realise we have only curious incidents at the moment, but the connection between them is what makes me believe all we've uncovered so far is the tip of the iceberg. I want to know what's beneath the surface.'

Bishop was nodding. 'I'll go along with that. My gut tells me Callum Oliver is missing, possibly abducted. It also tells me Mrs Latchford is missing, and that both are in trouble. Then there's the daughter to consider.'

'Does the fact that she might know who and what her husband is and was bother you at all, Bish?'

'Yes. Of course. But I'm willing to give her the benefit of the doubt until I find out for sure. Both she and the daughter are most likely victims in this, too.'

Bliss looked over to DC Ansari, who sighed and then shrugged. 'I have to say I'm torn, boss. These don't feel much like major crimes at the moment. But ultimately I'm with Penny: I think they will be once we understand them better.'

'I'm of the same opinion,' Gratton said before he was asked. 'My view is, if these go across to CID or even uniform, both of them will be back with us by lunchtime tomorrow. By then we'd have wasted too much time.'

Virgil stood shuffling from foot to foot. 'Come on, Constable,' Bliss said to him. 'Tell us where you stand.'

Cheeks flushing red, the young man nodded. 'I can't really say if these are major crimes ops or not, boss. What I can say is if they're tossed over to CID, they will have to sit and wait until a significant number of details change before anybody gives them a second glance. They'll see a questionable suicide and a vehicle abandoned by a man not yet reported missing. All the rest is just noise. It's not because they're not interested, just that they already have too much on their plates. Crimes they know to be actual crimes.'

It was all Bliss needed. 'Well said. All of you. I agree with everything I've heard. Callum Oliver's absence and the presence of blood in his motor are more than enough for me. So let's crack on and see where we are in forty-eight hours, because I'm going to buy us that amount of additional time.'

'You may be further advanced than you expected,' DCI Warburton said as she came through the door and entered the room. Her expression was pensive. 'I've been hovering around outside listening to much of what's been said. I wasn't being a nosy cow, I just didn't want to interrupt. Or influence. And I'm pleased you all came down in favour of continuing.' She paused and turned to Bliss. 'Inspector... a word in your office, please.'

Bliss was concerned by the worry etched into his DCI's face. She seldom presented herself as anxious, at least not to him, and he was troubled by her demeanour. With the door closed behind her, Warburton took him into her confidence.

'Jimmy, you have to make sure these two operations are assigned as major crimes before the day is over. And I mean officially. The moment you provide me with hard evidence, I'll assign myself as SIO and I'll open up a policy book immediately afterwards.'

'What's the urgency this time?' he asked.

'For reasons we have yet to ascertain, the DCS is on the prowl and making life uncomfortable for Marion.'

'What do you mean by that? What have I done now?'

'You're right to think it involves you. Look, for whatever reason, Feeley is taking the transfer of John Hunt to CID quite badly. Either that or he's pretending to, citing a failure of management on your part. But he's also extremely unhappy about these ops and the unnecessary cost of having them run by your unit. We both know he has you in his crosshairs, Jimmy. However, he now seems determined to take Superintendent Fletcher down as well. Given how supportive Marion has been of you, I don't think you want that on your conscience.'

Bliss hissed out a lengthy sigh, shaking his head angrily. 'Where's all this coming from? Who's been telling tales out of school?'

'I'm not going to discuss that with you.'

'Why not?'

'Because if I do, I rather suspect you will confront them. None of us needs that right now. I hope you will agree.'

'You're right. But I can't say I'm not disappointed in you, Diane. I'd hoped you would trust me enough to name DI Bentley as the source.'

'How could you possibly…?' Warburton stopped herself just in time.

Bliss gave a crooked grin. 'I didn't. Not for sure. But now I do. I know he has the ear of the DCS. Rumour has it they're golfing buddies. And if you want to know how I came by that information, just remember it's always a good idea to have the gen on your enemies.'

'I'll do that. But you didn't hear any of this from me, and you won't be doing anything about it, right?'

'I'm not that dumb, boss. And I would never do anything to hurt DCI Fletcher.'

'Which is precisely what you will do if this goes pear shaped, Jimmy. So you have to get out there and gather sufficient evidence to hold on to Understudy and Fledgling. You and your team need to work your arses off today.'

'Consider it done,' he said.

Warburton calmed herself and nodded. 'Good enough. And I'm praying what I'm about to tell you will help, because I have news concerning our red minivan.'

TWENTY-ONE

It hadn't been the easiest of nights to get through, and she'd enjoyed little sleep, but Phoebe knew the mask she wore that day for her daughter had to exude bravery. The room she and Beccy had been provided with was bare other than a scruffy two-seater sofa and an inflatable mattress on the floor, which had been made up with a sheet and blanket, the contours of the temporary bed forming a resting place for their heads. The room was warm enough, though the old cast-iron radiators groaned and popped every time they heated and cooled. Both tall sash windows had been boarded up, so she'd had to switch the light on early that morning. The dusty naked bulb hanging from a central decorative rose was bright but added only a cold austerity to their surroundings. With no TV, Phoebe was thankful for having brought reading and colouring books to keep Beccy amused. Plus, there was always the 7" kids' tablet with games downloaded to fall back on.

The man, who had refused to share his name but admitted to being an investigative journalist, had provided cereal for breakfast and sandwiches for lunch. He made drinks as often as they asked for one, but he insisted the pair remain in the room other than when using the bathroom facilities. He had also opened up the windows and forced out the plywood boards a few inches to allow both air and daylight into the room. Phoebe understood he was attempting to create a more pleasant atmosphere for her and her child, and she genuinely appreciated his efforts.

'Can we speak privately?' she said in the early part of the afternoon when he popped his head in to see if they needed anything.

He nodded and indicated for her to step onto the landing, which was also lit by a single bulb. It smelled equally musty and stale. 'What is this place?' she asked him. 'Where are we?'

'You know I can't tell you that,' he replied in a low voice. 'For all the excellent reasons we've already discussed.'

Phoebe understood. She had listened to his sound reasoning. Yet still she could not resist exploring further than he would approve of. 'There *are* others here, aren't there,' she stated firmly. 'Women and children waiting to move on, just like me and Beccy.'

This time he regarded her with a look of disappointment. 'What did we discuss, Phoebe? I thought I had made the conditions clear to you.'

She bowed her head. 'Sorry. I really am. I don't mean to exasperate you or have you think me ungrateful. I'm just anxious and frightened, that's all.'

He held out both hands and gently squeezed her upper arms. 'And I understand why. I really do. I see it all the time, and there's nothing you can say to me I haven't heard before. But equally there's nothing I can say to you because of the need for secrecy. If you're worried about us being discovered, please don't. Nobody is coming to look for you here, nobody will find us here. You and your daughter are both safe now. You do understand that, don't you?'

She did. And felt so indebted to this man. 'Let me ask one thing,' she pleaded with him. 'Just one more thing. How long do we have to spend here before moving on?'

He shook his head. 'That's out of my scope, Phoebe. The place I have in mind is one of the best for women with children your age and facing similar circumstances. Hence the need for secrecy. You need to understand, they cannot know this way station exists and you cannot know the end destination. And I don't mind admitting it's because if anybody gets caught, the only disruption is to the single cell they work within. This way protects everybody.'

'Okay, okay. I accept that, and it sounds reasonable. Instead, tell me more about Morgan,' she said. 'We never really got around to how you came to learn of his intentions towards me and our daughter.'

'It was by pure chance. It really is that simple. He thought he could make money from having me tell his back story. But in the process he revealed too much of himself, and I later discovered his true objectives online.'

'I still can't entirely believe my Morgan is the man you say he is.'

He looked up at her, his eyes wide. 'Yes,' he said in a calm, calculated voice. 'Yes, you do, or you wouldn't be allowing any of this to take place. You saw it or sensed it in him. You just didn't know what it was. Or, at the very least, you had concerns about his past. I don't think you realise quite how lucky you are, Phoebe. You and Beccy both. If I'd not intervened, your husband would, at some point, have relapsed. It was only ever a matter of time. He was bottling it up inside, and it was all about to spill over.'

The more she searched for answers, the more she knew he was right. Morgan had darkness inside him, and although she would never have suspected him of being the kind of person to hurt a child in such an ugly way, what had taken her by complete surprise was how little persuasion it had required for her to believe it of him now. Phoebe shuddered at the thought of what the man she had loved so fully might have got away with were it not for this reporter standing before her now. She held back her tears as she turned away from him, hoping he would mistake her weakness for relief.

TWENTY-TWO

Detective Chief Inspector Warburton had delivered the news in a flat monotone, but Bliss immediately realised there was a great deal to be excited about. A farmhouse close to the Dog and Doublet pub on the way out to Thorney was under observation after the Citroen had been spotted parked outside on its drive. The watchers had positioned themselves behind a line of trees in a drove south of the river, which is where Bliss and Chandler joined them. Upon arrival, they were greeted by DC Rowena Shanks, a surveillance specialist based out of the Hinchingbrooke divisional HQ. They chatted for a short while, catching up on events since they'd last bumped into each other, before Bliss brought them back to the reason they were there.

'Have you established what's happening on site, Row?' he asked, keen to get caught up with a fluid operation. He'd worked alongside Shanks on a few previous occasions, and had always found her to be friendly and professional. The only thing he knew about her personal life was that she was married to a Northampton Saints rugby union player, but was herself an ardent Leicester Tigers fan. She was thin to the point of appearing gaunt, habitually wore little or no makeup to work, and kept her reddish hair shoulder length beneath a ball cap displaying the Cambridgeshire county police logo.

'We have a rough idea,' she answered. 'A local man called in to tell us of his concerns about the farmhouse. According to him, the owner is in long-term care and the place has just been left as it was when he was taken to hospital. Our caller, a friend of the owner, drives over once a week to pick up the post and make sure kids aren't smashing windows or targeting the place with graffiti. Only, when he approached it this morning, he spotted a red Citroen Picasso outside on the driveway. As he drew closer, he saw there was nobody in the car, nor outside knocking on the door. He became anxious, so he turned off onto a dirt track that brought him out on Thorney Dyke. He pulled over there and made the triple nine call. His description of the motor raised a flag, and after some discussion we were sent out to keep an eye on the place and prepare ourselves should the car move on elsewhere. I'm guessing whoever made those arrangements notified you immediately afterwards.'

Bliss silently applauded Warburton for her quick thinking. 'Okay. That was a great call. So what have you done so far?'

'First thing we did was stage a minicab pick up. We had one of our own surveillance vehicles sporting kosher cab livery drive up. Female driver is one of my colleagues. She knocked, but got no reply. She made a meal of it, shouted out that she was there to pick up and take the owner to an appointment in the city centre. Still nothing. She even popped a card through the door. The number on it goes to a line we have set up specifically for this type of situation, so they're ready to take the call if it comes.'

'And that's your only contact so far?'

'It is. We have a drone up, flying a circular pattern over the farmhouse and its land. There's been no sign of movement. You have to wonder why that is.'

Bliss bit his lip as he assessed their predicament. 'You do. Sounds to me as if they're either bunkered down or no longer there. Does the place still have its utilities?'

'Yes. According to his friend, everything is paid out of the owner's bank by direct debit.'

'In that case, let's turn our thoughts to how the driver of our Picasso knew the farmhouse was currently empty. They had to have known the farmer himself wasn't living there.'

'I did wonder about that myself,' Shanks said. 'It's not the most obvious place to find, but it could have happened by chance. The driver might have turned into the drove to get off the main road, discovered it ends at the farm, then stopped to ask for directions or perhaps to have a sniff around because the place looked empty.'

'Is the kindly neighbour and friend still available to talk to?'

'We have his address and his phone number. He said he'd be at home for the rest of the day, so we can either pay him a visit or have him drive here to talk with us.'

'The latter sounds better to me. Could you arrange that, please, Row?'

Shanks nodded and turned, heading over to where her team gathered and chatted among themselves.

'Whatever this neighbour tells us isn't going to make our next decision any easier,' Chandler said to Bliss. 'No matter what he says, we're still left with the same two choices. Action or inaction.'

He accepted this with a shrug. 'That's true enough. But if we go in now, we blow the surveillance op for good if they're still in there. And I mean, if they are *all* still there. I'd like to know what's going on inside that farmhouse, but I'm not sure about risking an ongoing operation. Not based on speculation.'

'You're worried the Citroen driver might be there alone.'

'Yep. If he's dumped the two of them off somewhere else and is now hiding out inside the farm, he might just clam up once we have him in cuffs. And we may not get him to talk afterwards.'

'So you want to wait it out? Make sure all three are inside the farmhouse?'

'I do.'

'I'm glad to hear you say that,' Shanks said as she wandered back to join them. 'The mood of my people is that we sit tight and use our discretion. If we see or suspect something serious is going down or has gone down inside that property, then we have authority to go in. But for now we're happy holding our position to observe and record.'

Bliss nodded. 'As much as I hate to stand around and wait, I have to agree. My natural inclination is to roll on them now and make the best of whatever we find there, but it's a tough call.'

'For what it's worth, I think you're making the right one, Jimmy.'

'That's not to say I won't change my mind. If the woman and girl are in there with whoever our suspect is, anything could be going on.'

They all knew what he meant. About to leave it at that, Bliss had a sudden thought. 'Row, you'll know better than I do about this sort of thing. Can we get a police chopper high enough so that nobody in the farmhouse will see or hear it, but low enough to use thermal imaging?'

'Yes. If the camera can see it, then it can also detect any infrared sources inside it. But now that you mention it, Jimmy, we don't have to order up a helicopter. I can get our own thermal imaging device here in half an hour. Another thirty minutes after that and we'll be looking at heat signatures.'

Bliss gave himself up to the inevitable. They were now part of a waiting game. The only question was whether he and Chandler remained with the surveillance team or headed back to Thorpe Wood. He'd expected an indication by now, so the more time slipped by, the less they'd be able to anticipate the next move. That brought a question to mind.

'Row, has anybody arranged for traffic to station patrol cars close to exit points?'

'Yes, of course. Your DCI requested traffic to sit and hold a little further out at strategic points so that if our Picasso heads back onto the road, they can pull a stop on it. Unless we decide to follow it instead. In which case we also have officers in unmarked vehicles and two on motorbikes circling the area, ready to go when the call comes in.'

'They all from your surveillance team?'

Shanks smiled at him. 'Naturally. As if I'd trust your lot for a specialist job like that.'

'Yeah, fair play. Stupid question. All right, let's have that thermal camera here as soon as. Meanwhile, we'll use the time to form a strategy depending on what the infrared heat sources tell us. I want a plan for no sources, a plan for one, and a third plan if all three are there.'

'And what if there are only two?'

'Then we're buggered,' he said, turning away to place a call to Bishop.

TWENTY-THREE

The unmanned aerial vehicle did its job perfectly, lazily circling the farmhouse at its maximum operating height of 400 feet. DC Shanks's only concern with using it at all for this operation was the distance between their UAV pilot and the drone itself, which legally could not extend beyond 500 metres. Nor could it be out of sight at any point during its flight. Both were proving difficult to maintain from their position, and the pilot had frequently shifted location in order to improve the situation. Each change of batteries gave them up to forty-five minutes of flying time, but Shanks erred on the side of caution and intended to call it back in on the half hour. With the thermal imaging camera now on board, the hope was they'd need less than half that.

'Bloody wonderful machines, aren't they?' Bliss said, watching the image sent back by the drone on a small screen sheltered from glare by an overhanging hood.

Shanks raised her eyebrows. 'You can thank POCA for that one up there. Five grand well spent and already earned its money back ten times over.'

The Proceeds of Crime Act fund was a tough nut to crack, the bidding process highly competitive. Shanks had stated it as a single word, sounding much like "poker". The system was popular with all police officers, who enjoyed the thought of draining bank accounts belonging to criminals in order to fund the fight against crime.

'You did well,' he told her. 'I hear it's like pulling teeth getting them to hand over funding.'

'It was a team bid. We got three smaller drones at the same time, so we're well set.'

The FLIR camera flickered into life at the push of a button. Bliss, Chandler, and Shanks crowded behind and around the officer tasked with monitoring the feed. He and the pilot worked in unison to provide a full 360 degree view of the building, its barns, and outhouses.

Bliss needed neither to tell him what he could see for himself.

There were no heat signatures at all.

'Are we sticking to our earlier plan?' Shanks asked him.

He gave it a moment. They had decided on an action should this be the result, and he saw no reason to alter their decision now. Nothing had changed as far as he could tell, and the farmer's friend had not been able to add to the information he'd already provided.

Bliss nodded. 'Yep. Please give your mobile teams the word to go. We'll join them on the plot.'

Shanks did as requested, and seconds afterwards, also withdrew the drone.

'What do you think?' Chandler asked as they walked across to the car.

He knew what she was asking. 'My biggest fear is we'll find all three dead. A murder-suicide on our hands, and probably no way left to explain any of it. But what I think we'll find is an empty farmhouse. My guess is Picasso Man used the location only to transfer vehicles.'

Chandler's eyes widened. 'Good grief! Jimmy Bliss the optimist.' She extended her hand. 'Pleased to meet you. I don't believe we've met.'

'Forget that old pony,' he growled, dismissing her observation as he climbed into his seat and turned the engine over. 'You know me better than that. I'm a realist, Pen. Always have been, always will be. Some people choose to view that as pessimism, but they're talking out of their backsides. That includes you and your fat arse, in case you were wondering. I told you what I fear we'll find, but there's a difference between that and what I really think.'

'And what you think is based on…?'

He nosed the car back out onto the main road and pressed down on the accelerator. 'Logic,' he insisted. 'As always. To my mind, if murder-suicide was our Picasso driver's end game, why not do it at the Latchford home? Why drive all the way out here, taking more risks riding with the woman and her daughter in the car? Makes no sense to me.'

'Okay, I see that. I'm with you there. But we don't know what was going through his head. No clue as to why. We don't even know what connection he has to the Latchfords – if any. Without that knowledge, how can we assess the situation properly?'

'We can't. We don't. Speculation, theories, hypotheses, are all best left to the investigative parts of the operation. In this situation, you go with what you know. What we know so far tells me the farmhouse is empty.'

When they turned onto the dusty track of the drove, Bliss was surprised by the number of vehicles already jammed into the driveway they had so far only viewed from above. The Citroen was wedged in tight and officers had spread themselves out around the property. The plan had been for the first unit on the plot to enter by any means possible, and as he and Chandler drew closer, Bliss could see the front door hanging wide open.

As they crunched their way across a gravel surface, Chandler hoisted the bottom of her jacket and looked down at her rear end. 'Does my arse really look fat?' she asked, demurely.

'Bloody thing ought to have a *Wideload* sticker on it,' he replied.

By way of a response, Chandler wrinkled her nose and gave him a familiar two-fingered salute.

'How old are you?' he taunted her.

'Old enough to know that a true gentleman would never mention the size of his work partner's arse.'

'They would if it was big enough to hold up traffic.'

'Well, my boyfriend has no complaints.'

'Because he's a bloody ogre. They're used to fat arses.'

'Me too,' Chandler said pointedly, looking him up and down. 'I have to work with one every day.'

By the time they crossed the threshold, some officers on the scene were already on their way out. 'You DI Bliss?' the first asked. When he got a nod in reply, he went on. 'We've cleared the property. No sign of anyone. The rooms are currently being searched again, nook and cranny this time, including attic and crawl spaces. But take it from me, there's nobody here.'

Unsurprised, and pleased not to have dead bodies to deal with, Bliss thanked the officer before making his way into the first room along the passage. The presence of the Picasso told them their quarry had been here. The real question was what had become of him and his passengers. Either they'd exchanged vehicles, as Bliss believed, or the driver had taken the woman and the child out into the fields somewhere to carry out his final acts. That was if the pair had made it this far; Mrs Latchford and her daughter might have been disposed of prior to the changeover. Bliss understood he had to act as if all three had driven to the farmhouse and all three had driven away again, but to also allow for alternative scenarios. He placed a call to Rowena Shanks, who had remained in situ awaiting developments.

'Bring your equipment up here, Row,' he told her. 'There's no sign of anyone inside the farmhouse, so you can make this your new base. Using the drone from here will give you the range we need to look at the extended land.'

'You thinking he might have killed them and dumped them somewhere else on the property?'

'Actually, no I don't.' He outlined his main theory.

'Okay. So you believe they've moved off the plot, but you're covering your arse just in case.'

Bliss smiled. 'That about sums it up. And believe me, it's far easier to cover my arse than my partner's.'

He received a whack from Chandler for his trouble, but refused to flinch. He knew the drone probably wouldn't be sufficient. A Police Search Advisor team would provide a more thorough ground-level search, because at this stage if Mrs Latchford and her daughter were close by, they were most likely dead, their bodies cold. It was another expense to add to the surveillance teams, but sending them out had to have been with Detective Superintendent Fletcher's authority, while this one lay in his hands.

He turned to Chandler. 'Give HQ a call will you, please, Pen. Have Bish arrange for a PolSa team to come out here and give this place the once over. Oh, and let's have SOCO on site to check out the Picasso before they tow it over to the inspection yard.'

His DS looked up at him with a frown puckering her forehead. 'You sure about PolSa, Jimmy? Looks to me like you were right; they transferred wheels and are long gone. Is the search team absolutely necessary?'

'You thinking about how much Diane and Marion are going to take me to task for spending too much of their budget?'

'That, and the fact that we may be denied a funding request

later on because we spent money on this. If you're looking to search the entire farmland, the PolSa team will have a major job on their hands. That equals days, and days equals manpower.'

Bliss hung his head. He wasn't stupid. He understood the financial constraints. Budgets were precious and needed to be spent wisely. The simplest decision was to move on once the more thorough search of the house and its outbuildings was complete. On the other hand, nobody wanted to have some dog walker stumble across dead bodies in a week's time.

He took a deep breath. Sometimes you had to play the game and follow procedure. He called DCI Warburton. 'It's me, boss. Listen, there's nobody on the plot, just the red minivan. I can send the drone up again to look for heat sources out in the fields, but if they're long dead and hidden away, then it'll take more to clear the entire farm. I'm thinking PolSa, but as Penny rightly pointed out, it's possibly an expense we can do without. If money were no object, then we'd leave the proverbial no stone left unturned, but my feeling from the moment we arrived was that they came here to exchange vehicles, and I've seen nothing to change my mind.'

'You're on the plot, Jimmy. My eyes and ears.'

'True, but as we haven't officially opened up a book on this, and I'm not the SIO anyway, you're still the guv'nor.'

'And you're still the highest rank on site. I'll make up my own mind, but what's your call?'

'My gut tells me we move on and forget this place. My head tells me we'd kick ourselves if we missed something because we failed to carry out a proper search.'

'Okay. Leave it with me. You get the drone up again for now and I'll speak to the Super. As far as I'm concerned, if you want the search of the farmland, then you get it. But neither of us gets paid enough to make the final decision. Nor do we have to live with it.'

Satisfied, Bliss and Chandler waited it out once again. They helped by inspecting each room in the house and clearing the other buildings scattered close by. They found nothing of any value, and not a thing to suggest anybody had been inside. To cover himself, Bliss spoke to the officers who went in first. The front door had been closed and locked. No windows had been left open. It seemed unlikely that Picasso Man had entered, not without using a key. The drone went out and came back, to no avail. Bliss hated hanging around doing nothing, but sometimes you had to wait for the mechanism behind you to function.

'If they're out there,' Shanks told them with a sombre shake of the head, 'they're no longer alive.'

'Any sense of where their bodies might be hidden?'

'There's the river itself, of course. Close by and running parallel is Counter Drain, inside which concealment is a real possibility. A couple of neighbouring properties have fairly dense thickets. Also, there are bound to be some uncharted wells and small drainage channels out in these fields as well.'

It was all Bliss needed to hear. He thanked the DC for her efforts, and those of her excellent team. By the time DCI Warburton called him back, he and Chandler were on the road, his mind made up.

'You have authorisation if you decide to order a search,' she told him.

Good news. They wouldn't have to argue.

'Thanks, boss. Let's have them in there. I've asked for an ordnance survey map of the entire farm to be made available to the search team leader. They know their stuff far better than I do, but I thought it'd be a place for them to start.'

'But you still think the man we're after is long gone, taking the woman and child with him?'

'I do. It makes perfect sense. If they're not completely dim-witted, they'll know the Citroen was likely to have been spotted and subsequently identified. Swapping vehicles all the way out here allows them to head off again in any number of directions without being observed, and with few if any cameras about to watch them go.'

'So if they're gone, we have no way of knowing where or how?'

'That's about the size of it, yes.'

'And still no idea who the driver of this Citroen might be?'

'Not at the moment, boss. The only other player we know for sure is involved in this somehow is Callum Oliver, the *PT* journalist. But why he'd be mixed up with Mrs Latchford, I don't know. I suppose he could have confronted her with what he found out, told her who her husband really was. That is a genuine possibility. If she was clueless and distraught at learning what kind of man she'd been living with all these years, then perhaps Oliver convinced her to pack up and leave, helping her get away.'

'Could that be who Latchford was talking to just before stepping onto the tracks? His wife, I mean. She tells him she knows all about him, and realising his entire world is about to collapse, he ends it all.'

'It's a decent theory. It holds water. But then you have to wonder how and why his motor ended up in the river. And why fake the disturbance inside the Latchford home?'

'Hmm. You're right, that remains a puzzle.'

'We could have another go at the witness. See if she remembers more. Ask if she could have heard him arguing or pleading with his wife.'

'You'll be lucky. IE came and took her away earlier this morning.'

Immigration Enforcement was part of the Home Office command, including the Border Force, charged with protecting the

UK borders against illegal immigration. Bliss had dropped in on Balodis before leaving work the night before, hoping to put her at her ease as she sat in the holding cell. While he was down there he had asked to be advised when the border officials arrived to speak with their witness, and was angry that nobody had done so. He bottled it up until he was done speaking with his DCI.

'Those fuckers down in custody,' he said, turning to Chandler. She'd heard every word through the car's Bluetooth audio system.

'Don't jump in without knowing the full story, Jimmy,' she warned. 'You know how IE can be. They were probably in a hurry at the same time as the custody area was busy.'

'All I needed was a heads-up. Just a call. Now I'm going to have to trace her in the system, and we both know how difficult that's going to be.'

'Why don't you let me do it? The documentation will tell us who collected her. I admit that once she's been in the system for a while it gets harder, but provided I find out where they took her today, we should be fine. It'll be more productive if you focus on the ops. Plus, you've been in a good mood of late and this will only make you lose your rag.'

Bliss understood she was attempting to calm him down. She was right; steaming into the custody area and giving them both barrels would achieve nothing. Somebody had screwed up, but they would not have done so on purpose. There were no lingering resentments between him and uniform. It had to have been a mistake. And everybody made them.

'Okay,' he said. 'Cheers, Pen. When you find out where she's being detained, ask who will represent her and also make sure that whoever manages her case knows she is a helpful witness. Tell them it may yet turn out to be a murder trial, so she could be needed.' He held up a hand to ward off any argument. 'Yes, I realise we're not looking at murder. But they don't need to know that. Let them know we'd like her case to be assessed sympathetically, and that placing her back into the community may be the right thing to do. Stress the possibility of us needing her to give evidence in court at a later date, which means keeping her sweet.'

'I'll do my best.'

'And get onto one of the immigrant support charities. Feed them her details once you have all the info. See what they can do on her behalf.'

'I'll give JCWI a bell. They might be interested in this one.'

'JCWI? Never heard of them.'

'Joint Council for the Welfare of Immigrants. They're good at helping people who have fallen through the cracks after the EU settlement scheme cut-off date.'

Bliss nodded. He felt his anger dissipate. Zinta Balodis had come forward when most would have stepped back into the shadows. For all he knew, her immigration status was deliberate and knowingly illegal, but her actions should at the very least be rewarded with a fair hearing. His thoughts turned once again to the suspicious link between Callum Oliver's absence and that of Latchford's wife and kid. He ran a hand across his forehead, lingering on the scar.

'What's up, Jimmy?' Chandler asked, clearly sensing his apprehension.

'I've got a bloody raging headache thinking about all this. I'm liking more and more this idea of Oliver telling Mrs Latchford all about her old man and then the two of them staging a crime scene before having it on their toes together.'

'It's a sound theory, boss. Certainly not one we can ignore.'

'You're right. I don't know precisely what kind of investigation we're running here, Pen, but I can't help but wonder where the three of them are right now.'

TWENTY-FOUR

Nursing an open facial wound having received between three to five punches, and a shattered ulna caused by a single blow with some form of cosh on the arm he'd held up to protect himself, Callum Oliver had come to realise the pain and anguish relating to his injuries were the least of his concerns.

When he eventually emerged from his unconscious state, he quickly realised both hands had been bound at the wrist by a length of chain wrapped around one of four large industrial metal pipes. Each ran at a slight downward gradient from a box-like piece of olive green machinery before disappearing into what he could see was an exterior wall. He recognised the components as those belonging to a water pumping station; the type whose function was to drain nearby fields and push the surplus water out into a river. But judging by the near silence and the feeling of disuse and stench of decay, this station had been superseded many years ago by something modern and presumably more effective.

The room in which he sat on the cold, concrete floor, could barely contain the essential equipment, leaving little scope for a human element. A bank of slit windows set into the wall above the four pipes had been boarded over, through which vague light spilled in narrow bands where the boards had not been fastened adequately. Otherwise, he was left in darkness for much of the time. This led to a gnawing sensation inside his stomach, which increased as claustrophobia set in and fear took a vice-like grip. A feeling which at no time felt as if it might recede.

The station was damp and the cold air smelled musty. He heard no sound other than the occasional babble of water on the other side of the obvious exterior wall; he thought the other three were also most likely part of the external structure, but without windows it was hard to tell for certain. If he had to guess, he'd say he was somewhere in the fens, probably with the Nene, Welland, Great Ouse, or possibly the Glen flowing outside. Yet being trapped and alone inside this stuffy and stifling box was still not high on his list of worries.

Number one came in the form of the man whose occasional visits struck fear into his very soul. This was the same man who had hurt him inside his own car, after which he had brought him to this dreadful place. The same man who asked questions, the truthful answers to which he refused to believe, extracting responses and pleas for mercy by inflicting little acts of punishment.

The day this nightmare began had started so well. Fresh from gathering further information on the story he was investigating, he'd stopped off at the Coach House Inn – a fine old sandstone pub and restaurant in South Luffenham. Shortly after leaving, he'd come to a halt at what looked like a minor accident between a car and a van now blocking the road. A man wearing a long jacket with its collar pulled up around his neck and a beanie hat covering his head, came jogging over to him, intent on explaining what had happened. Or so Callum had thought. He powered down his window in anticipation, but instead of talking to him, the man who appeared by his side punched him hard in the side of the face. Additional blows followed, swift and vicious. As Callum raised a hand to ward off his attacker, he felt his forearm snap beneath the weight of another strike, this time with a cosh-like implement.

Callum didn't think he could rely on his memory regarding anything that happened immediately afterwards. He felt a fierce burning sensation running along the length of his left arm. It flared and bloomed, after which the pain hit him as if shards of glass were being driven into the entire left side of his body. Immobilised and completely disorientated in those first few seconds, he was certain he'd then been bludgeoned two or three further times. As he slipped into unconsciousness, he felt his seatbelt being removed, his taut and twisted body unceremoniously yanked from his seat and dragged several yards along the road. The next thing he recalled was the feeling of movement while he lay still on a hard metallic surface. His wrists were fastened together by adhesive tape, his ankles likewise. A rough scrap of cloth smelling of oil had been forced around his face, preventing him from seeing anything or anyone. He assumed he'd blacked out while being forcibly taken from his car, and in remembering the van at what he now knew was a fake accident, Callum guessed he was probably being transported in the back of that.

He passed out again a few minutes later. This was followed by periods of lucidity, moments in the back of the van during which the agony of his wounds returned to overwhelm him back into unconsciousness. He believed he'd been semi-conscious, though, at the time he was shifted from the vehicle into the pumping station. He could have imagined it, or perhaps it had been a dream that felt real in retrospect. Either way, here he was and here he had remained since.

That the man who came to him afterwards wore a balaclava was a good sign as far as Callum was concerned. To him, it suggested his attacker did not wish to be recognised and described later on. This implied there would *be* a later on for him, which was the only positive note he felt able to cling to. Everything else, absolutely everything about his ordeal since, had been painful and agonising and torturous.

Callum was aware he had lost track of time. Days and nights had come and gone. He'd survived on a diet of sandwiches that came in triangular plastic boxes, along with bottled water which he tried not to guzzle down in long thirsty gulps. Round plastic tubs had been made available to him in which to both urinate and defecate, but despite the chain being long enough and flexible enough to allow him to use their lids to seal the foulness away, the pervading stench was overbearing. The man replaced them during each visit, which was also when fresh supplies of food and drink came. Callum received them with gratitude, forcing a smile even as tears spilled down both cheeks, as if some form of Stockholm Syndrome had already set in.

He couldn't imagine what he had done to deserve such awful treatment, and nothing said during the man's visits gave him any clue as to the reason behind his forcible abduction and subsequent incarceration. But Callum didn't want to think about the man, nor dwell upon what his visits represented. Being on the receiving end of such violence was one thing, reliving every moment of his humiliation quite another.

TWENTY-FIVE

After a swift drink in The Windmill pub a short drive from Bliss's house, he and Chandler shared a takeaway from the local Chinese restaurant. Neither of them had eaten during the day, and they wasted little time in wolfing down the savoury food.

'That's the first time I've had a meal like that in ages,' Chandler said, blowing out her cheeks and gently rubbing the slight curve of her stomach. 'I feel bloated now.'

'That's because you've lived on a diet of swamp food since you started dating Shrek.'

She punched him on the arm. He winced; the blow had carried little weight, but her bony knuckles made their presence felt. The two colleagues sat together on the sofa in his living room, trays set to one side on the floor by their feet.

'I dare you to call him that to his face when you meet him on Sunday,' Chandler challenged him.

Bliss frowned at first, then remembered. 'Oh, yes. I'd forgotten all about my little shindig.'

Chandler rolled her eyes. Her subsequent groan was purely theatrical for his benefit. 'Of course. Why wouldn't you? It's only your birthday party, after all.'

'It's not a birthday *party*. I'm not five. There will be no clowns – other than us – no balloons, and definitely no bloody birthday cake with candles. It's a shindig that happens to be taking place on Sunday.'

'A shindig is just another word for party, and it's happening on your birthday, so it's a birthday party whether you like it or not.'

'I'll disinvite you if you carry on like that.'

'So we'll gate-crash.'

'I'll put Bish on the door.'

'And I'll buy him off with cake.'

He surrendered. He couldn't remember the last time he'd won a verbal battle with Chandler. If he ever had. She was simply too quick and too persistent; like a fly in need of swatting.

'Okay, okay,' he said. 'You've had your fun at my expense. Let's get back to business. What did you make of the office meeting?'

It hadn't lasted long, which was about all it had going for it. The general mood inside the room was sombre, and the team was unhappy with their rate of progress. Any excitement they had felt at learning about the connection to Dean Norman and Stevie Phillips had been tempered by the realisation that the break had taken them no further. They were no closer to knowing why Latchford had walked onto the railway line, why his wife and daughter had driven away from their home in the red Citroen Picasso, who its driver was, or where they were now. Equally, Callum Oliver had yet to be traced – and nobody could be completely certain he was even missing. The only light in the darkness was the clearing of PC Griffin's name, which, although extremely welcome, had no bearing on either operation in hand.

'Diane was right to issue the twenty-four-hour warning,' Chandler said in reply to his question. 'It was good of her to stick her neck out for more, but if she'd insisted she might have got bugger all instead.'

He agreed. There was no doubt in his mind what their hard work was telling them so far. The reporter was missing. The reason lay in his private investigation into Dean Norman. Latchford's family were also missing, presumably for similar reasons. Three missing people, none of whom had been reported as such. That fact alone told Bliss the case would be scrutinised once again by senior leadership, because until this point, both operations had been running on nothing more than conjecture and pure instinct. They all knew they were on the right track, even those who no longer worked the streets. But officially, no crimes had been committed until evidence was presented to the contrary.

And now the team had a final day to find it.

'We're close,' he said eventually. 'I can feel it in my ancient bones. Yet at the same time, we couldn't be further away.'

'Yes and no,' Chandler said, wrinkling her nose as she considered what they had. 'Let's face it, we do now have a whole new cast of suspects.'

Which was true. Whether the observation added to or lessened his dismay, he wasn't sure. They now knew the notorious Dean Norman had been in or close to the city. They were also aware of at least one person's interest in the man he had become. If Callum Oliver had been in contact with the family of Norman's and Phillips's victim, Haley Deerbourne, because of his findings or perhaps even at their behest, the possibility of any of them subsequently infiltrating Morgan Latchford's life had to be investigated.

Bliss nodded, his face stern. 'I can easily imagine one or more of her family members abducting and threatening Latchford's wife and daughter, then contacting him to demand he kill himself or they would harm his family. Perhaps one of them even drove him there and then dumped his motor in the river afterwards.'

'If that was the case, once Latchford did as he was ordered, why didn't they let his family go? Why have we heard nothing from them since?'

'It may be too soon. They could be buying themselves more time to cover their tracks. It's possible they stashed the pair of them away somewhere and will either contact us to tell us where they are, or have somebody else let them go.'

'Okay. Yes, that works for me, too. So then we're left with Oliver. Why would they hurt him, assuming the same members of Haley Deerbourne's family are involved?'

Bliss spread his hands. 'He knew too much. It could just be that simple.'

'So what role do you think Marty Lipman has in all this?'

'I don't think he's involved in anything unsavoury. Not this time. Though I suspect he's been dealing with Callum for longer than he's admitted to. I don't believe this nonsense about having just the one meeting.'

'Is it worth taking another crack at him?'

Bliss sniffed and shook his head. 'We won't get him in the room again unless we arrest him. He has nothing to gain from speaking to us. He'll never agree to it. Besides, I doubt he has a great deal more to offer.'

'But he could have. If Callum Oliver has been consulting with him about the legalities of hunting down Dean Norman, then Lipman might know something that could help us. He's a shyster and a prick, but he has no reason to turn his back on us when we're trying to help his client.'

'Okay. You're right. It's worth asking him.'

'Good. And besides, this may not be only about Norman. There's been no mention of that evil bastard's partner in crime. For all we know, Stevie Phillips, aka SH on our board, might also be in the frame.'

Bliss was doubtful, and said as much. 'The chances of one of those men being identified and traced is huge, but both of them…?' He shook his head. 'Nah, I'm not buying that. But I'll ask Lipman if his name ever came up.'

Judging by the sour look on her face, Chandler wasn't entirely happy with his response, but for once she didn't argue. 'Which reminds me, did the Super agree to follow up on Morgan Latchford's monitoring team?'

'She did. All she can actually do is speak to the Chief Super and make a request for it to be run through the channels. I've no doubt the Chief Constable will be both surprised and keen to learn more about our reporter's investigation, so hopefully he'll be eager to discuss it with the probation officers he usually works with. With a bit of luck they'll decide to talk to us in person.'

Chandler yawned and stretched out her arms. 'Then I really think we've done all we can, Jimmy.'

His phone interrupted them. It was his personal mobile, and he smiled when he saw the name of the caller. He swiped to accept.

'*So move awayyyy, Jimmy Blue. Before your small, small town turns around and swallows you-hoo!*' a voice sang playfully. The song lyrics were followed by a hearty laugh and then: 'Oi, oi, Jimbo. How's it hanging?'

Bliss laughed, unable to help himself. 'You got the Del Amitri album I sent you, then.'

'Yeah. How did you figure that out? Oh, wait a minute, that's obviously why you're the world's most famous detective.'

'Don't push your luck, Molly. Or there'll be no more vinyl.'

'Sorry, Jimbo. I'm on a high right now. I couldn't wait to play the album, and I love, love, love it. So ancient and retro.'

'You cheeky cow! That was only released in 1989.'

'Yeah. Like I said: ancient and now retro.'

'Listen up, I've already threatened to disinvite Pen and Shrek to my bash on Sunday, and I'll do the same with you if you're not careful.'

'Aw, you wouldn't do that to little old me. You luuurve me too much.'

He couldn't argue with the strange little waif he'd rescued from a sodden rooftop; a terrified child looking for permanent release, yet in reality desperately searching for a human touch capable of salving open wounds. He'd provided that connection at a time in her life when she needed it most, since when her world had turned and improved out of all recognition. With a supportive and loving adopted family behind her every anxious step, Molly had embraced new opportunities and fresh possibilities with an open mind and an outlook surprisingly devoid of cynicism. In turn, she had slipped easily into his heart and stoked paternal emotions in him he didn't know he possessed.

'You still okay to pick me up at the station?' she asked him.

'I'll make sure I'm okay. I'll be there by ten to seven on Saturday, right?'

'If you want to be a day late, that's perfect. If you don't want earache from me all weekend, make it Friday as planned, eh?'

When he and Molly were finished chatting, Bliss killed the connection and found Chandler gazing at him with a faraway look in her eyes.

'What?' he asked defensively.

'You still have your hard protective shell, but that kid really brings out your gooey centre.'

'I don't have a gooey centre,' he countered unconvincingly.

'Not much you don't. You forget who you're talking to sometimes, Jimmy. This is me. Remember… I see the real you.'

'So you keep telling me.'

'It's true. Speaking of which, what on earth has made you more relaxed lately?' Her eyes were kind, and Bliss was drawn in by them. 'You've been so much more balanced and, dare I say, carefree recently. Come on, old man. Cough up. Tell me everything.'

'I do feel better,' he grudgingly admitted. 'More whole, if that makes sense.'

'I think it does. So tell me why. Why now?'

'This is hardly the right time.'

Chandler looked around. 'Is there a better time? We're sitting in your living room. Just the two of us. Food in our bellies. Alcohol in our bloodstream. Feet up for the first time in weeks. Come on, Jimmy. You need to open up if you've found a way to centre your Chi.'

He squinted at her. 'I know you're mocking me, but I believe in that.'

'I'm not mocking. Well, maybe I am, but it's good-natured ribbing. I don't understand all that lifeforce essence business. But you do, and if it's important to you then it's important to me, too.'

Bliss exhaled. 'All right. If I owe anybody an explanation, it's you. This is going to sound strange, but in part it's because of a song I've been playing lately.'

Chandler arched her eyebrows. 'Anything coming from you is always on the strange side. The song part... not so much. You have a bond with music that I just don't get. What song has you charmed this time?'

'You know Steven Wilson?'

'From the Beach Boys?'

'No, that's Brian Wilson. Steven Wilson weighs about eighteen stone less and his band is Porcupine Tree.'

'I'm none the wiser.'

'Okay, well, it doesn't really matter who recorded it. The song is called *Pariah*, from his first solo album.'

'*Pariah*? Sounds cheerful. We're off to a cracking start.'

'It's not. It's desperately sad and yet at the same time it's… uplifting.'

'You listen to music all the time. What about this one out of all the songs you know makes it special? So much so that it's turned you around. Does it have anything to do with Hazel?'

Bliss nodded. He and his wife had been married for almost eight years when she was murdered in their own home by a fellow cop. In the two decades since, he had not been able to escape from beneath the shadow of their life together, or the weight of her terrible death.

Gathering his thoughts, he said, 'Let me see if I can explain it to you. It's a dual vocal track. The verse lyrics sung by the male talk about being tired of having feet of clay, tired of days to come and of yesterday. I get that. I really do. Not being able to move on, being stuck in the here and now. Later, he mentions being tired of his failing health, and of everyone, including himself. And again, I see where he's coming from.'

'Clearly he has a bleak outlook,' Chandler remarked. 'Suicidal, even.'

'Yes. Perhaps. But the female vocal is more uplifting, insisting he can conquer this period of his life. And yet I suppose the most poignant part for me is when he says he's not bothered by being alone, because the real hell is not knowing if she is. It's not entirely clear to me if they've drifted apart or she's gone in the way Hazel is gone, but when I heard the woman singing a chorus telling him to take comfort from her, insisting he can dig in and move on because he's still there and that he should not worry because nothing really dies or ends, it felt as if, in that specific moment, she was singing only to me.'

'Really? Saying what, specifically?'

'That she… Hazel was telling me to take comfort from her and to move forward. I know it sounds trite, and I'm probably making too much of it, but when I heard the song I pretty much held my breath all the way through. Hairs rose on my neck and arms. He was me and she was Hazel. And to my complete astonishment, I did take comfort. And since I first heard that song, I've felt… unburdened. Sounds stupid to you, I suppose.'

'No. No, not at all. Jimmy, I can't tell you what you heard or what those lyrics truly mean, but if that's what you took from the song, if that's what it did for you, then I'm glad of it. I couldn't be happier.'

'There's more.'

'Oh?'

Bliss held her gaze. 'Hazel's gone.'

'What do you mean she's gone?'

'I mean she's not here any more. You know that ever since my wife was murdered, I've continued to feel her presence. All around me, as if she and I have been unwilling to let each other go for almost twenty years. But since I played that song, Hazel's no longer with me, Pen. It's as if she stayed with me just as long as I needed her to. And the moment I felt able to move on with my life, she stepped out of it.'

Chandler blinked and tears slid from the corners of her eyes. When she spoke, her voice was choked with emotion. 'Oh, my god, Jimmy. That would break me. How on earth can that possibly make you feel better?'

'Because now I know she's also been released. That she has finally moved on. And I don't mean spiritually. I mean she's moved on from the space she was occupying inside my head. And I couldn't be happier. For her. For me. For what we had together. And for the peace we've both found now we're finally apart.'

Chandler sobbed. Tears streamed down both cheeks. But he sensed they were not tears of sadness. Rather, she was so happy for him the dam had given way, her defences breached.

He reached out his arms and she slid into them. He hugged her close with one hand and stroked her hair with the other. 'It's all right,' he whispered. 'Really. Everything is okay now.'

'How do you know? How can you know that? What if she was your strength, Jimmy? What if she was the only thing holding you together?'

Bliss pulled back his head, waiting for their eyes to meet. 'But don't you see? That's what I'm saying. Hazel *was* my strength. My rock. The memory of her was the only thing holding me together for the longest time. But she let me go. We let each other go. And I'm still in one piece. I made it, Pen. I finally made it through to the other side.'

TWENTY-SIX

He'd endured a restless night, the focus of his thoughts firmly on the ops he and his team were tasked with solving. The emotional release with Penny Chandler the previous evening had carried with it no shame, and in some ways Bliss felt relieved to have finally said it all out loud in the company of his closest friend.

Ahead of the morning briefing, he made two phone calls. The first was to Sandra Bannister, looking to find out if Callum Oliver had been in touch with her since they'd last spoken. The reporter insisted she hadn't heard from her subordinate and reminded him she wouldn't expect to.

'What do you intend doing with the information we uncovered?' she asked. 'I assume you have to run it by your senior officers. After all, if something bad has happened to Callum, the *PT* needs to be made aware of the circumstances.'

Bliss had expected the approach. 'I realise that, Sandra. But you need to be patient, because things have moved on a stage or two since. You know I can't talk about ongoing actions, though I will say we've found ourselves heading in a surprising direction.'

'Your media spokesperson was equally tight-lipped last night. They refused to release the name of the man who committed suicide on the railway line until his family had been notified. I wasn't the only one who thought that was odd.'

'In what way?' he asked, knowing precisely what she would say. Bannister was too good at what she did to have missed it.

'They'd had thirty-six hours by that stage and still hadn't informed his family. How's that possible in this day and age? And I have to wonder why there's no mention of this at all on the Policing Peterborough Facebook page.'

Bliss deflected rather than get into it. 'Sandra, between you, me, and the gatepost, the only identification we had was inside a man's wallet. We believe we know who it belonged to, but we aren't yet positive. We're waiting on DNA to confirm.'

'Sounds flimsy to me, Jimmy.'

She was not wrong. DNA results had actually arrived shortly before the media briefing, but they came without providing any formal identification. The notes received from forensics revealed the hit in their database, but ID was being withheld pending further investigation. Eventually, news of the DNA search and hit would be brought to the attention of the Chief Constable, but Bliss knew internal procedures and protocols moved at a snail's pace. He was certain their own request to the CC would be acted upon before the man was even aware of the forensic findings. However, there was no way he was about to share any of this with Bannister.

'Listen to me, Sandra. You're right in thinking there's something iffy going on. But now is not the right time for me to tell you what that is. It's one of those rare occasions when I simply cannot discuss the details with you. Please understand the reason relates to another investigation. If I can give you a heads-up before wider media release, then I will, but I may not get the chance. Now that we have some movement, this thing could take off like a rocket.'

When he ended the call, he realised Bannister was not satisfied with his explanation. Still, it had done no irreparable harm to their relationship. He could live with that. He'd feed her whatever he could ahead of the official media release, allowing her to get a march on her peers. That would appease her, leaving them in a good place. He was glad of it, because he considered them to be friends. His second call was to Marty Lipman, a man he did not care for in the slightest.

'Before you throw up all kinds of barriers, Mr Lipman, please just listen to me,' he said brusquely. 'I don't need to hear about legal rights just now. Nor human rights, for that matter. Hear me out, and if you still don't want to help us when I'm done, then I'll let it go.'

'You will? That surprises me, Inspector. After all, last time we spoke, you threatened me.'

'To be clear, I threatened to tell the truth as I knew it. To make a fuss where so far I had made none. Let's both be adult about this, because you were in the wrong and you got found out. We both know I could have you for it, and to my mind you deserve knocking down a few pegs. But we had a deal and I'll stick by it. Thing is, I wasn't aware of all the facts at the time. We now have additional information, which means I have different questions for you.'

It took a moment, but eventually Lipman said, 'Ask away. I'm not promising anything, mind.'

'Fair enough. When we spoke about Callum Oliver, you said he was a client and you could not discuss why. The point is, we now know something of what Callum was working on. It has connections to another operation we are running. Both are in their early stages, but this could be far more serious than you might have appreciated. We believe the man is in serious trouble. Possibly even great danger. Moreover, other people are also at risk. So I'm asking if you and he had discussed the legal ramifications of his breaching a court injunction preventing him from even searching for a particular individual, let alone disclosing information about that same individual.'

The pause this time went on much longer.

'Mr Lipman?' Bliss finally prompted. Usually he would allow silence to do the hard work, but he didn't believe Lipman would fall for that.

'All right, all right. I'm thinking. Okay. Mentioning no other names, I can confirm what you want to know; Mr Oliver and I did have that conversation.'

'Good. Thank you. Just so's we both know who we're talking about, the person you can't name is closely connected to another person you can't name, correct?'

'Yes.'

'Thanks again. Now for the big one: was Mr Oliver investigating only one of these two unnamed men, or was he looking into both?'

'Just the one.'

'Are you sure about that?'

'Yes. Only one of the two men.'

'A man he was looking to expose in print?'

'I can't go into that. Mr Oliver is still my client, and I won't speak about his objectives concerning publication of anything he came to be aware of.'

Bliss licked his lips. Lipman had phrased his reply skilfully. 'So he did have intentions beyond mere interest. This wasn't a hobby project for him.'

'I can't answer that, Inspector.'

'Okay. I had to ask. But you're absolutely certain about his focus on just the one man?'

'One hundred percent. That I can and will confirm. He came upon some information by chance, which spurred his interest.'

Bliss ended the call there. He entered the inquiry room pondering the conversations he had just finished. The room was not packed; this was not a full murder inquiry, and only the close team and a couple of civilian workers were in attendance. He felt the burden of trying to carry two new investigations on top of his already burgeoning workload, especially as neither had yet been tagged for the unit. He had only this shift to prove his instincts correct, and that was a heavy weight to carry.

At the investigation boards he made a couple of notes alongside operation Fledgling. He capped the pen and used it to indicate the information he had just written up. 'Callum Oliver's attention was on Dean Norman only. Marty Lipman just confirmed this without saying an awful lot. Which makes sense if you think about it. These two lads will have been relocated to different ends of the country, perhaps even further afield. They'd never have been seen together since they were sentenced, given they served their ten years in separate detention centres. We can't know if they've ever been in touch during that time, but neither is stupid enough to arrange some kind of sick reunion. So the focus of our attention remains on Dean Norman, the man we know as Morgan Latchford. Whoever the SH is that Stevie Phillips became is unimportant right now.'

DC Ansari raised a hand to grab his attention. 'Speaking of which, are we anywhere with Oliver, boss?'

'No. If you've checked the case files recently, you'll know the blood found inside the Audi was confirmed by type as matching his. Expect DNA confirmation later today. Results have been delayed because there was no match in our database, but hopefully whatever CSI bagged and tagged from his flat for comparison will give us a result by this afternoon or early evening. For the time being, we work on the assumption the blood in the Audi is his. Forensic tests on his motor suggest the blood loss was not extensive, so it's unlikely any major veins or arteries were torn open. That doesn't mean he's alive, of course. Only that he may not be dead.'

DS Bishop stepped up next to talk about the progress of his actions. 'We're having no joy with capturing footage anywhere close to the farm. There are just too many roads and droves you can use to make your way out of that area. I think we have to consider extending the radius this morning. In addition, we'll now be inspecting footage gathered from the area surrounding the Latchford property. Maybe we'll get lucky and pull an image showing our driver in better detail.'

'Good. Thanks, Bish.' Bliss was about to move on when something came to mind. 'Have you reached out to Stagecoach?'

'For footage from their CitiBus cameras? Yes, all done. We know the red Picasso had to travel in and out of Alderman's Drive. It might have entered and exited the same way, but even if it used Mayor's Walk, that's also a busy road on a regular bus service. We're having Stagecoach grab up feeds from any bus taking either of those routes during the window of time we have, so who knows what we might find?'

'Good shout. Well done.' Bliss nodded and then looked around to face the group. 'Remind me who's liaising with the search team.'

Gratton stuck a hand up. 'That's me, boss. Nothing to report from yesterday. They began again at first light and will give it their all for the rest of the day. But they've been told that's it for them if they've still turned up nothing.'

Bliss was neither surprised nor disappointed. 'How about phones?' he asked. 'Mrs Latchford? Callum Oliver?'

'Not much to report, boss,' DC Ansari said, shaking her head in frustration. 'Oliver's work phone has not reappeared since it went dead. After running subscriber searches, we've put in RIPA requests with the relevant providers, but I'm still waiting for responses to come back. I'll push again as soon as we're done here.'

'Cheers, Gul.' He took a couple of steps back and turned to look at the boards once again. 'The cupboard is looking distinctly bare,' he said. 'I understand why these ops are likely to be taken from us if we don't see greater progress today. However, since the two are now linked, finding something concrete in one investigation may allow us to keep hold of both. To my mind – and please do shout out if you disagree – the priorities have not altered. Locating Mrs Latchford and her daughter is clearly out on top, closely followed by tracking down our *PT* reporter. Who Latchford once was, why he killed himself, whether his wife knew, what happened to their home, and precisely what Callum Oliver was looking to expose, are all secondary considerations.' Bliss broke off to allow his team to take that in. Then he shrugged and said, 'Or are they?'

'Are you suggesting the answer to one or more of those questions might help us find them, boss?' Chandler asked.

'I am, yes. Let's look at Oliver, for example. What he was about to do was both illegal and dangerous.'

'In what way dangerous?' DC Virgil wanted to know.

'Well, how far might you go to protect your identity if you were Dean Norman? For argument's sake, let's say his wife wasn't aware of what he did when he was twelve, no clue as to her husband's true identity, and then along comes some reporter who claims he's about to reveal all.'

'But Norman… Latchford as he was for the past twenty-odd years, is the only one we know for certain is dead, boss.'

'That's true enough. But people don't always do the dirty deed themselves. We have no idea about the people Latchford hung around with. Or perhaps communicated with online. Let's dig into him and his known associates, find out if he had become the kind of man who had someone in his pocket willing and able to prevent our reporter from spilling his guts.'

'So what are you thinking at the moment, boss?' Bishop asked him.

'I genuinely don't know, Bish. As a working hypothesis, I rather like the idea of Callum Oliver confirming Norman was Latchford, telling the man's wife, and then helping her get away from him. That fits neatly with the other theory that she was the person Latchford was talking to on the phone shortly before he took his own life. The trouble is, other pieces of physical evidence don't quite tally. Latchford's car ending up in the river miles from where he killed himself is something that doesn't fit and still needs explaining. And then we have Oliver's motor, left the way it was, the blood cleaned up inside.'

'Which reminds me,' Ansari said. 'We're still collating security footage from around the retail park alongside the railway line. Once we have it, we'll dive in to see if we can spot Latchford's car entering and exiting. Sorry it's taken so long, boss, but there's only a couple of us able to work on it at any one time.'

Bliss acknowledged this with a firm nod. Resources were at a minimum, and sifting through CCTV surveillance with time window parameters wide open at one end was a painstaking task. 'I can't spare you anyone else, Gul. But I don't want you spreading yourself too thin. I know Bish just told us he was going to expand the radius of the CCTV search around the farmhouse, but actually I don't believe that's worth pursuing any further. We need something to click into place, something with a greater anticipated hit ratio. Did Morgan Latchford drive into Maskew

Avenue Retail Park? Because if so, he certainly didn't drive out again, which means somebody else did. And if he didn't drive there, how did he end up there? Did he walk? Did he take a taxi, mini cab? We know when he died, so Bish can join you and together you can work backwards from that and find me something I can use.'

'That's an awful lot of actions for two ops we don't know will still be ours come end of play today,' Bishop observed, crunching out the words as if he were chewing gravel.

'The pressure is still on,' Bliss admitted. 'But we already have more today than we had yesterday, and yesterday we learned more than we had on day one. I'm confident we'll be given the go-ahead to run with these, and I know DCI Warburton is all in favour. To help things along, I've persuaded her to open a policy book and as of the start of this meeting, Diane is the SIO for both ops.'

Bliss gave a nod of satisfaction as his statement was greeted warmly, with a few pumped fists generating increased chatter. 'I'm glad to see you're all raring to go,' he told them. 'But make no mistake, we still need some hard evidence. So get out there and find me some.'

When Chandler asked him what their own day looked like, Bliss had a couple of things in mind. 'It's all too much up in the air for my liking,' he said. 'But we need to narrow things down by assigning ourselves some firm actions. I definitely want to look into little Haley Deerbourne's family. Who else is more likely to want to see Dean Norman punished, even dead? But that's going to require a great deal of digging to provide us with names and addresses, and if they're still living in the same area we'd have to travel down to the Littlehampton and East Beach area. I can get the digging started, but for the time being I think it's best we start closer to home with the people monitoring Dean Norman.'

TWENTY-SEVEN

A RELATIVELY NEW BUILD IN a street of late Victorian homes, the offices of the Cambridge Probation service were tasteful, comfortable, and cool on a warm early May day. Grant McKinney and Ione Pearson had insisted the interview take place on home territory, and had both initially seemed reluctant to be in the same room as Bliss and Chandler. They gathered in McKinney's office; he was the more senior of the two probation officers. Hot drinks had been provided. Ignoring a plate of cookies, Bliss took a couple of sips from his cup of black coffee before deciding it was time to get into their reason for travelling to Cambridge city centre.

'As you were advised, our Chief Constable has granted us the authority to discuss this matter with you both,' he began. He paused, wondering how forceful he might need to be. He decided to give them the opportunity to speak freely. 'I'm sure by now you've also been informed of Morgan Latchford's death. Let me be clear, my colleague and I are aware of his former name and what he did when he was a child. When he was released on licence, he was still Dean Norman in everything but name. You inherited him from Kent after his adult appearance was compromised there with the taking and posting online of a photograph.

Since when, you, together with our CC, have been responsible for monitoring him. To begin with, I'd like to know what that all means and how it works.'

'I'm afraid we cannot possibly go into precise detail,' McKinney said a little too quickly for Bliss's liking. 'As you will know, these court injunctions allied to lifelong anonymity rulings require us to keep shared information to a minimum. I *can* tell you we apply OASys to all offenders, irrespective of their particular standing.'

'This is the Offender Assessment system, yes?' Chandler said.

'It is. In effect, we use it as a guideline for assessing the needs and the risks of the offenders. It helps us identify the threats they pose, as well as how best to minimise those dangers and effectively tackle their behaviour.'

'And how does that work?' Bliss asked. 'Break it down for us.'

Ione Pearson took a drink and grasped her hands together in her lap. Tall, willowy and elegant with an oval face and prominent cheekbones, the woman was clearly uncomfortable being part of such a discussion. 'That's easy enough,' she said with more confidence than she projected. 'We begin by assessing how likely an offender is to re-offend. We then identify and classify offending-related needs on both sides. Part of that overall assessment requires us to look at the risk of serious harm *to* the offender and also to the public *by* the offender. We then formulate a plan designed to manage these risks. Once this has been achieved, we link this to the offender's supervision or sentencing plan, and we will indicate the need or otherwise of additional specialist assessment. Of course, we then measure and monitor and decide whether changes are required during the probationary period.'

Bliss nodded at various points as Pearson spoke. She appeared to be self-contained and unsure of herself, but not so of the system she spoke of. He needed to put that to the test. 'Thank you for that concise explanation. Dean Norman was not quite a teenager when he murdered Haley Deerbourne, and only twenty-two when he was released on licence. Presumably the fact that he was freed at all was because he was believed to be harmless to both himself and the public.'

Ione Pearson glanced at McKinney, who gave a single nod in response. She turned her attention back to Bliss and Chandler. 'The decision to release him on licence came after a thorough evaluation of his time spent incarcerated. Although Norman was clearly a troubled child and had lived an unfortunate life in abject poverty, what he did to that poor girl was completely out of character. Yes, records tell us he'd been violent before. But these were almost always in defence of himself or others. Whilst detained, he had one or two early outbursts of aggression and even violence, but soon settled down. Such behaviour is not unusual at the start of life in detention, as you can imagine.'

'You said "almost always",' Chandler pointed out. 'That suggests there were occasions when Norman was the aggressor.'

'That's true. But like I also said, he came from a troubled background and these moments were nothing unusual given his circumstances.'

'Let's skip a few beats,' Bliss suggested. 'We can spend the next half an hour picking away the scabs which you will do your best to cover up, or we can move straight to the bottom line. Which for me is this: Dean Norman was still very much a child when he and Stevie Phillips beat, tortured, attempted to rape, and eventually murdered another, younger child. On that basis alone, I assume he would have been considered to be non-threatening because over the previous decade he had matured, become an adult and now had an adult's perspective. Is that about the strength of it?'

'Crudely put, but accurate enough,' Grant McKinney allowed.

'Thank you. Crude is my middle name.'

'I meant no offence, Inspector.'

'I'm sure. Moving on, am I also right in saying that the result of your OASys findings led you to believe Norman was more at risk himself than he was considered to be one?'

'That's a safe assumption. Remember, he came to us having had his physical appearance exposed whilst living in Kent.'

'Of course. Presumably your monitoring process included vetting any people he got close to, friends he made, women he might have been seeing. Especially with Phoebe Cox, who married Dean Norman.'

Here, McKinney shook his head vigorously. 'I am unable to discuss that aspect of our job. Even your Chief Constable would not expect me to. And please remember, Phoebe Cox married Morgan Latchford, not Dean Norman.'

'As far as she was aware.'

'No, in reality, Inspector Bliss. For all intents and purposes, Dean Norman no longer existed. Now, of course, we looked hard at anybody who came into Morgan Latchford's life, and we were obliged to evaluate his request to marry Phoebe Cox. I'm simply not able to go into detail about that evaluation as it concerns somebody outside the probation service.'

'Okay, okay. Suffice to say, the three of you were happy for the wedding to go ahead, or it would not have taken place. You believed she was not a threat to him, and that he posed none to her. Presumably you later extended that same threat evaluation to their daughter, Beccy?'

'Of course.' Ione Pearson was firm about this matter. 'Inspector, please believe me when I tell you we take our roles seriously. We've carried out our monitoring with the same thoroughness throughout his time in our charge. In fact, myself and Grant took over at the same time from our predecessors, which was shortly before Morgan approached us to discuss his relationship with Phoebe.'

'This was when?' Chandler asked.

'He spent four years living in Kent. Five years later, he met and fell in love with Phoebe. That was in 2006. We came on board in the January of the following year. They married later that autumn.'

'So you've been monitoring him for, what, a little over thirteen years? Time enough to form a judgement. I don't suppose you can share with us what that might have been?'

McKinnon stepped in to fend that one off. 'Sorry. That one is strictly off limits.'

'But it's safe to assume your risk assessments to date had left you with no immediate concerns,' Bliss persisted.

'If you mean did we consider him to be a risk to anybody, or at risk from anybody, then no, we did not. No risk either way, nor any likelihood of his re-offending.'

The two detectives had agreed on the journey down to Cambridge not to inform the probation services of Callum Oliver's interest, so Bliss had to tread carefully. 'Just to clarify, then, to your knowledge he had not been recognised, nor had he been targeted by anybody?'

'That's correct. But please, tell me, why do you ask that?' Pearson said sharply.

The glimmer in her eyes told Bliss he might not have been careful enough. He gathered his thoughts. 'Because we're trying to figure out why your man killed himself. Let me share with you our two working hypotheses: first, Latchford's wife somehow came to learn about his prison sentence, causing a rift between them that led to him taking his own life. Second, somebody else discovered the truth and threatened the lives of Latchford's family to the point where he was forced to walk in front of that train. Either theory leads us to conclude that his identity had been exposed.'

'And your question is?' McKinnon asked, after exchanging glances with his colleague.

'Do you think we could be on the right lines? Is it possible for this to have happened without you being aware?'

'Of course.'

The answer took Bliss by surprise. Shocked, he frowned and said, 'You're saying it is possible?'

'Naturally. Anything is possible, Inspector. The potential for exposure features extensively in our risk assessment process. We're not immune to the fact that Morgan was previously recognised. Although the various court orders and injunctions prevented the mass media from showing the photographs that were taken of him, we are fully aware that they exist somewhere out there in the ether. He was in his mid-twenties at the time, so without cosmetic changes his current appearance compared to any existing images of him will reveal the likeness. That said, the chances are in his favour, and I'd say the past two decades living freely in and around Peterborough suggest those odds were about right. But we take nothing for granted, Inspector. We have no evidence to suggest Morgan Latchford's true identity had been compromised. Were that the case, he would already have been moved.'

'I'd like to add something,' his fellow probation officer said as she leaned in. 'You outlined your two working hypotheses. Given your jobs, you came up with a couple of options, either of which might lead to further investigation. I wonder if you'd ever considered a third, perhaps a more likely alternative?'

'Which would be...?' Bliss asked. He so enjoyed being coached in how to do his job by people who had never seen what he had seen.

'That Morgan killed himself for the same reason so many suicidal people do. Because he was depressed.'

Bliss could see how she'd got there. It was, of course, a viable consideration. But then she was not privy to the information they had concerning the man's demeanour, the condition of the house, the missing wife and daughter, and the mystery Picasso driver. He dipped his head as if acknowledging her suggestion.

'We've considered all possibilities. And we haven't yet ruled out any of them. However, a variety of factors lead us to conclude this was not the case.'

'And what factors might they be?'

He gave a thin, humourless smile. 'There are things I can't disclose to you concerning an ongoing operation, just as you cannot reveal everything to us.'

Bliss thought back on their discussion and realised the probation officers had not offered anything of real value or import. Certainly nothing that would help them redefine their approach. He was beginning to think their short trip south had been in vain. Despite this, he had a few more questions before throwing in the towel.

'I understand Latchford worked from home as a self-employed editor for a publisher.'

'He did, indeed,' McKinnon said. 'It kept him indoors for much of the week, which worked out nicely for all concerned. Especially given the recent social circumstances.'

'But he presumably had friends. Then there's his wife's family, her work colleagues, her friends also. Any of whom might have stumbled upon something that made them suspicious.'

'That's true. Look, Morgan was on probation, out on licence. His identity changed with guaranteed anonymity. There were obvious constraints to his life, but essentially he was allowed to live it without being harassed by us at every turn. We checked up on him, double-checked relevant intelligence, but he had a life to lead and we did not interfere or intervene. He was obliged to tell us about new people in his life, and on that basis we carried out frequent risk assessments. But quietly, in the background.

Which means it was always a hands-off approach. We and your Chief Constable last met with Morgan three months ago – we see him twice a year. He reported nothing of any consequence to us, and we had nothing new to report back to him. As far as this office was concerned – is concerned – Morgan Latchford had nothing to fear from others, and nobody had anything to fear from him.'

'Sounds like a model client,' Chandler said, injecting more than a little scepticism.

'In many ways he was,' Pearson shot back, her voice clipped. 'Learning that he had taken his own life came as a complete shock. To both of us. Legally there is much we can't tell you, DS Chandler, but I will say this: Morgan loved his wife and adored his daughter. If Phoebe somehow found out about him and her reaction meant it was about to end his marriage and his relationship with Beccy, that could easily have pushed him over the edge. Equally, the Morgan Latchford I came to know was definitely the sort of man to walk in front of a train rather than have harm come to his family.'

Bliss caught the edge in her tone and manner. He thought he could guess its source. 'None of us are looking to blame either of you for what happened,' he said softy. 'And we are certainly not about to accuse you of missing something important. If we had to look at the pair of you sideways, we'd also have to do the same with our own Chief Constable.'

'Perhaps that's just as well. It wouldn't be the first time a probation officer was scapegoated.'

'That's not what's happening here. We're simply carrying out our investigation and asking pertinent questions of relevant people. That would describe you two, would it not?'

Pearson bowed her head, acknowledging the point he had made. Meanwhile, Bliss fumed inwardly. The interview had taken on a defensive tone, and he wondered if he'd brought that into play by something he'd said, or perhaps the way he'd said it. It was getting harder to tell these days, what with people being so easy to trigger, their emotions bubbling so close to the surface. He asked for a list of Morgan Latchford's friends and ended it there, because once an interview reached this point it had nowhere else to go. Nowhere better, at least.

TWENTY-EIGHT

'You fucking stink!' the man said to him. It was his first visit of the day, and he wasn't wasting any time.

As terrified as he was of both his abductor and the fragile situation he found himself in, Callum spat out a heated response. 'What do you expect? Really, what do you expect? You keep me bound like an animal in a room containing my own filth, pretty soon I'm going to smell like one.'

For a moment he didn't think his complaint was going to elicit a reply. Then, without warning, the man bent forward and slapped both his cheeks, forehand and backhand. As the sting welled up on his flesh, Callum cried out and roared all his frustration and fury, the strangled noise sounding alien to his ears.

The man loomed over him still, striking a threatening pose as the fingers of both hands bunched. 'Just for that, you're going to have to wait for your food and water.'

Callum fixated on the single word that gave him succour. *Wait.*

No threat to withdraw sustenance, merely to delay it. That was fine. He was ravenous and starting to feel a little dehydrated, but he could cope with a simple delay.

The man ran a hand over his own unshaved face and breathed

out a steady lungful of air. 'Let's get back to where we left off last time,' he said, standing upright once again. 'See, the thing is, I have to be certain in my own mind that you're being honest with me. There's no way out of this for you if that doesn't happen.'

'I told you what you wanted to know. You asked, I answered. What more do you want from me?'

'Hmm. That's just it. You say you told me what I wanted to know, but I think you told me what I wanted to hear. I think you mixed the truth with a few porky pies, and I really can't have that.'

Callum shook his head in desperation. He stared up at the figure standing tall above him. 'I told you everything. I answered every question with more honesty than you deserved. I left nothing out. I told you no lies.'

'So tell me again. And think about it carefully this time. Because for all you know, I've been recording our conversations, playing them back at my leisure. For all you know I've been comparing your answers. So if you don't tell me exactly what you told me before, then you and I are going to fall out big time.'

Yeah, because we're such great pals now, right?

Blinking away a smattering of tears, Callum slumped back in despair. He'd told only the truth each time, answered every question fully and faithfully. But he could already tell something about this man: he would never accept at face value anything Callum told him. He would never accept the truth. But what else was there? What was left to be said?

Shuffling closer, the soles of his boots scuffing on the cold concrete floor, the man dropped to his haunches. With the balaclava covering his face, the eyes drew Callum in. They were flat, and dull, and yet glinting with anticipation.

'Tell me precisely what you came to know about Morgan Latchford,' he said, asking the same question in the same way as he had half a dozen times before.

Callum almost gave up, came so close to refusing to answer, to rejecting this man's awful game. Except for one simple fact: the man was not playing. He was serious. Perhaps even deadly serious. 'I've given you my answer,' he breathed. 'I told you everything I know. There's nothing left, nothing new to give.'

'Tell me precisely what you came to know about Morgan Latchford.'

With no thought for the consequences, Callum half-screamed and half-snarled by way of a response. The man remained squatting by his side, unmoved, unimpressed by the outburst.

'Do that again,' he said, 'and the next time I strike you, I'll have something heavy in my hand. The time after that it will be heavy *and* sharp. I'm not fucking around with you. You stepped up a league, and you were never going to be big enough, tough enough, or good enough to survive. So far you've had a beating. True, it got severe at one point, but I held back. I won't be doing that again in the future. From this point on, please understand something: today's beast differs from the one you faced when I first chained you up in here. And believe me, you don't want to see what tomorrow might bring.'

The room fell silent after the echo of his words died away. The man closed his eyes for a second or two. Callum had no way to respond, other than by doing as he had been told. 'Where do you want me to start?' he asked in a small voice.

'Where all good stories start,' came the reply. 'Right at the beginning.'

*

Bliss treated them to lunch at the Cuckoo in Alwalton. He did his level best not to dwell on the case, but trying to avoid thinking about it made him focus on it all the more. This soon led to feelings of guilt at wasting time eating and drinking while people were missing. His companion must have noticed his dip in mood, especially when he shoved his plate aside with the food on it barely half touched.

'Oi, snap out of it!' Chandler reprimanded him. 'You can't force this to go where you want it to by sheer force of will. Nor by sulking like a child.'

He drained his pint glass. 'Why not?' he complained. 'Is that really too much to ask?'

'Yes, Jimmy. Even for you. Just like us mere mortals who work with you, every so often you have to accept the fact that sometimes things don't go our way. In this case – or these cases, I should say – we're not picking up any momentum despite all our best efforts.'

'I do accept that, Pen. The trouble is, as per usual, I can't help but wonder if we're missing something.'

'And as per usual, the chances of that are remote. I'd say the lack of hard evidence means we can't be missing anything, because there's not enough for anything to have fallen through the cracks. Tell me, what more could we be doing with Fledgling? We've forensiced the fuck out of the abandoned motor. We know who owns it. We know where he last used his work phone. We know what he was working on. We also know there's a very good chance his disappearance is because of his own journalistic investigation. We've worked off scraps and yet we still have all that. What could we have possibly missed?'

Bliss sighed. 'I don't know. But I do have a question of my own.'

'Go on, then. What is it?'

'Is there such a word as "forensiced"?'

Chandler's usual response to one of his asinine remarks was to stick two fingers up at him. Today she went for just the one – the middle finger.

'Pen, if you think about it, you just steered an aircraft carrier through your own argument. You said we didn't have enough to go on for there to be room to miss anything, but then you ran off a list of what we've learned so far. And left out a few things. I'd say that leaves plenty of room for missing something important enough to create a new and worthwhile lead. I mean, just look at the things we now don't know as a result of our discoveries. We don't know where Callum Oliver had his car jacked. We don't know where he is. We don't know if he's dead or alive. We don't know how far his investigation into Morgan Latchford's past had progressed. We don't know if he confided in anybody else. We don't know if he was in contact with the man, or indeed his wife. We don't even know if he took any action at all at this stage. That's a shitload we don't know, and every single piece of it sticks in my gullet.'

Chandler groaned around the rim of her own glass, then set her drink to one side. 'But they're not things we've missed, Jimmy. They're just things we haven't had time to find out about yet.'

'Are those known unknowns, or unknown knowns?'

This time he got the full blown raspberry. 'You're an idiot.'

'But do we actually know that?'

'Fuck it! When you get like this, Jimmy, there's no dealing with you.'

'You say we haven't had time to find out. What if we simply lack the nous?'

'Oh, so now we're rubbish at what we do?'

'I didn't say that. But did you stop to think about it? Isn't it possible that some of those answers are right in front of us, only we're so consumed by everything else we're blind to what our eyes and ears are telling us?'

Chandler shook her head. An abrupt movement, firm and decisive. 'No. It isn't. I'm telling you, the missing pieces of the puzzle have yet to be found because the break we very much need hasn't happened yet. It's not that it's there and we've missed it. It's just not there.'

He ran a hand over his face, lingering at the scar on his forehead. He wanted to believe his friend and colleague, wished he had her outlook. For all his recent changes in general demeanour, he was never going to be the optimist she was. Experience had long ago taught him that investigations seldom made constant progress. There had always been and would always be times when you felt as if you were running in mud wearing concrete boots. Yet this time it felt different. This time he simply did not know what to do next.

'You're being impatient,' Chandler insisted.

Bliss looked up. She'd read him well. 'I know. But three people, including a child, are not where they ought to be. So how about we get back to basics? This is all about those people, and where you have people you have friends and family. Let's dig deeper into their details and speak to them. Usual stuff: when was the last time any of them spoke to Callum or Phoebe? Were they behaving differently? Did they discuss any recent issues?'

'Oh, is that all? Is that on top of or instead of speaking to Haley Deerbourne's family?'

'Yes, it is all. And in addition to. Even if it means drawing in extra bodies we have no budget for. I realise we're short of manpower – or personpower or whatever the fuck I'm supposed to say now – but we can spare Phil and the new boy for the rest of the day. After that, it may not be our business anymore.'

'You mean it may not be the team's business. I suspect you won't give it up so easily.'

'You're bloody right I won't be. Telling us to cut short our investigation because some officers and civilians might end up booking too much overtime is… indecent. That can't be the way this goes, Pen. It just can't.'

'So suddenly you're the man who refuses to accept reality. You? The great Jimmy Bliss. The DI of hope. What a bloody joke.'

Bliss realised how serious Chandler was when he saw tears glittering in her eyelashes. He reached across the table to put a hand over hers. 'Hey,' he said gently. 'What's wrong? I thought we were just letting off steam like we often do. Duking it out verbally.'

She shook her head fiercely. 'That's just is, isn't it? You and I, we have our rhythms, we have our snark, we have our tantrums, but we love each other more for it at the end of every day.'

'Of course. A hundred percent.'

'Except we have fewer and fewer of those days to look forward to, Jimmy. Each one that passes is another one down the drain of your time left with us. It's not all about you. How do you think I feel knowing that the day you have to hand in your warrant card is hurtling down the road towards us like some unstoppable force? Do you think about me at all when you contemplate your future? When that day comes around, both of our futures will be affected, and I, for one, don't want to go through the motions, don't want to argue, don't want to waste your last hurrah fighting each other because you're too busy fighting the system. You're better than that. You have to be. Especially this time.'

Bliss blinked, staggered by the ferocity and passion in her voice. 'What am I supposed to do?' he asked. 'What do you expect of me now?'

It took a minute, but eventually she gave a firm nod and said, 'I expect you to do the right thing. It's all I've ever expected of you, no matter what the outcome. What's your favourite saying, Jimmy? Come on, your all-time favourite?'

'I'd rather die than be a Spurs fan?'

A smile cracked her glum features. 'The gospel according to Jimmy Bliss: things are what they are, not what we'd like them to be. We work with that, not with the unworkable.'

Bliss frowned. 'I don't say that. Not that last part.'

This time Chandler nodded enthusiastically. Her smile grew wider. 'No. That's mine. Poetic licence. And I'm owning it.'

'You can keep it. It's shit!'

This time she couldn't help herself. When it came, her laughter bordered on the hysterical. But Bliss could see she was venting, that she needed to express how she was feeling, and he accepted he was the continuing cause of many of Chandler's woes. He didn't know how he was going to approach having the ops ripped from his grasp, and he'd deal with it when it happened, tackle it head on. It was his way. But the thought of hurting his best friend at the same time took hold of his gut and gave it a sharp twist. That was something he never wanted to do, and he knew that every step he took from this point on would, for her sake, be a wary one.

TWENTY-NINE

OTHER THAN DCS GRATTON and Virgil, the incident room was deserted by the time Bliss and Chandler arrived. 'Bish and Gul are on their way back from the diner,' Gratton reported. 'Alan and I have been gathering intel on the Deerbourne family. Haley's father passed away a few years back. Her mother is now in her mid-sixties, and has MS, so we can rule her out as well. We're still digging into extended family, but we discovered something regarding Haley's two brothers. They were both older by four and five years respectively when she was murdered. And here's the really interesting part: when Dean Norman was spotted in Kent, newspaper and TV journalists door-stepped the Deerbournes for a response. Both brothers were interviewed together, and they warned Norman to stay hidden next time or they would find him and pay him back in kind for what he did to their kid sister.'

It was something to consider, but no more and no less than Bliss expected. Some families reacted to tragic events with quiet dignity, others with wild threats of revenge. It didn't mean a thing. He'd witnessed the quiet and the dignified avenge their loss with ruthless efficiency, and tough guy braggarts melt into the background when put to the test. It was one more item to follow up on, however.

'Do you have contact details on them?' he asked.

'That's what we were working on when you came in, boss,' Virgil told him.

'Okay. Good work both of you. Send everything across to me. I'll allocate jobs a bit later after we've all updated.'

'Did you two get much out of the probation service?'

'Not a lot,' Chandler growled. 'And the little we did get had to be prised out of them with the help of a crowbar and some lube.'

'Both of which I expect you had in that handbag of yours,' Gratton said, chuckling to himself.

Chandler rounded on him. 'Tell you what, Phil, I'll smack you over the head with it and you let me know if it's heavy enough to be carrying a crowbar.'

'In your case, I was thinking the lube would be heavier.'

He dodged a swipe and stepped back to the computer he'd been using when they walked in.

'For probation, it's all about risk assessment,' Bliss informed him and Virgil. 'The risk of their client reoffending or going off the rails in another way. The risk of somebody working out who he was and acting upon it.'

'This kind of thing must be right up there with their worst fears,' Gratton said, shuddering a little. Bliss understood; none of them had seen what remained of Morgan Latchford, but they all had good imaginations.

'They don't know the full story. Only what I was prepared to share with them and whatever the Chief Constable's office told them. What we can say with some certainty after meeting them is that their monitoring of him was at arm's length other than when people got close to him. The rest of the time, they did their work in the background to ensure the new identity held up and pretty much allowed him to live a fairly normal life.'

Virgil shook his head dismissively. 'Doesn't seem right to me. Haley Deerbourne never got to live a normal life.'

'Are you saying you don't believe in rehabilitation, Alan?'

'In specific cases, and with certain people. Dean Norman served ten years. That might have seemed fair to him, his legal team, and possibly even his family. But how would you feel if you were Haley's nearest and dearest? If somebody did that to my sister, I wouldn't consider a decade and then a free life as sufficient punishment.'

'He was still on licence, remember,' Gratton argued. 'He always knew if he screwed up, he was back inside. Only next time it would've been in prison and not an offenders' home.'

'But at least he had that opportunity. Yeah, he knew he'd have to walk a straight line for the rest of his life, but he was given that chance. Which is more than he gave Haley.'

'All right you two,' Bliss intervened before the conversation spiralled out of control. 'I think we can all agree the law is often an arse when it comes to proper justice, but whether it was or wasn't in this case is neither here nor there. We deal in the factual. Dean Norman *was* released on licence. He *did* become Morgan Latchford. He *did* step in front of a speeding train. It doesn't matter how we got here, this is where we are and this is what we have to work with. Ultimately, probation was of no help other than allowing us that insight into how little they actually did watch over him.'

Bliss looked up as Bishop and Ansari entered the room, jackets hooked over their shoulders. Bishop wore a sly grin and immediately sought him out. 'You nervous about tonight, boss?' he asked.

'Tonight? Oh, you mean the game? Of course. Drawing 1-1 at the Bernabeu was a cracking result, but this is Real Madrid we're talking about.'

'You afraid Hazard might come back to haunt you?'

Feigning shock, Bliss said, 'Not a chance. Reece James will have him in his pocket.'

It was Champions League night, the second leg of the semi-final and his team, Chelsea, had the slight advantage of an away goal. He rarely attended games these days, having once been a regular both on the terraces and in the seats at Stamford Bridge. He had fallen out of love with the game itself, but not with his club. That was never going to happen, no matter how many managers they went through or years spent without winning a trophy. A long-suffering Leicester City supporter, Bishop gave a knowing nod before turning away.

'We have much to report,' he said, marching up to the front of the room to stand by the boards. 'Shall I crack on or do you have anything we need to know first?'

'No, you fill your boots,' Bliss said, a look of amusement on his face. 'I can't remember the last time I saw you so energised and animated, Bish. It's like somebody stuffed a Duracell up your arris.'

Bishop waited for the resulting laughter to die down before he told them everything he and Ansari had learned at the OK diner. 'No prizes for guessing what happened to the member of staff most likely to have given up information to Callum Oliver… she went back home to Poland. However, I asked the deputy manager – her boss was off duty – how easy it would have been for this Polish woman to have found what Oliver was looking for. He asked for the approximate time and date and he was able to come up with the same info within a couple of minutes. Morgan Latchford was indeed our man in that booth, and we have a copy of his debit card payment to prove it. It's evidence only, but it at least proves we're thinking the right way.'

'Good work,' Bliss said. 'Anything yet on his associates or his wife's family?'

'Yes and no. Gul spoke with the publishing company he sometimes works for, but these days that job is mainly done online. They've never actually met in person, so that was a waste of time. I had words with Mrs Latchford's family, such as it is. Her father told me they'd been estranged for a good few years, and he knew little to nothing about Morgan. She has a sister, but their relationship is also strained. Apparently the two of them speak once or twice a year on the phone, but Phoebe never had a bad word to say about her husband. I think that's a dead end, too.'

'Fair enough. You tried. How did you get on with CCTV?'

Bishop hung his jacket around the back of his chair. He rifled through the clutter on the desk he'd been using, eventually emerging with a sheet containing his notes. 'Regards Latchford and his journey to the railway line, I'm going to have to go back to ask for more footage. Unfortunately for us, he appears to have walked all the way down Maskew Avenue. So we have no vehicle to check out. I'm going to go back further to see if I can spot where he might have been dropped off, but I think we run out of cameras at the roundabout leading into the retail estate.'

'How about the buses? Did Stagecoach come through for us?'

Bishop raised a thumb. 'They did, and we have some nuggets of treasure here, boss. Front and rear camera footage from two separate buses shows us the red Citroen parked outside the house. It gave us a plate, but it doesn't come back to a Picasso, red or otherwise. From other footage both earlier and later, I can tell you that car was not there at 7.47, was there by 8.06, was still there at 8.28, and gone again by 8.49.'

Bliss ran the calculations. 'So we have a window of one hour. By the time our Picasso driver arrived, Morgan Latchford had already left the house. Given what you said about him walking along Maskew Avenue, I'm wondering if he walked from home. That's a genuine possibility. The question is, why? Why does a man who works from home leave the house at that time of morning and take a long walk like that?'

'Perhaps because he *does* work from home. He could just have been taking some exercise.'

Bliss raised his eyebrows. 'Like you'd know anything about exercise.'

'Yeah, yeah.' Bishop patted a stomach straining against his shirt. 'This is all relaxed muscle.'

'Well, then you'd better get it unrelaxed, because your annual fitness test is coming up soon.'

'My gran could pass that bleep test, and she has dodgy hips.'

Bliss chuckled. Olly Bishop was a good sport when it came to jokes about his weight. He loved his food, loved his snacks, and loved his beer; not exactly a recipe for slenderness. Suggesting Latchford was getting some exercise was not at all unreasonable, so he added it to a growing list of considerations.

'Well, unless it's related to his death, it may not matter why our man was out and about, but I would like to know more about how. Let's look at his most likely routes and see what we can get from another CCTV sweep along them. Let's not forget his car, either. When does that come and go from his house, and who was driving it at the time? This is good stuff, Bish. We're starting to squeeze this thing now.'

'And I haven't even told you the best part.'

'Then don't fanny about. Get on with it.'

'While I was watching the footage again, I noticed a van parked up a couple of doors down from the Citroen at 8.28. It was still there later at 8.49. Which means it was there when the Citroen left. And the thing about it is, I spotted what I think were a couple of plumbers getting stuff out of their van and laying pipes out in a front garden.'

'You're thinking they might have been outside when the family left, so they also could have spotted the driver.'

'Precisely. If we can track them down, then they might be able to provide us with a description.'

This was positive news. A description was progress, no matter which way you looked at the rest of what they had. Alone, it might not buy them more time, but one more thing on top… Bliss felt buoyed by this. 'Great stuff,' he said. 'Coming back to something I mentioned a while ago, is there any sign of Mr Latchford's motor on the bus footage?'

'I was so focussed on the Picasso I didn't think to look. But it's a good point, because if he wasn't driving it that morning, then who was?'

Bliss nodded. 'Precisely.' He then turned to DC Ansari. 'Gul, please tell me you have something on the phones.'

Her smile told him she had good news. 'I finally got responses. We know Callum Oliver's personal number died at the same time as his work one because their individual SIMS are in the same physical device. But we got details back on both. I figured he was keeping the investigation from his employers so he wouldn't have used their number, leaving me free to concentrate on his personal one. We have him running many web searches, from the OK diner to the *Stamford Mercury*, from Bernadette Finch to Morgan Latchford, from Dean Norman to Stevie Phillips, the Deerbournes, and the murder of Haley. We also have a phone call between Oliver and a number I've traced to Bernadette Finch's landline, plus two texts to her mobile. The texts were just thank-you notes, dated the same day as they spoke. It's about as comprehensive as you'd expect from somebody looking to identify the man Dean Norman became, and it's solid evidence to put in our report.'

Running a hand across his scalp, Bliss said, 'Okay, that's all sounding terrific. How about Mrs Latchford?'

'Just as we thought, boss. That phone conversation Mr Latchford had moments before killing himself was with his wife.'

Bliss inclined his head. 'Correction, Gul. It was her phone being used. Doesn't mean it was her he was speaking with.'

'Then who... ah, our man in the red Picasso.'

'If you believe our witness and read between the lines of what was said,' Chandler jumped in, 'then it makes more sense for Morgan Latchford to have been talking about his wife, not with her.'

Ansari's shoulders slumped, crestfallen. 'Oh. Well, then I guess my news wasn't exciting after all.'

'On the contrary,' Bliss argued. 'Because if it wasn't his wife, then it had to be somebody close enough to her at the time to have use of her phone. And we now know our Picasso driver was there at precisely that same time. If it doesn't tell us anything new, it does at least confirm our hypothesis. That's still progress in my book, together with some healthy momentum.'

That did the trick in cheering her up. Then Gratton piped up. 'Oh, boss, you mentioning the witness reminds me. Zinta Balodis is on her way back to us. Superintendent Fletcher intervened on our behalf. I was having trouble getting the border and immigration people to take me seriously. I felt bad about not keeping Balodis here, so I had a word with DCI Warburton who had a word with the Super. Evidently, the possibility of Balodis being required as a witness worked a treat.'

Bliss huffed out a long sigh. He was relieved to have good news on that score. He was also taking in the information his team had gathered while he and Chandler were in Cambridge. This was real movement, genuine progress. He nodded at Bishop. 'Are wheels in motion concerning this plumber who might have clocked Picasso Man?'

Bishop regarded him with a look of amazement. 'Of course. This ain't my first rodeo, boss.'

'Rodeo? You'd be the one bucking the rider off your back.'

'Is that a euphemism?'

Bliss chuckled. 'For your sake, I do hope not. So you had somebody looking into it before you went off up the A1 to the diner, then?'

'I did. I asked Inspector Kaplan if he could spare a couple of his people. I think he was keen to still be involved, even in a minor way. Evidently they got hold of a name from the van and called the number, but each time it's gone straight to voicemail. We don't have any office details – looks like a small self-employed outfit – but we've left messages and Gul is going to have a crack at finding whose phone it is.'

Bliss was delighted. 'This really is great work everybody. You're all thinking on your feet. Seems you hardly need a team leader these days. So, we have excellent movement on that side of the investigation. Understudy is functioning well at the moment, and I reckon it alone will buy us at least another day, though I'll be asking for three. As for Fledgling, progress is slower, but we seem to have a pretty full picture taking shape.'

Bishop's barge-hull of a chest rose and fell. 'I've been thinking more about that Picasso. I think we'd be right to assume our driver headed straight to the farmhouse where they changed vehicles. Whichever way he drove when he left the Latchford home he'd almost certainly have gone through the city centre on the A15, past the courthouse, onto Bishop's Road, continuing along Fengate, right onto Storey's Bar, right again taking him past Flag Fen, and then on North Bank alongside the river. It's the most direct route that I can think of, and he'd want that.'

'So you're thinking of ANPR plus all that juicy CCTV in the centre.' Bliss pursed his lips. 'I'm right with you. Get it done as soon as we're finished here. Now that you have a decent time window, you can narrow it down to reduce the sheer volume of footage.'

'Wouldn't he want to avoid CCTV as much as possible?' Virgil asked.

'Possibly so. However, getting from where he was to where he ended up would take him past security cameras, whichever route he chose. In which case, I'm betting he went for the quickest.'

Bishop folded his arms and leaned forward, almost hugging himself. 'I suppose he might have gone north, onto the A47 and then south again when he reached Thorney. That has to be fewer cameras to contend with, even though it's a slightly longer journey.'

'Then get them all checked.'

'Easier said than done, boss. You know how small this team is right now.'

Bishop was right, and Bliss grew frustrated once again. 'Fair point,' he said. 'So it's shit or get off the pot time, folks. Do we have enough for me to go with to the DCI to have a word with the Super? This is big enough, and it's growing. Two ops, but now a single investigation to my mind. We need more bodies, and I'm already treating this as a major crimes case. How about the rest of you?'

The response he got back was emphatically positive. He grinned. 'That's what I was hoping to hear. I'll have a word with the boss. But before I do, there is another big question we have to find an answer to, and that is whether Callum Oliver could be Picasso Man.'

THIRTY

It was supposed to be a drive of around three and a half hours. Closer to five after setting off from Thorpe Wood, Bliss and Chandler eventually arrived in Littlehampton. Tailbacks resulting from two accidents on the M25 had soured Bliss's mood, and he was feeling more than a little tetchy as they inched their way through heavy traffic before finally arriving at their destination.

It was a shame, because he'd begun the day in high spirits, his team having qualified for the Champions League final the previous evening. Prior to that, the afternoon had petered out, leaving everybody in major crimes dissatisfied. At the office meeting before they all went home, Bliss reminded his fellow officers of other difficult operations they'd come through together; detectives had days filled with peaks and troughs, and you couldn't allow yourself to be pulled down by the latter. They'd made excellent progress, and he was proud of the hard work put in by all concerned to help keep hold of both cases. When you were constantly waiting for intel that might lead to further actions, sometimes you had no alternative but to do so patiently.

His choice of words had provoked a ripple of gentle laughter, patience not being one of his strengths. As he was leaving the building shortly before 6.00pm, he ran into Detective Chief

Superintendent Feeley, who was also on his way out. The DCS had attempted to engage him in conversation, but Bliss mumbled something about having to rush off for a prior meeting he'd forgotten about. Feeley took the brush off well, pausing only to congratulate him at having secured a further twenty-four hours working the ops, together with a promise of extra staff. That was enough for Bliss, and given the result of the game he'd been in a positive frame of mind until finding himself sitting in the car park that was the M25. That damn road had the ability to suck the very life out of a person.

The Deerbourne brothers owned and operated a fishmongers virtually on the banks of the river Arun at East Beach. When Bliss and Chandler showed up, the two men left an apprentice in charge and found a seat by Oyster Pond close enough to keep an eye on their business. The pair behaved as if they were granting the two detectives an audience, which did nothing to improve Bliss's sour disposition.

Intelligence on them revealed a long pattern of unlawful and aggressive behaviour, both having spent a short amount of time behind bars on different occasions. Reading between the lines, they were nothing more than small-time hoodlums acting as if they wielded power in the area. Bliss spotted their bluff a mile off, but kept the observation to himself. He hadn't endured the road to Hell only to leave without a clear idea whether these two men were responsible for Morgan Latchford's death.

During the tedious journey down to the south coast, Chandler had wanted to pursue the previous day's intriguing notion that Callum Oliver might have contacted the Deerbourne family after having confirmed Dean Norman's new identity. Bliss was still considering the possibility, unable to shake the undeniable logic of such an approach, when he asked the first question on his mental list.

'Tell me, when was the last time either of you set eyes on Dean Norman?'

Robert Deerbourne, the elder brother, was the first to respond. 'Not since the day he was sentenced.'

'You're sure about that?'

Both men nodded, though neither was overly convincing. 'No chance,' Robert said. 'If we had, that prick wouldn't have made it out alive.'

'That's not really something you ought to be telling two coppers, is it, Robert?' Chandler said, her clipped tone a mild rebuke, but nothing forceful enough to justify a negative reaction.

'But understandable for all that,' Bliss said. 'I mean, if they'd gone after a close member of my family and murdered her the way those two bastards did, I'd want them punished.'

'I think they were implying some measure of severe violence would be doled out, boss,' she insisted, eyebrows raised.

'Funnily enough, so was I. The thing is, Haley's murder took place in 1987. Carrying a significant level of anger around for that length of time is unusual.'

'We're an unusual family,' Robert said gruffly. 'But you have to remember how short a time we had our sister with us. Eight years is fuck all, and those two pricks stole these past three decades and more from us.'

'Surely her tender age means the social and emotional ties with your sister were reduced. How did your desire for revenge carry on regardless? You want him dead, right? I mean, let's be honest, you want to kill him. Life for a life is what you see as justice. Isn't that correct?'

'What of it?' Raymond asked, his piercing tight gaze fixed on Bliss. 'Wanting to ain't no crime. We can want whatever the fuck we like. It's no business of yours.'

'True,' Bliss agreed. 'Just as long as you don't act upon it. Thing is, if you found out where he was, I'm beginning to wonder if you might do precisely that. But I don't expect you to tell me, so let me take a step back. You say you've not been in his presence since he was sentenced. Have either of you been in contact with him at all?'

'No. Why would we?'

'Oh, I don't know… to threaten him, maybe?'

'No. We ain't seen him and we ain't spoken to him, either. Satisfied?'

'Not really, but let's move on.' Bliss gave a friendly smile before continuing. 'You say you haven't seen him? By that, you mean in person. But how about in a photograph?'

Robert jerked his head up, squinting against the sun. 'You mean that one from years back when he was in Kent? Of course. Those fucking reporters rammed it down our throats all over again.'

'No, I mean since then. I mean recently. See, it's our understanding that a journalist approached you within the past few weeks and told you he'd spotted Norman. Not only that, but he'd also worked out Norman's new identity.'

'I wondered why you were asking about him only, and not that other piece of filth as well. Look, Inspector Whateveryournameis, I'm not really sure why you think we would help you. We want very different things where those fuckers are concerned. But so what if any of what you just said was true? What about it? Why are you asking us about Dean Norman now?'

Bliss thought about how much he ought to reveal. The idea of every interview was to gain more than you gave away, learn more than you revealed. In this specific instance, he wasn't sure how the men might react to hearing about the death of their sister's killer. If they were responsible, he might see it in their eyes or in their body language. If they weren't, they might become too emotional to continue. In the end, he decided to be cagey while at the same time looking to tease information from them.

'All right,' he said. 'That's a fair question, so I'll give you a straight answer. We believe somebody has been stalking the man once known as Dean Norman. As I'm sure you'll appreciate, in cases like this it's hard for us to look past the victim's family. It's also our understanding that the journalist in question came to learn of this, and if that's true then we reckon their next logical move would be to seek you out.'

'I've no idea what you're prattling on about,' Raymond snapped, looking away sharply. His brother said much the same thing.

Bliss had been leaning in. As he nodded in response, he pulled back to appraise them both. 'I hope that's the case. I really do. Because when it's something as serious as this, we go all out. That includes tracing people's movements, asking a shit load of questions, and digging into people's lives to the point where, frankly, it becomes indecently like a colonoscopy. So if you do have any knowledge about any of the things I just mentioned, it's better for you to own up now. Think of your poor tender arseholes. And let me assure you both, provided you did not initiate the search for Dean Norman or pay somebody to do it on your behalf, you're not in any trouble. We just want to know the truth.'

The Deerbourne brothers eyed one another, shifting uncomfortably on the hard wooden bench. Robert rubbed a hand down his face, stretching the flesh tight across the bone, before taking charge. 'Look, the reporter came to us, all right? Told us he believed he'd found that prick Norman and was going to expose him as a happily married family man with a decent job living the kind of life he never allowed our sister to have. That was his angle, not ours.'

'And your response was?' Chandler asked.

'I offered him cash,' Raymond admitted, putting his head back and exhaling up into the sky. 'Told him he'd earn more out of us than he ever would getting his story into print.'

'Let's roll back for a second. What was the name of this reporter you spoke to?'

'He didn't say.'

'He didn't give you his name? What, so he just told you he was a reporter and had this information for you, and you didn't even check him out?'

'He said if he gave us his details, we'd know where Norman was. He also admitted he was being cautious because he couldn't predict how we'd react.'

'And just like that, without confirming a single word, you offered to buy him off.'

This time, the younger brother scowled at Chandler. 'Do I really look that fucking stupid? He'd only get our money for information he could prove.'

'Fair enough. So what happened next? Did he agree?'

'Not exactly. He told us he'd think about it.'

'How about you, Robert?' Bliss asked. 'What was your view on this deal your brother was trying to set up?'

The man squirmed uncomfortably. At first it didn't look as if he was going to offer up an answer, but eventually he shook his head and nailed Raymond with a fierce glare. 'I didn't want no part of it. I thought it was a scam – and it wouldn't be the first time some half-wit tried to pull a stroke like that. But we didn't fall for it before and I wasn't about to again.'

'But you had different ideas, Raymond. Tell me, why did you think this was genuine?'

The man shrugged and turned the question over for a few seconds before responding. 'I think it was the way he spoke. He was calm about it. And remember, he didn't ask for money. He wasn't looking for a pay day – at least, not from us. He told me he was going to make our sister headline news again, and the public sympathy would be massive. He got in touch because he wanted to write a piece about how we'd moved on as a family since Haley was murdered. But to be honest with you – and I don't give a flying fuck what either of you think at this point – I didn't give a shit about his story. I wanted the information he had, the details he was still rooting out. I wanted to know who Dean Norman was today, and where I could find him.'

Bliss believed him. Raymond Deerbourne spoke with such conviction, despite knowing his words might get him in trouble with the police. Honesty was admirable in Bliss's opinion, whatever the circumstances.

'When was the last time either of you spoke to him?'

'That would have been me,' Raymond said. 'Last week sometime. Friday, or maybe the day before.'

'You willing to hand your phone over to us?'

'Am I fuck? You want my phone, you arrest me.'

'I can do that if you really want me to, Raymond. Arrest the pair of you and have both your phones.'

The man sat back, folding his arms beneath a muscular chest. His brother got to his feet. 'You do that if you feel the need. But if you ain't got the balls for it, me and Raymond have to get back to work now.'

Bliss bit down on a heavy retort, deciding to back pedal. He regarded Raymond Deerbourne with a look of compassion. 'Look, let's not end this on a bad note. I don't want to go through all that crap, and neither do I have any wish to put either of you through the wringer. You've both endured enough, I reckon. Just tell me, what arrangement did you end up making with this journalist?'

'He was going to complete his… investigation, I suppose you could call it. Then he was going to write it up and think about his next move. I assumed he was considering taking the cash, but we made no firm plans either way.'

'And neither of you ever met him? Never drove out somewhere to discuss these arrangements face-to-face?'

They both insisted they had not, but Bliss noticed the younger man glancing away again, as if unwilling to meet his intense gaze. It might have been an instinctive gesture, but it came across as furtive. As if there might be more to his story. Something he did not wish to admit to. Bliss wondered if Raymond's reluctance was because of the presence of his brother or two police detectives.

He was hiding something, though.

Of that, Bliss was certain.

THIRTY-ONE

IT WAS ALMOST 5.00PM by the time they arrived back at Thorpe Wood. Bliss had called ahead to ask the team to hang on for the final meeting of the day, and there were no dissenters. He gave a wry smile when he entered the incident room to discover DC Hunt had returned as one of four detectives on loan to the unit from CID. He assumed everybody other than him was getting a kick out of that.

'Thank you all for staying on,' he told them. 'I'll try to keep this short. The fact is, I haven't yet decided if that was a complete waste of a day for me and Pen. I could have asked locals to interview the Deerbourne brothers and report back, but you all know there's nothing quite like seeing the whites of their eyes when you ask difficult questions, so I admit I took a bit of a gamble.'

'I'm sure it can't have been a complete washout, boss,' acting DI Bishop said helpfully. 'Even if you only cleared them, that's still a result.'

'That's just it, Bish – I'm not certain we did either. If we take at face value all the brothers told us, they're guilty of nothing more than wishful thinking. As we suspected, Callum Oliver contacted them, though they claim he kept his identity and location to himself. He told them he was a reporter about to write an article exposing who Dean Norman was now, with an editorial slant on comparing how the man's life was everything his actions had determined Haley Deerbourne's own future never had a chance to be. The younger brother, Raymond, admitted to offering the reporter a bung for the information instead. It's clear what his intentions were. The gist appeared to be that Oliver was considering the offer, but I doubt that was true.'

'So what do you reckon is really going on there, boss?' Ansari asked. 'You sounded sceptical when you mentioned taking the brothers at face value.'

'I was. I still am. Pen and I bounced it off each other on the drive back, and I think we eventually ended up in agreement. Robert Deerbourne seemed genuinely not to know anything more than the pair admitted to. Raymond came across as being more shifty and our impression was he was holding something back. It could just be that his dealings with Callum Oliver were more advanced than he'd told his brother, but I got the feeling there was more to it than that.'

'Like what?' DCI Warburton asked. She stood with one elbow resting on a filing cabinet, one hand jammed into her hip. 'Ahead of meeting with them you thought they might well be responsible, extending to having spirited Mr Oliver away. Do you still think that's a possibility?'

Bliss nodded. 'I do. Certainly, when I reconsider Raymond Deerbourne's little tics and reactions. If I had to guess, I'd say his brother is in the clear, but he himself has some explaining to do. Whether that amounts to having been directly involved, I can't be sure. So yes, possible, but no more than that.'

'You don't think it more likely than not?'

'No. I didn't get that kind of read.'

'Do you intend reinterviewing him?'

Bliss had asked himself this same question, and had his answer ready. 'I won't drive all the way back down there on a hunch, boss. But I may call him later on. Hopefully I'll catch him at home, without Robert around. I got the sense he had more to say but didn't want to include his brother in that conversation.'

'So your thinking remains the same: one or both brothers is potentially behind Morgan Latchford's suicide, the abduction of his wife and daughter, and the disappearance of Callum Oliver.'

Bliss caught himself before confirming. He wasn't convinced, because he couldn't see one man doing it all. It felt like more of a two-man job. After a moment of head scratching, he explained his feelings to the DCI and the rest of the team.

'I don't believe Robert is involved,' he eventually admitted. 'But if this is the work of two men, and Raymond is one of them, then I've yet to identify his partner.'

'I suggested the partner might be Callum Oliver himself,' Chandler told them, going on to elaborate. 'Up to the point where something bad happened to Oliver, he could have been working with Raymond Deerbourne. I don't know why he would willingly do so, but I can easily see Raymond somehow either forcing him to help or coughing up a hefty pile of cash and making it a difficult offer to turn down. Oliver approaching those two brothers opened up a real can of worms, and I doubt he was expecting the reaction he got. If I had to guess, I'd say he rejected the cash payment offer, at which time Raymond began thinking of a completely different approach. He could have spoken to Oliver on the QT, arranged to meet with him to offer his account of life without his sister, his outrage that Norman went on to have a happy life. The two meet. Raymond turns the tables.' She ended with a shrug. 'It's a theory.'

'And it holds up,' Bliss said. 'But if that's how it happened, no way are we getting him to admit to it. The bloke was jumpy, nervous even, but he's not the type to break down and spill his guts. I'd say he was desperate not to say the wrong thing, and whatever he kept from us could be useful. But like I said at the outset, I'm just not sure about him either way.'

Warburton gave it her blessing. 'Call him, Jimmy. Squeeze every last drop out of him. If he won't give himself up, he might be persuaded to give us more… perhaps even enough to take us another step in the right direction.'

Bliss nodded gratefully. He looked around the room. 'Okay. I realise you're all probably keen to bugger off home, but before you do, quickly fill me in on what you've been up to while snails have been passing me and Pen on fucking motorways.'

Gratton sprang to his feet, reading from a sheet of paper. 'We spoke to the plumber whose van was parked close to the Latchford property on Monday morning. He saw a man walk out to the Picasso. Unfortunately, he took little notice, but the brief impression he had suggests the bloke was about six foot tall, quite slender, with slightly long and scruffy hair, and he had a full beard.'

'Well, that's something,' Bliss said encouragingly. 'It's more than we had before. Have you asked him to come in to do an E-Fit for us?'

'Already done, boss. Just waiting to hear from you about circulation.'

'And you might want to hold up on that,' Bishop said. 'We got a break with CCTV again…'

'Fuck knows how we ever solved crimes without CCTV, mobile phone data, and GPS,' Bliss observed. 'Without dog walkers and joggers, we'd never know a dead body was out there in the first place, and without tech, we'd never find out who murdered them. Makes you feel superfluous. Well, it does me, anyway.'

Chuckling, Bishop continued. 'First, we got an ANPR camera

hit which told us the Picasso travelled the route we thought it might. And we struck gold with the second CCTV camera feed. You know the lights by Bridge Street outside the court?'

'I do indeed.'

'Well, few people notice it, but there's a tiny camera mounted on either side of the road there as well. One of them caught the Picasso stopped on red, no car ahead of it. There's some glare off the windscreen, but we've got perhaps three or four decent stills. The images show us a man with a thinnish face, straggly hair, and beard.'

'Which matches the plumber's description. How about Mrs Latchford and the daughter? Were either or both picked up by this camera?'

'Nothing clear, but definitely the impression of figures sitting together in the back.'

Bliss felt a chill between his shoulder blades, as if somebody had popped an ice cube down the collar of his shirt. They now had two separate sources of identification, which was all they needed to push ahead. He made an instant decision.

'Let's move on this,' he said firmly. 'Bish, before you leave, get the best still and send it out together with the E-Fit provided it's remotely similar to the man's actual image. Once they're out on our own system and across to all ports, have a word with media relations and get them cracking on this. Have them start with the *PT*, then all the other county newspapers, followed by the nationals. I also want it with TV news stations. Local news will have to do if you can't drum up interest elsewhere, but push for wider, especially the Beeb and Sky. Produce a statement suggesting we're looking for this man in connection with a serious crime, but at this stage be no more specific than that. Provide the usual contact information and make sure the relevant switchboard has our direct mobile numbers.'

DCI Warburton raised a hand. 'As I am officially the SIO here, let's pretend for a moment that I'm actually in charge. We all know this is a pivotal moment in our case. Should we be letting this man know we have a recognisable image of him? Do you not think he might panic? If he still has the Latchfords, he might react badly.'

Bliss understood his boss's reservations. He shared them. But he had his reasons mapped out. 'If Callum Oliver is not already dead, he's unlikely to survive his current ordeal. Whoever has him – and we still don't know if it's Picasso Man – must surely have kept him alive in order to question him. If that's the case, when he's done, he'll have no further use for him. I have no doubt about that. But if he's not holding Oliver close, if he has to travel to him each time, then this might just compel him to run instead. I realise it's a close call, and this is something that can always come back to take a chunk out of your backside, but I believe we have to get this man's face out there. Remember, we are as certain as we can be that he has Phoebe and Beccy Latchford, but we don't have a clear idea about what he intends with them. Nor do we have a Scooby where they are or where to look for them. Making photos or E-Fits available for public consumption has always been a balancing act and something of a last resort, boss. But I think now that we have them, we use them.'

DC Ansari spoke up, struggling to make her voice heard above the gentle hubbub of various discussions taking place. 'Yesterday, we were debating whether Callum Oliver could also be our Picasso Man. Given the description and the footage, we now know that isn't the case. That puts him back in play and back in danger. So we still have three lives to consider. I take it the man in the CCTV still couldn't possibly be one of the Deerbourne brothers?'

'You take it right,' Chandler said. 'Picasso Man looks nothing like either of them.'

'Which, once again, doesn't mean Raymond is not involved,' Bliss warned. 'Picasso Man may well be the accomplice I mentioned earlier.'

'Fair enough,' Ansari said. 'But for me, with three people still missing, I think you're right in wanting those images being broadcast by the media.'

'Are we in danger of spreading ourselves too thin once more?' Warburton asked. 'Every time we answer a question, two more spring up in their place.'

Bliss had been wondering the same thing. 'I'm still trying to digest everything,' he admitted. 'We have to narrow our focus, but I'm struggling to get there quickly.'

'I have a suggestion if you'd like to hear it.'

'Of course.' He gestured towards the boards, half a smirk playing across his lips. 'I'm willing to listen to anything at this moment. Even a proposal from the boss.'

'Thank you for that, Jimmy. I'm acutely aware of time constraints and the vast amount of work this fresh influx of information has generated. But I'm a step back, so perhaps I can see things more clearly. Even after you put together everything we've learned over the past three days, the priorities remain the same: locate Mrs Latchford and her daughter, locate Callum Oliver. With those achieved, putting together a case against whomever will follow. Am I right or wrong about that?'

'You're right,' Bliss said. 'No question. But surely our way towards doing the first of those is to identify Picasso Man.'

'Agreed. I'm not suggesting for one moment that you don't go ahead with that plan of attack. But you have to remember, as SIO it's my responsibility to update the policy book and in doing so I must justify every decision we make. All I'm doing at the minute is attempting to find some perspective, because what feels like a complete overload of information right now isn't necessarily as overwhelming as it may seem. As things stand, our goals haven't changed. All we have now is a possible way to move forward. Find Picasso Man, find the Latchfords. Hopefully.'

Bliss was happy to be compliant. 'No argument here, boss. I agree, we have a lot of balls in the air, but I think we all understand how to keep them there. The only fly in the porridge being Raymond Deerbourne. But… there's always the possibility that I read him wrong.'

Warburton turned to Chandler. 'What was your take, Penny?'

'I admit to being a little more sceptical than Jimmy,' she said reluctantly. 'And by that, I mean about the man's involvement. I agree he was acting strangely, but to be honest, I put that down to anxiety over talking to us, knowing he'd offered to pay Callum Oliver for information.'

'If it helps,' Bliss said quickly, 'I'm happy to leave the Deerbournes on the back burner for the time being. Neither of them is Picasso Man, and as we've all agreed, finding him is our number one priority. That's why I want his face out there. He'll be recognised, and all we can do is trust that whoever does so is willing to approach us with what they know.'

'You genuinely believe somebody will identify him based on that CCTV still and the E-Fit?'

Bliss nodded emphatically. 'I do. And I think it'll be the break we've all been waiting for.'

THIRTY-TWO

Bliss stood the first round and was happy to do so. He got little change out of forty quid, but he knew you couldn't measure the worth in terms of money alone. Having the entire team together, including DCI Warburton and his friend, Lennie Kaplan, was a rare thing these days. One he was determined to milk.

'Here's to you lot,' he said, raising his own pint. 'You've all played a blinder this week. I know it's been hard going, but each of you has grafted and helped develop the ops to this point. One more break and we'll be there for the final push. Thank you all.'

The sound of clinking glasses and muted cheers filled Bliss with a sense of pride. He had returned to Peterborough and Thorpe Wood four years ago, knowing he had an entire perimeter of fencing to mend. Thrust into a complex murder investigation before his official first shift back had begun, he'd gradually won the team over. Losing a vital member of the unit a couple of years back had been hard to deal with, and he wasn't entirely convinced the grieving process was over for any of them. But this was a dynamic and professional bunch, and he was honoured to lead them. Having invited everybody for a drink before they fled for home, he'd been both surprised and delighted when they all accepted.

'This is nice,' Diane Warburton said to him, having pulled him to one side during a lull. She had a longer drive home than most, so she'd stuck to a soft drink. 'They seem in good spirits.'

Bliss could only agree. 'I think they feel the same way I do. Well, you know what I mean – you are one of us, after all.'

Her cheeks coloured. 'It's not always easy to feel as if you are. I certainly didn't back in Lincoln. I think in some eyes when you sit behind a Chief Inspector's desk you're as good as grounded, and you become part of the leadership team instead.'

'Perhaps nobody gave you the room before. Me, I'm always happy to see you in our meetings, and offering your opinions.'

'Provided I agree with you, right?'

Bliss returned the knowing smile she gave. 'Of course I prefer it when you do,' he admitted. 'But I know when you oppose me, you don't do so for the sake of it. To be honest, and if you tell anybody I said this I'll deny it, it's good to have that other voice now and then to add contrast. I think we understand each other, and that makes us work well together. There aren't too many SIOs who would give me the freedom you do.'

'I'm glad to hear you being so positive, Jimmy. Mine is not always an easy position to hold.'

'And I'm not always the easiest of people to work with.'

'That's also true.'

They both raised their glasses and tapped them together. 'What you have working in your favour,' Warburton said, 'is the respect of your team. Even John Hunt respects you, though he doesn't always show it. And from what I've seen, DC Virgil already looks up to you like you're Sherlock Holmes and Harry Bosch rolled into one.'

Nudged by a fleeting memory, Bliss said, 'You're the second person to mention this Bosch character to me. I'm going to look into him.'

'Are you a reader, Jimmy?'

He took a swallow from his glass. 'Used to be. Not so much these days. I find it hard to concentrate.'

'The books are good, but try the TV show. Might be more your thing.' She finished her drink, then pulled a couple of twenty-pound notes from her purse. 'Here, take these. I'm slipping away, but please get another round in on me. Oh, one more thing before I go: did you speak with our suicide witness?'

He had. Balodis had been brought back to the station where she was once again detained in custody while arrangements were made for her to stay at a halfway house in the city. 'I apologised to her, but I also clarified that I had little influence over how long we might keep her here. I said I'd speak to immigration on her behalf and that I would do everything in my power to make sure her stay was long enough for us to find her good representation.'

'And how did she seem?'

'I can't say she was happy about it, but I think she understood. The language barrier got in the way again, but Zinta will have access to whatever she needs in order to make a case for remaining here.'

Warburton patted his upper arm as she turned to leave. 'You've done all you can, Jimmy. Let others decide on the legality or otherwise of her situation. You're in her corner now, so she has that going for her, too.'

Lennie Kaplan collared him next as he made his way back to the bar. 'Where's the party Sunday evening?' he asked.

'If it's decent weather, I thought we'd have it at the boat. If not, then at my place.'

'Sounds good. You thought of renaming that boat of yours? Call it the *Tuchel* rather than the *Mourinho*, maybe. Especially after last night's result.'

Bliss sank the rest of his beer. 'To be fair, if I renamed it after every manager we've had since Jose, I'd be redoing it every other week.'

'True enough. Nice win for your lot last night, though. How d'you fancy your chances in the final?'

'Man City are tough, but if we can hold them out we could sneak a winner.'

'I know you were steaming when they got shot of Lampard, but it's looking like a shrewd move now.'

Bliss shrugged. 'We'll see. We've won fuck all at the moment, and there's still plenty of time for things to go wrong.'

Kaplan laughed. 'Typical Jimmy Bliss.'

'No. Typical Chelsea supporter, mate.'

'Yeah, I make you right. Listen, I'm glad this investigation is working out okay. There's been a time or two since I called you in that I've kicked myself for involving you. It never felt quite kosher, but neither did it feel right leaving it to my lot or calling in CID. For that matter, I suppose I could have left it for the BTP to sort out.'

'You did the right thing, Lennie. It was a tough call, but you showed good instincts. You never fancied leaving the uniform in the wardrobe and joining the dark side?'

Kaplan's shake of the head was firm. 'Not a chance. I enjoy being at the sharp end. Sniffing out clues ain't for me, pal. I like to take on what's in front of me, plain as day.'

'There's a lot to be said for that, mate. I never really knew how my old man felt about me suiting up. He wasn't a great one for talking about feelings. He spent all his years in uniform, but we hung about with all kinds. I was always impressed with the detectives. Mind you, that was a long time ago now, when they still had a bit of mystery about them. We're all coppers beneath the clothing, Lennie. We all want the same result.'

'No argument here, pal. So, how do you see this one panning out?'

Bliss dipped his head and lowered his voice. 'Truthfully, I don't have a Scooby. I don't think I've ever worked a case before with so little crime to go on. Four days in and we're still basing everything on our guts, because while we suspect several crimes have been committed, we have nothing confirmed. It feels strange, mate. Bloody weird.'

'But you know there's something. You just have to root it out.'

'Oh, yeah. There's definitely something going off. And it's bad, too, I feel that as well. I think that's why I called for this nineteenth hole meeting. Celebrating even minor victories is mandatory where this op is concerned. And this lot have earned it.'

'True enough. But don't leave yourself out of that, Jimmy. You've also put in the hard graft.'

Bliss winked and went up to the bar. He bought the second round, which for most of them meant soft drinks. Briefly, he toyed with the idea of spending the rest of the night in the pub and cabbing home, but he wanted a clear head for the following day. A day when he knew a breakthrough must come or they would go backwards once again.

*

Callum Oliver knew from the moment the man stepped into the water pump room that something had changed. For a start, on each previous occasion, he had brought with him a clean bucket in addition to food and drink. This time his hands were empty, and Callum felt despair wash over him in a single massive wave. He sobbed when the man failed to remove the gag and binding tape.

'I'm sorry you got caught up in this,' the man said. His voice was flat, and it was impossible to discern if he felt genuine regret. 'I really am. But I had to know what you knew. I had to behave the way I did to make sure you were telling me the truth. And my own truth is… this is too important to me not to see it through. I haven't arrived at this decision lightly. I'd hoped it could all go another way, but…'

Callum attempted to speak through his tears, to beg for his life, but the cloth rammed into his mouth prevented him from articulating a single word. His shoulders bucked and his chest heaved as he vented in the only way open to him.

He had no idea how the pattern of his life had led him here. He'd been desperate for a way out of the pathetic local rag he'd already spent too long working for. His skills deserved so much more, and when he'd spotted that photograph in the *Stamford Mercury,* the hairs springing erect on the back of his neck told him this was the beginning of that brighter future. He knew it was illegal to even try searching for Dean Norman, but in that moment he didn't care. He convinced himself that provided he could build an effective and thorough investigation, those journalistic instincts would be enough to earn a spot with one of the nationals. He realised it would be too risky for them to publish the accompanying article – the *News of the World* might have had the balls, but he didn't see that level of self-assurance in even the worst of tabloids still in existence. And yet, he reasoned that if they gave him his shot based on the hard work he'd put into developing the story, he'd be satisfied with publishing anonymously online.

At least, that had been the plan.

For a while after being beaten and snatched from his car, Callum had become convinced of the Deerbourne brothers' involvement. At the time, it was the only logical conclusion – who else wanted to punish Dean Norman? Who else knew he had discovered Norman's new identity? And who else had a better reason to want the man punished?

Yet now he wasn't at all certain. In fact, he wasn't sure of anything anymore. Apart from one thing. One final, terrifying inevitability.

He was going to die.

This man who held him captive – for whatever reason – was going to kill him. Once again, it was the only logical conclusion.

'Things have moved on, buddy,' the man said almost casually.

Buddy?! Buddy?! Did he really just call me that?

Callum snarled his outrage through the cloth and the tape, jerking spasmodically from side to side, his eyes narrowed, hostile breath billowing from his nose.

The man paused, as if to reflect, before continuing. 'The truth is, I don't need you anymore… and, well, as I'm sure a bright man like you has already worked out for himself, that also means I can't allow you to just walk out of here. But you know what…? This is all going to be over soon. Tomorrow, day after at the latest. So I'm going to give you a fighting chance. I'm not going to end you, but neither am I letting you go.'

Callum's eyes shot open. *What did that mean? What was this man…?* He snapped his eyes closed again and tears forced their way through the slits, so hot they felt as if they were molten. He knew precisely what the stranger intended. And while he wanted to shake his head and implore the man to end it now, quick and clean, and not let him linger until his organs slowly started shutting down, that would not happen. He had no voice, no leverage. He'd started something he no longer had control over, and that misstep was going to cost him everything.

'Truth is, buddy,' the man said, looking down at him as if he were an animal, 'I don't know how long a man can live without food or water. Three or four days at most is my guess when it comes to fluid intake. But you might get lucky. Somebody might come along by chance and for no apparent reason decide to look inside this building. I mean, being completely honest with you, I doubt it, you know. We are tucked out of the way here – which is why I chose it. But it could happen. Strange shit happens all the time. Some homeless bloke might spot it and fancy it for a bit of shelter. All I'm saying is, it could happen. And I'm going to allow you that, at the very least.'

The fucker thinks he's doing me a favour. He's not twisted, not some psycho, after all. He's just fucking demented.

The man turned, his boot heel scraping the floor. 'In some ways, I hope you make it out of here,' he said. Only this time the regret came across as genuine. 'Not that it matters to me one way or the other where I'm headed. The real shame is, I really do wish I could let you go. But I need a bit of time still. I need to finish what I started, and that means I have to leave you here to fend for yourself. Anyhow, bud, take it easy. Be lucky.'

Callum Oliver roared. But his cry might as well have been silent.

THIRTY-THREE

Bliss was used to being summoned to meetings in the conference room. What took him by surprise on this occasion was the number of people waiting for him. Besides DCI Warburton, Superintendent Fletcher, Chief Superintendent Feeley, and the two probation officers, McKinney and Pearson, four other individuals sat at the table. One of the two in uniform he recognised as the area Chief Constable, Michael Wood-Lewis. The epaulette insignia of the other uniform was unfamiliar to Bliss, which bothered him greatly. Finally, two further women made up the numbers gathered together in the room.

Bliss masked his brief appraisal by taking his time to reach an available chair. A thousand and one thoughts tossed around inside his head like autumn leaves caught in a fierce gust of wind. He had walked into something significant, and it had to be connected to his investigations. He just couldn't work out how.

'Thank you for coming, Inspector,' Fletcher said, as if he'd had a choice in the matter; her summons had brooked no debate. 'Have you left your mobile phone behind as requested?'

'I have.' It was rare for those attending a meeting here to be instructed not to bring any device with online capabilities, but wasn't entirely without precedent. Several similar orders had been given during a case in which counter-terrorism and the security services were among the attendees.

'Good. Thank you. I'm sorry to call you away from your early morning briefing, but you'll soon understand why that was necessary. I'm sure you're familiar with our own Chief Constable, though I don't believe the two of you have officially met before today. But let me introduce you to Brendan Thouey, the Chief Constable of the Police Service of Northern Ireland, and two senior probation officers from the area, Mary Donovan and Sharon McGeedy.'

After exchanging nods and smiles of greeting, Bliss thought his heart might be hammering so loud it could be heard outside the room. Now that he knew who these visitors were, he also understood precisely why they were there and where this meeting was heading. He felt a quick jolt of adrenaline rush through his bloodstream.

Following the introduction, Wood-Lewis took over from Fletcher. A stern-featured man in his early sixties, he had the grizzled look of a veteran who had seen and done it all. Bliss knew the Chief Constable had risen through the ranks, working his way steadily to the top and garnering a reputation for being a hard-nosed pragmatist. For that reason alone, Bliss admired him.

'I can tell by the disturbed look on your face that you've worked out the purpose of this meeting, Inspector Bliss,' the officer with overall responsibility for the entire area police authority said, allowing himself a slight upward turn of the lips. 'But let me put you out of your misery, just in case you haven't slotted all the pieces together. Your decision to have the media run with the captured still image and E-Fit, brought instant and startling results. You took a risk, but it paid off. I'll now ask CC Thouey himself to fill you in on precisely why he is here with us this morning.'

The PSNI Chief Constable nodded his thanks, his linked hands tapping the table at the same time. He wore a wristwatch, and the chunky metal strap made a knocking sound with each movement. 'Thank you, Chief Constable. I'll jump straight in, if you don't mind. Inspector Bliss, I was at home last night while Sky News was on our TV. I tend to let news wash over me these days, as it's all a bit too shallow and negative for my liking. But I perked up when I heard about a manhunt from over the water, and so I started concentrating on what I saw and heard. Picture my surprise when the images I saw on the screen bore a striking resemblance to a man I have come to know over a number of years now. So familiar was the face staring back at me that I immediately took out my phone to order officers to the Coleraine home of the man in question. I suspect you already know who I'm talking about.'

Bliss cleared his throat, which felt dry and scratchy. He calmed himself before speaking. 'I think I do, sir. If I'm right, the man you're here about was formerly known as Stevie Phillips.'

Thouey nodded and rapped his hands on the table once more, as if his head and arms were linked by an invisible thread. 'Quite so. You are, of course, familiar with his partner in crime, Dean Norman.'

A flush of heat ascended Bliss's throat. He could barely contain himself, such was the effect of this dramatic shift in direction. He nodded in reply, adding, 'With the man he became, though we only learned of Morgan Latchford following his suicide.'

'Indeed. As you will understand, Inspector, we in Northern Ireland had no idea what happened with Dean Norman, either. But when Stevie Phillips was released on licence, he opted to change his name to Stuart Hammond and sail across the water to live in Coleraine, which is where his great grandfather was born. I've been CC for seven years now and have met with Stuart every six months since. The last of these meetings was just over two months ago. Both Mary and Sharon alongside me also attended that meeting.'

'That you've all travelled so urgently to the mainland tells me Hammond was not home when your officers called at his address.'

'He was not. He shares a flat with a student attending the Coleraine campus of Ulster University, and it was he who answered the door. He subsequently told my officers that Stuart packed his bags three weeks ago and left the house. He told his flatmate he would be back, though he did not say when.'

'I take it this student has no idea who Hammond really was, what he did when he was twelve?'

'No. And his leaving came as a massive shock, because Hammond seldom left the town borders, let alone go away for weeks at a time.'

Bliss nodded. 'And this student wasn't aware that our man had come here to England?'

'Not at all. That's what he told my officers, and they believed him. He had no reason to lie.'

'The two of them were flatmates only, then?'

'So it would appear.'

'Do you know if Hammond took his passport with him?'

'He did not because he does not possess one. At least, nothing legitimate. However, we subsequently discovered he travelled from Belfast to Liverpool via the Stena Line ferry service. While he had no need of a passport in order to make that journey, he had to show photo ID and he did so, using his current name and providing his driving licence.'

'And I take it this kind of travel is not flagged in any way?'

'No, it is not. Because he is under licence, and because of the special circumstances, he is supposed to inform us if he travels further afield than usual. But of course, technically speaking, he didn't travel abroad and we are not allowed to implement restrictions at that level.'

Bliss had assumed this to be the case, but it frustrated him nonetheless. His gaze took in the two unfamiliar probation officers. 'Am I right in thinking your last meeting with Hammond raised no concerns?'

'None whatsoever,' Mary Donovan answered without equivocation. 'Stuart was his usual self.'

'And what was his usual self like?'

'Pleasant enough. Stuart is a quiet man. Mostly, he speaks only when spoken to. The three of us always discuss each meeting after Stuart has left the room. There is seldom anything to say, other than we all agree there's been no noticeable change in his demeanour since our previous meeting. His risk assessments were the easiest I've ever dealt with, because he lived a staid, practical life and never gave us any cause for concern.'

'I'm guessing you have no idea what tipped him over the edge.'

'Correct. The three of us travelled last night from Belfast to Gatwick, and shared a car up here early this morning. We've discussed little else in all that time, Inspector. And still we have no insight to offer, I'm afraid.'

Bliss wasn't sure that was the case, but he let it go. 'Are you aware of a connection between Morgan Latchford and a local newspaper reporter?'

The tap of the hands told Bliss the Chief Constable from Northern Ireland was going to answer that one. 'Your Chief Superintendent filled us in on Mr Oliver, yes. Are you of the mind that he is also connected to Stuart in some way?'

'If you'll forgive me, sir, I'm still assembling my thoughts on the fly here. But it occurs to me that when Callum Oliver decided to investigate and expose one man who murdered Hayley Deerbourne, he might well have considered including his accomplice.'

'Even if that were the case, Inspector Bliss, as we understand it, his door into Dean Norman's life opened up when he saw a photograph of the man in a diner not far from here. He would not have had that same route available to him in Stevie Phillips's case.'

'If you'll forgive me,' Cambridgeshire's Chief Constable interrupted, 'I think we're focussing our attention in the wrong direction. Irrespective of how Phillips, or Hammond as he is now known, entered this troubling series of incidents, our concern at this moment has to be for the welfare of Mrs Latchford, her daughter, and Callum Oliver. Inspector Bliss, I realise you fought hard to retain these investigations, and your judgement has proven correct so far. Now that you know the man who took Mrs Latchford and her daughter is Dean Norman's old friend, are you able to tell us what you think his intentions are?'

Bliss gave himself a few seconds. It was a pivotal question, because although there was no longer the slightest risk of the ops being taken away from him and his team, the CC was right to narrow their focus. He licked his lips and said, 'I wish I could, sir. But the truth is, I've known about this additional connection for only a few minutes, and my team and I need time to consider all the angles. But given what Morgan Latchford was heard to say moments before taking his own life, and acknowledging his demeanour at the time, I have to consider the possibility that Stuart Hammond threatened to harm Mrs Latchford, perhaps even their daughter as well, if Morgan didn't commit suicide. Yet, worryingly, with Latchford having done so, Hammond did not free the man's family. Instead, he drove away with them… or so we believe.'

'You think he intends harming them still?' DCS Feely asked abruptly.

'I couldn't say, sir. With his partner in murder gone, he could have left it there and walked away. Presumably Mrs Latchford didn't know who he was, so why not sneak back into Belfast with us none the wiser? Then again, there's motive to consider.'

'Motive?'

'Yes, sir. Why, after all these years, would the man once known as Stevie Phillips want the man once known as Dean Norman to die? Officially, it's been thirty-four years since the two so much as laid eyes on one another at their trial – they were sentenced separately as I understand it. It doesn't make sense to me.'

Chief Constable Thouey coughed and for once unclasped his hands. 'I may be able to help you there, Inspector. When I replaced my predecessor, the file I received on Mr Hammond was extensive and included information dating back as far as his initial arrest. Because he eventually confessed to murder, it's not widely known that twelve-year-old Stevie Phillips initially refuted the charge, claiming he played a distant second fiddle to Dean Norman. He fully accepted his role in teasing, bullying, tormenting, and eventually beating, sexually molesting, and torturing Haley Deerbourne. He admitted exposing the young girl's genital area and touching her there. He and Norman both attempted to have sex with the girl as well, but neither was successful in penetrating her. He opened up fully on each of those elements, but when it came to sealing her inside the tipped freezer cabinet and weighing it down so that she could not open it up again, he flatly denied culpability. Phillips insisted that was solely Norman's idea, and they even argued about it. But Norman was the more forceful and aggressive of the two – this is acknowledged by witness statements at the time – and Phillips admits he was unable to change his friend's mind. He says he walked away and never even saw Norman hoist her into the freezer chest and close the lid afterwards.'

'I'm guessing his solicitor subsequently told him he was equally responsible and that it might be better for him to admit to everything,' Bliss said, unable to prevent disturbing images of Hayley Deerbourne's last moments from flitting across his mind's eye.

Thouey nodded. 'Something of that nature. In effect, the pair of them were there at the same time. Young Phillips did not prevent Norman from doing what he did, and neither did he inform anybody immediately afterwards. There was time for the poor wee child to be rescued, perhaps sufficient air inside that chest to buy her ten minutes, but the lad never said a word.'

'So the suggestion is that Hammond would have wanted Latchford dead in order to punish him for the years he did in detention and the kind of life he's had to live since.'

'That works for me.'

Bliss conceded the point. 'Me, too. Especially when you take opportunity into consideration. Which leads me back to the role Callum Oliver played. I don't see Hammond deciding it was time to take revenge on his schoolboy friend and travelling across to England at the same time as a journalist happened to be investigating the man that old friend had become. I've never been one to dismiss coincidence entirely, but this would have to be the most incredible of them all. The real question, for me, is how Oliver located Hammond.'

The implication was obvious, and Bliss was quick to follow up on it. 'I'm certainly not saying that information came from anybody in this room. There's Hammond himself, of course. But – and please forgive me if this tramples over anybody's toes – there are previous Chief Constables who knew who he was and where he lived. And how many previous probation officers?'

Sharon McGeedy bristled, clearly indignant at the implication, but she did not shirk responding to the question. 'Off the top of my head, I couldn't give you a precise figure. But Stuart Hammond has existed for the past twenty-four years, each of them spent living in Coleraine. At a guess I'd say besides myself and Mary, there are possibly four or five other senior probation officers who monitored Stuart over those couple of dozen years. That said, Inspector, I have utmost faith and confidence in my current and previous colleagues.'

Bliss offered a regretful smile. 'I have no doubt, but we can't know everybody as well as we would like. As such, it's something we have to consider, and we will need a list of names and contact details.'

'I assume you want the same regarding my predecessors?' Thouey said, his face grim.

'I realise that will be challenging, sir,' Bliss said. 'However, we can't rule anybody out simply because of the position they once held. People talk to me about optics, and that's a good example of the wrong kind, I think you'll agree. I'm happy to arrange that myself if you'd rather. But before we dive too deep into that rabbit hole, let's take a hard look at Hammond. Was he as clean as he led you to believe? Did he have a social media presence under an assumed name? Did he frequent chat sites, forums? Let's grab up his online and mobile phone history and drill down into that, because even if Callum Oliver went hunting for the man Stevie Phillips became, he could have no way of knowing who his probation officers were. And he'd have no reason to look in Northern Ireland, either. All of which makes me suspect the leak came from Hammond himself. I intend to find out how.'

'That's all well and good,' Detective Chief Superintendent Feeley said in a low, but authoritative voice. 'But how do you plan to proceed immediately, Inspector Bliss? Mrs Latchford and her daughter must surely remain your primary concern.'

Bliss met the man's direct gaze. 'Of course. That won't change. But none of what I've learned this morning takes us any closer to finding them. All it's really done is throw a whole lot more information on top of the heap. With respect, I need time to go over this with my team, and to catch up on any updates. Our priorities have not shifted, but we are going to have to take a whole new approach.'

'More specifically?'

'We switch our attention to Hammond. If we're right, then he was in touch with Callum Oliver. If we're right, we believe he must have had a partner. The partner could be Oliver, but I doubt it. The partner could be one of the Deerbourne brothers, but I'm not convinced of that, either. I spoke with Ray last night, and while he confessed to having attempted to bully Mr Oliver into telling him everything he knew about the man Dean Norman had become, he said it went no further than that. I think I believed him. But the fact is, for a man supposedly lying low, Mr Hammond has a been a busy boy. We need to find out precisely how, why, and when this all began.'

THIRTY-FOUR

Phoebe Latchford pulled the blanket back over her bare legs after shifting her daughter's warm body. Beccy lay wrapped in her arms, still asleep following a restless night. She felt the ache of her child's weight; it had been years since the two had clung together like this. She took care not to disturb the girl as she moved, not wanting to wake her; every time Beccy stirred from her slumber and caught her mother looking down at her, she asked the same plaintive questions: 'Is Daddy coming?' and 'When are we going home?'

She had pacified her daughter so far without providing any straight answers. How would she ever be able to tell Beccy the truth? How could she ever tell the sweetest child in the entire world that she would never see her father again? Or that she would never again set foot inside the only home she had ever known? Then there was her school and all the friends she had made. It was surely impossible to explain any of this to an eight-year-old kid, even one as bright and aware as Beccy. An unbearable task, yet something Phoebe knew she couldn't avoid too much longer. There was no way of preparing for a conversation like that, so when the moment arrived she had to get it right first time.

Phoebe solemnly appraised her surroundings. Had she made the right decision in agreeing to bring her child to such a place? The man's original plan had been for them to put as much distance as possible between them and her husband as they could in a single drive. The change of vehicle had come as a surprise to her, but his explanation for it had sounded like common sense; neighbours might have spotted her and Beccy leaving home in the red Citroen, so swapping cars was a good call. But when he'd stopped once more after driving for less than thirty minutes in the replacement vehicle, she had been both perplexed and alarmed.

The man had shifted sideways in his seat. He explained that he'd had two plans in mind all along, and having given their awkward situation further consideration, he thought the better option was to lie low for a few days. All ports and obvious routes would be the focus of the authorities' hunt for them, he'd reasoned. The one place they would never think of searching was right under their own noses. The confident way he'd said it was convincing, yet with each passing hour of each subsequent day, Phoebe had become more concerned.

The man had made them comfortable enough. The old fin style radiators put out enough heat to warm the building, which she acknowledged was in good order, and the utilities were still connected and working. He made sure they had plenty to eat and drink, and although they had only the use of inflatable mattresses at night and could not venture downstairs, it had been no real hardship so far. She hadn't even needed to question his intentions, because after showing her where she and Beccy were to remain, he had made a point of indicating his own sleeping area in a different room.

These were conditions she could endure for a short period; no more than a week, he had assured her. The real problem was Beccy. She got bored easily, and although she had her tablet and games and books, keeping her active was a full-time job. The constant questions were also burying themselves beneath Phoebe's skin, worming their way inside her brain.

What was she thinking bringing her daughter here with this man she did not know? How had she so easily been convinced to run away from her husband rather than confront him about his past and current inclinations?

That's simple, she told herself. The thought of the juvenile her husband had once been beating and torturing a younger child, a girl at that, was sickening enough. The idea of him being capable of trying to rape that same child with only his inability to gain an erection preventing him from doing so was equally appalling. But being warned that her husband now had similar designs on their own daughter had actually made her physically ill. She had fled to the closest toilet, vomiting and retching into the porcelain bowl, hugging it for dear life as if letting go might send her spinning off the planet as it revolved.

After that, her only thought was to get as far away from Morgan as she could. The man who had brought this horror into her life had a way to make that happen, and she had clung to his every word afterwards. He was clever, too. He knew precisely what to do and what not to do. Taking her mobile phone along with them was acceptable, he'd agreed, but initially it had to be broken down into separate pieces, the SIM card and battery both removed. To also remove temptation, those pieces had gone into his pocket where they would remain until this nightmare was over.

'What am I going to do now?' she had asked him. 'How am I ever going to make this work?'

'When you and Beccy are far away and safe, I'll come back on my own,' he'd replied in that comforting way of his. 'I'll find your husband and I will explain it all to him. Before I do that, I'll also get a message to both him and the police to tell them that, having discovered who your husband once was and the threat he now presented, you had no option but to remove yourself from the marriage, from the family home, and from his life. Phoebe, you need to relax. This is what I do. I've made it my life's work to expose these monsters, after which, if the other people in the relationship want to get away with no questions asked, I also provide that service. I do it because I care, because I myself have been betrayed in the past, so I know what it feels like.'

Whenever she had doubts, Phoebe returned to that moment and paused for breath. The man had been true to his word so far. She felt safe. Uncertain, troubled, grief-stricken at the loss of her marriage to a man she had believed to be good and kind. But safe, nonetheless. It would do for the time being, she decided. Because what was the alternative?

THIRTY-FIVE

With his major crimes colleagues virtually stunned into silence, Bliss tried to make sense of this new lead to them. 'The most obvious interpretation of the facts is that Callum Oliver, having convinced himself of Morgan Latchford's true identity, then went in search of Stevie Phillips and the man he had become. Having contacted Stuart Hammond as Phillips now is, Callum told him what he knew. My best guess is that Hammond subsequently used this information and played Oliver for a fool, that he probably agreed to an interview and instead turned on our reporter. His clear aim was to learn everything he could about Latchford in order to devise a plan to gain some kind of revenge.'

'So, are we still thinking this man inserted himself into Phoebe Latchford's life and told her all about her husband?' Chandler asked. 'What I'm saying is, knowing he's Morgan Latchford's old pal doesn't change that specific aspect of our hypothesis, does it?'

'I don't see why it should,' Bishop said.

'It was always the most speculative part of our thinking,' Bliss reminded them. 'And it's possible we've allowed a burst of new information and fresh leads to blind us to the weakness in that theory.'

'How so?'

'It all comes back to the timing and the reason he drove them from their home. Gul, that final phone call to Morgan Latchford was made from his wife's phone at what time?'

'Shortly after 8.00am,' Ansari replied. 'It lasted between seven and eight minutes.'

'And the language used by Latchford during that conversation strongly suggests he had to have been talking to Hammond about his wife and daughter, pleading for them to be left unharmed.'

'True, but Hammond needn't have been in the wife's presence when the call was made.'

'That's probably right,' Bliss agreed, picking up the reins once more. 'But he was still either inside the house or just outside, because this is where that red Picasso both helps and hurts our own argument. If we agree that Hammond persuaded Latchford to end it all shortly before ten past eight, at that time the Picasso was parked outside the house. So with Latchford dead, why take the risk of removing the wife and daughter? And for what purpose?'

'I thought we already went over that and reached a conclusion,' Chandler said dejectedly. 'We're saying Hammond knows his old pal is dead because he's just coerced him into it. But Phoebe Latchford is completely unaware of this. To her, he's a decent guy trying to do the right thing, while her husband is some kind of deviant. Our thinking is that part of his entire approach was to talk her into leaving her husband, with his help, covering their tracks in the process so that Morgan Latchford would never know where to find them. We can't know the precise details, but that's a fair assumption.'

'Yes, based on what we know – which isn't a great deal – there's a good chance that's how Hammond planned and executed it. Let's say he went into it with a plan A and a plan B. Plan A is to have Morgan Latchford kill himself. If that fails, he has plan B to fall back on, which is to whisk Phoebe and Beccy away from under Latchford's nose. He runs with both as a failsafe. So what I'm asking is, why does he then carry on with this charade? He's got what he came for, because Morgan is dead. Plan A has worked. Why still go ahead with the backup?'

Realisation dawned on the others. Bliss could see it on their faces. All along, they'd been desperate to put together a timeline of events. Now that they had one, the pieces were not adding up. The more he thought about it, the less reason he saw for Hammond to continue operating his secondary scheme. He could have just walked away, unless…

A memory jolted him out of his reverie. In an earlier meeting, somebody had briefly mentioned the possibility that Picasso Man had snatched Mrs Latchford and her daughter in order to buy time. That aspect fitted neatly with the faked ransacking and the dumping of the car, both of which were intended to obfuscate and delay. While the police were busy investigating a break-in and making initial inquiries regarding the woman and her child, Picasso Man was putting distance and time between himself and them.

Bliss raised both hands to quieten down his team. He mentioned the earlier suggestion as a possibility worth considering, and although the response he received was positive, he couldn't prevent a nagging sensation tugging at his instincts. Logically, the notion of Hammond using the female Latchfords as a deflection had merit, but he worried there might be a deeper, much darker reason in play.

'Here's another theory for you all to chew over,' he said flatly. 'We're going around in circles because we're assuming that persuading Latchford to top himself was enough for Hammond. But what if it wasn't? Remember, the Latchfords have an eight-year-old daughter. She's exactly the same age as Haley Deerbourne was when she was murdered. I have to say I don't like where my mind takes me sometimes, but in this case I have to wonder if he intended to harm her all along because of her connection to his onetime friend, the lad who betrayed him and helped ruin the rest of his life.'

The shocked reaction in the room told Bliss they were right there with him, though DC Gratton voiced his doubt. 'It is another possibility, boss. But surely if he was going to hurt the girl, he would have done so while her father was still alive. There's no additional pain or suffering for Morgan Latchford if Hammond hurts the girl afterwards.'

'You're right, Phil. I agree that would have been the ideal scenario for him. But we all know the best of plans don't get past the first point of contact. What if that's precisely what Hammond intended, but for reasons we're unaware of, his initial plan went awry. He still got Latchford to top himself, but not in the way he'd originally anticipated. And his desire to hurt the man's daughter the way Latchford hurt the Deerbourne girl doesn't pass even when his old mate is gone. I'm not saying that's how it was, only suggesting it's something else we have to consider. Because Phoebe may be with Hammond right now, believing she and her daughter have escaped the clutches of a monster, not knowing they've simply fled from the hands of one straight into the grasp of another.'

Bliss didn't want them to dwell on the terrifying prospect, so instead pushed ahead. 'However wicked a thought that might be, remember we've all seen or heard worse. We have to assume the Latchfords are being held somewhere and are in danger, perhaps already being mistreated. We can't know where, so we drill down into this man Stuart Hammond and the boy he once was. I want to know what he was like when he was in that detention centre, and I mean from a fellow detainee's perspective. Our Northern Ireland contingent has agreed to stay on to answer any questions we might have, so from them we find out everything there is to know about his family, friends, employment, colleagues, his hobbies, phone and online use. If he could be found by Callum Oliver, then we must have a way to uncover more about the real man behind the one he presented himself as.'

'I take it we're also to push through with existing inquires?' Bishop said.

'Yes, no action is to be closed off until it's been taken to its logical conclusion. And now that we have a name, let's get in touch with letting agencies. If they haven't fled the area, then they have to be staying somewhere, and Hammond would have felt secure in using his name. Let's see if he rented out a place.'

'What about empty properties? Given where he swapped out the Picasso, it's possible he knew it was vacant and chose it for that very reason.'

'There'll be no registry of places like that, Bish.'

'Yeah, I'm aware of that. But we could ask our uniforms who patrol and work out in the Fens to put the word out within the communities and to pay close attention to properties that don't look lived in. Let's close the net locally before we look further afield.'

Bliss nodded. 'Good idea. Do that. And while you're at it, give our colleagues in Lincolnshire a call and ask them to do the same. Make sure they all have the still of Hammond, and to be acutely aware of the Latchfords being with him.'

'Anything else?'

'Yeah. Something you just said gave me a nudge. I'm still confident that Hammond is working with somebody else. But if I'm wrong, how he sorted out the vehicles he used bothers me. We know he used the Picasso on Monday morning and then swapped motors at the farmhouse near Thorney, but how did that vehicle get there?'

'Hammond drove it there first, collected the Picasso so's it would be the vehicle people saw and picked up on CCTV before dropping it back there again.'

'Fine, but if that's the way it went, how did the Picasso get there to begin with?'

Bishop's heavy brows furrowed. 'I see what you mean. If he doesn't have a partner, at some point he had to arrive or leave via a different method.'

'That's what I'm thinking. Let's contact taxi firms to see if they had a fare collecting from or going out to our farmhouse. Just to cover all bases.'

Having dealt out the actions, Bliss took it upon himself to question the three people charged with monitoring Stuart Hammond. He imagined they would be feeling raw, having had this occur on their watch. He took Chandler with him to help soften the edges of any contentious questions, and instructed her to handle the bulk of the interview for that same reason. Before heading upstairs again, DC Ansari approached them. The glint in her eyes told Bliss she had something important to reveal.

'Boss, I've had more data back from Callum Oliver's phone network provider. There are several calls between Oliver and a phone registered to Stuart Hammond. That proves your theory about the two of them being in touch. No messages and no voicemails, so we can't know what they discussed. But here's the thing that stands out for me: the initial contact between them originated from Hammond's phone.'

Bliss was shocked by the news. His hand reflexively came up to worry at the scar on his forehead. After a moment, his thought process became clearer. 'Okay. That's something to bear in mind, but we're talking only about contact between the two of them through Hammond's mobile. Callum could still have made the very first contact via different means.'

'Of course. But like you say, it's something we now have to consider.'

'Yet another bloody question without a sodding answer to be found anywhere.' He took a breath. 'Good work either way, Gul. And don't pay any attention to my grumbling. We need to peer around every corner and think of every permutation. I've been so fixated on Oliver having sought Stevie Phillips's new identity, it never even occurred to me that it could have happened the other way around.'

'What do you want me to do with it, boss?'

'Check the GPS on the phone and let me know if he ever strayed outside Northern Ireland before. In fact, give me a list of everywhere he went other than his home town of Coleraine.'

About to summon Chandler for their meeting, Bliss cursed when his phone rang. It was Sandra Bannister, and he thought it best not to ignore it. 'Hi, Sandra,' he said pleasantly. 'Before you ask, I have nothing I can share with you at the moment. I'm not being slippery. I just can't tell you where we are because the lid is firmly on.'

'Well, thank you for that. But that's not why I called. The investigator part of me couldn't leave Callum's absence alone. I went back over records and turned up nothing, checked out his work mobile and that didn't tell me anything I didn't already know. So I turned to his laptop and spent some time with that. I have a tech guru I consult with, and he talked me through a few checks. As you probably know, it's difficult to erase everything unless you shred the disk, so I was able to ferret around. I came up with a couple of interesting pieces of information.'

'And you want to share them with me?' Bliss couldn't keep the surprise from his voice.

'I'd prefer not to, of course. But Callum is still missing, and I have no story here as it stands. So you might get something from what I found.'

'Okay. Sounds good. Fire away.'

'To begin with, I discovered a deleted piece of software. You're aware of TOR, I assume?'

'The Onion Router. Yes, of course. As it happens, it came up in our case last autumn. So you're telling me Callum had the software on his laptop but then deleted it?'

'I am. Not only that, but he installed, used, and removed it on a regular basis. Looks as if every time he wanted to dive into the dark web, he installed TOR, did what he had to do, then uninstalled the program.'

Bliss felt himself frowning. 'Given the device belonged to the *Telegraph* and he took it into work with him, I can understand why he went to those lengths. But wouldn't it have made more sense to just buy his own laptop and use that?'

'That's what I thought. And when I ran through all the dates and times, I think he did precisely that. He used TOR on average once a day. Every day for a number of weeks. Then it all stopped a couple of weeks ago.'

The implications were obvious. Yet they hadn't found a second device inside his flat or in his vehicle. 'Were you able to grab up any details relating to what he did when using TOR?' he asked.

'Yes and no. I couldn't find any records of which sites he visited, nor who he might have chatted to online. But here's the really interesting thing, Jimmy: I also found evidence of spyware on the device. Somebody had dropped Trojan malware onto the laptop, presumably while he was on the dark web, and it executed the next time Callum booted it up. It ran continuously, and then the day before he stopped using TOR altogether, another piece of malware executed, removing the spyware.'

'What the...?' Bliss paused, rubbing the phone against his brow. He tried to find logic in the jumble of information. Finally, he thought he had it. 'Sounds to me as if Callum was in contact with somebody who used that time to spy on him, and who then persuaded him to protect himself more fully. Only, it was all a strategy to keep him on the hook. I'm guessing whoever it was simply repeated their spyware activities as soon as the two of them were back in contact.'

'I can buy that. What better way to convince someone you're on the level and looking after their best interests than to talk them into additional confidentiality when it's actually anything but?'

'Precisely. They probably did it in case Callum slipped and actually went into work with TOR on his machine. But the fact that we didn't find this second laptop suggests whoever took him also has the device.'

'I'm afraid it does.'

'I don't suppose you found out the username Callum employed when using TOR, did you?'

Bliss could almost hear her broad smile when she said, 'As it so happens, I did. He went by Shadowman. I have to tell you, I'm getting extremely concerned, Jimmy. I feel as if I should raise this with my bosses.'

'To what end?' he asked quickly, worried that she might blow their investigation. 'In this particular case, we have a much better chance of finding him than you have. That's why you called me, remember? Listen, Callum is not due back to work until Monday morning. You and I will speak before then. I'm hoping I have a great deal more to tell you. I have to go now, Sandra. But thanks for this. Let me do the worrying. The moment I have any news, I'll call.'

As he and Chandler made their way upstairs, he told her about his conversation with Bannister. 'You think he and Stuart

Hammond somehow found each other on the dark web?' she asked. 'That Hammond infected his devices with malware, spied on him, and in that way discovered everything he needed to know about Morgan Latchford?'

'That's exactly what I'm thinking, yes,' Bliss said. 'How that contact was made and who initiated it is now of huge importance.'

'More questions, questions, questions.'

He grunted. 'I feel your pain, Pen. Believe me, I'm close to drowning in them.'

'Then let me be your buoy. We're stronger together, remember.'

'What fool told you that?'

'You did.'

'So I did.'

'And it's true. But there is one thing…'

'What's what?'

Chandler dug her elbow into his side. 'Don't. Call. Me. Pen.'

THIRTY-SIX

DCS FEELEY REMAINED IN the conference room while Bliss and Chandler spoke with Chief Constable Thouey and the two probation officers from Northern Ireland. His own CC, Wood-Lewis, had an appointment he could not cancel, and it was felt that somebody from senior leadership needed to be available for the discussion. Bliss was fine with that, provided his Chief Superintendent didn't interfere.

'Fresh intelligence can make a significant difference to our approach,' was how Bliss began. He then broke down the revised line of thinking following the information he'd obtained from Sandra Bannister. He skipped through his relationship with the journalist, pointing out that he had provided her with no intelligence in return for a wealth of additional knowledge. He suggested it was a good deal, and while he noticed Feeley making notes, nobody in the room questioned his motives.

'What's your new plan of action, Inspector?' Thouey asked.

'I believe a dramatic shift in approach is required. I've requested and have been given additional staff. And while none of our open actions will be abandoned, there is now a need to investigate Callum Oliver's online presence in greater detail.

Specifically, I'm talking about his dark web use. We have his username, which will be incredibly helpful. Our own tech people are experts when it comes to the dark web, while Mr Oliver's use of TOR suggests he's not an overly experienced user. If we can find out which chat rooms he frequented, we may well discover his communications with Stuart Hammond.'

'Sounds to me like a bit of a chicken and egg situation,' Mary Donovan said in a voice barely louder than a whisper. 'Which came first: did your man connect with ours or did ours connect with him?'

'It's an interesting question,' Bliss acknowledged. 'However, we've moved beyond that. I strongly suspect Hammond of toying with our reporter, stringing out their online relationship until he gained enough intel on Morgan Latchford to then act independently. I'm inclined to believe he never intended doing Oliver any harm, but then something perhaps went wrong that brought him into play as a target. Going back to the dark web, my guess is we'll find a forum dedicated to murder and murderers, perhaps even child killers. Our thinking is that Oliver threw out a hook by suggesting he was onto something relating to the Hayley Deerbourne murderers, and Stuart Hammond took the bait. If he genuinely holds a grudge against his old pal after all these years, he might easily have formulated a plan during that short period and then used Oliver to help him see it through.'

'Hard to see how any of that takes us from where we are now to locating Hammond – and hopefully Mrs Latchford and her daughter – any time soon,' Feeley said. It didn't come across as a judgement against Bliss and his team, merely an observation. Bliss paused briefly before responding.

'Our feeling for some time now, sir, is that Hammond is not operating alone. The practicalities surrounding the vehicles suggest a two-man job. We understand it could have been carried out with Oliver's help initially, after which Hammond turned on him. But in my investigations I like to look for the anomalies. With these ops, that anomaly is the dumping of Morgan Latchford's car in the river Nene. When we look at Callum Oliver's Audi, we see deliberation, planning, reasonable execution, a clean-up, albeit not as thorough as it might have been. Latchford's motor was dumped without a great deal of thought or finesse.'

'Could that not be a case of different situations rather than different methods?' Thouey asked. 'Perhaps he acted out of sheer panic with the second vehicle.'

Bliss nodded. 'Of course. But there are other incidents that make us think Hammond had help. When you put it all together, it's a lot of work for one person.'

'Take us back to the Audi,' Feeley said, leaning forward, his eyes steady on Bliss. 'The solicitor's backpack being in its boot might also be considered an anomaly, no?'

'Yes, sir. And it was until we decided otherwise. The difference being we have a reasonable explanation for its presence. I don't buy it entirely, but I think the only role he played was to offer Callum Oliver pertinent advice. I suspect him of nothing more than that.'

'But you have not ruled out further involvement?'

'Not at all. Our minds, ears, and eyes are wide open. It's a matter of having to be that way, given how little hard evidence we have to go on. We're mostly working on speculation and instinct, but you have to form a strategy even when you have almost nothing to go on.'

'I have another question for you, Inspector,' CC Thouey said, along with the now familiar hand rap on the table. 'If Stuart Hammond was regularly delving into the dark web, is this something we ought to have picked up on?'

Bliss admired the question and was quick to put the man at his ease. 'I see no reason why you should have. The remit is to allow him most of the freedoms any of us expect. By its very nature, the use of the dark web is clandestine. The only way you'd know about it is if you monitored his use, and even then, if he used TOR and set up relevant securities, you'd probably not have noticed. No, sir, I don't think there's any way you can reasonably have been expected to know. However, I do have a question of my own.'

The man spread his hands. 'Go ahead, please.'

'There's a certain level of expertise and technical sophistication shown here by Hammond. The ability to upload malware to Callum Oliver's laptop, to install spyware, to use the spyware, and to then have it automatically removed in much the same way as it was installed isn't common computer use by any means. However, as previously mentioned, the fact that he used TOR suggests to me he wasn't an expert. I'm guessing he had an accomplice – albeit probably an unwitting one – for the technical part of his plan as well. So tell me, please, what did Hammond do for a living?'

Thouey flushed slightly as he and the two female probation officers exchanged glances. 'Hammond was – is – an IT helpdesk worker.'

Bliss felt his eyebrows arch in surprise. 'Do you know which level?'

'I believe he was first level. The first person you spoke to if you needed help.'

Chandler spoke up for the first time. 'Those guys are usually the least skilled of all the techs. They offer documented steps and processes, leaving the more complex problems for others to solve during escalation.'

'He worked for a software company. So if it malfunctioned, he'd look into the issue they reported.'

Bliss reacted instantly. 'A software company suggests

programmers somewhere along the chain. I wonder if they worked in the same building as tech support.'

'Unlikely,' Chandler responded. 'Often the programmers are in some far off country. But that doesn't mean to say the other tech people he worked with aren't keen on the darker side of the industry. Plenty of hackers have ordinary jobs.'

'This is something we can certainly look into,' Thouey said.

'We've already discussed you digging deeper into his life. Friends and co-workers, etc. You might come across a suitable candidate for us to look at.'

'I'll get it started as soon as we're done here.'

'Thank you. At all times, we must remember we're speculating. I've laid out a scenario that may be entirely incorrect. But although we're lacking many details, the picture I'm forming inside my head tells me we're finally looking in the right place. That said, one of the more elusive parts of the puzzle is why Hammond would still take Phoebe and Beccy Latchford even after Morgan had ended his own life.'

'I agree,' DCS Feeley said. 'And I'm willing to bet you have a new theory, Inspector.'

Bliss breathed in slowly. Exhaled in the same easy way. 'I do. It's not one I like, but it's perhaps one of several possible answers to the question.'

'I think we still need to hear it.'

'Of course. But I'm aware we have two civilians in the room, sir. I'm happy to tell you all everything I'm thinking, but only if Mary and Sharon are willing to hear it and you two senior officers are willing to have them hear it.'

Thouey cleared his throat. 'I suspect we all have some idea of what we are dealing with, Inspector Bliss. We may not have known the boy who carried out such debased atrocities, but we have always been aware that such desires once resided in him and that, for all we know, they still do. I gather that's the way this conversation is going, correct?'

'You are, sir. And yes, the fact that Beccy Latchford is the same approximate age as Hayley Deerbourne was at the time she was murdered, has not escaped our attention.'

'We also have a somewhat different theory,' Chandler added. 'The boss encourages us all to come at problems from different angles. So when one theory pops up, we try to find reasons to shoot it down. That way, only the stronger options make it through. It gives us checks and balances during an op. So, we also asked ourselves whether, instead of taking the Latchfords because he intended to harm them, he had instead persuaded them to go with him to avoid the fallout of the suicide. That perhaps Hammond approached Mrs Latchford and told her who and what her husband used to be, and offered her a way out. She may be entirely unaware of her husband's suicide, simply that this man who told her and possibly showed her who her husband truly was had also offered to take her and their daughter away from him.'

'But why on earth would she listen to and then trust the man who was her husband's partner in crime all those years ago?' Feeley asked sharply.

'I'm not suggesting she did, sir.'

'Then what are you suggesting, DS Chandler?'

'That Hammond presented himself as someone else entirely. I don't know who, or how he did it, but if he came to her in the guise of someone trustworthy and then subsequently manipulated and persuaded her to flee from the life she shared with a child killer, it could have worked. In the short-term, at least. Which may be all he needed.'

Bliss was nodding. 'The possibility of Hammond presenting himself to Mrs Latchford as a friend rather than a foe is compelling. In fact, there's a distinct possibility that both theories are correct and are running in parallel.'

The room fell silent for a few long seconds. 'And so where does that leave us?' Thouey asked, eventually.

'Still very much in the hunt,' Bliss stated flatly. 'But as yet with no clue where they might be. And now pretty much trusting entirely that our search of the dark web will throw us the bone we need.'

THIRTY-SEVEN

B LISS AGREED ENTIRELY WITH the Chief Inspector Morse approach to police work; he did his best thinking over a pint. Author Colin Dexter's curmudgeonly fictional detective had been a firm favourite in the Bliss household, despite the procedural aspects causing much amusement and the occasional howl of protest. Not an avid reader, Bliss only became aware of the novels after the television show first aired. It wasn't a type of coppering he recognised, but he loved the idea of solving crimes while supping the local real ale.

This was one of those lunchbreaks during which he had to be alone. His brain felt squeezed; he needed fewer questions and alternatives obscuring the way forward. Other opinions threw barriers ahead of his own train of thought. Two operations that had barely fallen under the purview of major crimes were now being scrutinised by top police officers in the county, intensifying the pressure to succeed. Yet for Bliss, the burden began and ended with three missing people. And for all the progress made by the team over the past five days, those same three people felt just as far out of reach as they had been at the beginning.

That did not sit well with him at all, and he knew his colleagues were slogging their guts out and feeling out of sync with both the investigation and each other. Too many ideas being tossed around, too many possibilities having to be considered because each was just as feasible as the next. When you had little or nothing to guide the way, every path seemed significant.

The key components of the single case the two operations had now become suggested a common theme as the root cause: revenge. Stevie Phillips grew up resenting Dean Norman initially for his own incarceration, followed by a subsequent detachment from the life he had once envisaged for himself. When resentment was left to fester it became rotten to its very core, leading to anger and rage resulting from a feeling of impotence at not being able to act upon any initial bitterness. Then along comes journalist Callum Oliver, serving as the catalyst precipitating the means by which the man Phillips had become could at last achieve retribution against the man Norman became.

Bliss took regular pulls on his Doom Bar ale, scarcely aware of the flavour as he consumed the beer with mounting concern. Before declaring a meal break for all and leaving HQ on his own, he and Chandler had read up on Stuart Hammond's notes, which included those made by a variety of therapists and psychiatrists. Much of the boy's psychological scarring had originated during his fumbled and ultimately failed attempts to penetrate Haley Deerbourne with his penis. His initial erection had wilted from the moment he and Norman had removed the girl's underwear. Rather than becoming more engorged by the sight of her and the anticipation of his first sexual encounter, he'd felt almost faint, overcome by the thought of what he was about to do. This, he insisted, included knowing how wrong it was. He'd prodded the girl's vagina with the limp thing in his hand, his friend's laughter echoing in his ears. He hadn't wanted to go through with it. Hadn't even wanted to try. But Dean had insisted this was the easiest way to lose his cherry without paying for it, and only at that point did he realise how terrified the girl had to be.

Humiliation burning his cheeks, he'd felt a little less sorry for himself when Dean hadn't been able to fuck the girl, either. His friend claimed his inability was entirely due to Haley being far too young, and that he'd already screwed his way through several girls at school, plus one of his older cousins. But Stevie Phillips had noted the fury in Dean Norman's eyes. There was fire in them, energy pulsing, and in that moment he had known this wasn't how their actions towards the girl were going to end.

Which is the point at which the torturing began in earnest.

Bliss bowed his head for a moment, both absorbed and sickened by the last moments of that eight-year-old's life. She couldn't possibly have understood why, nor how it was about to end. Her initial fear had been beaten out of her, leaving her terrified, he was sure. How could she not have been? Traumatised, too. At that point, she would almost certainly have stopped resisting. The defence counsel and both sets of parents had complained bitterly that their sons were not old enough to truly comprehend what they were doing, insisting the boys lacked the ability to empathise because their age had not yet provided them with sufficient life experience. In essence, they lacked the emotional tools.

He thought back to his twelve-year-old self and did not believe this to be true at all. Children matured differently, that much was true. But those two boys had known their initial taunts about Haley Deerbourne's fishy odour would wound the girl, had known their sexual assault would create alarm at the very least, even if she wasn't absolutely certain what they were trying to achieve, that their subsequent punches and kicks and whacks with scraps of wood would hurt her terribly, causing pain and misery beyond the girl's comprehension. As for heaving her body into a dumped chest freezer and slamming the door closed on her, Bliss paused before passing judgement. If he was remembering his own experiences properly and fully, the two boys would have known that sealing her away inside that chest was a truly vicious thing to do, especially to a girl four years younger than they were. But would it have occurred to either of them that in doing so, they were robbing her of oxygen? That ultimately, they were sentencing her to death?

Children matured differently.

That much was true.

But Bliss was as certain as he could be that one of those lads at the very least had been aware of how final an act slamming that freezer door closed truly was.

After leaving the pub, Bliss drove out to the fisheries where his working week had begun. It looked and felt completely different in the daytime, and although it wasn't heaving, there were several people around, with cars parked up close to where the Audi had been in the early hours of Monday morning. He was glad he had made the short trip, because it convinced him all the more that the car hadn't been left abandoned for long – he was betting it had been dumped during the night over the weekend.

He then drove back out to the Latchford home, outside which a single uniformed officer stood guard. Bliss found a parking space from which he could observe the house. He had no expectation of learning anything new, but occasionally he liked to reaffirm his thinking by returning to a significant location connected to whatever investigation he was running at the time. He got a feel for it again, and this had the desired positive effect during his drive across to Thorpe Wood afterwards.

The team were working hard on their second wind. The first thing Bliss did now that his head was clear was to ask for suggestions; new ideas, anything capable of kick-starting a fresh line of inquiry.

DC Ansari raised a hand. Not so long ago she would have shifted uncomfortably in her chair at drawing attention to herself, but her development had been rapid and she was now much more assured. These days, if she had a point to make or a question to raise, she did so with a confidence and enthusiasm he admired.

'Boss, this business with Callum Oliver using the dark web has got me thinking…'

'A truly dangerous thing for the likes of your sergeants,' Bliss quipped, provoking some much needed laughter. 'But I suspect what you have to say will illuminate, Gul. Do go on.'

'Well, it's just that we're assuming he used TOR to find information on Dean Norman's first twenty-two years, and then Morgan Latchford for the past twenty-four. But what if he actually used it to communicate with him as well? What if Latchford himself contacted like-minded men via the dark web, and Mr Oliver regarded that as a way to get close to the man by perhaps posing as one?'

'So you're suggesting Callum Oliver… lurked – if that's the right term – on some chat site or forum and somehow recognised Latchford by something he wrote?'

'Possibly.' Ansari shot to her feet, in her stride now. 'If last year's autumn tree case taught us anything, it's never to underestimate the sickness and depravity people are capable of, especially flowing through the unhinged portals of the deep web. So what if Morgan Latchford, using his anonymous online identity, actually admitted to being Dean Norman? He would have been an absolute rock star to some of those sickos out there.'

Bliss was interested enough to see where the young constable's suggestion led, but approached the subject with caution. 'It's not the worst proposal I've heard this week, Gul. But even so, we're starting from a point at which we have absolutely nothing to suggest Latchford took part in any such online activity. And even if he did, why would Callum Oliver get himself involved in something like that? He already knew the man lived locally, and we also know he had ways to narrow that down to an address. So why risk contact online?'

'To gain his trust. Build confidence. Perhaps enough of both to lure him out into the open – who knows, but down there in the depths these people wallow in, nothing is out of bounds and anything is possible. I just think Mr Oliver would have wanted more ammunition for the article he was writing, so the more he squeezed out of Latchford the better.'

'I'm actually going to suggest we take Gul's great idea further,' Gratton said. 'It's not much of a stretch to imagine that, during Callum Oliver's online interactions with the man informing others he is Dean Norman, the name of Stevie Phillips came up frequently. So what if Hammond came across the same group and joined in? What a scoop for our journo bagging those two for an expose.'

Bishop was the first to register his dislike of that theory. 'Let's stick with what we know for the moment, because we're in danger of getting carried away here. All we are certain about as things stand is that Callum Oliver spent some time on the dark web. Extrapolating that to include him, Latchford, and also Hammond indulging in some despicable three-way is speculating too far in my book.'

Ansari sighed and spread her hands. 'I mentioned Latchford only, and I wasn't suggesting we deviate from any genuinely sound theories or actions. All I'm saying is it's not such a wild leap of the imagination to think that Mr Oliver didn't take to the dark web thinking only about gathering underground information chatter concerning Mr Latchford. After all, if Latchford still had any of Dean Norman lingering inside him, the dark web was just about the only way he'd be able to spend time with his own sort of people. And taking up Phil's point, if Latchford, then why not Hammond as well?'

'Let's not forget that Hammond denies having anything to do with the murder itself,' DC Hunt pointed out.

'Are you suggesting he wasn't perverted enough?' Chandler asked, eyebrows arching. 'John, that boy still bullied, beat, tortured, and attempted to rape that little girl. I'd say that's plenty sick enough for the man he is now to still have a bit of that running through his blood.'

'It might explain why he's still single and unattached,' Bliss chimed in, noting how heated the debate had quickly become. Emotions bubbled over when it came to child brutality and murder. 'No wife, no partner, no girlfriend. Maybe women see something in him they don't like.'

'He could be gay for all we know,' Chandler pointed out.

'So no spouse, no partner, and no boyfriend. Same fears, different gender.'

'It's not outrageous to think he might be one of these incels. Perhaps that early incident in his life created enough psychological damage to cause a reaction of that magnitude.'

Bliss shook his head. 'There are no obvious signs of a hatred towards women, Pen. I think he's possibly shy, perhaps cripplingly so, around women. That much I can imagine.'

'Any of it would be easy to pull off with such lax monitoring,' Bishop said with an air of dejection. 'How simple it must be to keep your secrets: they ask and you answer. End of.'

'From what I understand, Bish, them taking the monitoring seriously and answering questions honestly is crucial to keeping that licence. You lie and you're done. Hammond is fully aware of those risks.'

'One more thing to check with colleagues and friends then.'

Bliss was keen to acknowledge the debate, but also eager to move things on. 'Being done as we speak. Look, call it conjecture, call it speculation, call it a load of old bollocks spouted by a bunch of brain dead arseholes with no clue what they're saying or doing, but these are all logical threads to pull at based on the known facts. We've had less intel to go on in the past and still got the right result. We just have to keep working each angle until something breaks for us. I left my meeting earlier convinced that break would be found somewhere on the dark web, so let's push hard on that. If there was any contact among these three men, I want to know about it.'

DC Gratton, who had fallen silent, turned his head away from the computer monitor he had been studying. 'Um, boss,' he said. 'I just spotted a team-wide email. Alan Virgil sent a message from the Vault. He says he's got something tasty for us.'

THIRTY-EIGHT

IT HAD BEEN A perfectly normal Saturday morning when Phoebe Latchford's entire world collapsed. At the time, she told herself she couldn't possibly have seen it coming. But subsequently, during the darkest of the many hours that followed, she wondered if that was entirely true.

A decade of working as a teaching assistant, coupled with a knack for arts and crafts, had led to her being given greater responsibility for wall displays around the school in which she worked. Once a month she spent some of her own money in The Works, which stood on Bridge Street in the city centre. There, she selected fun materials to use with the younger children so that their artwork projects were different to most others.

On that particular Saturday she had, on a whim, grabbed a coffee and a snack at the Lightbox Cafe, which was directly opposite. Working on a lemon cupcake in between sips of her latte and scrolling through the Facebook news feed on her mobile, Phoebe noticed a figure standing over her on the other side of the table at which she was sitting. Looking up sharply, she took in the ordinary bearded man, whose piercing blue eyes seemed both desperate and anxious at the same time.

'Mrs Latchford, yes?' he said with deliberation. 'Phoebe Latchford?'

She recalled frowning, quickly reassessing the man in case they had once known each other. Perhaps from work. She'd felt awkward when she realised she didn't recognise him. 'Yeess. I'm sorry, do we know each other?'

He shook his head. 'No, we've never met. But I feel as if I know you despite that.'

'Are you a friend of Morgan's?' she asked, feeling that had to be the answer.

'No. But I'd like you to invite me to join you, anyway?'

Curious rather than alarmed at this juncture, she gave him a blank look and said, 'I'm sorry. Why would I do that? And how is it you know my name?'

The intense look on his face did not alter in the slightest. 'I have something to tell you about your husband. Something you are not going to want to hear, something you probably won't want to believe, and yet it's something you most definitely need to know.'

As she sat in the room darkened by the wooden boards fastened over the glass on the outside to protect the panes from vandalism, with Beccy fast asleep on the blow-up mattress, Phoebe ran through the sequence of events for probably the hundredth time since that day. She'd felt the first tug of trepidation at the stranger's presence, his knowledge of her, the hint of warning in his tone. And yet her lack of self-confidence had latched upon his words and what they might mean. Was there anything about her husband she didn't know? Was there anything she was afraid to learn? She mentally answered in the affirmative to both those questions.

'Are you about to tell me my husband is having an affair?' she asked in a choked, uncertain voice. 'Perhaps even with your own wife or girlfriend?'

Her mind had taken her there immediately, having questioned her husband's fidelity throughout their marriage. It also seemed to be the only logical explanation for this man's approach. She had feared his response, but that paled by comparison to how she felt when he eventually shook his head and said, 'No, Mrs Latchford. I'm afraid it's so much worse than that.'

Looking back and being truthful about her feelings and suspicions, she realised she had always felt a yawning chasm between her and Morgan. His claims not to have any family at all were a little difficult to believe. She had known a few people who'd been orphaned while they were still young, yet never before had she met somebody who had no surviving relatives at all. Worse still, the man she'd married had a truncated past; no adolescent memories, no further education, no stories about his first jobs after leaving school, no friends from any part of his past. It was as if he had entered the world in his early twenties. And yet until the day the man approached her in the cafe, she had never allowed her thoughts to linger on those discrepancies.

Phoebe now understood that those existing suspicions had made it easier for her to accept everything the bearded man told her after she had reluctantly invited him to join her at the table.

He refused to give her his name, insisting he was a journalist who, during an investigation, had stumbled upon information he had not expected to discover. Having learned of this fresh angle to his proposed story, he realised this was not something he could keep to himself.

'I imagine your husband never speaks about his past,' the man had begun. 'Or, if he does, his recollections are not always consistent. The reason for this, Mrs Latchford, is that he will do anything to keep one element of that past from you. The dismal truth is, when he was twelve, he and another lad the same age abused, tortured, and murdered an eight-year-old girl.'

Phoebe had reeled back as if slapped. 'That's absurd. You don't know what you're talking about.'

'Actually, I do. And the fact that you haven't stood to leave tells me you have your own doubts.'

She recalled shaking her head. 'No. Not that. Never anything like that.'

'So hear me out. Let me persuade you otherwise.'

'Say what you came her to say. I'll give you a few minutes.'

'Okay. So, on the one hand you refuse to believe me. On the other, you're already making excuses inside your own head. You're telling yourself that whatever he might have done when he was a kid, he's an adult now, with a family of his own, and time changes people. As far as you're concerned, even if he's guilty of the offences I just laid out for you, the man you know and love is incapable of repeating the behaviour he showed in pre-adolescence. The real question, Mrs Latchford, is how much you are willing to risk on taking that gamble?'

She was shocked at how close he was to her own line of thinking. 'What do you mean by that?'

'Are you willing to risk your life? How about Beccy's?'

'Now look... you keep my daughter out of this.'

'It's not me you have to be worried about. Thing is, I was of the same mind as you at first. I told myself your husband was a different man more than three decades on from his horrific crimes. That is until I observed conversations your husband entered into online. I followed them, unobserved, purely to add weight to my story. But then, during one of those online chats, your husband informed other members of the group that he was having feelings similar to those he had experienced all those years ago. Only now they were towards his own daughter.'

Shaking her head furiously, Phoebe snapped at him. 'No! That can't be true! It can't be!'

With a calm, almost serene authority, he said, 'Mrs Latchford, what I read on those online pages convinced me of the danger your daughter is in. Your husband openly admitted his intention to harm her in the most brutal and sadistic ways imaginable. I think it's also safe to assume he has already decided to remove you from the equation beforehand.'

And just like that, the comfortable – if mundane and ordinary – life she relied on was gone. Snatched away from her as if it were some insignificant bauble. Whenever she reflected on that conversation, as she did a dozen times a day, she always came back to the same dark place and the same unambiguous questions: how fragile was her marriage, her relationship, her love and affection for her husband, when a single verbal exchange could tear it apart so completely? What had she seen in him that made the shift between devotion to revulsion fall into place so readily?

As ever, the memory of that initial dialogue led inexorably to the content of their second, during which she had asked him what she could do to avoid the awful future he had predicted for her and Beccy.

He'd paused, reflecting. Perhaps even reconsidering his position. But finally he answered her question. 'Answer me this: is there any part of what I have told you that you think the police will believe?'

'I… I don't know. I can't be sure. What if you told them what you know?'

'And what do I know, Mrs Latchford? What do I know that your husband cannot simply argue against? What evidence do I have? You're an intelligent woman, so I think you know how this sort of thing goes. Whatever either of us alleges, he will deny. And when the police look into his background, they will discover everything I know about his past, to which their response will be to move him on elsewhere.'

'But that's good, isn't it?'

'Is it? How can you be certain that your husband, exposed by me and with wild claims from you, won't get to bring your daughter with him into his new life? Or still be a part of it in some kind of custody agreement? You can't know, and neither can you allow him to spend time alone with your daughter under such circumstances.'

'So what are you suggesting I do?'

'I can help you,' he had assured her at that point. 'People like him don't go from where they are in their life to acting upon their impulses overnight. He's not ready, but he's fast approaching the stage when he will be. Besides, I watch his every word online and I know you have time. We have time.'

'For what?' she asked in a voice breaking beneath a raw combination of desperation and terror.

'To plan your escape,' he said then. 'You and Beccy. To leave him and this city and never have to look back.'

THIRTY-NINE

The sealed and separate room situated on the ground floor inside Thorpe Wood police station was known as the Vault because it was the most secure suite in the building, requiring various biometric readings and knowledge of a key code that changed four times a day in order to gain entry.

Only a handful of trained officers had access to the Vault, and for good reason. Inside the room sat eight computers hooked up to the dark web with no protective filtering applied. For the most part, the devices were used by detectives working child protection and organised crime. Each of those officers was supervised to the nth degree, psychologically monitored by therapists trained to manage emotional breakdowns and the general strain of having to work with material associated with the physical and sexual abuse and exploitation of children. Invariably, working such cases exposed these men and women to obscene material such as photographs and videos. It was difficult to handle, impossible not to be affected.

DC Virgil had worked the Vault on several previous occasions, and although his remit this time had been to find and follow exchanges between Callum Oliver and the wider dark web dwellers, he knew going in that any communications also involving either Morgan Latchford or Stuart Hammond might veer off towards the crimes they were sentenced for. His debriefing took place in the major incident room.

'What do you have for us?' DCI Warburton asked him the moment everybody had settled down.

'First up,' he told them, 'I have evidence showing Callum Oliver stepping away from a forum and engaging in personal messaging with four separate individuals. I began tracking activities from all four, and I think we can dismiss two of them as being enthusiasts for crime and criminals, but almost certainly nothing more than having an interest. The other two, however, caught my attention. Both entered the discussions at completely different times – days apart, in fact – but tellingly, both did so only after the topic turned to child murder and Dean Norman and Stevie Phillips in particular. They were initially cagey, not volunteering too much about themselves or their interests. One of them eventually offered insights into Norman, leading to several other users challenging him to confess he actually was Norman. Callum Oliver bit harder than most, and immediately afterwards the two went into the private messaging area.'

'This is specific member to specific member, yes?' Bishop asked, seeking clarification as to who was invited into these PM sessions.

'Yes, Sarge. In this case, it was suggested by the other member to our reporter that they take the conversation into the PM app.'

'And you were able to follow Oliver inside?'

'I was. The user calling himself Born Free, the same member who claimed to have greater insight into Dean Norman, asked Callum Oliver to switch to PM. Once there, he told Oliver to assume he was messaging with Dean Norman and to ask whatever he liked. Now, I know from the intel I read this week that police kept back the detail about both lads attempting to have sex with Haley Deerbourne. That information was never released to the public and, as far as I could tell, never even speculated upon. I realised Norman could have told his story to somebody else when they were in detention together and that person might now be impersonating Norman to get his own twisted kicks. But I followed up, just as I followed up on everything else while I was searching for more.'

'Sorry for interrupting when you're on a roll,' Bliss said, 'but what do you mean when you say you followed up, Alan?'

'Prior to sitting down in the chair, I contacted the tech team, boss. Had them standing by to process any IP addresses or usernames I came across – some users make the mistake of taking their online handles with them into other, completely different online arenas.'

'Okay. Go on with what you found, and then we'll move on to your follow-ups.'

'Yes, boss. So, this other user, named Sporus, also became involved in the general back and forth regarding the Norman and Phillips case. At one point, he went off on one when somebody suggested both boys were equally monstrous. He ranted about people being aware of all the facts before they delivered their judgement, and shortly afterwards Callum Oliver asked him if he wanted to go to PM. I read through their exchange as well, and while this Sporus never claimed to be Stevie Phillips, he was extremely angry about people apportioning blame despite not knowing the truth. Reading between the lines, I thought this might well be Stuart Hammond.'

'This sounds like great work, Alan. I hope it wasn't too stressful for you.'

Virgil shook his head. 'Not at all, boss. This was powderpuff stuff compared to the nightmares I've had to wade through before.

They were never overly graphic about anything. Even Born Free, who I believed had to be Latchford, never spoke about precisely what he did, despite implying he was responsible.'

'Okay. Then let's turn to what you discovered afterwards from the techs.'

'The software we use can strip out the metadata from any site or app we gain access to. For those who might not know what that is, metadata essentially describes in detail the rest of the data, breaking it down into individual components. So while on the surface the data tells me I'm in a private messaging app looking at the messages exchanged by two members of a specific forum, the metadata provides in-depth information about the source and the users. This gave me the intel I was most interested in: the IP addresses of all relevant participants.'

'Leaving tech to use their tools and skills to locate who those IP addresses were being used by at the time,' Chandler finished for the young DC.

He shrugged. 'Sort of. If not exactly who was using the address, certainly where they were using it.' He looked around at the expectant faces staring back at him. Puffed out his cheeks. 'I won't dwell on the user we know to be Callum Oliver, except to say that he can be traced to the router inside his flat as well as one assigned to his mobile phone, which tells us he used the provider's 4G connection at some point and not his own internet service provider. That really only means he used it while not at home, or perhaps if the home service was down.'

'Come on, you dick, get to the good bits,' DC Ansari said.

Virgil nodded amiably. 'The user calling himself Sporus had an IP address that led our techs to PlusNet, which led to a router located in… Coleraine, Northern Ireland.'

A huge cheer went up around the room, followed by words of praise for Virgil's detailed work. He took the plaudits and back slaps with a graceful smile, but once again, Bliss believed there was more to come.

'Tell us the rest, Alan,' he said with an easy grin. 'I know you have something else.'

'I do, boss. Perhaps the best is to come. First of all, we found no direct comms between Latchford and Hammond, though it's clear they knew who the other was. But the techs and I also discovered another connection between Callum Oliver and somebody who features in our investigations. That person is Raymond Deerbourne.'

Bliss glanced at Chandler before saying, 'I'm not at all surprised. I take it these communications were through more regular means?'

'Yes, boss. Texts and phone calls. We're waiting for the body of the texts to be sent to us, but the two men were definitely in contact.'

'Okay. And moving on…'

'To move on we have to come back to Born Free. I'd automatically assumed that user's IP would trace back to either Latchford's home computer or his mobile phone.'

'And I'm guessing from your tone it didn't?'

'No. We checked the trace twice, and both times it came back the same. It never even took us to a Peterborough address. Instead, the route led us to the probation services.'

As gasps of shock and surprise echoed around the room, Bliss instantly seized upon the most logical question to ask next. 'Northern Ireland or Cambridge?' he said, the words catching in his throat as his breath stalled.

'Cambridge, boss.' Virgil's nod was firm and purposeful. 'To be precise, it was Grant McKinney's computer.'

FORTY

'We have to prepare a solid arrest package,' Bliss told his senior officers. Detective Chief Superintendent Feeley was treating their visitors from Northern Ireland to a late lunch, so Bliss sat with DCI Warburton and Superintendent Fletcher in the latter's office. 'We can't go in half-cocked where he's concerned. We all know twenty-four hours is seldom enough time once you make allowances for rest breaks, solicitor consultation, and sleep. Just as we all know in a situation like this we'd obtain authorisation for some additional time. But few people in Grant McKinney's position are going to break easily, and I don't want him walking out of here again once an arrest has been made. I want this bastard on remand.'

'That's a tall order, Jimmy,' Fletcher stated flatly. Her grim countenance spoke of the betrayal they all felt. 'I don't see a judge remanding somebody of McKinney's stature in a case like this. What he's done is criminal, it's amoral, but he hasn't murdered anybody.'

'That we know of,' Bliss said.

'What do you mean by that?'

'I'm not suggesting he physically took anybody's life, ma'am. Nor that he was actively involved in any of what we've been investigating. But his contact with Hammond suggests he fed the man information on Latchford, even posed as him. That information indirectly led to Latchford's suicide and the probable abduction of the man's wife and daughter. It's likely the intelligence he shared also resulted in Callum Oliver coming to harm. Surely that's enough to push for a joint enterprise charge?'

Bliss was confident, yet Fletcher shook her head adamantly. 'A few years ago, perhaps. But since the Supreme Court ruling over charge misuse, a jury would need to be convinced of the defendant's intent to assist in or encourage the principal crime. Here, even if Hammond has harmed Oliver, even if he has harmed the Latchfords, we'd find it impossible to prove intent on McKinney's part unless we uncovered concrete evidence of him deliberately goading the man into it.'

'So we're looking at accessory before the fact, perhaps secondary liability?'

'I'd say so, yes. Accessory after the fact is unlikely here, no matter how deep you dig. But please keep on digging, Jimmy. Whatever you turn up will be passed over to the CPS, because if McKinney used his position to provide information on Morgan Latchford and his family, then he has to be punished in more ways than losing his job.'

'They have him on breaking the court injunction for a start. That alone can be pushed towards a prison sentence. But he surely aided and abetted, which to my mind makes him a principal offender.'

Fletcher considered this. Eventually she nodded. 'Your arrest package has to be strong enough to buy us time to charge him to the full extent. However, I'm conscious of being up against the clock.'

'A clock we can't see,' Bliss reminded her. 'A clock whose alarm settings we have no clue about. But to be frank, I don't believe McKinney can help us with that aspect. It looks as if his involvement ended prior to Callum Oliver's carjacking, which was the first offence to the person committed here. I have no expectations of him knowing what Hammond did with Oliver, nor what he intends to do with Phoebe and Beccy Latchford. However, he may know more than we think, possibly even more than he thinks. So the question before us is, are we better off getting him in the room now to find out precisely what he knows and does not know, and then coming at him hard for being an accessory the closer we get to the end of his detention?'

Fletcher looked across to DCI Warburton. 'Diane, what's your view on this as SIO?'

'McKinney is done, no matter how we proceed. He'll lose his job, he'll lose his freedom. We have time to push the envelope on that. Where we don't have time to play with is in discovering the whereabouts of our three missing persons. With all that in mind, I'm leaning towards as solid an arrest package as we can put together in a hurry. We don't need it all, we just require enough.'

'I think we can work with that,' Bliss said. 'Particularly if we get him in the room and talking without arresting him first. If we can persuade him to open up initially, we then make an arrest at the point at which he opts to walk away – which he will, because he'll recognise the signs. But those extra few minutes when his guard is down might make all the difference.'

'How do you propose to get him talking?' Fletcher asked.

'A sense of duty, perhaps. Plain old cooperation. I'm thinking we speak to them both, him and Ione Pearson. That way, he'll be less suspicious of our motives. We'll start benignly, then throw a hand grenade into the room and see how he reacts. If we insist right from the word go that any help he provides in locating our three missing persons can only be to his benefit in the long run, he may see sense. For all we know he's been fretting about his involvement, bricking it since he discovered what his leak of intel led to.'

'An old-fashioned interview, then. Sweat them until they confess.'

Bliss caught the wry smile, which he returned. 'Those days are long gone, and some would say thankfully so. But if he is anxious, we'll see it and we can react.'

'I take it that means you'll be in the room, Jimmy.'

'I was thinking along those lines, yes. Probably with DC Ansari, given she's received all the relevant training. But I think I just begin with a casual chat, move it on up to an informal interview, and when the time is right, I ask him to continue under caution. If he agrees, that's when I'll bring Gul into it. If he doesn't, then we make the arrest and we go on the clock.'

'How long before your arrest package is complete?' Warburton asked. She checked her wristwatch. 'The pair of them ought to be in Cambridge by now, so you're going to have to work out how to get them back here without raising suspicion.'

'CC Thouey is getting things done on his side of the water, pulling together an information package on Stuart Hammond, and requests have gone out to his mobile and internet providers for additional data. We're at least circling him now, which means we'll soon understand him better and hopefully figure out what makes him tick. As for McKinney, I'd say an hour – two at most. I can begin my chat before it's ready, if necessary.'

'Which still leaves us with the thorny issue of how we get them here. And today, otherwise you might have to wait until Monday.'

Bliss shook his head. 'I don't want to wait. How about we tell them we have information which leads us to believe Hammond was using Callum Oliver to find his way to Latchford, and that we could do with talking it over with them. They won't want to drive back again today, but if we stress the urgency in relation to Phoebe and Beccy Latchford, they won't really be able to refuse.'

'That might work. It'll take them an hour to get back here, and to buy more time. Diane and I can meet with them again in the conference room. We can stall them with a general conversation about both Latchford and Hammond. You never know, something might come of it. At the very least, it fends them off until you're ready to speak with them.'

'I think that's a great idea,' Bliss said. 'In my experience, people like talking about their jobs. It'd be interesting to make comparisons, and yes, we might even learn something valuable.'

'And your immediate plans are?'

'I have Penny and Bish already working on the arrest package, while the others are all still getting through their actions. I have to find time for a quick chat with the CPS ahead of my court appearance on Monday, and I'm also going to have another word with Marty Lipman, if at all possible.'

'What more do you hope to get out of him?' Warburton asked.

'Probably nothing. But if I emphasise how much trouble his client may be in, he could open up. I think he and Callum Oliver spoke about the investigation more than Lipman implied, and once again it's a question of whether Oliver revealed anything useful that we don't already know. Frankly, until I can get McKinney in the room, I'm clutching at straws and I don't want to just kick my heels.'

Fletcher ended the meeting on a solemn note. She reminded them all of the statistics relating to missing persons, her concern coming towards the latter part of the fifth day being that the odds were no longer in their favour in achieving a positive outcome. Bliss was reminded of the autumn tree case and how just a few minutes either way could either save a life or allow one to slip away. Frustration lodged inside his chest, a weight he felt sitting there like a bad case of indigestion. Callum Oliver didn't deserve to die, but he had invited trouble into his life by investigating something he was not supposed to even stray close to. Phoebe Latchford may have been aware of her husband's former life and been happy to continue sharing his new one. A questionable decision, perhaps, but not one that should carry a death sentence. Beccy Latchford might prove to be the only truly innocent victim of the three, and it was she who featured heavily in Bliss's thoughts as he left Fletcher's office.

FORTY-ONE

They met at the Park Inn, an unspectacular six-storey hotel on Wentworth Street. Bliss had often wondered if the architect had a child who came up with the two-dimensional design while playing with Lego. But it was close to Lipman's offices, which is where he had been when Bliss called. Plus it enjoyed the benefit of a small bar. Lipman arrived late though he'd had less distance to travel, as Bliss had known he would; he was that kind of man, that kind of solicitor.

Prior to arranging the meeting, Bliss had contacted the CPS to discuss his court appearance scheduled for the following week. It was eleven months since the case had concluded successfully, and Bliss was the prosecution's lead witness. Although acts of torture and murder had been committed in various parts of the country, several of the offences had also taken place in London. Such was the severity of the crimes, the trial was being held at the Central Criminal Court at the Old Bailey.

Having spent much of his working life in London, the nation's most famous court no longer held any fears for him. He'd made several appearances there as a witness, and knew precisely what was expected of him. Many people whose only experience of court came from watching television shows – and most of them taking place in the USA – believed a trial amounted to an awful lot of objecting and use of the gavel. In fact, neither was true of a British courtroom; gavels were not and never have been used in UK trials, and objecting to something the opposing barrister might say was a far more temperate affair.

Bliss had prepared fully with his CPS liaison, and the call he made this time was to check on any final updates and words of advice relevant to changes since their last meeting. He could have done without the added pressure of a court appearance at this stage of an on-going op, but it was part of the job and just one extra stressor to cope with. Fortunately, there were no last-minute surprises for him to worry about. The chances were good that he would be called on the opening day of the trial, first witness up after the prosecuting barrister had initially laid out the case. He was ready, confident in his ability to remain objective even when the defence tried to get beneath his skin. It was a tactic and not at all personal. Quite unlike his feeling of distaste when having to spend time in the same room as the man he was about to meet.

He was halfway through a tall glass of lager when Lipman joined him. 'I ordered a coffee,' he said, taking his seat at the two-person table Bliss had chosen. They were the only patrons in the entire bar, but still Bliss sat with his back to the wall, facing out.

'Hopefully, this won't take long,' he said. 'Though that depends on whether I think I'm hearing the truth out of you.'

He saw the man about to protest, before the realisation of how he'd ended up in Bliss's pocket came to him. Instead, he shrugged and spread his hands. 'I'll do my best, Inspector. As always.'

'We're going back to our previous conversations about Callum Oliver, Marty. And don't roll your eyes – you and I both know you held shit back from me last time.'

'Have you really never heard of professional privilege?'

'I have, as it happens. It extends only to confidential discussions between you and your client.'

'Precisely.' Lipman sat back in his chair, as if that word alone had ended their discussion.

Bliss narrowed his gaze. 'Do you have remote access to your IT system, Marty?'

'Of course. A modern service for a modern world.'

'Is that one of your taglines?'

'One of them, yes.'

'Good. Well then, while you wait for your coffee to arrive, why don't you access your system now and pull up Callum Oliver's client file for me.'

'I'll do no such thing,' Lipman scoffed. 'That would be part of the client privilege we talked about moments ago.'

'Oh, I don't want to see any details, Marty. I just want to see his name and a client reference number.'

Lipman made no reply this time. Instead he licked his lips and his eyeballs darted from side to side.

Bliss took a swig from his glass and leaned forward across the table. The film of sweat forming on the solicitor's upper lip told him his hunch had been right. 'Let me make this easy on you, Marty. You can't do as I asked because you never signed Callum Oliver on as a client. Whatever he was up to was off book. Which means nothing you two discussed falls under client-solicitor privilege.'

'No, that's not quite right,' Lipman argued, his cheeks reddening. 'He and I discussed a number of issues, and the only reason I never took him on as a client was because he failed to show for our next meeting.'

'All of which means he wasn't a client when you and he chatted. Time's up, Marty. Tell me. Tell me everything right now, or I might just cash in my bargaining chip.'

It took Lipman a few seconds to gather himself, but by the time his coffee sat on the table in front of him, he was ready to talk.

'This much I'm sure you know: Mr Oliver approached me with some concerns he had over an investigative piece he was putting together. He told me he couldn't run it by his newspaper's legal staff because he had no intention of submitting the piece or pieces to them. He was straight with me from the beginning, clarifying that if we could somehow find a loophole whereby a national newspaper or online news outlet could publish his articles without any of them being charged for ignoring a court injunction, he would seek alternative sources in order to publish… and be damned, if you will.'

'He told you who he was investigating, yes?'

'He did. Dean Norman. Whom he knew to be living life to the full under the name of Morgan Latchford.'

'Oliver's original intention was to expose Latchford. But to what end?'

'I wouldn't quite call him a zealot, but young Mr Oliver had strong opinions about the judicial system. It was his belief that animals like Dean Norman ought never to breathe the same air as innocent people ever again. He described him as a savage beast walking among us.'

Bliss thought about how to approach the next stage of the conversation, and decided on a method that had served him well in the past. 'So at what point did his attention turn to the man Stevie Phillips had become?'

Lipman pulled back a little, studying Bliss for a moment. 'You're a formidable opponent, Inspector. I like what you did there: putting the question to me as if we'd already agreed it had happened.'

'So then tell me. And remember: be honest with me, because you really don't know what I know.'

'Very well. Yes, Mr Oliver approached me a second time. On this occasion he said he'd been researching and gathering information online, and that he was convinced Norman's partner was now also on the hook.'

'How did he confirm that?'

'He didn't. He wasn't able to. No, that's not quite true. What I mean to say is that while he was certain who he was communicating with, he had no way of finding out the name the man was now using.'

'Nor where he had chosen to live?'

'Not as far as I know, Inspector.'

Bliss gave that some thought. Hammond had sidled into the conversation, had revealed himself to Callum Oliver and perhaps even the person he believed was Morgan Latchford, but he had not given away either his identity or location. It wasn't beyond the realm of possibility for either man to have brought in the services of a hacking expert to track down the source of the person using the online name Sporus, but perhaps it had never made it that far. After all, neither Oliver nor Latchford had gone after Hammond; it was all the other way around.

'Okay,' he said to Lipman urgently. 'This is important, Marty. I want you to think hard and tell me whatever you remember. Did Callum ever tell you about any of his conversations with either man? I mean, the details they might have shared with him, threats they may have made.'

Lipman's face grew serious. 'Mr Oliver is an earnest young man. Clearly ambitious, he wanted to reveal as much about both of them as he could. However, our conversations were almost always limited to legal ramifications.'

'So, during those moments when were they not, what did he tell you?'

Here Lipman paused and frowned, then nodded to himself. 'Actually, there was one occasion when he told me how much he'd like to see both of them suffer by having to go back to prison, which was why he was attempting to dig up dirt on them. But I just remembered something else. The reason I accidentally left my backpack in his car was because we'd stopped off for a coffee and he received a phone call. I don't know what it was about, but he sprang up out of his seat, told me I'd need to take a cab back to my office and to add the cost to his bill.'

'And you have no idea what it was about? He gave no indication?'

'No. But of course it had to be important.'

'How did he seem afterwards?'

'I don't know what you mean.'

Bliss leaned in closer. 'Was he excited? Surprised? You said he left immediately afterwards, which sounds as if he was eager at the very least.'

Lipman gave himself time before responding. 'Now that I think about it, the look on his face gave me pause for concern. If anything, I'd say he seemed fearful. In fact, I'd say Mr Oliver was scared stiff.'

FORTY-TWO

Bliss took his time with Grant McKinney. This was a fragile stage of the investigation which, if it fragmented, might cost the police everything; and with it, any hope of finding any of their three missing persons alive. Understanding the risks only added pressure to an already febrile situation, and with the clock not on their side, there was no long game left to play.

'What did you think of Morgan Latchford?' he asked as the two sat in one of the rooms set aside for taking witness statements. 'Your overall impressions of the man himself.'

'To be honest,' McKinney said in casual repose, his back pressed into the chair, legs stretched out, 'he struck me as something of an empty shell. In our line of work, we often see how people – men especially – are pretty much comprised of the things they learned in their formative years. It's hard to shake, and impossible if you don't have the will to make changes. But with Latchford, it always felt to me as if he had been hollowed out by his experiences. There was no depth to his personality, no real energy or conviction about him. I never could work out what Phoebe saw in him.'

Bliss was alert to the man's final statement, and quickly

followed up on it. 'Did that concern you at all? Did it worry you that his lack of charisma might lead to Phoebe leaving him and creating a vacuum in his life?'

'It was certainly one of the many things we discussed. Myself, Ione, and your Chief Constable, I mean. It's not something we would ever have spoken about with Morgan himself.'

'Of course not. Tell me, what was the outcome of those discussions?'

Here, McKinney frowned and regarded Bliss more closely. 'I'm not sure where this is leading, Inspector.'

'I'm trying to understand the man more fully. I'm also attempting to find out for myself how these meetings between you all worked; the things you discussed, or avoided, as you just pointed out.'

'I see. Okay. Well, although we made notes of all concerns raised, provided they did not warrant closer attention, we took no action. Predicting how a person might react to any given situation is purely speculative, because as you must know from your own job, people can surprise you.'

'Absolutely. I suppose what I'm driving at is, I imagine it to be almost impossible for you to actually get to know these people well. After all, you meet with them twice a year and they tell you what they want to tell you. Perhaps even what you want to hear.'

McKinney bristled at Bliss's insinuation. 'That's a little simplistic, Inspector Bliss. We're trained to spot deflections, half-truths, and if we pick up on them we know how to lay verbal traps.'

'Okay. That's fair. Even so, I assume it would surprise you to learn that Morgan Latchford was a regular visitor to chatrooms on the dark web? That during these chats he anonymously admitted to being Dean Norman, and seemed to revel in his infamy.'

Bliss spoke casually, though his gaze was anything but. He looked for signs of panic in the other man's eyes, but saw something he had not expected to find there: disappointment.

'Morgan did that?' McKinney drew himself upright, tension appearing in his face and on his rigid frame for the first time.

'He did. Not as Morgan Latchford, of course. He wasn't stupid enough to provide his name, but we know it was him.'

'I… I don't know what to say. Surprise is too small a word. I'm shocked by this. Genuinely staggered. I would never have thought it of him.'

Puzzled, Bliss questioned his own radar's effectiveness. They knew McKinney had entered those chat rooms posing as Latchford, though for what purpose Bliss couldn't imagine, given he had to be Hammond's partner. His thirty-plus years in the job had made him proficient in reading people. By now, the conversation ought to have caused the senior probation officer some consternation, yet nothing in his voice nor in his body language revealed anything other than genuine astonishment and regret.

As his thoughts swiftly ran through their evidence on the man, Bliss spotted the basic flaw in the conclusion he and his colleagues had drawn. He asked McKinney one more question, after which he left the room and went to find DC Ansari.

*

If Chandler was startled by the unexpected presence of him and Gul inside the room in which she had been chatting to Ione Pearson, she betrayed no reaction. Bliss caught her eye and asked her to remain with them, before settling himself into a chair facing the other probation officer from Cambridge.

'You made a terrible mistake, Ms Pearson,' he said without inflection. 'After all that planning and plotting and manoeuvring, not to mention the terrific act you put on, that single stupid error is the one that's going to bite you.'

'I'm sorry?' Pearson looked from him to Chandler, and back again. 'Am I supposed to know what you're talking about?'

Bliss ignored her remark. 'You were clever. I'll give you that. Clever enough to help set this whole thing up, clever enough to not only hide your tracks, but also to steer us in the wrong direction should we catch on.' He raised a hand to forestall any further protestations of innocence. 'And to give you your due, it almost worked. I've just been speaking to your colleague, Mr McKinney, fully intending to grill him until he confessed, or at the very least catch him out in multiple lies. But the more we spoke, the more I believed in him. And you see, that's where you went wrong, Ms Pearson.'

She faced him down with no outward sign of tic or tremor. 'Is that so, Inspector? I'm afraid I still have no idea what you are talking about.'

'The problem is, you put your faith in technology and forgot all about the human element. So yes, when we eventually discovered the breadcrumbs you'd left leading us to suspect Morgan Latchford of having virtually outed himself online, we also identified the other trail you left for us. The one leading directly to Mr McKinney's office computer. But what you failed to take into consideration is an experienced copper's instinct when it comes to people.'

'I've heard all about them,' Pearson said. 'Nowhere near infallible is what I've been told.'

Bliss nodded. 'True. But close enough to pursue alternative theories. And you see, the moment I lost interest in your boss as a suspect, I was left only with you. So I asked the most obvious of all questions: I asked your colleague if he was in his office on Monday afternoon when we know his PC was used to go online into a dark web chatroom. It was clever of you to use malware to mirror his desktop and then use it in the background as if he himself was working on his computer at the time. And it was especially clever of you to do so while you were supposedly working from home. The problem being, you were unaware of one thing, Ms Pearson.'

The woman remained completely unflustered. 'Is that so? Very well, I'll play along, Inspector. Tell me, in this fantasy world you've concocted, what precisely was I unaware of?'

'That your boss had a dental appointment that day. It ran long, too. So at the time his computer was being used to access the dark web, he was not even in the building. In fact, he was on the other side of the city. All of which means Mr McKinney has an alibi, Ms Pearson. But I'm guessing you don't.'

FORTY-THREE

Bliss had seen his young DC work many interviews, and always came away impressed by her intelligent methods and stoical demeanour. Having put Ione Pearson on the back foot, and with his initial conversation with her having reached its logical conclusion, Bliss allowed Gul Ansari to take over.

Prior to entering the room, he and his colleague had done their homework. They believed the woman's hubris was most likely to bring about her downfall. Immediately after mentioning Pearson's lack of alibi, he had called for a break and then advised the probation officer of her rights. He told her that while she was not under arrest, if she left, he'd have no alternative but to go down that route. As predicted, she declined the offer of a legal representative; she preferred to tackle them on her own, and that was just fine by him.

In interview room 1, its olive green wall tiles and flooring the colour of limes making for a sickly, depressing environment, Ansari and Pearson did battle. As far as Bliss was concerned, there was only ever going to be one winner.

'We know what you did, Ione,' Ansari confirmed at one point, without expanding upon the declaration. 'What we still don't know is why. What can you tell us about that?'

With Pearson having not asked for a solicitor, the two detectives had known she would talk to them. The real question was how much they could squeeze out of her before she saw the steel door swinging shut and the sound of the key being turned in the lock.

'Correction,' Pearson said bullishly. 'You *think* you know what I did. I've yet to hear anything other than wild speculation from either of you.'

'Hard evidence is being gathered as we speak, Ione. But all the nuts and bolts are there for us, so all we have to do is put them together. The thing is, you're currently in a fortunate position, because we need to find three missing people much more than we need to focus on charging you. The more you tell us now, the better it will go for you in the long run. You will be charged, you will go on trial, and you will be found guilty. The only difference you can make right now is to decide on the length of your sentence.'

'What is it you want to know?'

'Before I get to that, I have to make something clear to you. There is an entire range of charges for us to consider in respect of the crimes you've committed. However, what you knew and when you knew it, what you did and what you did not do, will all be considered when we sit down to discuss those charges. Again, any sentence you receive will depend on the charges you are convicted of. If you tell us everything we want to know, our conversation with the CPS will be completely different to those we will have if you play games with us. I urge you, therefore, to give it to us straight. Understood?'

'Oh, I think you made yourself perfectly clear, Constable.'

'Excellent. Then we're off to a good start. Let's continue in the same vein. Tell me, Ione, who is Stuart Hammond to you?'

'Nobody.'

'Then why are you working with him?'

'How am I working with him? You tell me what you think you know.'

'That's not the way this works. I'll ask again: how and why are you working with Stuart Hammond?'

Pearson looked down and away, as if steeling herself to speak. When she eventually did, her voice was smaller, weaker, and much less confident. 'Have you ever been in the presence of someone truly evil?'

'I believe I have, yes. Frequently.'

'Of course. In your job I suppose it's more difficult not to. But not in mine. True evil is more rare than most people imagine. And I don't mean the inadequates who don't care one way or another about their victims or what they do to them. I mean those who enjoy it, who get a real kick out of it. Perhaps even live for it.'

'Are you telling us Morgan Latchford was like that? Because as far as we know, he hadn't harmed anybody in decades.'

'As far as you know. And maybe he hadn't. But he still had it in him, believe me. People like him never truly lose that desire. When confronted with the records relating to his trial and the murder that preceded it, Latchford freely admitted to us that he led his friend into areas he did not wish to go. He spoke about Stevie Phillips with utter contempt. I'd say the only reason he befriended the kid was because he was malleable, introverted, and mostly naïve. I didn't have confirmation of this until our colleagues from Northern Ireland joined us this morning, but that single incident had a devastating effect on the lives of first Phillips and then Stuart Hammond.'

'As it did Haley Deerbourne,' Ansari was quick to say. 'Let's not forget that her own life ended that day after enduring relentless physical torture at the hands of those two boys.'

Pearson nodded vigorously. 'I know that. I'm not suggesting

otherwise. But that failed rape attempt he wanted no part of in the first place did things to that boy's mind. Things he's never been able to overcome. He's been unable to have a physical relationship in his entire life, and for that, in addition to everything else that happened to him after that day, he blames Dean Norman. Imagine what that kind of anger and bitterness does to a person's state of mind.'

'And still you sound as if you're sorry for him,' Bliss observed.

Her sharp gaze fell upon him. 'That's because I am. Do you really think I would go as far as I have if I didn't sympathise? Dean Norman was a monster. The man he became was a monster. I'm not convinced Stevie Phillips was ever in the same category, but Stuart Hammond certainly wasn't.'

'And you know this how?'

'Because all he wanted from this was to save Beccy Latchford's life. When he learned of the man's wife and daughter, he became convinced that Latchford would do to his own daughter what he did to Haley Deerbourne. Absolutely no doubt in his mind. And I didn't need any convincing.'

Bliss nodded for Ansari to continue. She regarded Ione Pearson with open scepticism. 'You expect us to be as naïve as you? We don't believe Hammond has good intentions, and I can't see how you came to that conclusion, either.'

'Believe what you like. Stuart will contact me as soon as he has Phoebe and Beccy in a secure and safe environment.'

'And how exactly will he do that?'

'In the same way we've been communicating all along.'

Ansari took a breath. She studied the contents of a folder she had brought into the interview room with her. Bliss thought it was time to change tack, and he was delighted when his DC did just that. 'How deep are you into this, Ione? I told you before we began how important that might be for you in terms of charges.

So, as you're being cooperative, what was your role in the car-jacking, the assault on and abduction of Callum Oliver?'

'I had no role in that.'

'Okay. How about the disposal of Morgan Latchford's vehicle?'

'That was me. Can I expect a harsh punishment for dumping a car in the river?'

'Tell us about that. How did you come to have his car?'

'I posed as a new client and arranged to meet with him on Monday morning at the Starbucks by Morrisons. I waited close by and let Stuart know when Morgan arrived. Stuart then called him and they spoke for several minutes. By the time he left the coffee house, I was standing outside the door. Morgan handed me his car keys and continued walking without even looking at me. I took the car and dumped it in the river as planned.'

'Stuart asked you to do this for him?' Ansari probed.

'Yes. But I swear I wasn't aware of what would happen next. If I'd known Stuart was going to talk Morgan into killing himself, I would never have gone through with it. You have to believe me.'

'I don't have to believe a damned thing. What about the vehicle exchange at the farmhouse?'

'That was complicated, but yes, I played my part. Nothing illegal there, I assure you.'

Ansari glanced at Bliss and shrugged. He was struck by something that had been said earlier, and right now he was trying to puzzle it out. The closer he got to latching on, the further away he drifted from it.

'You posed as Latchford online to discover information about him, and to draw out Hammond,' he pointed out. 'You caused an enormous amount of damage, and that alone is going to earn you jail time.'

'Then it is what it is. I'll fight my corner when the time comes. But I never hurt anybody. I helped out with the vehicles, I helped stage the accident that forced the reporter into stopping on the road. If Stuart wounded him during the carjacking as you claim, and then later did something bad to him as you suggested, then frankly I'd be shocked. I still believe he didn't have it in him to harm anybody.'

'Perhaps. Or maybe he misled you the whole time.'

'No. I refuse to accept that. He is nothing like Latchford.'

'So you say. And yet you never spoke out about it. Wasn't that part of your so-called risk assessment?'

She regarded her inquisitor with a defiant tilt of the head. 'Whatever people think of the job we do in the probation service, the pain and misery we see on a regular basis can't help but leave its mark. In my time I've encountered many real hard cases and mad bastards, and even with those who are barely criminals ours is a thankless task. But until I met Morgan Latchford, I had never dealt with anyone who gave me chills the way he did. He was just so detached, even describing his own crimes as if speaking about a third person. He referred to his younger self in a way others might a mythical creature. It wasn't just weird, it was downright creepy. Yet there was never anything explicit.'

Bliss sat back and spread his hands. 'All right Ms Pearson. Tell us how it all began, and why.'

'I wasn't the only one who'd noticed changes in Morgan lately. He rarely mentioned his family, but during the last review meeting he spoke about his daughter, specifically in connection to Haley Deerbourne and how Beccy was now about the same age as Haley had been.'

'Did he make any specific threats against his daughter at that time?'

'No, nothing like that. He was way too shrewd. But I didn't like the way he spoke about it, nor the look in his eyes while he did. To be honest, it really freaked me out.'

'Which led to you doing what?'

'I discussed my concerns with Grant. He was equally unnerved, but couldn't pinpoint why. He was also adamant that if we were going to accuse Morgan of something, we would require absolute proof. It was too high profile a case, and our jobs might well be on the line if we got it wrong. But I couldn't just let it go. I thought long and hard, and eventually decided the best way to learn more was to dip my toes in the dark web to see if I could find something in there.'

'What made you think of that? How would you even know what to do, where to start looking?'

'Are you kidding me?' she scoffed. 'Do you have any idea how many nonces and deviants I have to deal with? Yes, I can see my descriptions surprise you. Professionally we don't refer to them in that way, of course, but in private the language can get pretty ripe. Some of these people talk to us openly about this kind of stuff, DC Ansari. In great detail at times. You learn a lot, whether you want to or not.'

'Okay. So you went into the dark web with what intention?'

'Either to surreptitiously connect with Morgan himself, or to see if anybody online knew more about him behind closed doors.'

'And did you find either?'

'Not quite. But I happened upon somebody else who had similar interests as me. This particular user had been mentioned by others as possibly being a journalist, and other members of the chat sites we frequented were warned to steer clear. But I thought I could use it in my favour.'

'By posing as Morgan.'

'Yes. Prior to that I'd taken part under my own username, but it occurred to me that pretending I was him, especially with everything I knew about his crimes and his life as a child, I would either get closer or the real Morgan Latchford would reveal himself.'

'How did that work out?'

'It didn't really, but what it did do was bring Stuart Hammond out into the open and into the conversation. I hadn't expected that, though it didn't exactly surprise me when it happened.'

'So Hammond communicated with you both?'

'Yes. He quickly slammed the door closed on the journalist, who I now know to be Callum Oliver. But he was keen to communicate with me, as you might imagine. It didn't take long for him to suss me out as a fake, but by then we'd connected in a way neither of us had imagined. After a while he told me he wanted to know more about what the journalist had on Latchford, which is when I started getting closer to Callum – bearing in mind I still didn't know his name or who he worked for at that point. Eventually, his eagerness to sit down with Morgan Latchford got the better of him. When the time was right, I called him up to make arrangements for a first meeting.'

Bliss thought back to his discussion with Marty Lipman; the solicitor's explanation of his meeting with Oliver and how a call had left the journalist fearful and so keen to leave he'd left Lipman stranded.

'But it was Stuart Hammond who wanted to meet him instead,' he said softly, the unravelled threads finally tying together to make sense.

Ione Pearson nodded. Still, she sat upright, filled with self-righteous indignation at being questioned. Bliss got to his feet, a surprised Ansari standing moments afterwards. Bliss rested his hands on the table, palms down as he leaned across to catch the probation officer's tight glare.

'Whatever happened to Callum Oliver is on you,' he said. 'And if Phoebe and Beccy Latchford have come to any harm, that's on you as well. Believe me, Ms Pearson, defying a court ruling will be the least of your concerns by the time I'm done with you. You pious, self-righteous and arrogant bastards make me so bloody angry. You think you know everything, and yet time and time again you prove you know nothing at all.'

'Say what you like, think what you like. You've yet to prove a single thing against Stuart.'

Bliss continued to glare. 'It's just a matter of time,' he said. 'Believe me, it's just a matter of time.'

FORTY-FOUR

'How do you feel about going away on a little holiday?' Phoebe asked her daughter.

Beccy was being reasonable about their current circumstances for the first time since they'd settled in the room. There was no better time to address the future than when her child was calm and relaxed.

'Where to?' the girl answered after a moment of studied contemplation.

'I'm not sure yet. Just away somewhere.'

'Is Daddy coming?'

'No, sweetheart. Your daddy is… busy with work. You know how he gets sometimes.'

'You mean when he shuts himself in his room.'

'Yes. When he works in his office. Well, the thing is, sweetie, he's going to be busy for a while longer, so I thought you and I could spend our time together doing something different. Somewhere different.'

'But where, Mummy?'

Phoebe felt herself melting into her child's innocent, pretty face. She hated herself for the lies she felt forced into telling. But the man had insisted he knew of a refuge somewhere on the east coast. He wouldn't tell her precisely where, insisting it was the kind of place you never spoke about in case you were ever questioned or challenged about it beforehand. If you didn't know, you couldn't tell. He admitted it would take him a few days longer than expected to make the arrangements, but if he used his time well, he would also obtain new identities for her and Beccy. It was worth a few days of uncertainty, because the shelter would provide them with a safe house until they figured out a way to move on with their lives.

'I don't know, baby,' she breathed, dragging herself back into the moment.

'Well, when are we going?'

'Soon, sweetheart. Very soon. I know this must all feel strange at the moment, but you'll see… we're going to have a wonderful time together.'

'Is the beardy man coming with us?' Beccy had settled on that name right from the beginning, and nothing could shake it loose because it made her giggle every time she said it.

Phoebe shook her head. 'No. Well, yes, he is taking us in the car, but then he'll be leaving us there. What I do know is we'll be staying somewhere close to the sea, which will be nice as the weather gets warmer, right? Think about the beach we can play on, and we can do some paddling while we're there, too. We'll be staying in a nice big house with other mums like me and, best of all, other children like you. Lots of them, so you'll make new friends in no time at all.'

With a nod and a hike of her shoulders, Beccy turned back to her tablet. For her, the matter was settled, and once that decision had been made, there were no more questions. It left Phoebe feeling wretched all the same. Making what they were doing sound like a fun getaway to a holiday destination was essential in order to pacify her child, but each unspoken aspect of it felt like a sharp hook tearing at her heart.

I'm ripping you away from your daddy, who I know you love so much, baby. I'm giving him no choice, no opportunity to defend himself. He will have come home from his meeting on Monday to find an empty home, seemingly vandalised, both his girls gone. By now, he'll be beside himself with worry and fear. But also perhaps anger and thoughts of revenge.

Walking away from him had been nowhere near as hard as she would have liked, nowhere near as gut-wrenching as it ought to have been, which gave Phoebe a small measure of comfort. Whatever she had once felt for Morgan disappeared like a trail of smoke at the thought of his despicable intentions towards their own daughter. His actions when he was twelve years old were horrific enough. What he now wanted to do to Beccy made him the very personification of evil in her eyes.

Phoebe had already decided never to tell her daughter about that nauseating aspect of her father's nature. Beccy's initial misery would ultimately subside, but she never needed to know there were worse things in life than losing him.

As for herself, she could only be grateful for the reporter's intervention. This stranger had put himself out to make sure Morgan hurt neither of them, and she would never forget his kindness. By this time tomorrow, it would all be over, and Phoebe knew there was no way she could ever truly repay the man.

FORTY-FIVE

Bliss, Chandler, Bishop, and Warburton huddled together in one of the witness interview rooms. DC Ansari was the only member of the team who knew where they were, and Bliss was glad of the time and space in which to think and talk without constant interruptions. When he had finished updating his colleagues on the conversation with Ione Pearson, his DCI was the first to respond.

'I suppose it's always good to know why people do what they do, even if it only prepares us better for the next time. Even so, our takeaway from all this doesn't leave us any closer to finding our missing persons.'

Bliss wasn't so sure. 'You're right about one thing: discovering how all the main players came together is worth the time and effort. Hammond's interests are now obvious, as were Callum Oliver's. When it comes to Pearson, I got the impression she genuinely doesn't appreciate the harm her actions have caused. I believe her when she says her physical interventions were minimal, and it's entirely possible that she had no idea how Hammond intended to throw his weight around. Nor what his ultimate goal might have been. But she still provided the means, and she'll have to suffer the consequences of her actions.'

'And Latchford?' Bishop asked. 'Does this mean he was never engaged in all these online shenanigans?'

'If he was, we're not seeing it. We have nothing to suggest he was involved.'

Chandler exhaled heavily. 'And Pearson's fears about Latchford? How genuine are they?'

'Unknown. In fact, I can't see any way we'll ever know for sure. With him gone, all we have is supposition. He might well have been the reformed person he claimed to be. And yet we can't dismiss the feelings Pearson had about the man. Feelings McKinney confirmed he'd shared. They had both become uncomfortable around the man, but the fact remains, at the time of his death, Morgan Latchford had committed no crimes that we know of.'

'You mentioned I was right about one thing,' Warburton noted. 'What was I wrong about?'

Bliss smiled at his DCI having picked up on that. 'You said we were no closer to finding our missing persons, but I'm hoping that's not the case.'

'How so?'

'Something about the way Pearson phrased one of her answers stayed with me. She told us she and Hammond would continue to communicate the way they had been all along. We know this was on the dark web, and I got the distinct impression she meant they had been in contact since the events of Monday morning.'

'I'm not following you, Jimmy.'

'I couldn't work it out at first, either. I knew something was bothering me, but couldn't think what it was. And then it hit me: Hammond's Sporus username went dead last week. No activity whatsoever since. So I asked Gul to add a new flag and also trace the use of another username. If I'm right, we might get lucky.'

As if the moment had been planned and executed to perfection, right on cue there was a knock at the door and DC Ansari entered the room, panting as if she'd been hurrying along the corridor. 'Sorry to bother you, but I have something the boss wanted and he said I should interrupt.'

'Of course,' DCI Warburton said. 'I think we're all eager to know more about what's going on.'

Ansari remained standing by the door. 'Okay, so our trawl through the dark web alerts has given us some positive news.'

Chandler looked up, instantly alert to the possibilities. 'Sporus is back online?' she said excitedly.

But Ansari shook her head. 'No, Sarge. Born Free is.'

The room fell silent. Bliss blinked, momentarily unable to believe his hunch had paid off. 'In contact with?'

'Ione Pearson.'

'That makes no sense,' Chandler said, her face screwed up into a mask of bemusement. 'Born Free is the username Pearson used when posing as Morgan Latchford. Why on earth would she contact herself when everybody knows Latchford is now dead?'

'Did he use his phone?' Bliss asked Ansari.

'I don't have that information, boss. But remember, we think Callum Oliver had a personal laptop which we still haven't found.'

Bliss ran a hand across his scalp, his mind working furiously. 'It's Hammond,' he said, looking around the room. 'It has to be.'

'We do still have our journalist out there somewhere,' Warburton reminded him.

'No, it's not him. Switching usernames is of no benefit to him, and why would he even have access to it? Take it from me, this is Hammond. Pearson gave him the credentials for the username she chose when presenting herself online as Latchford. She probably worked out that we were likely to track down the Sporus user and trace it back to Hammond, but it never occurred to her that we'd find a way back to the name she had been using.'

'The sneaky bitch!' Bishop snapped. 'She kept that quiet. Did you manage to trace it, Gul?'

Ansari couldn't hide the grin as she nodded and said, 'Oh, yes. Not to a private address, sadly. But we may still be able to use it. The trace route came back to a hot spot wireless facility provided by the Horsefair Shopping Centre in Wisbech.'

Earlier, the team had speculated as to whether Hammond had kept moving further and further away over the week, or if he'd holed up somewhere close by to wait out the initial search. If this was him and not the reporter it was potentially a major break, and Bliss felt excited by the possibilities.

'Let's settle down and think about this rationally,' he said, regarding his team urgently. 'Two things have to happen: first, we need to discover everything Hammond has been doing while using the Born Free name, including anybody else he was in contact with and why; second, we need to get some troops into that shopping centre. That username is now flagged, so next time it comes up – if there is a next time – I want people there. Bish, find out everything you can about the place, entrances and exits, car parking, shops, opening times, and anything else you can think of. Speak to their security people as well. Let's get access to their CCTV...'

Bliss turned to DC Ansari. 'I take it you have a time code?'

'Yes. He was last online from 9.37 to 10.14 this morning.'

'Terrific. Then we need complete coverage during that window for the entire centre, including the car park if the wi-fi service extends that far.'

'I'll work with Bish while we're waiting for the dark web searches to come back to us.'

'This is big, people,' Bliss said, surveying his colleagues once more. 'If we get really lucky we'll find him in the security footage and then track him all the way to his car. Once we have the plate we can move on to traffic cameras. If we're less fortunate we can still set up there so that next time that flag pops up we're in position to be effective. At the very least we'll be able to confirm this is Hammond.'

'You thinking we should grab him up next time he appears or surveil him only?' Bishop asked.

'Surveillance, and a good team of them, too. Unless he has Phoebe and Beccy Latchford with him, which changes the game entirely. I think that's unlikely, but we must be prepared to take him out of the picture if they do show up. If he's on his own and we follow him to where he's keeping them, we can work on tactics depending on where they are, what kind of access it offers us.'

Bliss puffed out his cheeks, hoping to eject some of the electricity shooting through him. He recognised the significance of this breakthrough, and once it became a genuine lead it surely offered them more – a way through to Hammond and the Latchfords.

A dizzy spell caught up with him momentarily, leaving his ability to think or even speak in tatters for several long moments during which he became silent and introspective. His colleagues had come to recognize the symptoms, and also how to react; by saying nothing and doing nothing unless he specifically requested help. On this occasion it was a series of rapid attacks, landing on him in waves, so the trick was to focus. He had learned from a fellow Meniere's sufferer early on that when the spins hit, you had to concentrate in the same way a dancer did when they were literally spinning in place; to focus on something when they began and refocus on the same spot upon return of the head to that position. Bliss did much the same until his equilibrium returned. He exhaled heavily until his lungs were fully expelled, before drawing in a long, deep breath and repeating the process twice more.

The world righted itself. It became a fragile platform on which to stand, vulnerable to misstep and a tendency to favour one leg when he walked which caused him to take each stride on a slight slant, constantly having to shift his position while in motion. When seated he simply had to wait it out. Finally, a series of fast blinks culminating with one final long stare directly ahead. Once he could hold that position with no involuntary wander of his eyes and the accompanying feeling of light-headedness, he was ready to get on with his day once more.

'I don't know about you lot, but I'm starting to feel something familiar,' he said, dismissing the sickly churning in his stomach. 'I'm starting to feel that net tighten.'

It pleased him greatly to hear ripples of agreement, and to hear it reverberate around the room without DC Hunt's voice chiming in at the end to warn them of something catastrophic in their line of thinking. There never had been, but it was his way to find fault wherever he could, whether or not it existed. The thought reminded Bliss of something. Somebody he needed to have words with.

Ansari's ringing phone caught their attention. She spoke for a few minutes, and when she broke away her face was positively beaming. 'That was tech, boss,' she said to Bliss. 'They grabbed up the earlier exchanges between Hammond and Pearson. There's nothing in their chat to lead us to him, but that may not matter. Because Hammond said he would be back in the chatroom at 8.30 tomorrow morning to update Pearson on his final plans.'

'We don't actually know it's Hammond,' Warburton said, cautiously.

'It's him,' Bliss said, clenching both fists and punching the air with them. 'The bastard's going back to that shopping centre.'

'Even if that's true, we don't know precisely where. I've been to that shopping centre. It's not the biggest, but it's not small, either.'

'It doesn't matter,' Bliss assured her. 'We'll be waiting for him. We'll have eyes on the security feeds, watching every way in and out. Plus we'll have people outside in the car park, in case he picks up the wi-fi signal from his vehicle and doesn't enter the centre itself.'

'That'll take a few bodies, boss,' Chandler said.

'It will. I'll have the Hinchingbrooke surveillance team on the plot to help us out. In fact, I want them to trail his car when he leaves. We'll rope in CID volunteers as well.'

'He's expecting to talk to Pearson online,' Bishop pointed out. 'Can we use that to our advantage?'

Bliss shook his head. 'I wondered the same thing, but I think it's too risky. If we let her do it, she might tell him we're onto him. If we try to do it ourselves, we might miss a pre-arranged word or phrase telling him they're safe.'

'We could ask her.'

'And she could lie. No, it's not worth the gamble. Besides, we don't need it. If he has the Latchfords with him, we take him before they can come to any harm. Otherwise we track him as planned.'

DCI Warburton cleared her throat and said, 'I don't want to piss on your cornflakes, but I do have to point out the high element of risk involved in that strategy. If we allow him to re-enter the building in which he's keeping Phoebe and Beccy, then we have a potential hostage situation on our hands.'

Bliss was prepared for this. 'I accept that, boss. But this is one of those rock and hard place situations. If we snatch him up too soon we may never learn where they are and we might end up losing them. I can see no alternative. Ideally we'd have a short window of time between discovering their whereabouts and him moving from his vehicle back to them, but we can't rely on that gap being large enough. What we can do is have a drone up in the air from the moment he leaves the car park, and when he stops at a likely looking spot we can check for thermal images. If we get the word to go then we go, but if not, if there's not enough time, then yes, we might need to negotiate. It's not ideal, but unless you can give me something better then we have to roll with it.'

'We'll need a risk assessment plan for this one, Jimmy.'

'Of course. And we'll get as close as we can in the car park areas. Staff are instructed to leave their own wheels at the end of the rows, letting customers have the spaces closest to the shops. We'll have our people on him from the moment he pulls up.' Bliss glanced across at his partner. 'Including me and you, Pen. I want to be there for this, because provided Phoebe and Beccy Latchford are still alive, he's going to lead us straight to them. I feel it with every fibre of my being.'

FORTY-SIX

After Bliss had collected Molly from the railway station, the two of them sat on the bench in his garden watching the sun disappear beyond nearby rooftops while they chatted. Warm evening air kissed their flesh, and Bliss felt his muscles relaxing one by one.

'I'd like to get some koi when I have my own place,' she told him, breaking a period of comfortable silence. 'It's so peaceful looking at them do their thing.'

He agreed. 'To those fish, it may be just swimming around making different patterns in the water, but for me they provide tranquillity and escape.'

Molly turned sideways to peer hard at him. She wore a vintage Creedence Clearwater Revival 'Gator' T-shirt, which he found himself slightly envious of. He regarded the item of clothing as further evidence of his influence over her musical tastes. 'You look tired, Jimbo,' she said. 'But you also look different.'

'Differed how?' he asked.

'I'm not sure. More content, maybe.'

Bliss acknowledged her observation with a nod. She had blossomed in the short time he had known her, and was becoming a beautiful and sensitive adult. He told her about his recent revelations, how he'd finally accepted his lot and moved on. He also admitted the past week had drained him.

'So, yes,' he said. 'I suppose you could say I am both tired and different.'

'No more roughing up the bad guys, eh? Keeping a lid on your temper.'

He tried to dissuade her of the notion that he had ever roughed up anybody without due cause, but she wasn't having any of it. He declined to mention the conversation he'd had earlier with DI Bentley from CID. The pair had discussed the supporting role required for the surveillance op, after which Bliss had verbally laid into his colleague for talking out of turn with Chief Superintendent Feeley regarding both DC Hunt and the twin operations. At one point, their disagreement had become heated, provoking a lot of finger pointing and aggressive posturing. Bentley admitted nothing, but had been the first to back down. Beyond his fellow Inspector's bluster and annoyance at having been found out, Bliss had detected shame and unspoken remorse. They parted with a better understanding of one another.

'So you're really okay with your life?' Molly asked him.

He raised his beer bottle. 'I am now.'

She raised her own. 'From what I know, it's about bloody time.'

'You'll get no argument from me on that score. Fact is, I've been bound to Hazel's ghost for more than twice as long as I was actually married to her. I should have arrived at that conclusion much earlier, but now that I have, there's no looking back.'

Molly regarded him with one of her easy grins. 'Sounds to me as if you're wearing big boy pants now.'

'If you say so,' he said, chuckling. 'And how about you – what's new? How's school?'

'All right. Surprisingly good, considering my lack of education down the years.'

'Formal education. I dare say you learned a great deal on the streets. I'm glad school is going well for you, though. I was worried how you'd take to it. You must be due exams soon.'

She sniffed dismissively. 'Yep. Later this month and into June. I'm not worried about them.'

Bliss smiled. 'I doubt you're worried about anything these days. So, what else is new in Mollywood?'

'Um, well, I have a boyfriend.'

His brow crinkled. 'Tell me his name. I'll have him checked out.'

'I'm sure you would, which is why I'm not giving it to you.'

'Fair enough. But you know I'll find out, anyway. I am a detective. So, is it serious?'

'Not really. We're more friends with benefits.'

Bliss spat out the swallow of beer he'd just taken. 'You what?!'

Molly roared, her laughter echoing off the fencing. 'I'm having you on, Jimbo. We've only just started seeing each other, you doughnut. Anyway, you know better than most what kind of life I had before I met you. I'm hardly a virgin, am I? Damaged goods, more like.'

'Hey!' he grew serious and levelled a straight finger at her. 'Don't you dare talk like that. I won't hear of that damaged goods bollocks. None of what happened was your fault. And besides, you've put all that behind you. Any boy would be lucky to have you for a girlfriend.'

She blushed and sipped some of her beer. They sat in silence for a while. When she next spoke, Molly did so with hesitancy. 'Do you ever think what might have happened to me if you'd not been the first up on that roof?'

He had. More times than he could count. In physical and emotional distress, she had stood on the edge of a high roof in the pouring rain, a frigid December breeze whipping at the material of the thin white nightdress plastered to her frail body. To this day, he refused to believe this girl he had come to know and love would have stepped off that roof, but understood how she had become convinced living was at that point a worse alternative.

Until he'd come along, uncertain and unfit to talk her down.

In the end, he'd wrestled her to the ground, which had come as a shock to them both. A county lines mule, abused by those who used her to move drugs from London to other towns and cities, Molly had snapped when two men attempted to satiate their desire for an early morning quickie. She fought off the man whose home she had slept in, stabbing him in the process. Days later, the same man had abducted her from a temporary foster home, and it was Bliss and his team who had rescued her from his clutches. He had saved her life, only to have to save it again. With the dealer and his crew safely behind bars, this was the first time she had felt confident enough to return to Peterborough.

'The main thing is you're happy now,' he told her as the orange and crimson sky darkened to deeper hues, purple jagged ribbons like marbling slicing through. 'Safe, happy, and with a brighter and better future to come.'

'I'll drink to that,' Molly said, tipping her bottle once more. 'And hopefully we can say the same for you.'

'I'm content. Just like you said. I'll settle for that.'

Appraising him closely once again, she said, 'You know, I realise you couldn't take me in when I was in trouble. But even though I now have parents who adopted me and love me as much as they love their biological kid, I still don't think I could have got through this without you being there for me.'

'I don't know about that, Molly. I've always thought of you as resilient enough to withstand and overcome anything.'

She looked down at the ground. 'Maybe. But you gave me the strength I needed when I was at rock bottom. I feel secure with you in my life, Jimbo. I've never felt that before, and it's still you who makes me feel safe now.'

Bliss smiled. Her words pleased him, though they made him feel emotional. 'If that's the case, then I'm glad of it. Couldn't be happier about it, in fact. I told you this before, Molly, but if I'd ever been fortunate enough to have had a daughter, I'd have wanted her to be like you. To have your character, your courage, your spirit, and your heart.'

'Not to mention my brain and my stunning good looks.'

'Well, let's not go too far. Also, I'd probably want a daughter of mine to have less to say for herself.'

This time they clinked bottles.

'You got any new tunes for me, Jimbo?' Molly asked.

'As it happens, I do. That song I told you about earlier, when I mentioned my conversation with Pen… I'd like to know what you think.'

'Okay. But what kind of name is Porcupine Tree?'

'I know. It's so desperately proggy, isn't it? But you liked a few of the tracks I sent you before, so I want you to hear *Pariah*. I don't mind admitting it changed my entire outlook on life.'

'If it did that for you, then I have to hear it for myself. I'm sure I'll enjoy it – you don't steer me wrong too often.'

Bliss nodded, but said nothing. As daylight faded over a distant an unseen horizon, he took a deep breath, exhaled for a long time, and allowed the moment to soothe him. Tomorrow would bring about another difficult day, but with Molly sleeping here in the spare bedroom, he thought he might have a restful night ahead of him. Already her mere presence felt like a soothing balm. She wasn't his daughter, they were not related at all, yet she was family. He hoped she always would be.

FORTY-SEVEN

Anxiety twisted inside Bliss's stomach. The entire area was filled with and surrounded by professionals who were exceptionally good at their jobs, but he knew how bad this could turn out if events conspired against them. What if Hammond had woken up that morning and gone on the run without contacting Ione Pearson one last time? What if he got into a fatal road traffic collision on his way to the centre, losing his life before he could tell the emergency services where he was holding Phoebe and Beccy Latchford? Or what if he'd not been holding them at all, but had already made sure neither of them could talk about what he had done?

'Don't,' Chandler said to him, derailing him from his miserable train of thought.

'Don't what?'

'Don't twist yourself into knots. I know that face, Jimmy. I've seen that squirming before as well. You're sitting there considering all the negative things that might happen, rather than focus on the positives. Where's the new Jimmy Bliss got to this morning?'

The two of them were sitting at a table in Costa, hot drinks going untouched on the table in front of them. It was 7.23am according to Bliss's watch, and each minute that ticked by added another layer of worry, another twinge of the gut.

An hour earlier, the major crimes team had met up with surveillance specialists at a staging post on the site of a now defunct hand car wash outfit on the outskirts of Wisbech. Rowena Shanks was not on duty, her place as leader of the shadowing unit taken by DS Tom Cavanagh, an officer Bliss had never worked with before. The two men pored over an A3 printed map of the shopping centre. Ingress and egress points were marked clearly in bright orange highlights; far too many of them for Bliss's liking.

The centre was nothing like he had imagined. With Queensgate in Peterborough, entrances and exits to the self-enclosed shopping mall were obvious. But the Horsefair shops were part of an open centre, starting with the car park at one end and running through several streets up to and including the marketplace, leaving far too many areas to cover. But Bishop had worked hard with the town security offices to map out CCTV camera locations, each identified by red circles on the map. These allowed Bliss and Cavanagh to develop a plan to have enough people on the ground to cover any blind spots. Between the digital and physical surveillance, the entire centre could be monitored at all times.

The company who provided wireless internet access had confirmed their coverage areas, which extended out to both the car park and bus station. The former was where Bliss believed they had the best chance of locating Hammond, suspecting the man might not even leave his vehicle. But realising the lure of breakfast might prove too much to resist, he and Chandler were sitting in the coffee shop, with Bishop and Ansari having eyes on Greggs bakery.

Bliss blew on his drink and took a sip, the heat adding to the misery his stomach was experiencing. Whatever the odds, this was always how surveillance jobs affected him. Darker thoughts crept in unbidden, worrying at him to the point where he became convinced failure was always only one step away. As he told anybody who commented on his mannerisms, fear kept him sharp. Keeping the adrenaline pumping was a necessary evil, even though for most of the time he felt like throwing up.

'Twenty minutes before we're relieved,' he told Chandler after another check of the watch. They had decided to switch couples inside Costa every forty-five minutes, and Bliss was keen to get back outside into the fresh air. He wanted to be here should Hammond walk through the door, wanted to be standing close to Greggs should he step inside the bakery, wanted to be sitting out in the car park when the man arrived and when he left again. It was his way, and how he had avoided an ulcer over the years was a miracle.

Not that he believed in those.

*

Phoebe awoke that morning to find the reporter sitting close by, watching her without blinking. Alongside him, Beccy sat with her knees pulled up to her chest. Her little girl had always looked so cute in her Disney Princess pyjamas, but not today. Red and swollen by tears, Beccy's eyes closed and squeezed out another trickle of sorrow. She sniffed and snuffled, and when her eyes popped open again, they implored her mother to help her.

The shiny silver-coloured tape fastened around her daughter's wrists and ankles screamed at Phoebe, yet for what felt like an age she lay like a rock on the inflatable mattress before eventually pulling herself up onto one elbow. The item now capturing her full attention was a knife the man held in his right hand.

'Sleep well?' he asked her.

She stared at him, unable to find her voice. *What was going on? This was insane!*

He let out a long sigh, allowing his features to become deeply solemn. 'This was never going to end well,' he admitted in a small, soft voice. 'I was foolish to believe otherwise. I'm sorry to say this, but it was inevitable. I've held out for as long as I am able, Phoebe. Please believe me when I say I wanted a far better outcome for the three of us.'

'What…? I don't understand. I don't know what you mean,' she said to him, her breath catching with every other word. 'What are you doing? What's going on?'

He pulled a face as if wincing in pain. 'There have been times this week when I've come close to leaving you both here unharmed and just driving away. On a couple of occasions, I even considered letting you go – you and Beccy. But the simple truth – one that's taken me an awfully long time to realise – is we are who we are meant to be. Not on the surface, where we can pretend and make do, but deep down where the truth sits in judgement on us all.'

Phoebe shook her head. 'You're not making any sense.' She sat all the way up, reaching a hand out towards her daughter. Before she could offer an encouraging squeeze to let Beccy know everything was going to be all right, the man slapped her arm away and pushed the knife closer to her face. He leaned forward, forcing her backwards.

'Those things I told you about your husband… I actually have no way of knowing if they are true. What I can tell you is that I believe he was also who he was meant to be rather than the man he presented himself as. But, I can't know that for certain. All I have to go on is me. And me… well, I am an outcast. I'm not fit to dine at the table with good and decent human beings. And do you know why?'

Phoebe said nothing, somehow seeing her daughter's pitiful eyes, his desolate face, and the sharp steel blade of the knife he held, all together in one terrible collage. The sight provoked sharp, stabbing pains in her chest.

'I'll tell you why. Because I'm not human,' he said flatly. 'How can I be when I did those terrible things all those years ago? How can I be when I've carried those ghastly things around with me ever since? How can I be when I've held them close, not with shame or anger, but more a sense of unfulfilled angst? I have to confess, I'm not a reporter, Phoebe. A few decades ago I was your husband's friend, sentenced just as he was for the murder of a child the same age as your sweet Beccy. Do you know what your husband and I tried to do to Haley Deerbourne, Phoebe? It wasn't just the beating or the torture or shutting her away in that freezer chest. No, we tried to have sex with her as well. Tried and failed, I might add. The pair of us. Looking at Beccy here, Dean obviously overcame it all eventually. But me… I never did. And the thing is, I wanted to. I wanted to so badly, but I never could. I still want to. But not with a woman like you, Phoebe. As pretty as you are, as lovely as that figure of yours is, I've no desire to finish the job I started and failed at when I was twelve, by losing my cherry to you. But with Beccy… that's another matter entirely.'

As he spoke, he drew the tip of the blade towards the young girl's face. He stared at Phoebe and shook his head. 'Don't you try anything. Don't you even think about it. I'd prefer to take her alive, but I'm prepared to do so while she's still warm if I have to.'

A scream erupted from the core of Phoebe's soul, but she clamped her lips together and kept them pressed tight until she was confident the sound had died away inside her chest. Instead, she looked at her daughter and summoning up all the courage she possessed, said, 'It's okay, sweetheart. Everything is going to be just fine. Mummy's here. Mummy won't let anything bad happen to you.'

Hammond cleared his throat. 'How touching. Now then, I have to leave you for a short while. I was going to go through all this when I returned, but the moment I saw you both sleeping, I couldn't help myself. I'm so close to the point of release that I can barely contain whatever's inside me. But I'll be back, that you can count on. I have to leave one final message, though, and then I can be at peace. But before I pop out, you and I have to come to an understanding. Okay?'

She said nothing.

He opened his eyes wider and waggled the knife in his hand, slipping a sidelong glance at her child. 'Okay?' he asked again.

Still Phoebe said nothing, but this time she offered a stilted nod.

'Good. Then please take note: I'll leave Beccy here, but you are coming downstairs with me. I feel it's best to separate the two of you now that you know who and what I am. I won't be gone long, so she'll be fine left like this. Though I will, of course, fasten her to something solid so that she won't slip away. But I'll be doing so only after I've done the same to you. You won't be able to scream or shout with your mouths taped up, but you'll be able to breathe and tire yourselves out by wriggling to get free. But if I were you, I'd save your energy, because neither of you is escaping.'

He stood, tall and upright. Closed his eyes for a moment while he gathered his thoughts. He said nothing further at first, breathing steadily as if coming to terms with a wave of fresh emotions. Then he swallowed thickly and said, 'You'll both be waiting here for me when I get back. I'll see to that. And Phoebe... let me make this clear to you so's there are no misunderstandings: how you behave from this point on will dictate how badly you'll be hurting when I'm done with you both. Because although I failed miserably the last time I tried to have sex with an eight-year-old girl, I was much more successful handing out a beating along with some particularly interesting methods of torture. You'll do well to remember that. Understood?'

Phoebe nodded.

*

Bliss strolled aimlessly along Hill Street until he came to the Holland & Barrett health food shop. He thought back to his taste in dry cereal and sandwiches with odd fillings, and immediately felt out-of-place looking at a window display of supplements and protein powders. But he paid no attention to the contents, instead checking out the reflection of Greggs to the left behind him. He continued to watch as Chandler strode by before pausing outside Superdrug, and with her in place he moved on. The bus station lay to his left, with Argos directly opposite. Tension continued to build and Bliss felt the ache of it in his muscles.

Pausing as if looking up bus timetables, he heard a crackle in his left ear followed by a voice he didn't recognise.

'Blue team, SO Three. I have contact. I say again, Blue team, SO Three. Contact, contact.'

Blue team had been assigned to the car park, with four surveillance officers split between three vehicles. SO Three was stationed directly opposite the bays closest to the centre on the upper deck. It was he who had spotted Hammond first.

'This is command,' DS Cavanagh said in response. 'Do you have eyes on suspect's vehicle?'

The officer confirmed, offering the make, model, colour, and licence plate. He finished by advising everyone on the same channel that their man was heading for the stairs which led down into the centre, at which point Bliss realised he'd be only yards away from their quarry in the next thirty seconds. Hammond had to be on his own, otherwise SO Three would have mentioned the presence of others.

Allocated the number one slot as part of his team colour, Bliss spoke into the microphone clipped inside the collar of his lightweight jacket. 'This is Green team, SO One to all green and orange team members. Contact will be on high alert. Do not – I repeat – do not meet his gaze. If you receive direct eye contact, do not look immediately away. Raise your eyebrows and smile if necessary, but then continue doing what you were doing.'

His major crimes team had been assigned to the colour green, while orange were detectives drawn from CID. None of them were surveillance specialists, and while at the staging point they had gone over these critical aspects of watching and following a target, Bliss knew it would do no harm to issue a reminder. They could not allow the man to get spooked. Now that they knew he was on the plot, green and orange would funnel back to their respective vehicles, leaving only the specialists to maintain eyes on. Some of them would have to walk past Hammond, and they needed to brush by as if they were shadows.

Bliss turned away from the timetable boards and headed towards the car park. In his peripheral vision, he noticed Chandler walking a couple of paces further ahead. He did not turn, he did not look back. Hammond was in the net as planned, and the mouth of it was closing around him.

FORTY-EIGHT

The units followed Hammond out of Wisbech town centre and on to North Brink, which initially ran parallel to the river Nene. Surveillance officer One from blue team had affixed a magnetised tracker to Hammond's grey Toyota Previa, which allowed the teams to follow at a distance. This was particularly useful on the longer, straighter sections of the narrow road. The drone control vehicle kept pace with the UAV as it tracked their man from above. Cavanagh had also sent a biker on ahead, overtaking the Toyota early on so that they'd have an additional presence up front.

Before long, they moved beyond the bulk of residential dwellings, after which they shot by a scattering of business properties and small homes. The land then opened up to wide expanses of crop fields. Eventually the green flood barriers to their nearside gave way to strips of embankment which developed into increasingly wider stretches of pasture. The road surface was smooth, but the lane ultimately narrowed to become single track. Every so often they had to pause to allow traffic through from the opposite direction. Eventually, the caravan of surveillance vehicles curved right, taking them away from the river. Bliss eyed the Sat Nav, looking at their route ahead. Just as he noticed the point at which North Brink became Rummer's Lane, a voice in his ear cried out, 'Taking a left, left, left onto Mouth Lane.'

Bliss took the same turning approximately thirty seconds later, following the lead vehicle containing DS Cavanagh. After making the left he depressed a button to put out a message across the secure channel. 'Drone control… this is Green One. We've been driving for a good ten or twelve minutes now. I don't think it can be too much further. Any chance you can get the drone ahead of him, see what properties there might be out this way. It's looking pretty barren and flat, so I doubt there will be many places to choose from.'

Seconds later, he received a reply, informing him that pushing the drone further ahead would send it out of its legal range.

'Fuck that,' he snapped back. 'We're not going to need the drone footage for video evidence. I just want the thermal imaging.'

'No can do, Green One. These models have on-board GPS, recording distance from my controller to the device itself. They'll revoke my licence to fly this thing if I let it loose.'

Bliss slapped the steering wheel. 'Come on! You must let it slip occasionally, right? Make one of those occasions now.'

'Anything lasting longer than thirty seconds and I'm done.'

'Good enough. So give me thirty seconds, then come back within range, wait ten and send it out again. But I doubt you'll need that long.'

The light static of complete radio silence filled his ears, then: 'Green One… I'll do what I can.'

Bliss was about to thank the man behind the controller, when another voice rang out. 'Contact has stopped, stopped, stopped. Wait one…'

'Shit!' Bliss thumped his steering wheel with the meat of his left fist. He glanced across at Chandler. 'We're going to be too late grabbing him up before he gains entry to whatever property he's stopped at.'

As he spoke, he spotted the first surveillance vehicle pulling up onto the grassy verge ahead, its brake lights glowing like narrowed devil's eyes. He slowed and pulled up behind it, followed moments later by a second motorcycle, a van, two more cars, and finally the drone control vehicle. As Bliss climbed out of his pool car, he noticed they were lined up outside a square and stubby modern brick building whose sign told them it was the Mouth Lane pumping station. Up ahead, the lane veered slightly to the right, concealed by what looked like a new property surrounded on three sides by trees. A steep bank rose to his left, and he was surprised to hear the river flowing on the other side.

DS Cavanagh came jogging back to meet him.

'We missed our opportunity,' he said with a sigh of regret. 'A couple of hundred yards further down the lane, there's a pub called the Wounded Crane. I'm told by our officer on the motorbike that it appears to be closed down and currently out of business, but the Toyota pulled into its grounds and parked up around the back out of sight of the road.'

Bliss couldn't hide his disappointment. Their tough job had just become harder still. 'Why didn't he give us a shout out when he rode by it? We could have done with that heads-up.'

'He didn't think about it as it was boarded up. It was an honest mistake.'

'What about the drone?' Bliss asked, looking up at the bright blue sky.

'Don't worry. It's up there. Let's have a word with the operator, shall we?'

The two men walked back to the control vehicle. Pulling open the back doors, they were confronted by an officer transfixed to the drone feed monitor. He looked up sharply at the incursion of daylight and immediately nodded. 'I have heat sources inside the building,' he told them. 'Three of them. One on the move, the other two stationary. I can also see the bloom of a hot engine outside.'

Bliss had just thought through the implications when he heard pounding feet coming their way. He turned to look up at DC Ansari's anxious expression and immediately knew they were in trouble.

'Boss, I just got word from the techs monitoring Hammond's internet access back at the shopping centre. At first all he did was enter Ione Pearson's username, followed by a question mark. He repeated it every five minutes for half an hour. That's all he was doing when we saw him with the laptop in his car. But just before he exited the chatroom, and presumably because he'd not received a response, he wrote something we need to concern ourselves with immediately.'

'Is he going to top himself?' Bliss asked, having suspected this was where they were headed.

'Yes. At least, that's what he wrote. But before he closed out, he added something else.' Ansari showed Bliss her phone, on which he read Hammond's final message.

> BEFORE I TAKE MY LEAVE FOR THE FINAL TIME, I'M GOING TO FINISH WHAT I STARTED THIRTY-TWO YEARS AGO. THIS TIME I WILL BE SUCCESSFUL. I'M FINALLY GOING TO DO WHAT COMES NATURALLY TO OTHER MEN. AND THEN WHEN I'M DONE I'M GOING TO PUT HER AND HER MOTHER OUT OF THEIR MISERY.

FORTY-NINE

His mood had altered dramatically. She noticed the shift right away. Earlier, he had threatened and intimidated. Yet, he had also been upbeat. This juxtaposition had given her some small measure of hope. But his demeanour was darker now, more intense and brooding. Not that he had to say a word. It was more about the laden slouch as he moved, his laboured breathing, the dour expression on his face, and the way he seldom blinked. He'd been back for a good few minutes before he came across to her, kneeling on the floor beside the mattress on which she had remained since he'd left.

'I think you know what I have to do to Beccy. By now you must realise I have no say in the matter. What was once a desire has become a compulsion.'

Phoebe shook her head urgently, her voice strangled by the tape wrapped over her mouth. She breathed heavily, beseeching him with tearful eyes not to harm her daughter.

'I know you would offer yourself in her place, but like I already told you, that's not where I am in my sexual development. What I'm telling you is, it's happening, and no amount of struggle on your part can prevent it. And of course, I can't just allow you to walk away after I'm done. I'm going to have to take care of you, too, though I haven't yet decided how. Perhaps for your sake I could snap your neck – something quick, dead before the pain sets in. I could also just leave you to it, make sure you can't move and let time and nature take its course. I appear to be good at that, if nothing else.'

He sighed as if regretting the array of choices before him. Perhaps even the decisions he had already made. 'I suppose you must be wondering why I didn't get it over with five days ago, or at any time since. The thing is, Phoebe, I wanted a taste, just a small sample of the life Dean – sorry, Morgan – had with you and Beccy. I've always wondered what it might be like to experience that kind of relationship. To have a partner, a lover, a wife, to become a parent, to have that close family unit to come home to each day. For a time, I dared to imagine I might have all that with you two. But I was deluding myself. I can't possibly replicate what he had with you and the child you created together. I don't know what I was thinking. If I was thinking at all. Don't get me wrong, I'd always intended for it to end this way if all else failed. But I wanted to give myself time to breathe it in, to get a sense of what my life could have been if only things had not gone the way they did all those years ago.'

He paused. Looked up and exhaled deeply. Then he said, 'I don't know if this will make it worse or better for you, but I thought you needed to know the truth. There's no reason to be dishonest with you now. When I took your phone on Monday morning while you were packing up your things and getting Beccy ready to leave… I spoke to hubby. I told him I had you. You and his spawn. I told him I was going to hurt you both in so many twisted ways. Unless… unless he did exactly as I said. The meeting he went to early that morning, well, there actually wasn't one. Through the wonder of email, an acquaintance of mine posed as the local author he was supposedly having a business breakfast with that day. After all, I had to get him out of the house, didn't I? But you don't have to worry about him any longer, Phoebe. Not about him, and nor do you have to concern yourself with what might have been. He's not going to miss you and little Beccy. I have to say he pleaded with me not to hurt either of you. He begged, he sobbed, he pretty much broke down at the thought of it. He told me he'd do anything to spare you both. I put him to the test. And I have to say, he passed with flying colours. He really must have thought the world of his little family. Right up until the moment his body was obliterated by a speeding train.'

This time she wriggled and squirmed, struggling to free herself as scalding tears burned her eyes. Snot bubbles formed and burst, her breath came in ragged, uneven gasps behind the tape. She screamed and screamed again, making almost no sound at all other than a muffled, desperately shrill shriek of pain and misery and loss.

'I know, I know,' he said softly, leaning forward to stroke her hair. 'But at least he won't have to go on without you. You and his lovely daughter.' His hand fell away and his knees popped when he stood upright. 'Speaking of whom, I'm going to spend some time with her now. I doubt it will take me long.' He put a finger to his mouth as Phoebe shrieked once more. 'Hush. Hush now. I won't lie to you again, so please understand your little girl is going to suffer. But I will do one thing for you, Phoebe: I will make it quick.'

FIFTY

DETECTIVE SERGEANT CAVANAGH HAD instructed one of his officers to contact the owners of the Wounded Drake to see if they had blueprints of the pub. It was a standard move, but Bliss was convinced they had no time to wait.

'He's going to kill both of them,' he said to a small gathering, including Bishop, Chandler, and Cavanagh, together with two of his fellow surveillance officers. 'I don't think he intends to string it out much longer, either. So, with the greatest of respect for the job you and your team do and have done so far, Tom, this is now a major crimes operation once again.'

'I won't argue with you there,' the sergeant said, with no trace of chagrin. 'But I have to be prepared for the possibility of him moving on, with or without them.'

'Agreed. But it's my task to make sure he never gets that opportunity.'

'How do you intend to do that?'

'We have to get in there.'

'And what if you can't? What if we end up with a serious hostage situation?'

Cavanagh was right. But the specialist hostage and crisis

negotiators were back at county HQ, just shy of an hour away. Gul Ansari had taken a couple of relevant courses, but had no experience. He asked across comms for any member of CID to respond if they were fully trained at the job, but received no reply. With no other options available to him, Bliss put in a call to request a specialist attend the scene, after which he also called the firearms unit to ask for the closest Armed Response Vehicle – minus the blues and twos.

'I've followed procedure up to this point,' he said to the surveillance DS. 'But you know we can't wait for them to arrive. Phoebe and Beccy Latchford might have only minutes.'

'It's your call now, Inspector. I don't envy you this one. No matter what you decide, if you get the wrong outcome it will have been a poor decision.'

'Yeah. And even if we get the right result from going in, DCS Feeley will chew me out for it.'

'I imagine you're thinking better that than doing nothing and ending up with two victims on your hands.'

Bliss nodded. His colleague had said it all.

He looked across at the drone operator. 'Can you get me a decent shot of the back of the building?'

'Of course. Anything specific?'

'It's a pub. It has to have a cellar, probably around the back where they take deliveries. A cellar provides us with an alternative way inside. Hammond thinks he has this place to himself, so let's disabuse him of that notion.'

Moments later, he'd gathered together the entire Thorpe Wood contingent. After explaining the bind they were in and how he intended resolving matters, he asked for any dissenters to speak up. Nobody did. They each recognised how this was supposed to go: draw up a risk assessment and wait for the specialist personnel to arrive on the plot. But this incident wasn't theoretic, it was the reality of an extraordinary situation. Neither was it just about the high risk of Hammond murdering his two prisoners. It also concerned his other, more repulsive intentions towards the eight-year-old girl. The very thought made Bliss shudder.

Protocol insisted he and his fellow officers bide their time, and provided they got their potential victims out alive, it should be regarded as a job well done. Yet all Bliss could think of was the one sickening abuse Haley Deerbourne had been spared, and he had no intention of standing by while Beccy Latchford paid the price for decades of Stuart Hammond's emotional anguish.

'I'm looking for three volunteers,' he said, huffing a stifled laugh when all hands shot up. He gave a single nod of gratitude. 'Thank you. I won't forget it. But I need only three. Bish, I'm sorry mate, but you're going to have to stay out here. I need you to mind the shop while I'm gone. Penny, Gul, Phil… you're up.'

'Send me in with them, boss,' Bishop pleaded with him. 'You take control from here. This is your op.'

Bliss nodded. 'Exactly. It's my op. If it all goes tits up in there, then the blowback comes my way, not yours. End of, Bish.'

He had the drone operator play back the footage he'd just recorded. The pub did indeed have a cellar. There was also a rear door along with several windows to choose from. He nodded at the screen. 'What do you make of the thermal images?' he asked.

The man pointed at two heat signatures close together. 'Here we have one lying prone, the other standing, so presumably the latter is our man Hammond. From what I can tell, I have to think he's with the woman.' He jabbed a finger at the screen. 'That means this is the girl, and I reckon she is in a room upstairs.'

Bliss tried to visualise the layout, but there were many areas of uncertainty. He and his three colleagues would be walking into the unknown, but the images would help. 'That bird up there must be due a battery change,' he said.

'It is. It probably has about another five to ten minutes of flying time left on that charge.'

'Okay. So bring it back in now and make the change. We're going to work out how best to get into place around the back of the building. Once we're in position, send it back up and let me know if positions inside have changed, and how.'

'Will do.'

Bliss trotted back to the spot at which his team stood grouped together. He was bitterly disappointed not to have seen four heat signatures inside the abandoned pub, having hoped to find Callum Oliver still alive and being held prisoner. Chandler showed him what they had been looking at while he was gone; an overhead view of the property. He immediately noticed the problem they were going to have approaching it over flat, open ground. Moving in line towards the side of the building afforded them the least opportunity of being spotted if Hammond happened to gaze out of the windows. Plus it was the only way they were going to get close without risking full exposure. At night it would be a doddle. Here in the bright morning sunlight they were fully visible, with even their charted route feeling too risky.

He had an idea, but he needed to discuss it with Cavanagh. 'How do you feel about smashing up two of your motors?' he asked.

The wily sergeant merely raised an eyebrow. Bliss grinned. 'I thought you might say that. Listen, I think the best chance we have of getting in there unseen is by creating a diversion. I'm thinking you could have a car sideswipe a van as it tries to overtake, with your motorbike rider coming in the opposite direction. I'm hoping the sound of the collision will attract Hammond's attention and draw him to the front of the building. The resulting verbal abuse, some pushing and shoving that follows might just keep his focus on your people and not our victims long enough for us to make our way over and find a way in.'

Cavanagh thought about it for only a few seconds before pursing his lips. 'That could work. I can have my people put on a good show.'

'Have one of your female officers be part of it. Tell her to make her voice as shrill as possible. Have her eff and jeff a bit, you know, acting like a wounded animal. Let's make sure our man inside hears them and then sees them. Not only won't he want to tear his eyes away, but he'll also not want to do what he has in mind with all their nonsense going on right outside the pub.'

'No problem. Leave it with me.'

'Good man. I'll give you the nod when we're ready. We'll get as close as we can without having to come out into the open. I'll tell you when we need you.'

As he shuttled back towards his own team once again, Bliss felt no weight of expectation dragging him down. Sometimes you second guessed yourself, the burden of which could occasionally be overwhelming. But even though the plan he had devised went against procedure, his scheme had the full support of three entire teams on this occasion because, while there were options, there was no genuine alternative. Leave it for the specialists to arrive and by then it would probably be too late. For Phoebe and Beccy Latchford, it was now or never.

FIFTY-ONE

By the time the drone was in the air once more and the aftermath of the staged collision was in full swing, Bliss and his three fellow MCU team members had run into their first stumbling block. The steel double doors leading down to the cellar had been welded shut, a security feature Bliss had not anticipated. He swore and looked around. A few yards further on, he noticed the wooden boards erected over the back door were slightly askew. He loped across to assess their condition. A number of nails hammered in to secure the treated plywood were raised, some bent over, leaving the sheet timber loose enough to prise off with his fingers. His annoyance over the cellar doors evaporated; this had to be the way Hammond had gained access originally.

He spoke quietly into his radio microphone, asking for a situation report from the drone controller. As they'd hoped, one of the heat signatures had moved to the front of the building within seconds of the staged collision out on the lane. The three figures inside were now separated, and Bliss knew this presented his team with their best opportunity of a successful outcome. But only if they went in without delay.

Motioning for the others to join him, he kept his voice low but spoke urgently. 'He's forced his way in through here. He comes and goes as he pleases and probably hasn't given a thought to us since he's been inside. I'm guessing I can find my way in without making a sound. You all follow me unless I say otherwise. I realise we have only a rough idea where everybody is, so this is what we're going to do: me and Pen are on Hammond. Phil, you locate Phoebe Latchford and stay with her. Gul, that leaves you to find the stairs and get your arse up there to protect the kid. Everyone okay with that?'

They were. Bliss gently prised back both sheets of plywood currently protecting the full length of the door. They shifted without hesitation, the leverage allowing him to pull them away with barely a sound. With the barrier removed, he tried the round door knob, which turned with a squeal that forced air from his lungs. If Hammond had heard that from his position, their entire plan was blown.

'Drone control,' he whispered. 'Any change in locations?'

'No. I say again, no change. You're good to go, Green One.'

Bliss took a breath and made his move. As swiftly and silently as they could manage, he, Chandler, Gratton, and Ansari crept inside then closed the door behind them. They did not speak, and had muted all devices. As a result, they were unable to hear about any changes inside or out, but everybody had agreed with Bliss that a radio squawk at the most inopportune moment was a greater risk to all concerned.

The interior was gloomy, but several of the boarded windows had been prised loose to leave gaps, allowing cracks of light to spill through. These bright shafts illuminated the room sufficiently for them to realise they were in a large kitchen that had once provided food for the pub's customers. Stealthily, they moved on through the room's only other exit, its door standing ajar. This led into a short passageway. Bliss got his bearings and started creeping towards his right. He didn't look back over his shoulder; his colleagues knew their roles and he trusted them to execute their responsibilities.

Inside the next room they walked into, Phoebe Latchford jerked almost fully upright upon seeing them. Bliss put a finger to his lips. Gratton slipped across the room to join her, while Bliss and Chandler moved ahead towards a door on the far side of the room. They were in a dining area, and Bliss guessed the bar was on the other side of the far wall. That's where he expected to find Hammond. The door he hoped led into it was closed, and he realised this was now the most dangerous moment for them all. They had little idea what they might find on the other side, how much noise the door might make when opened, nor did they know Hammond's precise location at that point. Bliss glanced at Chandler, who had moved to his side. She nodded. He grasped the handle and turned it.

To Bliss's relief, the knob rotated silently. But the door did not. Its old and unlubricated hinges groaned loud enough to disturb any ghosts that might walk the property. Certainly loud enough to alert their quarry. Bliss threw the door wide open and barged through the gap just in time to see Hammond fleeing through an open archway from the bar into a second hallway. He realised at once where the man was headed and he cried out, 'Gul! He's on his way to you! Get to the girl now!'

He and Chandler both called for Hammond to halt, announcing themselves as police officers, although Bliss had never known this to stop a villain in their tracks. They both sped after him, but Hammond had a good lead and Bliss knew their man would arrive upstairs before them in whichever room Beccy Latchford was being held in.

'Gul!' he roared at the top of his voice. 'Get there! Get to her before him!'

When he and Chandler emerged through the brick archway and turned left as Hammond had done, they were confronted by a long passageway leading to the rear of the property, with a wooden staircase to the right leading up.

Up is where the girl was being kept.

Up is where Hammond would have run.

Up is where they needed to go.

As he took the stairs two at a time without considering the potential dangers lying in wait, Bliss wondered why he'd not heard a response from Ansari. For a moment he was struck by the awful realisation that she might not have found the stairs before Hammond had fled up them, leaving the child completely at his mercy. He locked that thought away inside a small compartment in his mind, not daring to focus on it for any length of time.

On the upper landing, they were presented with a stark choice. Straight ahead led to two doors, one open the other closed. To their left a corridor containing three further doors, one closed, one wide open, one ajar. He swallowed; sometimes the slightly open door was worse to contend with than one closed tight.

He turned his attention to Chandler, pointed to himself and then back along the corridor. Then he nodded at her and peered straight ahead. His partner immediately began to sidle in that direction. She had taken only two steps when they both froze at hearing Ansari's raised voice.

'Boss! I'm in the room at the end of the corridor. You better come. You better come now.'

Bliss turned, Chandler falling in behind him. He knew his DS would realise there could be only one reason Ansari would call out. As they entered the room from which they'd been summoned, he could see it ran lengthways to his right along the back of the building. He angled his body to peer inside, and what he saw caused him to whisper to himself beneath his breath.

'Oh, shit.'

On a thin plastic mattress at the far end of the room lay Beccy Latchford. She was bound with tape, including her mouth. She faced them, eyes wide and completely terrified. Before her, one hand outstretched to ward off an attack, DC Ansari crouched low. Her eyes never left those of Stuart Hammond, who stood gripping a long and heavy carving knife in the centre of the room.

Bliss didn't need an invitation to join this party.

'Stuart,' he said, throttling back his voice so that it emerged in a much calmer tone than he would have thought possible. 'You must know by now that whatever you intended here is not going to happen. Before you can reach Beccy, all three of us will be on you. You might well do some damage with that knife before we take you down, but believe me when I tell you, this is over for you. One way or another. We will not allow you to harm this child.'

Hammond stood quite still, other than the steady rise and fall of his chest. At first, it seemed as if he might ignore Bliss, but he then turned his body sideways and took two steps backwards so that he could see everybody in the room at the same time. He squinted at Bliss and licked his lips. 'If I'm going down, I'm going down fighting. I'll fuck up all three of you before you put me on the floor.'

'But to what end?' Bliss asked him, keeping his composure. 'I think we know what you really want here, Stuart. But whatever you try, whatever you do, that's just not going to happen.'

'Maybe I'm willing to take my chances.'

'Maybe, but it's the wrong way to go about this. I mean, what exactly have you done so far, Stuart? Think about that for a moment. Sure, you coerced a man into taking his own life. But you didn't physically murder him, so good luck to us proving whatever you said to him on the phone made any difference. And if Phoebe and Beccy came willingly with you, then all you've done since is hold them against their will. Right here, right now, is where the more significant charges against you are totting up. But you still haven't physically hurt anybody, have you?'

Bliss was struggling to find the right words, betting heavily on Callum Oliver still being alive. Because if Hammond had murdered the reporter, then he really had nothing to lose. And Bliss needed the man to focus on self-preservation above all other considerations.

'Tell me where we can find the journalist,' he said. 'That way, we can know for sure that it's not impossible for you to turn this around. Where is he, Stuart? Where did you leave him?'

Hammond's eyes dropped away, which is when Bliss thought he might convince the man to relinquish his weapon and surrender himself without anybody getting hurt. If that narrowed gaze of his hadn't faltered, then Bliss would have known he intended to keep his word about fighting his way out. But when the man glanced away, the gesture told Bliss he was considering his position. It presented an opening, one he intended to take.

'Come on, Stuart. Even if you resist, even if you use that knife, there's only one result here. But the difference between dropping your weapon and taking us on could be spending the rest of your life in prison. I won't lie. You're not going to walk away from this as a free man. But if you back off, then there is at least the possibility of coming out on licence again at some point in the future. If you don't, you can say goodbye to your freedom until the day you drop.'

Hammond made a chuffing sound as if repressing laughter. His shoulders rose and fell rapidly. 'If you knew me at all, you'd realise how little I care about my future.'

'And yet if you'd wanted to end it all you could have done so at any time over the past couple of decades. But you're right – I don't know you. I don't know what it's like to be you, to live the life you do. But you being here now tells me you don't really want to kill yourself, no matter what you tell other people.'

'Ah. So you saw my final message in the chatroom.'

'We did.'

'You caught on to me because I used the centre wi-fi to contact Ione, is that right?'

'Yes. We know a great deal, Stuart. But we'd like to know more. Most of all, we'd like to know where Callum Oliver is.'

After a couple of seconds, Hammond shook his head. 'It's too late for him. By now he'll be gone. And I'm sorry about that. More than you'll ever know. I just… I just didn't have the foggiest idea what do next.'

Looking at the man's woebegone expression and the slump in his shoulders, Bliss had a moment of realisation. 'I don't think you want any harm to come to little Beccy, either, do you, Stuart? Speaking as an outsider myself, it seems to me you've lived a bitter, sheltered life, and when you saw an opportunity to get even with your childhood friend, you thought you could go through with it. But you've had his family for several days now, and as far as I can tell you've not hurt either of them. In fact, I reckon you've come to enjoy being in their company.'

Hammond gestured towards the doorway with the knife. 'I told her, Phoebe, that I wanted a taste of the life Dean had… you know, as Morgan Latchford. That's the only reason they're both still alive.'

Bliss shook his head. 'I don't think so. I believe you want it to be true, because somehow you think doing so will make you a bigger man. Perhaps even a better one. But it's not any desire to see what life was like for Morgan, nor is it a lack of courage that's kept you from finishing what you started. The truth is, you can't go through with it because you care for them. By the sound of it, you didn't complete the job on Callum, either. And that's not a bad thing, Stuart. You've not failed, and you can't look at it like that. You just don't have it in you to be that type of person.'

Bliss could hear the following silence whistling in both ears. He knew he was right about this man. He just didn't know how he might react to the reality of his situation.

His eyes now moist, Hammond looked up at Bliss. 'The reporter… it's too late, but I left him in the pump station.'

'Okay. Thank you for that.' Bliss had reactivated communications, and for the benefit of the microphone he repeated the location, then said, 'Stuart, how about you let go of the knife now? Drop it on the floor or pass it to me. You're not going to hurt Beccy with it, and I don't think you want to harm any of us. There's no reason to take this any further. No reason at all.'

'You're right about that,' Hammond said. He glanced across at the girl still supine on the mattress, wide eyes staring up at him. He flashed a quick, sad smile at her. 'Look elsewhere, Beccy. Or just close your eyes. Either way, you really don't want to see this in your nightmares.'

Bliss reacted to the man's words the moment they left his mouth, but he was too late. Because as the girl jammed her eyes closed, Hammond raised the knife to his own throat and pulled the steel blade across from one side of his neck to the other.

FIFTY-TWO

'Any word?' Warburton asked him.

'Turns out he really wasn't good at anything,' Bliss told his DCI. 'Couldn't even kill himself properly. Missed the jugular and carotid, which meant he didn't bleed heavily. We'd whistled up an ambulance in case things went the wrong way for anyone involved, so he never even came close to bleeding out before the paramedics reached him. He's critical, but they tell me he'll make it.'

'Actually, I was asking about Callum Oliver.'

'Ah.'

They stood together in the car park at the front of the pub, some distance away from those who remained working the scene. 'Sadly not,' Bliss said dolefully. 'There's no sign of him. We had to break into the pumping station, and we turned the place upside down. To be honest, that sounds a lot more effort than it actually was. It's hardly spacious, and there's scarcely anywhere to hide an animal, let alone a human being. I've got a uniform posted at the hospital waiting for Hammond to come out of surgery, ready to ask him for more details. I don't think he lied, I just reckon he didn't mean the pumping station we were all parked outside of back down the lane.'

Warburton gave him a few seconds before moving on. 'I spoke to the team about what happened inside. How did you know about Hammond, Jimmy?'

'What do you mean? About what?'

'Him not truly wanting to go through with those things he claimed he intended to do.'

'I didn't. That is, I didn't know for certain. It just seemed obvious to me from the moment I clocked his face. I noticed the hesitation in his eyes, and his body language was all over the place. He was going through the motions, doing what he thought he ought to do now that he had reached the point of no return. Possibly he was even buying time while he tried to convince himself he was up to it.'

'But you could tell he wasn't?'

'It felt that way, yes. All along, his real anger had been directed towards Dean Norman, and with that monkey off his back, he was a spent force. Everything else was just… I don't know, some kind of perverted machismo that insisted he had to put behind him the misery of every year since he was twelve, and that the only way he could do so was to complete the act he started with Haley Deerbourne. Ultimately, I didn't consider Stuart Hammond to be the demon he thought he was. I just didn't buy it.'

'You appear to have been right about that, at least. And it wasn't your fault he tried to kill himself at the end, either.'

'I know that.'

She regarded him sceptically. 'Do you? That doesn't sound like the Jimmy Bliss I've come to know.'

'And love?' he queried playfully.

'Oh, good grief, no. But you'll do, especially if this new and improved version of you intends to stick around.'

He shrugged her words aside. 'Diane, the simple truth is I've had enough self-flagellation to last me a dozen lifetimes. The only thing it ever taught me is that it taught me nothing at all. I've come to recognise it as self-pity masquerading as something much more grand and noble. I'm tired of it, and done with all that shit.'

'If that's genuinely how you feel, then I'm very glad to hear it. Especially given how tense things must have been up in that room. In the circumstances, it must have been doubly difficult for you. I'm sure it brought back a lot of unhappy memories.'

Bliss cleared his throat. 'Mia, you mean?'

'Of course. I barely knew DS Short, but I liked her enormously. She was one of the good ones, and I can only imagine how it must have felt in that room just now seeing Gul in danger.'

He thought back. Mia Short and Gul Ansari were not dissimilar in their approach to the job, and he could easily imagine Ansari taking the same career path and trajectory as Short had been destined for.

'Mia was about to be the best of us,' he said reflectively. 'Capable of great things. It was different for me earlier, because unlike Mia's case, I was actually in the room with Gul with a knife being flashed around. I also had Pen to consider, plus Beccy Latchford. But yes, I can't say Mia never entered my mind.'

'That's to be expected. But you handled it, Jimmy. Everybody you just mentioned walked out of there safely, including you.'

'Will there be repercussions over us going inside the pub? If so, please make it clear that I ordered the others to come with me. None of them wanted to. They told me we should go by standard protocols.'

Warburton smiled at him, raising her eyebrows. 'They did? That's odd, because all three just got done telling me they volunteered, as did everyone else in your team and from CID. Every single one of them agrees these were exigent circumstances, Jimmy. Waiting might have cost lives. I've already updated the Super, so she's fully prepared for DCS Feeley if he tries it on. My policy book will also reflect the decision-making process that went into what happened, all with my authority.'

Bliss felt himself relaxing. His heart continued to pump furiously as a result of recent events, but for the first time since stepping back outside the pub, he was able to control his breathing. 'Thank you for that, boss. I appreciate your support. Still, Hammond was never going to hurt either of them. No doubt there was a part of him that felt he had to, but at no point did he ever want to, and that's the difference.'

'You weren't to know that going in. The fact is, you did your best in what was a terribly difficult situation. And nobody got hurt other than a man who brought it upon himself.'

'It's funny,' Bliss said, stroking the side of his face. 'But when you think about it, if it weren't for Callum Oliver, the only two people to suffer physically in all this were the two men whose actions when they were little more than kids started the whole ball rolling.'

'Truth is stranger than fiction. We all know that for sure. So where is Ione Pearson in all this, Jimmy? What charges are we looking at for her?'

'I'm not at all sure. She's admitted to helping with the vehicles, but claims to have believed his story concerning Morgan Latchford's intentions towards his own daughter. I think she readily bought into that story because the man creeped her out so much. Conversely, Hammond charmed her. There are elements of this that were not crimes at all, so we'll have to consider our charges more carefully than we've ever done before.'

Warburton agreed with him. 'That same story he spun for Pearson was enough to fool the man's wife, too, from what I hear. Hammond must have sold it well.'

'He really went to town on Phoebe Latchford's head,' Bliss said. 'The thing with her, as I understand from the brief chat we had before she was whisked away, is that she had always found her husband's lack of a past troubling. She suspected something had happened when he was a kid, but of course she'd assumed it had happened *to* him. Hammond used those fears to hammer home the final few nails.'

His DCI nodded towards the Wounded Drake. 'And this? How do you suppose he ended up here?'

'That's something we need to ask him, assuming he pulls through. But when you think about it, there aren't many people who are unaware of failing businesses, including pubs. Especially those in rural areas. I bet we could set off in any direction and within half an hour we'd find several empty properties to choose from. This place is ideal. It's close to the road. He could park up around the back and not be seen – other than by farmers working the fields I suppose – and because the place has not been entirely abandoned, it still had its utilities in working order. He just had to switch them on at the mains and reset the boiler and run the taps for a while.'

'This is going to be a charging nightmare all round,' Warburton complained bitterly.

'Yeah. Unfortunately, it looks as if that will now include manslaughter at the very least. Murder if I can swing it. If Hammond left Oliver without food or drink, then he knew full well he would die if not found. To my mind, that's intent. The suicide coercion will be a ball ache to prosecute, though.'

'I suppose we'll have to wait and see. When will you let Sandra Bannister know about her colleague?'

Blowing out his cheeks, Bliss said, 'When I have more to tell her. I have Pen chasing up the Internal Drainage Board for locations of all fenland pumping stations, and we'll get as many people out to them as we can. But right now I don't even know when he last ate or drank.'

'Without water, he'll have three to four days at most.'

'Yep. I don't rate our chances.'

Warburton reached out a hand to slap him on the shoulder. 'We got back two of our three missing persons, Jimmy. That's something to savour, isn't it?'

Bliss kicked out at a loose stone, watching it skitter away. 'I'm glad about it. Don't get me wrong. But I can't celebrate the moment. Not yet. The fact is, we have no idea where Callum Oliver is, and no clue as to what condition he's in. Those are not good odds, and if we lose him, then I can't consider the op a success.'

'No, you're right. I understand how you feel. But we take our wins where we can get them. Didn't you once tell me that?'

'Sounds like the sort of daft crap I come out with on occasion, yes.'

'Come on,' she said. 'Let's get back.'

Bliss shook his head. 'Take Pen with you, please. I'll follow on soon enough. I just want a few minutes alone to clear my head.'

He walked slowly out of the car park, across the lane, before climbing up the steep embankment whose heavy grass sucked and tugged at his boots. He stood on the crest and gazed down at the river for several minutes. Its flow was smooth and unstressed. He wished he felt the same way. He hadn't lied to DCI Warburton about his feelings concerning Stuart Hammond's suicide attempt, and it wasn't as if he felt any pangs of guilt at whatever fate had befallen Callum Oliver. But he considered it a job left unfinished, a life lost which could possibly have been saved had time and circumstances not worked against them. He and his team had done their best, but to a certain extent, it had beaten them.

Tilting his face to the sky, Bliss drew fresh air into his lungs in two greedy gulps. The sun washed down over him, and he basked in its gentle heat. Despite the impending arrival of summer, the times they were living in felt troubled and uncertain. This had been an awkward, at times brutal case, but he knew there were darker days to come. There always were.

He turned to stroll along the embankment's plateau, and as he cast his eyes down river, he noticed among the heavy gorse a small, square, brick building. It looked like an old bunker or coal shed, but the pipes protruding from it told him it was nothing of the sort.

He looked back over his shoulder and could just about make out the yellow brick of the Mouth Lane pumping station. Then he turned to stare once more at the tiny, grey, weathered and water-damaged structure which stood no taller than the embankment itself.

It couldn't be, he thought. *It just couldn't be.*
Could it?

FIFTY-THREE

THE AFTERNOON WAS SUNNY, warm, and bright. Bliss held the shindig on his boat, the partygoers naturally ending up spilling out onto the towpath. Molly was in charge of the music, because as she told him, 'Who the fuck can dance to Pink Floyd?' He had provided the booze, while Lennie Kaplan's wife arranged the catering for him. As the day wore on, his guests rotated positions and, as far as he could tell, everybody was having a great time.

Chandler had introduced her boyfriend to him as 'Graham, from a remote swamp in the land of Duloc.' That had creased him up, and to the man's credit, he had shown no sign of hostility at being likened to Shrek. He seemed like a decent bloke, and Bliss was thrilled for his partner; their relationship looked as if it had some mileage in it.

At one point as the fading sunlight glimmered on the still water of the river, he was joined on the cushioned bench seat at the stern of the *Mourinho* by Olly Bishop. The big man took a pull on his Boltmaker and said, 'That was some week, Jimmy. Some week indeed.'

Bliss raised his own bottle of London Pride, tilting it towards his friend and colleague. 'You're not wrong, Bish. It was certainly one for the record books.'

'I doubt we'll see its like again. Thank fuck. I can't even begin to know how to describe it. Still, in the end we got the best of results.'

'Yeah. By the skin of our teeth. I checked on Callum's progress before I left home, and he's improving nicely now that he's been rehydrated. His temperature was through the roof, his BP had gone the same way, but he reported no seizures and there's no obvious swelling of the brain. His age and physical condition helped him, and they expect him to make a full recovery.'

'I heard the list of pumping stations Penny was given didn't include the one you found him in.'

'No, that's right. They only listed working stations, and that one has been out of service for a few years now. We got lucky. Callum Oliver got lucky.'

'If you'd not taken a walk along that embankment…'

They both let it go at that; it didn't do to consider the journalist's fate had Bliss not needed time to himself.

'By the way,' Bishop said, lowering his voice so as not to be overheard. 'I've made a decision about my promotion. I'm backing away from the framework programme.'

Bliss was surprised by his friend's pronouncement. 'You are?'

'Yeah. I'm not cancelling, just putting it on hold. I have to tell you, Jimmy, standing there on the sidelines while you and the others went inside that building really got to me. I felt helpless listening to it all unfold across comms. I'm not sure if I'm cut out to be that person.'

'It's not for everyone, my friend. Not by any stretch of the imagination. But it cuts both ways. You were right there with Mia at the end, remember? Now that's an experience you never want to repeat.'

'In one way, of course. I don't ever want to lose a colleague again no matter what the circumstances. But being alongside her at that moment was also… a privilege in some awful, inexplicable way.'

Bliss nodded. 'I think I know what you mean.' He recalled contemplating their loss in the immediate aftermath, wishing he had been with her at the time. Not that the outcome would have been different. He wouldn't have been able to save Mia, but he would have felt honoured to have been the last person she ever spoke to. The colleague by her side at the end.

'It's impossible to explain,' Bishop acknowledged. 'To anybody outside the job, that is. But there you go, and that's the decision I've reached.'

'Who knows, maybe all the budget restrictions will create another new breed of DI. Turn full circle, perhaps. Make the role more hands-on again.'

'Yeah, well, I'm not working with a maybe as my end goal. The thought of having to repeat that experience while my team confronts such a level of unknown danger does not appeal one little bit.'

Bliss slipped an arm around Bishop's shoulder. 'Look, if that's what you want, I'm happy my DS is staying put. I'm going to need you in what might be my final year.'

'I don't know about that, Jimmy. But I have to ask, why are you having a party today and not next year for your sixtieth?'

'Because next year *is* my sixtieth. You really think I want to celebrate *that* landmark?'

Bishop chuckled. 'No, I suppose not. Won't be long before you have to decide what to do, though. We've been running a book on it. Consensus is you'll put in for a two-year extension contract.'

'Hmm. Does consensus say if such a request will be accepted?'

'Yep. We're running a book on that as well.'

'And?'

His friend grimaced.

This time, it was Bliss who chuckled. 'Yeah. That's what I thought.'

'Are we right? You think you'll stay on?'

Bliss took a beat before responding. 'Had you asked me last summer, I probably would have told you I wanted out of it. It's not the job – it's never been the job. But the politics, the public perception of us based on a few wrong'uns, it's all so fucked up now, Bish. It seems like everybody is against us, and that stings when the vast majority of us are genuinely here to help people when they need it most. It's still us who run towards danger, not those who criticise us from the safety of their armchairs.'

'I know what you mean, boss. My oldest recently told me she wants to join up. I said she ought to think about it long and hard, because I don't see things improving any day soon.'

'But that's the very reason why the job needs the best of us,' Bliss argued. 'We have to show people we're not who and what they think we are. Which is why I'm glad you're staying on as DS. I'd never have told you this if you were hell-bent on your promotion, and I'd never have tried to stop you from going for it, but our unit and the job itself would have felt the loss of another bloody good sergeant.'

Bishop nodded. He drained his beer. 'If you stay, I'll stay. But as soon as you hang up your warrant card, I'll a rethink my own future.'

'By then – if it happens – I'd expect to see Gul as a DS and working hard towards another promotion. Might not be a bad move to work as DS under her command at some point down the road.'

'I make you right, but what are the chances she'll stay with us when she moves up to DS. Can this unit afford a third sergeant?'

'With the crime rate in our fine city, I'd say the chances of the unit expanding are pretty good, mate. Plus, if I stay on, it'll be at a reduced salary, so there's that to consider. Besides, I still hold out some hope that Pen will finally decide to step up.'

'Penny?' Bishop turned to look at Chandler, who was engaged in conversation with Ansari and Gratton. 'I mean, of course she'd make a brilliant DI, but as far as I know she doesn't want the job.'

'She didn't. Probably still doesn't. But I'm hoping to persuade her to go for it. For totally different reasons it didn't work out for you or Mia, and with Gul a rank behind I'd like to leave this unit knowing it's in good hands. If I stay on, that gives me three years to lick Pen into shape.'

'You're a better man than me if you think you can turn her around, Jimmy,' Bishop said, laughing.

Bliss grinned. 'She's a better man than both of us, so she's worth the effort.'

They clinked bottles on it. 'What does our result yesterday mean for the witness to Latchford's suicide?' Bishop asked.

Bliss shrugged. Zinta Balodis had been his final call the previous day. After informing her of their progress, he'd impressed upon the woman how long it might be before Stuart Hammond was brought to trial. 'I told her I wasn't sure at this stage if we'd even bring charges against him for coercion,' he said to Bishop. 'But I also assured her it could be months before we made a decision, and I'd want her to be available should we proceed. All of which meant we'd be keen to keep her safe and secure and prepped. Pen also fed her name to a couple of relevant organisations, who were keen to contact Zinta in reference to her immigration status.'

'You think she'll end up staying?'

'I do. If she wants to after all this. Not quite the promised land she was told to expect, mate. Nothing like it, in fact.'

'Still, you've opened a door for her. Down to her now to make the best of it.'

The pair went to join the others on the towpath. Molly hugged him as if it had been weeks rather than minutes since she'd seen him. Earlier, he had unwrapped her gift to him and had been delighted to uncover a vinyl copy of an early Steely Dan soundtrack from a Richard Pryor movie. 'You going to cut some moves on the dancefloor later, J-Dog?' she asked him in that sing-song way of hers.

'J-Dog?'

'Yeah. My main man. My Jimbo dawg.'

He laughed and shook his head. 'Now you're just taking the piss.'

She gave him one of her 'what, little old me?' looks.

Bliss winked. 'Thanks for my pressie, and for sorting the music. You're right, nobody can dance to Pink Floyd.'

'And so they shouldn't,' she said earnestly. 'The Floyd are for listening to, not cavorting to. Nothing like a bit of Gilmour to send you into another time and place, Jimbo.'

'I'm glad you think so. I'll beat some taste into you yet.'

'Yeah, you and whose army? Oh, and I should tell you something. Your mate, Barry, has been pumping me for information. He wants to sort you out next time you two talk music. I told him to call Steely Dan Steeleye Span instead if he really wants to blow your mind.'

He laughed again and revelled in the enormous joy she had brought to his life, saying, 'I'm so glad you came. Seriously, you made my day just perfect by being here.'

Molly drew back and fixed him with a curious look. 'You're joking, right? You think I would have missed this for anything? Jimbo, I still don't think you appreciate what you did for me. To you it might have been just another day at the office, but you saved my life. Not once, not twice, but three times.'

'Three?'

'Yeah. Once on that roof. Then again when you rescued me after those tossers had snatched me. But mostly you saved my life because you made me realise I was actually worth saving; that I deserved to live. I know I take the piss and disrespect you like crazy, but I love the shit out of you, old man.'

'Oi, less of the "old man",' he said quickly, trying not to choke on the words.

Molly winked. 'Pen told me I should start calling you that. She thinks it's adorable, bless her.'

'Yeah, bless her stinking cotton socks.'

She switched her gaze from him to Chandler. 'You ever think what might have been between you two?'

'What, me and Pen? No chance.'

'Come off it. I saw shit going down between you two. She loves you to bits, too.'

'As I do her. But it's a different kind of love, Molly,' he explained. 'One that's hard to describe, and one you never want to take any further for fear of spoiling something so wonderful.'

'Hark at you. Soppy old sod.'

'What's with all the insults today?'

'Pen told me to call you that, too.'

This time he made slits of his eyes. 'I'm smelling the foul odour of bullshit, young lady.'

Molly poked her tongue out at him. 'Must be your aftershave, you old fart.'

Bliss chuckled and took another swallow from his bottle, savouring the moment. Finding Callum Oliver still alive in the pump house the day before had allowed him to fully enjoy the successful outcome of what began as two indefinite operations. He'd gone into the training session that morning feeling pretty good about himself and the world in general, with the workout and ring time allowing him to blow off some steam. But here, now, surrounded by good friends, he tried to recall the last time he'd been as content, and came up well short. Even Diane Warburton had shown up with her husband, who was outgoing and pleasant and fitted in well with the group. The party was loud and raucous, and a couple of people further along the towpath had voiced their displeasure. Chandler flashed her warrant card at them, which appeared to have done the trick. The day ebbed away and Bliss sighed, at peace with the world for a pleasant change.

He reflected on Bishop's question. The truth was, he was undecided about requesting an extension to his time in the job. Having always walked a fine line, he had stumbled across more times than not over the past few years. Even doing what he considered to be his job, the previous day had left him open to scrutiny from those above him. His DCI and DSI had backed him, and that was good enough. But he didn't understand how doing the job had become so fraught with difficulty, and he didn't care for it one little bit. Could he really take another three years?

Looking around at the revellers, knowing how much he would miss those he worked with every day, Bliss couldn't imagine a time when they would carry on without him. It would happen, of course. Eventually. But deep inside, where the truth pooled and occasionally caused him to be breathless, he already knew there was no danger of him walking away until the job didn't want him anymore.

He breathed deeply. Smiled. Felt himself completely relax for the first time in years.

A moment later, his personal mobile rang. *Who the hell can that be?* he thought. *Everybody I know is here.*

Bliss took out his phone and answered. He spoke briefly. And when he looked up, he saw Chandler staring at him. She walked across, wearing a deep frown. 'Jimmy, what is it? I noticed a change in your expression while you were talking on the phone. Something's wrong. What's happened?'

He blinked. Looking at his friend but not really seeing her, thinking: *not everybody. Not everybody I know was here.*

'That was a call from Ireland,' he said softly. 'My mum just died.'

ACKNOWLEDGEMENTS

I have to begin with my beta readers. They each bring something different to the table, each of them spots something the others haven't, and each of them is able to offer imaginative and on-point suggestions. So, once again, thank you Dorothy Laney, Kath Middleton, and Lynda Checkley for your invaluable assistance in getting this one over the line.

Thank you, also, to my editor (unnamed) for your help – especially with my awful grammar as a result of typing faster than my brain can think; I've worn four fingers down to tiny nubs after this one. And finally, thanks to my wonderful Facebook group (with a special mention to Donna Morfett for being a sounding board, and also on this occasion my blog tour organiser and ARC manager).

AUTHOR'S NOTE

How this one managed to struggle over the line I don't quite know. A brain fogging cocktail of my specific health problems, combined with the stress of moving home, came close to consigning this one to the digital shelf. I think sheer bloody-mindedness won the day, and boy did I need the objective views of my beta readers more than ever this time around. After the hectic nature of the previous few books, I decided to come back to a more procedural novel. Because of that it was never easy to judge the pace and back story and introspection versus storyline progress and action. Dot, Kath, and Lynda assured me I hadn't screwed the pooch, and I trust their judgement more than my own. Oh, and Bliss fans need not worry about my move south – Jimmy will remain in Peterborough for a while yet, because he's as bloody-minded as I am.

Cheers all.

Tony
February 2022

If you enjoyed this book, please spare a few minutes to write a review on Amazon and Goodreads. And if you're a member of any Facebook book groups, a recommendation is always welcome. Thank you.

Printed in Great Britain
by Amazon